OUT OF THE DARK

DAVID WEBER

A TOM DOHERTY ASSOCIATES BOOK
NEW YORK

This is a work of fiction. All of the characters, organizations, and events portrayed in this novel are either products of the author's imagination or are used fictitiously.

OUT OF THE DARK

Edited by Patrick Nielsen Hayden

A Tor Book
Published by Tom Doherty Associates, LLC
175 Fifth Avenue
New York, NY 10010

www.tor-forge.com

ISBN 978-0-7653-2412-2

First Edition: October 2010

Printed in the United States of America

0 9 8 7 6 5 4 3 2 1

For Fred and Joan Saberhagen.
Friends and inspirations, in more than one way.
I hope you like Basarab, Fred!

PROLOGUE

PLANET KU-197-20

YEAR 73,764 OF THE HEGEMONY

Garsul, are you *watching* this?"

Survey Team Leader Garsul grimaced. Just what, exactly, did Hartyr *think* he was doing? Of all the stupid, unnecessary, infuriating—

The team leader made himself stop and draw a deep breath. He also made himself admit the truth, which was that as effortlessly irritating as Hartyr could be anytime he tried, there was no excuse for allowing his own temper to flare this way. And it wouldn't have been happening if he hadn't been watching . . . and if both his stomachs hadn't been hovering on the edge of acute nausea. Then there were his elevated strokain levels, not to mention the instinctual fight-or-flight reflexes (mostly *flight* in his species' case, in point of fact) quivering down his synapses.

"Yes, Hartyr, I'm watching," he heard his own voice say over the link. He knew it was his voice, even though it seemed preposterously calm given what was going on inside him at the moment. But his next words betrayed the fact that his calm was only voice-deep. "And did you have something in mind for us to *do* about it?" he asked pointedly.

"No, but surely. . . ."

Hartyr's reply began strongly only to taper off plaintively, and Garsul felt most of his irritation dissipate into something much more like sympathy. His deputy team leader's natural officiousness and pomposity were an undeniable pain in the excretory orifice, and his fanatical devotion to paperwork was rare even among Barthoni. Hartyr was also prone to assume his answer was always the *right* answer to any problem that came along, and he was a pusher—the sort of fellow who would trample his own dam and herd brothers in pursuit of the tastiest grazing. But at this moment the sick horror echoing in the depths of his voice was completely understandable. It wasn't going to make him *likable* (nothing was ever likely to accomplish *that* miracle), but Garsul felt an unusually powerful sense of kinship with Hartyr as he heard it.

"I wish there were something we could do to stop it, too," he said more quietly. "Unfortunately, there isn't. Unless we want to break protocol, at least."

He heard Hartyr inhale at the other end of the link, but the deputy team leader didn't respond to that last sentence. It did put their options—or, rather, their *lack* of options—into stark relief, Garsul reflected. The Hegemony Council had established its survey protocols long ago, and the Barthoni had played a prominent part in their creation. There was an excellent reason for each and every aspect of the protocols' restrictions . . . including the need to restrain the enormous temptation for a survey team to intervene at a moment like this.

"Make sure Kurgahr and Joraym are recording this," he said now. He could easily have passed the message himself, but it was kinder to give Hartyr something to do. "This is going to be an important part of our final report."

"All right," Hartyr acknowledged.

The easygoing, centaurlike Barthoni were singularly ill-suited to the sort of spit and polish some of the Hegemony's other member species seemed to favor. A few of those other races made bad jokes about it, Garsul knew, but that was all right with him. He and his team didn't need a lot of "sirs" or bowing and scraping to get on with their jobs. They knew who was in charge, just as they knew each of them (likable or not) was a highly trained and invaluable specialist. And every one of them was a volunteer, out here because they were the sort who always wanted to see what was on the other side of the next hill. And perhaps even more importantly, because of their race's species-wide commitment to what the Hegemony Survey Force stood for.

Unlike some other *species I could mention*, he thought sourly, and returned his attention to the visual display.

The planet they were currently surveying—designated KU-197-20—was a pleasant enough place. Its hydrosphere was a little more extensive than most Barthoni would really have preferred, and the local vegetation would have been poorly suited to their dietary requirements. But the temperature range was about right, and however unsustaining the planetary plant life might be, parts of it were tasty enough, and it came in shades of green that were undeniably easy on the eye.

The only *real* drawbacks, if he was going to be honest, were certain aspects of the planetary fauna. Especially the *dominant* planetary fauna.

At the moment, the scene the survey remotes were showing him was less green than it could have been, for a lot of reasons. First, because the area he was watching was well into local autumn, splashing the landscape with vivid color . . . and showing more than a few bare limbs, as well. Secondly, because those remotes were focused on a narrow strip of open ground between two patches of woodland, and that strip had been recently plowed. The even more recent rain had transformed the turned earth into a mud bath deep enough to satisfy even a Liatu, just waiting to happen. Which, he thought, only underscored the insanity of what he was watching. Surely the lunatic local sentients (and he used the term loosely) could have found a better spot for their current madness!

"Garsul?"

The new voice on the link belonged to Joraym, the team's xenoanthropologist, and Garsul was darkly amused by his tentative tone. Joraym was the team member who'd been most insistent on their remembering that the local sentients—"humans," they called themselves—were still mired deep in their planetary childhood. One could scarcely expect them to act like adults, and it would be both unfair and unjust to hold their behavior to the standards of *civilized* races. The team leader couldn't quibble with Joraym's analysis of KU-197-20's dominant species, but the xenoanthropologist had been looking down his snout for "Barthoncentric prejudice" at anyone who criticized the "humans" ever since they'd arrived in-system. Garsul suspected it was Joraym's way of demonstrating his own enlightened superiority to his teammates.

"Yes, Joraym?" he said aloud.

"Can I deploy some audio remotes?" the xenoanthropologist requested.

"Why in Clahdru's name d'you want to do *that*? The *video's* going to be bad enough!" Garsul made a harsh sound deep in his throat. "I hope the Council's going to put this under scholar's seal when we get it home, but even some of the scholars I know are going to be losing their lunches if this is *half* as bad as I think it's going to be!"

"I know. I know!" Joraym sounded unhappy, but he also sounded determined. "It's not often we get a chance to actually see something like this happen, though," he continued. "*We* don't do it, and neither do most of the other races, but from what we've been able to determine about the local societal units, these . . . people think this is a reasonable way to settle political differences. Hopefully, if I can get the pickups close enough to the leaders on each side, I'll be able to establish that and monitor their reactions and decisions as the . . . effort proceeds."

"And just why is that so important?" Garsul demanded.

"Because some of my colleagues back home are going to reject my analysis without a hell of a lot of supporting data. It's so *alien* to the way we think."

"Excuse me, Joraym, but could that possibly be because they *are* aliens?" Garsul heard the asperity in his own voice, but he didn't really care.

"Well, of course it is!" the xenoanthropologist shot back. "But these creatures are more . . . comfortable with this than anyone else *I've* ever observed. They remind me a lot of the Shongairi, actually, and we all know how well *that's* working out. I'm only saying I'd like to have as much substantiation as possible when our report goes before the Council. Their attitude just isn't natural, even for omnivores, and I think we're going to have to keep a very close eye on them for a long time to come. Thank Clahdru they're as primitive as they are! At least they've got time to do some maturing before we have to worry about them getting off-planet and infesting the rest of the galaxy!"

Garsul's nostrils flared at the mention of the Shongairi. As far as he could tell, these "humans" probably weren't any worse than the Shongairi had been at the same stage in their racial evolution. On the other hand, they probably weren't a lot *better* than the Shongairi had been, either. And as Joraym had just pointed out, unlike the Shongairi, they were omnivores, which made their behavior even more bizarre.

Which presented Garsul with an unwelcome command decision, given that never mentioned, never admitted to codicil to Survey's official protocols. The one which had been slipped into place very quietly—by executive order and without any debate before the General Assembly of Races—after the Shongairi were granted Hegemony membership. This was the first time Garsul had actually found himself in the uncomfortable position of applying that codicil, but the classified clause of his mission orders made it clear one of his team's responsibilities was to provide the Council with the means to evaluate any new species' threat potential. Exactly what the Council meant to do with such an evaluation had never been explained to him, and he'd been careful not to ask, but Joraym's last sentence had brought him squarely face-to-face with that classified clause.

The team leader still didn't care much for the thought of recording everything that was about to happen in full color, complete with sound effects, but he was forced to admit—grudgingly—that in light of the orders Joraym knew nothing about, his request might not be totally insane, after all.

"What do you think, Kurgahr?"

"I think Joraym has a point, Garsul," the team's xenohistorian said. He, too, knew nothing about Garsul's classified orders, so far as the team leader was aware, but his tone was firm. Not remotely anything like *happy,* but firm. "Like you, I hope they'll put all this under scholar's seal when we get it home, but this is pretty close to a unique opportunity to get something like this fully recorded. The data really could be invaluable in the long run."

"All right," Garsul sighed. "I'll ask Ship Commander Syrahk to see to it."

· · · · ·

FAR BELOW THE orbiting Barthon starship, a young man with a long, pointed nose and a savagely scarred face stood looking out through the morning mists. His name was Henry, Duke of Lancaster, Duke of Cornwall, Duke of Chester, Duke of Aquitaine, claimant to the throne of France, and, by God's grace, King of England, and he was twenty-nine years old. He was also, although no one could have guessed it from his expression, in trouble.

Deep trouble.

It was obvious to anyone that he had overreached, and the chivalry of France intended to make him pay for it. His siege of Harfleur had succeeded, but it had taken a full month to force the port to surrender, and his own army had been riddled with disease by the time he was finished. Between that, combat casualties, and the need to garrison his new capture, his original field force of over twelve thousand men had been whittled down to under nine thousand, and only fifteen hundred of them were armored knights and men-at-arms. The other seven thousand were longbow-armed archers—nimble, deadly at long range (under the proper circumstances, at least), but hopelessly outclassed against any armored foe who could get to sword range. And truth to tell, Harfleur wasn't all that impressive a result for an entire campaign. Which was why, two weeks after the port's surrender, Henry had put his army into motion towards Calais, the English stronghold in northern France, where his troops could reequip over the winter.

It might, perhaps, have been wiser to withdraw his army by sea, but Henry had chosen instead to march overland. Some might have called it a young man's hubris, although despite his youth, Henry V was a seasoned warrior who'd seen his first battlefield when he was only sixteen years old. Others might have called it arrogance, although not to his face. (Not a man to whom the wise offered insult, Henry of Lancaster.) It might even have been a sound strategic sense of the need to salvage at least something more impressive than Harfleur from the expedition. Something he could show

Parliament that winter when it came time to discuss fresh military subsidies. But whatever his reasoning, he'd decided to reach Calais by marching across his enemy's territory as proof the enemy in question couldn't stop him.

Unfortunately, the French had other ideas, and they'd raised an army to confront the English invasion. Although it hadn't assembled in time to save Harfleur and wasn't much larger than Henry's army when he started cross-country to Calais, there was time for it to grow, and it had proved sufficient to block his progress along the line of the Somme River. In fact, it had succeeded in pushing him south, away from Calais, until he could find a ford which wasn't held against him in force.

By that time, unhappily for the English, the French force had swelled to almost thirty-six thousand men.

Which was why Henry was looking out into the autumn mist this morning. Confronted by four times his own numbers, he'd chosen a defensive position calculated to give the French—who had long and painful memories of what had happened to their fathers and grandfathers at places with names like Crécy and Poitiers—pause. At the moment his army held the southern end of a narrow strip of clear, muddy earth between two patches of woodland, the forests of Agincourt and Tramecourt. It was plowed, that stretch of dirt, and the autumn had been rainy. In fact, it had rained the night before, and the fresh-turned earth was heavy with water.

The French vastly outnumbered him in both mounted and dismounted knights and men-at-arms, whose heavy armor would give them a huge advantage in hand-to-hand combat against the unarmored archers who constituted better than eighty percent of his total force. That was why he'd formed his own limited number of knights and men-at-arms to cover the center of his line and massed archers on either flank. That was a fairly standard English formation, but he'd added the innovation of driving long, heavy, pointed wooden stakes into the ground, sharpened tips angled towards the French. The Turks had employed the same tactic to hold off the French cavalry at the Battle of Nicopolis, nineteen years before, and it had served them well. Perhaps it would serve him equally well.

The dense woodland covered both of his flanks, preventing the French men-at-arms from circling around to turn them, and his total frontage was less than a thousand yards. A frontal attack—the only way the French could get at him—would constrict their forces badly, preventing them from making full use of their numerical advantage, and the mucky terrain would only make bad worse. In fact, the potential battlefield was so unfavorable (from their perspective) that it seemed unlikely they'd attack at all. Besides, time favored them. At the moment, Henry was in a formidable defensive position, true, and the French were only too well aware of their previous failures in attacking prepared English defensive positions, but this time they had him trapped.

Henry was short of food, his weary army had marched two hundred and sixty miles in barely two and a half weeks, and many of his men were suffering from dysentery and other diseases. Charles d'Albret, the Constable of France, commanding the French army, was still between him and Calais; his enemies outnumbered him hugely; and his strength could only decline while theirs increased. Constable d'Albret could expect additional reinforcements soon—indeed, the Dukes of Brebant, Anjou, and Brittany, each commanding another fifteen hundred to two thousand men, were even now marching to join him—and if the English were foolish enough to move out of their current position the overwhelming French cavalry would cut them to pieces. They knew they had him and, in the fullness of time, they intended to repay the arrogant English with interest for those earlier battles like Crécy and Poitiers. But for now the Constable, in no hurry to bring on a battle, preferred to negotiate and stall for time and the arrival of yet more troops. After all, the English position was ultimately hopeless.

Which was why Henry had decided to attack.

• • • • •

"DOES ANYONE HAVE any idea why those humans—the 'English'—are *doing* that?" Garsul asked almost plaintively.

Despite the nausea roiling around inside him, he'd discovered he couldn't look away from the outsized display. There was something so hideously . . . mesmerizing about watching thousands upon thousands of putatively intelligent beings march towards one another bent on organized murder. No Barthon could have done it, he knew that much!

"I'm not certain," Kurgahr said slowly.

Of all the watching Barthoni, the historian came closest to possessing some knowledge of "military history," although even his knowledge of the subject was slight. There wasn't any *Barthon* "military history" to study, and while some other member species of the Hegemony were considerably more combative than the Barthoni, very, very few of them were remotely as bloodthirsty—a term no one in the Hegemony had even used until the Shongairi arrived—as humans appeared to be. None of them were represented in Garsul's survey team, either, but Kurgahr at least had their histories available.

"I think the 'English' have decided they have nothing to lose," he went on slowly. "Surely they must realize as well as the 'French' that they can't hope to *win,* yet they appear to have chosen to provoke combat, anyway." He twitched his upper shoulders in a shrug of bafflement. "I think this race may be even crazier than we thought. It looks to me like they'd rather attack, even knowing it means they'll all be killed, than do the sane thing and surrender!"

"That's a classic example of the worst sort of species chauvinism!" Joraym said testily. "You're unfairly applying our Barthoncentric psychological standards to a juvenile, alien race, Kurgahr. As a historian, you of all people should know how inherently fallacious that kind of pseudo-logic is!"

"Oh?" Kurgahr looked at the xenoanthropologist scornfully. "And do *you* have a better explanation for why they're doing *that*?"

He gestured towards the display, where the English army had slogged its way northward along the plowed, muddy strip of open ground towards its overwhelmingly powerful foe. The unarmored archers moved much more easily and nimbly than the armored men-at-arms, even with the long, sharpened stakes they carried. On the other hand, that same lack of armor meant that if the other side ever got to grips with them. . . .

If the longbowmen were worried about that, they showed no evidence of it—which, in Garsul's opinion, only proved Kurgahr's point about their lack of sanity. They simply waded through the mud, marching steadily towards the French.

The French, on the other hand, seemed taken aback by the English advance. They obviously hadn't expected it, and it took them a while to get themselves organized. By the time they'd taken up their own battle formation, the English had halted about three hundred yards from them, and the archers were busy hammering their stakes back into the ground.

. . . . .

CHARLES D'ALBRET WAS not a happy man.

He and his principal subordinates (inasmuch as fifteenth-century French noblemen could truly conceive of the concept of being subordinate to anyone other than—possibly—God) had prepared a battle plan. None of them had been blind to the defensive advantages of the English position, and they'd had a plenitude of experience with what English bowmen could do. Those Welsh and English bastards had demonstrated only too often that no other archers in Europe could match their lethal range and rate of fire. Worse, theirs was a weapon which let commonly born men, men of no blood, kill even the most aristocratic of foes. That was one reason French armies routinely chopped off the fingers of captured archers' right hands . . . on those rare occasions when they weren't in the mood for more inventive penalties, at least.

This time the Constable had almost as many archers—counting his mercenary Genoese crossbowmen—as Henry, however, and his initial plan had been to deploy them across his entire front to give the English a taste of their own medicine. It would be hard on his own archers, given the superiority of the longbow, but better them than their more nobly born betters. Besides, whatever else happened, the unarmored English archers would take serious losses of their own in the exchange, which was the entire point. Once casualties had shaken their formation, his armored cavalry would fall upon them and break the bastards up, at which point the English would be lost.

But after three motionless hours of glaring at one another, some of his mounted troops had dismounted to rest, or to water their horses, or to water themselves. God knew plate armor was a stifling, ovenlike burden, even in October, so it was easy enough to understand their actions. Yet it meant they were out of position, unable to launch the charge which would have devastated Henry's army if they'd managed to catch him on the move, when the English surprised them all with their sudden advance. By the time Charles had been able to reform his troops with some eye towards launching that sort of attack, Henry had stopped and those nasty, pointed stakes were back in place to protect his archers' frontage.

At which point, at a range of three hundred yards, they opened fire.

. . . . .

EVERY ONE OF the watching Barthoni flinched, almost in unison, as the first flights of arrows streaked into the French formation. The audio pickups Joraym and Kurgahr had requested brought them the screams and cries of wounded humans and their four-footed riding beasts—their "horses"—with hideous clarity. And no Barthon could have witnessed the sudden eruption of blood from rent and torn bodies without feeling physically ill. Yet, for all their revulsion, they couldn't look away, either. It was like watching some natural catastrophe—an avalanche, perhaps, sliding down to engulf and destroy. But this "natural catastrophe" was the result of willfully perverted intelligence, and somehow that made it even more mesmerizing.

"There!" Kurgahr said suddenly, pointing at the display. "I wondered when they'd do that!" He twitched his head in the Barthon gesture of resignation. "Insane or not, what's about to happen to those English is going to be ugly."

The historian had a pronounced gift for understatement, Garsul thought grimly, watching the better part of two thousand mounted knights charge the English line. It occurred to him that it probably would have been better to attack the English before they could settle into their new position, but the French charge began only after the English had begun pelting them with arrows. Still, it shouldn't matter all that much. It was clear from the display that the knights' armor was more than sufficient to turn the vast majority of the arrows sleeting towards them.

. . . . . .

CHARLES D'ALBRET SWORE viciously as his heavy cavalry pelted towards the English line. *Now* they attacked!

Yet even as he swore, the Constable knew it would have been foolish to expect any other response. That heavy rain of arrows was unlikely to kill or even wound many of those heavily armored men, but their horses were quite another matter. No cavalry in the world could stand in place under the aimed fire of seven thousand longbows, each firing as many as twelve shafts a minute. Its only options were to attack or run away to get out of range of those deadly horse-killing bows, and these were French knights. Running away was out of the question.

Not that attacking was any better option, when all was said.

The muddy field slowed the charging horsemen, and the English arrows continued to slash into them. Unlike their riders, only the horses' heads were truly armored, and they began to go down. Each fallen animal formed its own individual obstacle for its companions, but the wounded and panicked horses were almost worse. Many of them were uncontrollable, rearing and bolting with the maddening pain of their injuries, and the charge came apart in confusion, mud, mire, blood, and bodies. Unable to close with the English, the cavalry retreated back the way they'd come, which churned the already muddy earth into a slick, slithery morass dotted with dead and wounded horses like reefs in a sea of muck.

. . . . . .

HENRY WATCHED THE French cavalry recoil and smiled thinly. He knew all about the goading, maddening effect of archery. Even the best armored knight or man-at-arms could be killed or wounded under the wrong circumstances. The scars on his own face were the result of a Welsh rebel's arrow which had hit a sixteen-year-old Prince Henry in the face at the Battle of Shrewsbury. For that matter, Sir Henry Percy, the rebels' commander at Shrewsbury, had also been hit in the face. In his case, however, the experience had proved fatal.

The king saw very few armored bodies lying about in the mud, and most of those he did see appeared to be pinned by dead horses or injured when their mounts went down, rather than felled by arrow fire. But it was unlikely the French would simply stand there and take the English fire, and even if they managed to reorder their formation to get their own archers into position to engage, crossbowmen could never match the combination of his longbows' range and rate of fire. Which meant. . . .

. . . . .

GARSUL FELT THE others' shocked disbelief. It seemed ridiculous—impossible!—that such a thundering mass of heavily armored warriors could have been routed by nothing more than arrows propelled by muscle-powered bows.

Still, the French mounted troops were only a portion of their total force, and it was obvious the mounted men's comrades intended to avenge their repulse.

. . . . .

CHARLES D'ALBRET'S ORIGINAL battle plan had become a thing of the past. There was no way he could have reorganized his own forces under that plunging arrow fire. Partly because of the arrows themselves, but even more because of the nature of his army. The nobles and knights arrayed on the field had too many defeats to avenge, their numerical advantage was too overwhelming, and the taunting yells and yelps of contempt from the commoner longbowmen which had pursued the retreating cavalry were too much for men of blood to stomach.

And so they advanced.

The first French line, with almost five thousand dismounted knights and men-at-arms, was personally commanded by Constable d'Albret, along with Marshal Boucicault and the Dukes of Orléans and Bourbon, while the Count of Vendôme and Sir Clignet de Brebant commanded its supporting cavalry wings. The second line was commanded by the Dukes of Bar and Alençon and the Count of Nevers, following in the first line's wake, and a third line, under the Counts of Dammartin and Fauconberg, was ready behind the second. All told, ten thousand armored men-at-arms, including the very flower of the French aristocracy, stood poised to crush the mere fifteen hundred

English men-at-arms arrayed against them, and once those English men-at-arms had been disposed of, the archers would be easy meat.

Except. . . .

. . . . .

"I DON'T BELIEVE it," Kurgahr said flatly.

"Perhaps that's because we've had technology for so long," Garsul replied, still unable to look away from the display. "How long has it been since a few thousand Barthoni tried to walk across a muddy field together?" He snorted harshly. "Especially a muddy field like *this* one!"

The rain-soaked, plowed earth had been churned into mud by the French cavalry; now the marching feet of thousands of men-at-arms turned the mud into watery muck. What would have been slow going under any circumstances became a nightmare ordeal for men wearing fifty and sixty pounds of unventilated, sunbaked armor. Some of the men in the center of the field found themselves wading through liquid mud that was literally knee-deep, and even as they slogged slowly forward, the drumbeat of English arrows continued to slam into them.

. . . . .

HENRY WATCHED THROUGH merciless eyes, fingering the scars on his face, as the French struggled forward. Their heavy mail and plate armor might defeat his archers' arrows, but those same arrows forced the advancing French to close their helmet visors and keep their heads down lest the same thing happen to them as had happened to Henry and Percy at Shrewsbury. Visibility, as Henry knew from harsh personal experience, was hugely restricted under those circumstances, and just breathing through a visor's airholes could become a tortuous ordeal, especially for someone fighting his way through knee-deep mud in the hot, sweaty prison of his armor. Exhaustion was going to be a factor, he thought coldly, and so was crowding. As they advanced towards him, the field narrowed. They piled in on one another, packing closer and closer together, and the more congested their formation became, the more it slowed.

And not even the best armor could stop *all* arrows. Men *were* going down—dead, wounded, sometimes simply fallen and unable to rise in the mud—and those still on their feet became even more tightly packed, their formation even more confused, as they tried to avoid treading the casualties yet deeper into the mire. Even those still upright were being battered by the incessant impacts of thousands of arrows. They might not penetrate their targets' armor, but arrows driven from longbows with pulls of a hundred and forty and even two hundred pounds hit a man like the blows of a sledgehammer. The painful battering, added to all of the advancing Frenchmen's other miseries, had to have an effect.

. . . . .

GARSUL'S SKIN TWITCHED in disbelief. It was no longer shock; he was beyond that by now. No, this was duller than that. Almost numbing.

Despite everything, the lurching French advance had finally reached the English lines. They were so tight packed by the time they did that none of them could even take a full stride forward any longer. By Garsul's estimate, they'd probably been slowed by at least seventy percent simply because of the crowding. Yet, despite that, they'd covered the three hundred agonizing yards between them and their enemies somehow.

. . . . .

THE FRENCH MEN-AT-ARMS were exhausted; Henry's were rested and ready. The short English line of men-at-arms was four deep, and their supporting archers continued to fire—now into the French flanks—until they literally ran out of arrows. Yet even so, when the first line crunched into the English position, the outnumbered English were driven back by sheer weight of numbers. Not far, but back. Yet they fought savagely for each yard they were forced to yield, and the French formation was so crowded that many of its individual soldiers could find no room to use their personal weapons. Then the *second* French line drove into the melee, and the congestion got only worse.

At which point the longbowmen, arrows exhausted, swarmed over the French flanks and rear with hatchets, swords, daggers, mauls, pickaxes, and hammers. They were unarmored, true, but that meant they were far more mobile than their heavily armored, mud-mired opponents, and if they lacked the protective visored helms of their foes, they also had unimpaired vision. Worse, they were fresh, while many of the French were so exhausted from their long slog through the mud, the heat, and the lack of oxygen in their closed helmets that they could scarcely even lift their weapons. The situation could have been specifically designed—indeed, it *had* been, by Henry—to negate the heavily armored men-at-arms' advantages in close combat, and when a Frenchman went down, even if he'd only stumbled and fallen, he couldn't get back up under the longbowmen's mercilessly murderous attack.

. . . . .

"CLAHDRU!" HARTYR MUTTERED the better part of three human hours later. "It doesn't seem . . . How could anyone . . . ?"

His voice trailed off, and Garsul shook himself. "Humans" weren't Barthoni. In fact, despite his own decades-long commitment to Survey and his belief that all sentient species should be treated with dignity and respect, he couldn't really think of them as "people" at all. Joraym was right about that, and it shamed Garsul somewhere deep down inside to admit the xenoanthropologist was correct about his prejudices. But even so, they *were* sentients, and what these "English" and "French" had done to one another was going to leave him with nightmares for the rest of his life.

He didn't envy the Council when it read the confidential report he was going to have to file, either.

There were literal heaps of bodies, some taller than Garsul himself, piled in front of the "English" position. Clahdru only knew how many of the French had simply suffocated, drowned in mud, or been crushed to death by the weight of their own dead, and the third and final French line had declined to advance. Sensibly, in Garsul's opinion, given what had already happened to three-quarters of their armored warriors. It seemed incredible, preposterous, that such an outnumbered force could have so decisively defeated such an overwhelming foe, yet the English had, and the evidence of their ferocity and bloodthirstiness was horrifying.

"Do you still think they're simply 'juvenile' and 'immature,' Joraym?" he heard Ship Commander Syrahk ask bitingly.

"I don't know." The xenoanthropologist sounded badly shaken. "I mean, they *are* juvenile and immature—they couldn't be any other way at their current level of advancement. But *this*—!" Joraym tossed his head in a Barthon gesture of bafflement. "I've never read anything in the literature about this kind of brutality."

"Let's not get too carried away," Kurgahr put in. The ship commander and xenoanthropologist both looked at him disbelievingly, and he snorted. "I'm not trying to make excuses for anything we've just seen, but I've read enough history to know this sort of conduct isn't entirely unheard of among other species. For that matter, there were periods in our own pretechnic era when *we* did some things we'd be horrified to admit to today. Not over simple political disagreements, perhaps, and nothing remotely as bad as *this,* but when herds were faced with starvation conditions and forced to fight for range, they were capable of some pretty horrific actions. And I think if you looked into the histories of some of our omnivorous fellow citizens you might find some pretty bloody episodes there, as well."

"And then there's the Shongairi," Garsul pointed out. A symphony of scowls greeted the remark, and he shrugged his upper shoulders. "I'm just saying these creatures at least have the excuse of their social and technical primitivism. The Shongairi don't."

"Well, true," Joraym said in the tone of someone trying very hard to be detached, "but the Shongairi are bound to be a little . . . twisted, you know. I mean, they *are* . . . carnivores." The xenoanthropologist's distaste for the near-obscene term was evident. "I hate to say it, but these 'humans' are *omnivores*. They don't have that excuse, Garsul."

"I know, but—"

"Wait!" Syrahk interrupted. "Something's happening!"

. . . . .

"MY LIEGE!"

Henry looked up at the messenger's cry. The king was on his knees, beside the pallet on which his youngest brother Humphrey, the Duke of Gloucester, lay. Humphrey was barely three weeks past his twenty-fifth birthday, and Henry had personally led his guard to Humphrey's rescue when he went down. They'd gotten him out of the maelstrom and back to the surgeons, but he'd been wounded in the abdomen, and belly wounds were fatal far more often than not.

"What is it?" the king asked harshly now, fatigue and worry over his brother shadowing even his indomitable visage.

"My Liege, I think the French are regrouping!"

Henry rose abruptly, striding through his protective cordon of knights and men-at-arms to see for himself. The French rearguard had never advanced, but now the third line was stirring, and his jaw tightened. There were almost as many men in that line as in his entire army, and his archers' arrows were exhausted. It would take hours to get more of them up from the baggage train, and in the meantime his men were weary and out of formation and their prisoners were still unsecured. Literally thousands of armored Frenchmen lay in the mud—exhausted and fallen, perhaps, but unwounded—and their weapons lay with them.

Henry looked up the length of the field at the remaining French host and his nostrils flared.

"Fetch me Baron de Camoys!" he commanded.

"At once, Your Majesty!"

A messenger hurried off and returned minutes later with Sir Thomas de Camoys, who'd commanded the English left wing throughout the battle. With the death of Edmund of Norwich, the Duke of York, who'd commanded the right wing (and who, like hundreds of Frenchmen, had suffocated under a crushing pile of dead men and horses), Baron de Camoys had become Henry's senior field commander.

"Your Majesty," de Camoys said, bowing, and Henry jabbed a gauntleted finger at the stirring French third line.

"Those bastards mean to attack us, Baron," the king said flatly, his scarred face grim, "and we cannot chance what will happen here"—the same hand indicated the mud-mired Frenchmen heaped and piled before the English line—"when they do."

. . . . .

THIS TIME, GARSUL did vomit.

Perhaps it was simply cumulative revulsion. Perhaps it was more than that. Whatever it was, when the English began methodically slaughtering the helpless French men-at-arms and knights, thrusting daggers through visors or using axes and hammers and mattocks to literally hack open their armored carapaces and get at the men within, it was too much.

He turned away from the display at last.

"Kill the audio!" he said harshly. "We don't need to hear *this!*"

The sound of screams, babbled pleas for mercy, and prayers cut off abruptly, and Garsul shook himself.

Clahdru, he thought sickly. *Clahdru, preserve me. Of Your mercy, grant that I* never *see anything like this again! I thought those "secret orders" of mine undermined everything Survey stands for, but not now. Now I know how wise the Council truly was to issue them!*

"We're done on this world," he said, his voice flat. "We've got all the physical data we need, and Clahdru knows we've got more 'societal' data than any sane being is ever going to want to look at. Ship Commander," he looked at Syrahk, "I want us out of orbit and headed home within two day segments."

PLANET
KU-197-20

YEAR 74,065 OF THE HEGEMONY

.I.

"So, fearless hunter, are you ready for your venture into the deepest, darkest wilderness? And did you pack enough pemmican and jerky?" Sharon Dvorak inquired with a sweet smile.

"Was that last question a shot?" her husband responded suspiciously. He turned and cocked an eyebrow in her direction. "It was, wasn't it? It *was* a shot! Nay, a veritable aspersion—*that's* what it was!"

"It's sad to see a grown man—theoretically, at least—who's so *sensitive* about these things." Sharon sighed, shaking her head with infinite sadness.

"Yeah, sure!" Dave Dvorak snorted. "That from the woman who invented the word 'zinger'! *I* know. You're just being nasty because of that little faux pas the last time we took *you* hunting."

"Oh?" Sharon widened her eyes innocently at him. "You wouldn't be referring to that failure to bring along sufficient comestibles, would you? The memory failure—on my brother's part, I believe you said—where the food was concerned?"

"It was *not* a memory failure," Dvorak replied with immense dignity. "We simply regarded it as an opportunity for you to learn to subsist on the bounty of nature in the same fashion as us hardened hunter-gatherers. Nuts and berries, mushrooms instead of toadstools—that sort of thing."

"I could've sworn I heard my beloved spouse bitching and moaning about 'nuts and berries' for that entire trip."

"I'm sure your memory is simply playing you false."

"Oh? Then you aren't the one who said 'I'll trip him and sit on him while you go through his pockets for Slim Jims'?"

"Oh, I suppose the words might have slipped out somehow, since the greedy bastard wasn't willing to share with us. I mean, because of the low blood sugar associated with starvation, of course," Dvorak amended hastily. "Assuming any such episode had ever occurred, which I very much doubt."

"Oh, of course not."

Sharon shook her head and smacked him—gently, for her—across the top of the head. She had to stand on tiptoe to manage it, since he was a full foot taller than her own five feet two, but she'd had plenty of practice over the years.

He grinned down at her and wrapped both arms around her. She was exactly the right height to hug with his chin resting on the crown of her head, and he closed his eyes as he savored the embrace.

"You sure you don't want to come with us?" he asked in a much more serious voice. "Rob and I can still make room. And your tree stand'll fit just fine."

"You two can go out and sit in the woods in the rain if you want. Me, I'm staying home and curling up in front of the TV with that nice box of chocolates someone bestowed upon me—no doubt while in the grip of a guilty conscience."

"It may stop raining, you know," Dvorak pointed out, studiously ignoring the rain pattering on the roof even as he spoke.

"Yeah, and the horse may learn to sing." Sharon shook her head, but she also smiled at him. "Go on. Have fun. I'll even smear on the VapoRub when you come dragging home with pneumonia. But don't expect me to come to your rescue when your loving kids look at you reproachfully across a plate of Bambi stroganoff."

"Hah! As if that silly movie ever slowed any of your carnosaur offspring for a minute. Velociraptors don't care where the meat came from as long as it's fresh, you know."

"Of course they don't. But you *know* they're not going to pass up the chance to cast their woebegone gazes upon you." Sharon shook her head. "And don't blame me! It's *your* mother's fault."

Dvorak considered that for a moment, seeking a proper rejoinder. None came to him, so he contented himself with sticking out his tongue and making a rude noise. Then he kissed her cheek quickly, gave her another squeeze, and headed out to the waiting pickup.

. . . . .

"SO DID SHE give you a hard time?"

"I'll have you know," Dave Dvorak told his brother-in-law, Rob Wilson, severely, "that I am the master of my household. My lightest whim is law, my least desire instantly realized by all about me."

"Sure." Wilson rolled his eyes. "You do remember that I've known my sweet little sister for, oh, the better part of forty years?"

"If that's the case, then I think you might want to reconsider the phrase 'the better part of' when it comes in front of that particular number," Dvorak replied.

"I can still take her three falls out of four," Wilson replied, elevating his nose slightly.

"I seem to remember a Thanksgiving dinner when she got hold of your asp and pretty nearly broke your right kneecap," Dvorak said in a reminiscent tone.

"Only because I didn't want to *hurt* her."

"Yeah, sure." Dvorak looked away from the road for a moment to grin at his brother-in-law. "You sure you weren't afraid she was the one who was going to hurt *you?*"

"Well, I guess the possibility—the *remote* possibility, you understand—had crossed my mind," Wilson allowed. Both of them chuckled, and Dvorak returned his attention to the rain-streaked windshield.

The two men got along well. Dvorak, an NRA-certified firearms instructor, ran an indoor shooting range. Wilson, after twenty years in the US Marine Corps, had gone into law enforcement. He'd risen to sergeant with one of the smaller upstate municipalities and served as the force's designated marksmanship instructor before a high-speed car chase and a nasty collision led to a broken leg, significant loss of mobility, and a medical retirement. One of the best pistol shots Dvorak had ever met (he routinely ran the tables in the once-a-week pin-shooting contests at Dvorak's range), he'd moonlighted helping Dvorak out while he was on the force. He'd gotten his own NRA certification back when he was his police force's senior instructor, as well, so it had been logical for him to buy an interest in the business and go to work there full-time. It was a comfortable arrangement, and one which gave both of them the opportunity to expend a great deal of ammunition every week . . . and get paid for it. Sharon Dvorak and Veronica Wilson referred to it as "boys and their toys," but neither Dvorak nor Wilson minded that. Anyway, both of the women had been known to outshoot them.

Deer season was one of their favorite times of year, although as he looked out the windshield at the day's weather Dvorak wondered exactly why that was. Of course, it was only five o'clock. There was plenty of time for the weather to get better before dawn, he reminded himself.

At the moment they were on US-276, headed towards the small town of Travelers Rest, with their ultimate destination the Caesars Head / Jones Gap

Wildlife Management Area just south of the South Carolina–North Carolina state line. Dvorak's deer season had been disappointing to date—he'd only gotten to use up one of his tags so far—and Wilson had been fairly insufferable about it, since *he* only had one tag *left*. Had the ratio been reversed, Dvorak suspected, he would have opted to remain warmly in bed this sodden October morning. Such, alas, was the weakness of his character.

Well, he thought, leaning forward and peering through the upper quadrant of the windshield at the still black heavens, *at least if I do fill a tag today, I'll have damn well earned it.* He grinned, sitting back again. *I can see it now. "Here, woman—hunter brings back food. Go. Cook!"* He shook his head. *I'd be lucky if she didn't decide to cook* me! *Assuming, of course, that I wasn't the cook in the first place.*

Thunder rumbled overhead, loud enough to be audible even through the hissing sound of tires on rain-soaked asphalt, but he studiously failed to hear it.

.II.

The attention signal whistled on Fleet Commander Thikair's communicator.

He would remember later how prosaic and . . . normal it had sounded, but at that moment, as he looked up from yet another ream of deadly dull paperwork, when he still didn't know, he felt an undeniable sense of relief for the distraction. Then he pressed the acceptance key, and that sense of relief vanished when he recognized his flagship commander's face . . . and worried expression.

"What is it, Ahzmer?" he asked, wasting no time on formal greetings.

"Sir, we've just received a preliminary report from the scout ships. And according to the message, they've made a rather . . . disturbing discovery," Ship Commander Ahzmer replied.

"Yes?" Thikair's ears cocked inquisitively as Ahzmer paused.

"Sir, they're picking up some fairly sophisticated transmissions."

"Transmissions?" For a moment or two, it didn't really register. But then Thikair's eyes narrowed and his pelt bristled. "How sophisticated?" he demanded much more sharply.

"Very, I'm afraid, Sir," Ahzmer said unhappily. "We're picking up digital and analog with some impressive bandwidth. It's at least Level Three activity, Sir. Possibly even"—Ahzmer's ears flattened—"Level Two."

Thikair's ears went even flatter than the ship commander's, and he felt the tips of his canines creeping into sight. He shouldn't have let his expression give so much away, but he and Ahzmer had known one another for decades, and it was obvious the other's thoughts had already paralleled his own.

The fleet's main body had reemerged into normal-space barely four day-twelfths ago, after eight standard years, subjective, of cryogenic sleep. The flight had lasted some sixteen standard years, by the rest of the galaxy's clocks, since the best velocity modifier even in hyper allowed a speed of no more than five or six times that of light in normal-space terms. The capital ships and transports were still two standard months of normal-space travel short of the objective, sliding in out of the endless dark like huge, sleek *hasthar,* claws and fangs still hidden, while the medical staffs began the time-consuming task of reviving the thousands of ground personnel who would soon be needed. But the much lighter scout ships' lower tonnages made their drives more efficient in both n-space and h-space, and he'd sent them ahead to take a closer look at their target. Now he found himself wishing he hadn't.

Stop that, he told himself sternly. *Your ignorance wouldn't have lasted much longer, anyway. And you'd still have to decide what to do. At least this way you have some time to start thinking about it!*

His mind began to work again, and he sat back, one six-fingered hand reaching down to groom his tail while he thought.

The problem was that the Hegemony Council's authorization for this operation was based on the survey team's report that the objective's intelligent species—"humans," they called themselves—had achieved only a Level Six civilization. The other two systems on Thikair's list were both classified as Level Five civilizations, although one had crept close to the boundary between Level Five and Level Four. It had been hard to get the Council to sign off on those two. Indeed, the need to argue the Shongairi's case so strenuously before the Council was the reason the mission had been delayed long enough to telescope into a three-system operation.

But a Level Six culture was primitive enough for its "colonization" to be authorized almost as an afterthought, the sort of mission any of the Hegemony's members might have mounted. And in this particular case, authorization had been even prompter than usual. Indeed, Thikair knew some of the Council's omnivores—even some of its herbivores—had actually given their approval where KU-197-20 was concerned with hidden satisfaction. The visual and audio recordings the original survey team had brought back had horrified the vast majority of the Hegemony's member species. Even after making all due allowance for the humans' primitivism, most of the Hegemony had been none too secretly revolted by the bloodthirstiness those recordings had demonstrated.

Thikair's species *wasn't* revolted, which was one of the reasons those hypocrites on the Council had taken such ill-concealed satisfaction in turning KU-197-20 over to the Shongairi. Despite that, they'd never agreed to the conquest of a Level Three civilization, far less a *Level Two*! In fact, anything which had attained Level Two automatically came under protectorate status until it attained Level One and became eligible for Hegemony membership in its own right or (as a significant percentage of them managed) destroyed itself first.

Cowards, Thikair thought resentfully. *Dirt-grubbers.* Weed-eaters!

The epithets his species routinely applied to the Hegemony's herbivorous member races carried bottomless contempt, which was fair enough, since that emotion was fully reciprocated. The Shongairi were the only carnivorous species to have attained hyper-capability. Indeed, before them, the prevailing theory among the various Hegemony members' xenoanthropologists had been that no carnivorous species ever *would* attain it, given their natural propensity for violence. Over forty percent of the Hegemony's other member races were herbivores, who regarded the Shongairi's dietary habits as barbarous, revolting, even horrendous. And even most of the Hegemony's omnivores were . . . uncomfortable around Thikair's people.

Their own precious Constitution had forced them to admit the Shongairi when the Empire reached the stars, but the Shongairi were still the Hegemony's newest members, and the other species had never been happy about their presence among them. In fact, Thikair had read several learned monographs arguing that pre-Shongairi xenoanthropological theory had been correct; carnivores *were* too innately self-destructive to develop advanced civilizations. His people's existence (whether they could truly be called "civilized" or not) was simply the exception which proved the rule—one of those incredible flukes that (unfortunately, in the obvious opinion of the authors of those monographs) had to happen occasionally. What they *ought* to have done, if they'd had the common decency to follow the example of other species with similarly violent, psychopathically aggressive dispositions, was blow themselves back into the Stone Age as soon as they discovered atomic fission.

Unhappily for those racist bigots, Thikair's people hadn't. Which didn't prevent the Council from regarding them with scant favor. Or from attempting to deny them their legitimate prerogatives.

It's not as if we were the only species to seek colonies. There's the Shentai and the Kreptu, just for starters. And what about the Liatu? They're herbivores, *but they've got over fifty colony systems!*

Thikair made himself stop grooming his tail and inhaled deeply. Dredging up old resentments wouldn't solve this problem, and if he were going to be completely fair (which he didn't really want to be, especially in the

Liatu's case), the fact that some of those other races had been roaming the galaxy for the better part of seventy-four thousand standard years as compared to the Shongairi's nine hundred might help to explain at least some of the imbalance.

Besides, that imbalance is going to change, he reminded himself grimly.

There was a reason the Empire had established no less than eleven colonies even before Thikair's fleet had departed on its current mission, and why the Shongairi's Council representatives had adamantly defended their right to establish those colonies even under the Hegemony's ridiculous restrictions.

No one could deny any race the colonization of any planet with no native sapient species, but most species—the Barthoni came to mind—had deep-seated cultural prejudices against colonizing any world which was already inhabited. Unfortunately, there weren't all that many habitable worlds, and they tended to be located bothersomely far apart, even for hyper-capable civilizations. Worse, a depressing number of them already had native sapients living on them. Under the Hegemony Constitution, colonizing *those* worlds required Council approval, which wasn't as easy to come by as it would have been in a more reasonable universe.

Thikair was well aware that many of the Hegemony's other member species believed the Shongairi's "perverted" warlike nature (and even more "perverted" honor codes) explained their readiness to expand through conquest. And to be honest, they had a point, because no Shongair ever born could resist the seduction of the hunt. But the real reason, which was never discussed outside the Empire's inner councils, was that an existing infrastructure, however crude, made the development of a colony faster and easier. And even more importantly, the . . . acquisition of less advanced but trainable species provided useful increases in the Empire's labor force. A labor force which—thanks to the Constitution's namby-pamby emphasis on members' internal autonomy—could be kept properly in its place on any planet belonging to the Empire.

And a labor force which was building the sinews of war the Empire would require on the day it told the rest of the Hegemony what it could do with all of its demeaning restrictions.

That was one reason the Shongairi had been so secretly delighted when the more pacific members of the Council had decided that anyone as bloodthirsty as "humans" deserved whatever happened to them. In fact, Thikair was of the same opinion as the Emperor's senior ministers—the majority of the Council members who'd approved KU-197-20's colonization had seen it as an opportunity to neutralize the humans before they could become a second Shongairi. Better, in their opinion, to have only a single expansionist, bloodthirsty, hyper-aggressive species to deal with. Besides, a lot of them had probably salved their consciences with the reflection that conquest by the Shongairi would at least short-circuit the humans' almost inevitable self-destruction once they got around to acquiring nuclear capability. Looked at from that perspective, it was actually their moral responsibility to see to it that KU-197-20's unnaturally twisted development was aborted by an outside force while it was still primitive.

And if it happened that, in the process of being conquered, the humans should most unfortunately be rendered extinct, well, it wouldn't be the *Hegemony's* fault, now would it? No, it would be the fault of those vile, wicked, insanely combative Shongairi, *that's* whose fault it would be! And however regrettable such an outcome might be, at least the *civilized* races would be spared yet another batch of bloodthirsty deviants.

But the Shongairi saw humans in rather a different light. The majority of their client races (it would never have done to call them "slaves," of course) were as thoroughly useless in a military sense as the Hegemony's more developed herbivores. Most of them weren't exactly over-blessed with intelligence, either. They could be taught relatively simple tasks, but only three of them could be trained, at least without significant surgical intervention, using the neural educator technology the Hegemony took for granted. And none of them had any of the hunter's aggressiveness, the drive—the *fire*—that fueled Shongair civilization. Workers and drones, yes, but never *soldiers.* Never warriors. It simply wasn't in them.

But the humans, now . . . *They* might have some potential. It was obvious from the survey team's records that they were hopelessly primitive, and from their abysmal tactics in the single battle the survey team had observed, they were just as hopelessly inept. Still, they were the first species to come the Shongairi's way who might possibly—with serious long-term training—make useful slave-soldiers. According to the survey team's admittedly no more than superficial physiological data, it might even be possible to teach them using neural educators without surgically inserted receptors. While they would never be the equal of the Shongairi as warriors even if that were true, they'd at least make useful cannon fodder. And who knew? A few generations down the road, with the right training and pruning and a suitable breeding program, they really *might* at least approach Shongair levels of utility.

The Emperor had made the importance of exploring KU-197-20's utility in that respect clear before Thikair's expedition departed. And the fact that the weed-eaters and their only slightly less contemptible omnivore fellows had so cavalierly handed the planet over to the Empire only made the possibility that it *would* prove useful that much more delicious.

None of which did much about his current problem.

"You say it's *possibly* a Level Two," he said. "Why do you think that?"

"Given all the EM activity and the sophistication of so many of the signals, the locals are obviously at least Level Three, Sir." Ahzmer didn't seem to be getting any happier, Thikair observed. "In fact, preliminary analysis suggests they've already developed fission power—possibly even fusion. But while there are at least *some* fission power sources on the planet, there seem to be very few of them. In fact, most of their power generation seems to come from burning *hydrocarbons*! Why should any civilization that was really Level Two do anything that stupid?"

The fleet commander's ears flattened in a frown. Like the ship commander, he found it difficult to conceive of any species stupid enough to continue consuming irreplaceable resources in hydrocarbon-based power generation if it no longer had to. That didn't mean such a species couldn't exist, however. Alien races could do incredibly stupid things—one had only to look at the pathetic excuses for civilizations some of the weed-eaters had erected to realize *that* was true! Ahzmer simply didn't want to admit it was possible in this case, even to himself, because if this genuinely was a Level Two civilization it would be forever off-limits for colonization.

"Excuse me, Sir," Ahzmer said, made bold by his own worries, "but what are we going to do?"

"I can't answer that question just yet, Ship Commander," Thikair replied a bit more formally than usual when it was just the two of them. "But I can tell you what we're *not* going to do, and that's let these reports panic us into any sort of premature reactions. Survey's *always* off a little when it estimates a primitive species' probable tech level; the sheer time lag makes that inevitable, I suppose. I admit, I've never heard of them being remotely as *far* off as the scouts' reports seem to be suggesting in this case, but let's not jump to any conclusions until we've had time to thoroughly evaluate the situation. We've spent eight years, subjective, just getting here, and

Medical is already half a month into reviving Ground Commander Thairys' personnel from cryo. We're not going to simply cross this system off our list and move on to the next one until we've thoroughly considered what we've learned about it and evaluated all of our options. Is that clear?"

"Yes, Sir!"

"Good. In the meantime, however, we have to assume we may well be facing surveillance systems considerably in advance of anything we'd anticipated. Under the circumstances, I want the fleet taken to a covert stance. Full-scale emissions control and soft recon mode, Ship Commander."

"Yes, Sir. I'll pass the order immediately."

. III .

Master Sergeant Stephen Buchevsky climbed out of the MRAP, stretched, collected his personal weapon, and nodded to the driver.

"Go find yourself some coffee. I don't really expect this to take very long, but you know how good I am at predicting things like that."

"Gotcha, Top," the corporal behind the wheel agreed with a grin. He stepped on the gas, and the Cougar four-by-four (officially redesignated years ago as an MRAP, or Mine Resistant Ambush Protection vehicle, largely as a PR move after IED attacks had taken out so many Humvees in Iraq) moved away. It headed for the mess tent at the far end of the position, while Buchevsky started hiking towards the sandbagged command bunker perched on top of the sharp-edged ridge.

The morning air was thin and cold, but little more than a month from the end of his current deployment, Buchevsky was used to that. It wasn't exactly as if it were the first time he'd been here, either. And while many of Bravo Company's Marines considered it the armpit of the universe, Buchevsky had seen substantially worse during the seventeen years since a deceitfully honest-faced recruiter had taken shameless advantage of an impressionable youth—a family friend, no less!—to fill his recruiting quota.

"Oh, the places you'll go—the things you'll see!" the recruiter in question had told him enthusiastically. And Stephen Buchevsky had indeed been places and seen things since. Along the way, he'd been wounded in action no less than six times, and at age thirty-five, his marriage had just finished coming unglued, mostly over the issue of lengthy, repeat deployments. He walked with a slight limp the physical therapists hadn't been able to completely eradicate, the ache in his right hand was a faithful predictor of rain or snow, and the scar that curved up his left temple was clearly visible through his buzz-cut hair, especially against his dark skin. But while he sometimes entertained fantasies about sitting down with

"Uncle Rob" and . . . "discussing" his inducements to get him to sign on the dotted line, he'd always reupped.

Which probably says something unhealthy about my personality. Besides, Dad would be really pissed with me for blaming it all on someone else! he reflected as he paused to gaze down at the narrow twisting road so far below.

On his first trip to sunny Afghanistan, he'd spent his time at Camp Rhine down near Kandahar. That was when he'd acquired the limp, too. For the next deployment, he'd been located up near Ghanzi, helping to keep an eye on the A01 highway from Kandahar to Kabul. That had been less . . . interesting than his time in Kandahar Province, although he'd still managed to take a rocket splinter in the ass. Which had been good for another gold star on the Purple Heart ribbon (and unmerciful "humor" from his so-called friends). But then the Poles had taken over in Ghanzi, and so, for his third Afghanistan deployment, he'd been sent back to Kandahar, where things had been heating up again. He'd stayed there, too . . . until his battalion had gotten new orders, at least. The situation in Paktika Province—the one the Poles had turned down in favor of Ghanzi because Paktika was so much more lively—had also worsened, and they'd been moved to help deal with the situation.

At the moment he was on his *fourth* deployment, and he and the rest of First Battalion, Third Marine Regiment, Third Marine Division (known as the "Lava Dogs"), had been operating in Helmand Province, conducting operations in support of the Afghan Army. Although, in Buchevsky's opinion, it had been rather the other way around as far as who was supporting whom was concerned. Still, like most professional members of the United States military he'd gotten used to the sometimes inventive fashion in which operations' purposes were described to the public. In this case he even understood why it had to be described that way. And despite his own lingering concerns over the corruption of the national government, the overall situation really had improved a lot. The local governor in Helmand seemed to be working hard to provide the people of his province with genuine security, and most of the Afghan soldiers they'd been working with this time around seemed motivated to keep it that way. For that matter, they were even acquiring the rudiments of genuine fire discipline! They weren't as good as *Marines,* of course, but then, who was?

His lips twitched at that thought, which he reminded himself to keep *to* himself. At the moment, Bravo Company—*his* company—had been detached from Battalion and sent back up into Paktika yet again, this time tasked as backup for the Army's 508th Parachute Infantry while the Army tried to pry loose some of its own people for the job.

Despite all the emphasis on "jointness," it hadn't made for the smoothest relationship imaginable. The fact that everyone recognized it as a stopgap and Bravo as only temporary visitors (they'd been due to deploy back to the States in less than three months when they got the call) didn't help, either. They'd arrived without the logistic support which would normally have accompanied them, and despite the commonality of so much of their equipment, that had still put an additional strain on the 508th's supply services. But the Army types had been glad enough to see them and they'd done their best to make the "jarheads" welcome.

The fact that the Vermont-sized province shared six hundred miles of border with Pakistan, coupled with the way the political situation in Pakistan had once more become "interesting" (in the Chinese sense of the word) and the continuing upsurge in opium production under the Taliban's auspices (odd how the fundamentalists' onetime bitter opposition to the trade had vanished when they decided they needed cash to support their operations), had prevented Company B from feeling bored. There was always a large-scale trade in opium, and the recent upsurge in weapon-smuggling, infiltration, and cross-border attacks by the jihadists based among the Pakistani hill tribes hadn't helped, either. Still, the situation was beginning to show signs of stabilizing, and Buchevsky still preferred Paktika to his 2004 deployment to Iraq. Or his more recent visit to Helmand, for that matter.

Now he looked down through the thin mountain air at the twisting trail Second Platoon was here to keep a close eye on.

All the fancy recon assets in the world couldn't provide the kind of constant presence and eyes-on surveillance needed to interdict traffic through a place like this. An orbiting unmanned reconnaissance drone wasn't very good at intercepting a bunch of *mujahedin* backpacking in rocket-propelled grenades, for example. It could spot them, but it couldn't *suppress* the traffic. Not even helicopter-borne pounces could do that as well as troops permanently on the ground with good lines of oversight . . . and infantry wasn't likely to be downed by MANPADs, either. Not that anything was ever going to make the job simple. It was probably easier than the job Buchevsky's father had faced trying to cut the Ho Chi Minh Trail—at least his people could see a lot farther!—but that wasn't saying very much, all things taken together. And he didn't recall his dad's mentioning anything about lunatic martyrs out to blow people up in job lots for the glory of God.

He found himself thinking about the odd twists and turns fate took as he gazed down at the serpentine trail. His father had been a Marine, too, serving two enlistments as a combat infantryman before he got his divinity degree and transferred to the Navy to become a chaplain. Buchevsky the Younger, as he'd been referred to by his dad's buddies, had grown up on one Marine or Navy base after another, so if anyone should have known the truth when Uncle Rob spoke his seductive lies, it should have been Stephen Buchevsky.

Face it, he told himself. *You* did *know what you were getting into, and you'd do the same thing today. Which probably proves you* are *an idiot, just like Trish says.* He smiled sadly, thinking about that last conversation. *You could've gotten out, just like she wanted. God knows you've put in more than your share of time in places like this! And she had a point about what you owe the girls, too. You knew she did. That was why you got so pissed at her for playing that card. Because you knew she was absolutely right to say it . . . and you were too much of a coward to admit it. You're just lucky*—damned *lucky—she wants your daughters to grow up knowing their daddy. How many cases have you seen where it went the other way?*

He thought about the perversity of his own nature, but he knew the real reason he'd reupped so many times and why he was where he was. His dad had put it into words years ago, when Commander Buchevsky had finally retired and taken over a small church in his South Carolina hometown.

"Son," Alvin Buchevsky had said sadly, looking somehow like a stranger out of the uniform he'd worn as long as his son had been alive, "you're not just a lifer, you're a *combat arms* lifer. You're just never going to be satisfied doing anything else, and that's the way it is. I've seen it in plenty of others. In fact, to be honest, I was afraid I saw it in myself, once upon a time. Might be I really did, too, looking back on it. That's the real reason I was so relieved when I realized I had a genuine call to the ministry."

The Methodist pastor had looked up at his towering son and shaken his head.

"You've got that protective bug, too," he'd said. "That crazy notion—probably your mom's and my fault—that you're supposed to *fix* everything. Just don't have it in you to not answer to it, either. And you're good at leading Marines, and you're good at killing people you think need killing. I don't say you *like* doing it, because I know you don't, and I hate what I know that's costing you. But the truth is you'd never be happy leaving 'your job' to someone else—someone who might not be as good at it as you are and got more of your Marines killed because they screwed up where you might not've. I know better than most that sometimes people like you are exactly what we need, too. There's always going to be plenty of bad people in the world, and that means we need people like you to stop 'em. You know I'll never condemn you for it, either. Never love you any less. But what you do . . . it can be hard on a man's soul, and it's hard on his family, Steve. It's awful hard."

You were right, Dad, he thought now. Accepting that hadn't been the easiest thing he'd ever done, yet he'd had no choice, in the end. *And sometimes I think the real reason Trish is working so hard on "keeping the channels open" is because she wants to make damned sure she and the girls stay close to you and Mom, thank God. I don't know what I did to deserve you, but whatever it was, I'm glad I did it.*

He gave himself a shake. He had a lot on his plate organizing the Company's rotation home, and he turned back towards the command bunker to inform Gunnery Sergeant Wilson that his platoon's Army relief would begin arriving within forty-eight hours. It was time to get the turnover organized and Second Platoon back to its FOB to participate in all the endless paperwork and equipment checks involved in any company movement.

Not that Buchevsky expected anyone to complain about *this* move.

.IV.

The gathering in *Star of Empire*'s conference room consisted of Thikair's three squadron commanders, his ground force commander, Ship Commander Ahzmer, and Ground Base Commander Shairez. Despite the fact that Shairez was technically junior to Ground Force Commander Thairys, she was the expedition's senior ground base commander, and as such she, too, reported directly to Thikair.

At the moment, the flagship, along with the rest of the fleet, lay on the far side of KU-197-20's single large moon from the planet. Only the highly stealthy scout ships had been permitted to approach closer to the objective than that, and all but two of them—one in each polar position—had since been withdrawn, leaving even less easily detected remote platforms to continue the monitoring function.

Rumors about those scout ships' findings had spread, of course. It would have required divine intervention to prevent that! Still, if it turned out there was no landing after all, it would scarcely matter, would it?

"What's your interpretation of the scout ships' data, Ground Base Commander?" Thikair asked Shairez without bothering to call the meeting formally to order. Most of them seemed surprised by his disregard for protocol, and Shairez didn't look especially pleased to be the first person called upon. But she could scarcely have been surprised by the question itself. Unlike most of the Hegemony's other species, the Shongairi had little use for xenoanthropology. Still, at least some expertise in dealing with other races was necessary if one was going to manage them efficiently. One of the main reasons Shairez was the expedition's senior ground base commander was her experience in dealing with and studying the Empire's subject species, which made her the closest thing to a true xenologist Thikair had.

"I've considered the data, including that from the stealthed orbital platforms, carefully, Fleet Commander," she replied. "I'm afraid my analysis confirms Ship Commander Ahzmer's original fears. I would definitely rate the local civilization at Level Two. A surprisingly *advanced* Level Two, in some areas, in fact."

Unhappy at being called upon or not, she hadn't flinched, Thikair thought approvingly.

"Expand upon that, please," he said.

"Yes, Sir." Shairez tapped the virtual clawpad of her personal computer, and her eyes unfocused slightly as she gazed at the memos projected directly upon her retinas.

"First, Sir, this species has developed nuclear power. Of course, their technology is extremely primitive and it would appear they're only beginning to experiment with fusion, but there are significant indications that their general tech level is much more capable than we would ever anticipate out of anyone with such limited nuclear capacity. Apparently, for some reason known only to themselves, these people—I use the term loosely, of course—have chosen to cling to hydrocarbon-fueled power generation well past the point at which they could have replaced it with nuclear generation."

"That's absurd!" Squadron Commander Jainfar objected. The crusty old space dog was Thikair's senior squadron commander and as bluntly uncompromising as one of his dreadnoughts' main batteries. Now he grimaced as Thikair glanced at him, one ear cocked interrogatively.

"Apologies, Ground Base Commander," the squadron commander half growled. "I don't doubt your data. I just find it impossible to believe any species *that* stupid could figure out how to use fire in the first place!"

"It *is* unique in our experience, Squadron Commander," Shairez acknowledged. "And according to the master data banks it's also unique in the experience of every other member of the Hegemony. Nonetheless, they do possess virtually all of the other attributes of a Level Two culture."

She raised one hand, ticking off points on her claws as she continued.

"They have planet-wide telecommunications. Their planetary data net, while still rudimentary in a technical sense, is planet-wide, as well. And, to be honest, our initial probes confirm that their security measures are surprisingly good.

"Although they've done little to truly exploit space, it isn't because of any inherent inability to do so. They have numerous communications and navigational satellites, what appear to be quite competent orbital astronomy platforms, and at least one crude space station. Their military aircraft are capable of trans-sonic flight regimes, they make abundant use of advanced—well, advanced for any pre-Hegemony culture—composites, and we've observed experiments with early-generation directed energy weapons, as well. They have *not* established a unified planetary government as yet, which is virtually unheard of for a species at this level of advancement, but there are indications that they are headed in that direction at this time. And while their technological capabilities are not distributed uniformly about their planet, they're spreading rapidly and should achieve that level of distribution within the next generation or two. Indeed, they might manage it even sooner, if their ridiculous rate of technological advancement to this point is any guide!"

The silence around the conference table was profound. Thikair let it linger for several moments, then leaned back in his chair.

"How would you account for the discrepancy between what we're now observing and the initial Survey report?"

"Sir, I *can't* account for it," she said frankly. "I've double-checked and triple-checked the original report. There's no question that it was accurate at the time it was made, yet now we find *this*. Every projection says this species ought to be experimenting with muzzle-loading black powder firearms and crude steam engines. Instead, it's somehow made the jump from animal transport, wind power, and muscle-powered weapons to what's clearly a Level Two culture more than three times as rapidly as any other species. And please note that I said '*any* other species.' The one I had in mind were the Ugartu."

The fleet commander saw more than one grimace at that. The Ugartu had never attained Hegemony membership . . . since they'd turned their home star system into a radioactive junkyard first. The Council of the time had breathed a quiet but very, very profound sigh of relief when it happened, too, given that the Ugartu had been advancing technologically at twice the galactic norm. Which meant *these* people . . .

"Well, I suppose that explains how Survey's estimate of their tech level could be so far off," Jainfar said dryly. "Now if we only knew *why* it's happened!"

"Is it possible the initial survey team broke procedure, Sir?" Ship Commander Ahzmer asked, his expression troubled. Thikair glanced at him, and his flagship's commander flicked both ears. "I'm just wondering if the surveyors might inadvertently have made direct contact with the locals? Accidentally given them a leg up?"

"Possible, but unlikely, Ship Commander," Ground Force Commander Thairys said. "I wish I didn't have to say that, since I find this insanely rapid advancement just as disturbing as you do. Unfortunately, the original survey was conducted by the Barthoni."

Several of Thikair's officers looked as if they'd just smelled something unpleasant. Actually, from the perspective of any self-respecting carnivore, the Barthoni smelled simply delicious. But the timid plant-eaters were one of the Shongairi's most severe critics. And the reason the miserable little centaurs were so heavily represented in the Hegemony's survey forces, despite their inherent timidity, was because of their fanatic support for the Council regulations limiting contact with inferior races.

"I'm afraid I agree with the Ground Force Commander," Shairez said.

"And it wouldn't matter if that *were* what had happened," Thikair pointed out. "The Constitution doesn't care where a species' technology *came* from. What matters is the level it's *attained*, however it got there."

"That, and the way the Council would react to finding out about it," Jainfar said sourly, and ears moved in agreement all around the table.

"I'm afraid Squadron Commander Jainfar has a point, Sir." Thairys sighed heavily. "It was hard enough getting approval for our other objectives, and they're far less advanced than *these* creatures have turned out to be. Or I hope to Dainthar's Hounds they still are, at any rate!"

More ears waved agreement, Thikair's among them. However aberrant, this species' development clearly put it well outside the parameters of the Council's authorization. However. . . .

"I'm well aware of just how severely our discoveries have altered the circumstances envisioned by our mission orders," he said. "On the other hand, there are a few additional points I believe bear consideration."

Most of them looked at him with obvious surprise, but Thairys' tail curled up over the back of his chair, and his ears flattened in speculation.

"First, one of the points I noticed when I reviewed the first draft of Ground Base Commander Shairez's report was that these people not only have remarkably few nuclear power stations, but for a species of their level, they also have remarkably few nuclear *weapons*. Only their major political powers seem to have them in any quantity, and even they have very limited numbers compared to their nonnuclear capabilities. Of course, they *are* omnivores, but the numbers of weapons are still strikingly low. Lower even than for some of the Hegemony's weed-eaters at a comparable point in their development. That becomes particularly apparent given the fact that there are military operations underway over much of the planet. In particular, several more advanced nation-states are conducting operations against adversaries who obviously don't even approach their own capabilities. Yet even though those advanced—I'm speaking relatively, of course—nation-states have nuclear arsenals and their opponents, who don't, would be incapable of retaliation, they've chosen not to employ them. Not only that, but they must have at least some ability to produce bioweapons, yet we've seen no evidence of their use. For that matter, we haven't even seen poison gas or neurotoxins!"

He let that settle in, then leaned forward once more to rest his folded hands on the conference table.

"This would appear to be a highly peculiar species in several respects," he said quietly. "Their failure to utilize the most effective weapons available to them, however, suggests that in *some* ways they haven't advanced all that greatly since the Barthoni first visited this world. In fact, it suggests they're almost as lacking in . . . military pragmatism as many of the Hegemony's weed-eaters. That being the case, I find myself of the opinion that they might well make a suitable client species after all."

The silence in the conference room was absolute as the rest of Thikair's listeners began to realize what Thairys had already guessed.

"I realize," the fleet commander continued, "that to proceed with this operation would violate the spirit of the Council's authorization. However, after careful review, I've discovered that it contains no specific reference to the attained level of the local sapients. In other words, the *letter* of the authorizing writ wouldn't preclude our continuing. No doubt someone like the Barthoni or Liatu might choose to make a formal stink afterward, but I rather suspect they would . . . find their allies thinner on the ground than they might anticipate in this case, let's say."

Ahzmer cocked one ear questioningly, and Thikair flipped both of his own in an answering shrug.

"What I'm about to say is not to be shared with anyone not currently sitting around this table without specific authorization from me," he said. "Is that clear?"

Every set of ears indicated assent, and he let the very tips of his canines show.

"The truth is," he told his senior officers, "that the Council is . . . concerned about these 'humans.' Or perhaps it would be better to say its oh-so-noble members are disgusted by them. Possibly even appalled. All of you, I know, have seen the visual and audio records the original survey team brought back from KU-197-20. I'm sure all of you were as disgusted as I was by the sheer military ineptitude displayed in those records. The weed-eaters, on the other hand, were horrified not by the natives' appalling lack of skill, but by their ferocity. I'm sure many of the Council's members doubt they would ever survive to achieve hyper-capability without blowing themselves up. I think others, though, are afraid they might. That the Hegemony could find itself faced with a second Shongair Empire."

He let more of his canines show in reaction to that thought, and saw his own response mirrored by his subordinates. The Shongair Empire had no intention of allowing any rivals to arise. Not that anyone as pathetic at using its own military resources as this species could ever challenge the Empire, of course.

"Before our departure on this mission, it was suggested to me by the Imperial Minister for Colonization that the Council sees authorizing our colonization of KU-197-20 as a means of striking down two prey with a single claw. First, it gives us a toy to keep us satisfied and occupied, poor primitive creatures that we are. Second, it presumably short-circuits this species' probable self-destruction and also eliminates any threat to the Hegemony's peace it might someday pose. In fact, while the Council would never admit it openly, it was clearly intimated to Minister for Colonization Vairtha by none over than Vice-Speaker Koomaatkia that the Council has determined that *something* needs to be done about these creatures, and that . . . fewer questions than usual will be asked about our tactics in KU-197-20's case."

Several of his subordinates pricked their ears at that sentence, and his own flipped in a grim smile. Koomaatkia was a Kreptu, and the Kreptu were one of the Hegemony's original founding members. They'd also been among the Shongairi's more persistent critics, although never to the same degree as the Barthoni and Liatu, yet they were famed for a certain pragmatism, as well. No doubt the notion of using one problem to solve or prevent another one *would* appeal to them. And they were a highly consensual species. No Kreptu as prominent as Clan Lady Koomaatkia'n'haarnaathak of Chorumaa would ever have breathed even a hint of such a thing to Minister for Colonization Vairtha if it had not, in fact, embodied the *Council's* consensus. And that meant. . . .

"I'm sure," Thikair continued, "that she and some of the Council's other members hope these creatures will prove sufficiently difficult for us to manage that we'll find ourselves forced to slow our own rate of colonization and expansion. They'd all like that, whether they ever admitted it or not. But most importantly of all, to their thinking, our conquest of these creatures' homeworld will keep *them* from becoming a problem to the rest of the Hegemony in the fullness of time.

"And that, of course, was their thinking when they had no idea of how insanely rapid these 'humans'' rate of technological process might become. Let's not forget the Ugartu. Is there any officer sitting at this table who believes the Hegemony Council didn't feel deeply relieved when the Ugartu self-destructed?" His lips wrinkled back from his teeth in contempt. "All the weed-eaters—and most of the omnivores, too, for that matter—are far too hypocritical, far too aware of their own towering moral stature, to ever admit anything of the kind, but we know better, don't we?"

His officers looked back at him in equally contemptuous agreement, and his ears flipped another shrug.

"So even if this is a Level Two civilization, some members of the Council would shed no tears if the 'humans' were to find themselves subordinated to the Empire. They'd see it as the lesser of two evils, I think. As I said, the Barthoni and Liatu might disagree, but less vehemently than usual this time. And even if they did, it seems clear from Vice-Speaker Koomaatkia's comments to the Minister that they would find themselves with fewer allies than they'd probably expect. Against that background, I think it might be well for us to consider the possible advantages of proceeding despite the Constitutional protections *normally* extended to a Level Two civilization."

"Advantages, Sir?" Ahzmer asked, and Thikair's eyes gleamed.

"Oh, yes, Ship Commander," he said softly. "This species may be bizarre in many ways, and they obviously don't understand the realities of war, but clearly something about them has supported a phenomenal rate of advancement. I realize their actual capabilities would require a rather more vigorous initial strike than we'd anticipated. And even with heavier prelanding preparation, our casualties might well be somewhat higher than projected. Fortunately, Ground Force Commander Thairys has twice the normal ground force component thanks to our follow-on objectives in Syk and Jormau. That means we have ample force redundancy to conquer any planet-bound civilization, even if it has attained Level Two. And to be honest, I think it would be very much worthwhile to concentrate on this system even if it means writing off the seizure of one—or even both—of the others."

One or two of them looked as if they wanted to protest, but he flattened his ears, his voice even softer.

"I realize how that may sound, but think about this. Suppose we were able to incorporate these creatures—these 'humans'—into our labor force. Remember, preliminary physiological data suggests it may be possible to neurally educate them, so they could be rapidly integrated. But suppose we were able to do even more than that with them. Put them to work on *our* research projects. Suppose we were able to leverage their talent for that sort of thing to quietly push our own tech level to something significantly in *advance* of the rest of the Hegemony. The weed-eaters are content with the technology they have, and so are most of the omnivores. They're stagnant—we all know that. Our programs are already giving us a small edge over their technology base, but let's be honest among ourselves—it's taking longer than we'd like, and so far our advances have been only incremental. These creatures might very well give us the opportunity to accelerate that process significantly. Possibly even suggest avenues of development we haven't even considered yet. How do you think that would ultimately affect the Emperor's plans and schedule?"

The silence was just as complete, but it was totally different now, and he smiled thinly.

"It's been three standard centuries—over six hundred of these people's years—since the Hegemony's first contact with them. If the Hegemony operates to its usual schedule, it will be at least two more standard centuries—over four hundred local years—before any non-Shongair observation team bothers to visit this system again. That would be—what? Twenty of these creatures' generations? More? And that will be counting from the point at which we return to announce our success. If we delay that return for a few decades, even as much as a standard century or so, it's unlikely anyone would be particularly surprised, given that they expect us to be gathering in three entire star systems." He snorted harshly. "In fact, it would *amuse* the weed-eaters to think we'd found the opposition more difficult than anticipated! But if we chose instead to spend that time subjugating these 'humans' and then educating their young to Hegemony standards, who knows what sort of R&D they might accomplish before that happens?"

"The prospect is exciting, Sir," Thairys said slowly. "Yet I fear it rests on speculations whose accuracy can't be tested without proceeding. If it should happen that they prove less accurate than hoped for, we would, as you say, have violated the spirit—the *official* spirit, at any rate—of the Council's authorizing writ for little return. Personally, I believe you may well be correct and that the possibility should clearly be investigated. Yet if the result is less successful than we might wish, would we not risk exposing the Empire to retaliation from other members of the Hegemony?"

"A valid point," Thikair acknowledged. "First, however, as I say, the Council's attitude towards the humans is somewhat more . . . ambivalent than usual. Second, even if the Barthoni and their weed-eater fellows were able to muster support for a vote of censure from the Council, the Emperor would be able to insist—truthfully—that the decision was mine, not his, and that he never authorized anything of the sort. I believe it's most probable the Hegemony Judiciary would settle for penalizing me, as an individual, rather than recommending retaliation against the Empire generally. Of course it's possible some of you, as my senior officers, might suffer as well. On the other hand, I believe the risk would be well worth taking and would ultimately redound to the honor of our clans.

"There is, however, always another possibility. The Council won't expect a Level Three or a Level Two civilization any more than we did. If it turns out after a local century or so that these humans aren't working out, the simplest solution may well be to simply exterminate them and destroy enough of their cities and installations to conceal the level of technology they'd actually attained before our arrival. Given the Council's evident attitude towards the original survey reports and—especially—Vice-Speaker Koomaatkia's . . . encouragement, I suspect the Hegemony would be less brokenhearted over such an outcome than they might have been in another case, not that any of them would ever be honest enough to *say* so. In fact, it's possible they might well choose not to look all that carefully at the evidence of the locals' actual technological level lest unpleasant questions about their own attitudes and behaviors be raised. So while it would be dreadfully unfortunate, of course, if one of our carefully focused and limited bioweapons somehow mutated into something which swept the entire surface of the planet with a lethal plague, the Council might prove surprisingly . . . understanding in this instance. After all, as we all know"—he bared his canines fully—"accidents sometimes happen."

.V.

"I wonder if she'll drown him?" Captain Pieter Stefanovich Ushakov mused aloud, watching his daughter glower at the older of her two younger brothers.

"I doubt it," his wife replied calmly.

Vladislava Nikolaevna Ushakovna was a tall, trim woman, as blond as her husband, but with a markedly more placid disposition. Unlike Pieter, who'd been born in Ternopil *oblast* in western Ukraine and whose family had moved to Kiev only after his eleventh birthday, Vladislava was a native Kievan. She was the one who'd first introduced fourteen-year-old Pieter to the vast lake many years before, and he was glad she had. Not just because of the fond memories of moonlight, blankets, and murmured kisses, either, although they *definitely* played a part in explaining just how fond those memories were. At the moment, however, those long-ago days seemed rather remote as she did her best to dissuade their youngest—three-and-a-half-year-old Grigori—from ripping his favorite picture out of his favorite book. She, Pieter, and Grigori sat under a picnic shelter overlooking the huge Kyyivs'ke reservoir north of Kiev on the Dnipro River. The spring sunlight was warm, the day was young, and the dark blue waters of the lake were dotted with pleasure craft.

They were also quite deep enough to dispose of an irritating younger brother, Pieter thought.

"I don't know," he said with a slow smile. "If I were her, *I'd* probably drown him."

"I think that might be just a little extreme as a first response," Vladislava said. "Now, if he keeps it *up*. . . ."

The two of them looked at each other, and Pieter chuckled. At twelve, Daria had already shot up to a meter and a half in height. She was probably going to equal her mother's hundred and seventy centimeters, although it was unlikely she was going to accomplish six-year-old Daria's ambition to top her father's hundred and eighty-five. Ruslan, on the other hand, who was two years her junior, was just finishing a growth spurt which had left him a good two centimeters taller than she was, and he'd been making remarks about short people ever since he'd caught up with her. Now that he'd actually surpassed her, he was finally tall enough to literally look down his nose at her, and she didn't appreciate it one bit. She especially didn't appreciate it when her father was tactless enough to point out that now that Ruslan had taken the lead in altitude, she was never going to catch up with him again, growth spurts or no. For that matter, according to the pediatrician, Ruslan was going to be at least six or seven centimeters taller than Pieter by the time he was finished.

"Boy may have a future in basketball," he remarked now.

"Oh, that would be a marvelous thing to tell him in front of Daria." Vladislava shook her head. "Why don't you find out? If you get up and run after them right this minute, you could probably catch them before they get to the boat. Oh, and don't forget to take an anchor with you, so she can tie it to his ankles before she tosses him in! In fact, take *two*—I'm sure she could find a use for the second one, as well."

"Military men learn not to expose themselves to hostile fire unnecessarily," he told her. "Besides, for now at least he's way too interested in hockey to think about basketball."

"Like father, like son," Vladislava agreed. "And what brought up basketball, in that case?"

"Well, if he's going to be tall enough for it, you tend to lose less teeth on a basketball court," Pieter said philosophically. "Besides, he's got the hand-eye coordination for the game. And if we decide to go ahead and take Aldokim's offer, I understand professional basketball pays better than professional hockey."

"Are you really thinking about taking him up on that?" Vladislava raised an eyebrow, and he shrugged.

"I don't know, Slavachka," he said, reaching out to run one hand over her long, wheat-colored hair. "I don't know. But I have to say, it's been seeming more tempting lately."

"But the Army's been your life, Pieter." She enveloped Grigori in her arms, resting her chin on the top of his head and gazing across into her husband's eyes. "You've invested fifteen years in it."

"And made it all the way to captain," he replied with a crooked smile.

"The Colonel swears you'll be on the next list for major," Vladislava countered, and he snorted.

"Maybe I will, and maybe I won't. Oh, I don't think he's lying to us. I just think it's likely that under the current circumstances promotion's more likely to go to someone whose politics are a little more acceptable to the powers that be. Face it, Slavachka—I stepped on too many toes."

She said nothing for several moments, bending over the child in her arms to press her face into Grigori's sweet-smelling golden hair. What Pieter had said was true enough, she reflected. His outspokenly pro-Western attitudes would probably have been enough to put at least a bit of a damper on his promotion prospects, after the recent elections, but that wasn't the real problem. No, the *real* problem was his stint in the Inspector General's office.

Pieter Ushakov was only thirty-six. He'd been in his very early teens when the old Soviet Union dissolved, and he'd never served in the Ukrainian military when it had been an official part of the Soviet armed forces. He was part of an entirely new generation of officers—Ukrainian patriots and nationalists determined to build a *Ukrainian* military to protect and serve their country.

In general, that military had done an outstanding job of rebuilding itself into exactly that sort of national force. It had a right to be proud of itself, yet the job had been so immense, so complicated, that mistakes had inevitably been made. And human beings were still human beings, with an inescapable tendency to look after their own, protect their own little empires, nurture their own personal loyalties, and pursue their own agendas. That had created the sort of problems Pieter—a young, smart, competent, obviously dedicated and strongly patriotic young officer—had been called in to help clean up, and he'd done that job as unflinchingly as he'd tackled every other task to which his country had ever called him. With, in Vladislava's opinion, inevitable consequences for all concerned.

He'd pulled off too many scabs, exposed too much nepotism, too much cronyism. And turned up too many threads pointing to too many senior officers who maintained too close ties with the Russian military even today. He'd only been a junior captain at the time, but he'd taken his responsibilities seriously, and the establishment hadn't been able to shut him up. Instead, it had shuffled him back into a combat arms assignment with almost indecent haste . . . and an audible sigh of relief.

Despite that, she hadn't realized his older brother's urging that he and his family emigrate to the United States and join him in business there might have fallen on fertile soil.

"Do you seriously think you could be happy over there? Working with Aldo?" she asked finally.

"You mean working *for* Aldo?" Smile wrinkles crinkled around Pieter's blue eyes, and he glanced after Daria and Ruslan. "Sibling rivalry, you mean?"

"Something like that." Vladislava smiled back at him. "I seem to remember when we were all children that you and he had a distinct tendency to hit one another over the head. Frequently."

"Well, neither of us would have wanted to hit the other one someplace where we might actually have *hurt* him," Pieter pointed out with a chuckle. "Besides, as you say, that was when we were all children together. I'm far more mature than that now."

"Odd how *I* hadn't noticed that," she observed.

"Because you're too near the forest to count the trees, as they say in America," Pieter told her, lifting his nose with an audible sniff.

"That must be it," she agreed gravely.

"Of course it is. And as far as working 'for' Aldo is concerned, that wouldn't be the case—or not for long, at any rate," he continued more seriously. "He's offering to pay me a damned good salary, Slavachka, a quarter of it in voting shares, with a stock option bonus incentive plan, on top of that. In four or five years, I'd be pretty close to an equal partner."

Vladislava's eyes widened. Aldokim Stefanovich Ushakov had done well in the fifteen years since he'd departed for the United States. He'd founded his own firm, specializing in heavy construction projects, and he'd become a major subcontractor building infrastructure for the American military in Iraq and Afghanistan. Vladislava wasn't one of the greatest admirers of American foreign policy, and she'd lost two uncles during the Soviet Union's adventures in Afghanistan, one of them courtesy of a Stinger shoulder-launched antiaircraft missile provided to the *mujahedin* by the Americans. As a consequence, she found it difficult to shed too many tears for either side in the current conflict there. But whatever she thought about the politics behind it, there was no question about how it had contributed to her brother-in-law's success.

And it makes good business sense from Aldo's perspective, too, she reflected. *Pieter's experience would be a plus for him.*

Her husband was a combat engineer—and a good one. No one had ever suggested that his career's currently stalled status had anything to do with his competence or his ability. In fact, before his detour to the Inspector

General's office had brought him into conflict with the murky world of political patronage, he'd been viewed as a rising star. In many ways, Aldokim's offer was as shrewd as it was generous, especially if he realized just how discontented Pieter was feeling at the moment.

"I don't know," she said now, slowly. "I mean, it sounds like a wonderful offer, and you know how much I love Aldo. But I've never been to America. I don't even know if I'd like it there. And if we moved, what about everything we'd be leaving behind? Mama, Papa—*your* mother?"

"I know." He stroked her long hair again. "But Mama would still have Vanya, Fydor, and Lyudochka—one of the advantages of big families, you know! And both her sisters, for that matter. And your parents would still have both of *your* sisters. For that matter, it's not like the Cold War was still going on. What with telephones and the Internet it's not that hard to stay in touch. Just look at how Aldo's managed. For that matter, with the kind of money he's talking about paying me, we could bring the entire family back to visit every year. Or fly both our parents over to visit *us,* for that matter. Who knows? They might decide *they* like America! The country's supposed to be full of immigrants from just about everywhere, you know."

"You have been thinking about this, haven't you?" She looked up from Grigori's hair, her gaze intent, and he nodded.

"I guess I have," he admitted. "More than I'd realized, I think, or else I'd have already discussed it with you. I mean, it's not the kind of decision I need to be making all on my own—not when it involves you and the children and our families."

She smiled again, faintly, thinking of all the men she knew who would have expected to do exactly that: make their decision, then announce it to their wives. That attitude was beginning to wane, but it still had a long way to go in Ukraine.

Which might be another consideration in favor of making the move, she thought. *Whatever else I may think about Americans, their women are certainly . . . assertive.* She looked after Daria, and her smile grew broader. *God, think what* she'll *be like if she gets to grow up over there!*

"Is this really what you want to do?" she asked.

"I don't know," he said frankly. "Up until the last couple of years, I would have said no. Like you say, I was entirely focused on the Army. And there's a part of me that still is—you're right about that. But this offer from Aldo . . . it's not just generous, it's exciting. And I *would* like to accomplish something a bit more meaningful in my life than being the oldest man ever promoted to major."

"How soon does Aldo need an answer?"

"Well," Pieter said dryly, "unless you think the fighting in Afghanistan is going to end next month, I don't think there's an enormous rush. We can certainly think about it for a while, anyway. Besides, there's still my commission to think about. Just processing the paperwork if I decide to resign is going to take a couple of months. But in answer to what you were asking, I think this is something we both need to consider. I'd like to make up our minds before the end of the summer, though, I think."

Vladislava nodded slowly, her expression thoughtful, and he nodded back. Her calm, deliberate approach to life was one of the things he especially loved about her. It had always been part of her personality, even when they were schoolchildren, and he trusted her judgment. She wasn't the sort to rush to any decision, but once she *had* decided, she neither looked back nor second-guessed herself. Nor would she second-guess *him*.

"But for now," he reached out and scooped Grigori up in his arms, tickling the little boy until he squealed joyfully, "let's go down to the lake and make sure we still have three offspring."

. VI .

Lieutenant Colonel Alastair Sanders wanted his star.

Well, to be fair, *every* lieutenant colonel or colonel wanted stars eventually. In his case, however, there was an added incentive to achieve general officer's rank quickly.

No, he'd explained to one would-be wit after another, he *wasn't* from Kentucky. He was from Wyoming. And he didn't have any secret recipes, either. For that matter, he wasn't even all that *fond* of fried chicken, thank you very much. Soldiers being soldiers, however, and officers senior to one being senior to one, he knew beyond a shadow of a doubt that he would be dogged by those putatively jocular inquiries until the hoped-for day when—oh, glory!—he would become *Brigadier General* Sanders.

Of course, he reminded himself as he regarded the orders before him with something less than ecstasy, there were always trade-offs, and there would be on that longed-for day, as well. Such as giving up assignments like the one he currently held. As the commanding officer of First Battalion, Second Brigade, Third Armored Division, he had what was *the* plum duty of his career, as far as he was concerned.

Even today, the Army's transformation plan was still tinkering with the perfect setup for its modular brigades. And while it had discovered over the past few years that the format for its Stryker brigades was, indeed, well suited to fast, mobile warfare against guerrillas, insurgencies, terrorists, and low-intensity combat in general, it was rather less well designed than the enthusiasts had predicted for some of the other tasks it had been supposed to perform. In short, there was still a need for a *heavy* maneuver force, as well, as recent political events had tended to underscore.

That was what his combined arms battalion was supposed to be, and Third Armored Division had been reactivated less than two years ago specifically to increase the number of heavy combat teams. At the moment, his battalion's table of organization and equipment consisted of his headquarters and headquarters company, two companies of M1A2 Abrams tanks, two mechanized infantry companies, and a mechanized combat engineer company. Both of his infantry companies were mounted in the M2A3 Bradley infantry fighting vehicle, with all the updated digital electronics, and there was talk of assigning an organic helicopter gunship element to the brigade, although he suspected control would be held at the brigade level rather than assigned at the battalion level.

He'd just been informed that he was receiving three extra sections of ANT/TWQ-1 Avenger HMMVW-mounted antiaircraft systems for his upcoming assignment, plus two of the brigade's three armored reconnaissance troops, mounted in the M3A3 cavalry variant of the Bradley, as well. Despite the fact that he didn't care all that much for the assignment in question, he had to admit that was a potent, ass-kicking collection of combat power. Nor could he pretend he didn't feel a deep sense of satisfaction as he regarded the fact that it was his, all his.

Well, his, the brigade CO's, the *division* CO's, and national command authority's, anyway. Indeed, the orders he'd just received could be looked upon as a gentle reminder that those who commanded the United States military might occasionally have the odd little task they wished "his" battalion to perform. Unreasonable of them, perhaps, but there it was.

He didn't really object to being reminded, though, and that wasn't the reason for his discontent. No, the problem was where they were sending him. Or, more to the point perhaps, the *reason* they were sending him.

Herat, capital of Herat Province, just across the border from Iran. There hadn't been much fighting in the province lately, other than the increasingly frequent pounces seeking to interdict the flow of weapons across the border from Iran. Most of those weapons were headed to points deeper inside the country, not Herat itself, however, and the provincial government (which was at least reasonably free of corruption and cronyism, as far as Sanders could see) had relatively firm control of the region. In fact, there'd been substantially fewer incidents in the city of Herat over the last five or six months than in Kabul itself. But internal Afghan bloodshed (or the lack of it) wasn't the reason his battalion was being sent there.

No, the reason for that was the tension between the Iranian régime and the West in general, and the United States and the State of Israel, in particular.

Sanders didn't really think of himself as an expert on international relations and diplomacy, but the commander of a combined arms battalion couldn't afford to be uninformed on such matters, either. For that matter, his superiors would have taken a rather dim view of such a state of affairs. Because of that, he was only too well aware of just how completely relations with Iran had gone into the toilet over the last few years.

The régime's brutal suppression of internal dissent—the "Green Movement"—had driven its relations with the outside world even farther into the wilderness. The mass executions which had followed the resurgence of protests in 2012 had completed Iran's descent into pariah status, and the régime had reacted by becoming even more hardline, even more repressive. The U.S.-sponsored embargo on gasoline shipments which had finally been agreed to after the 2011 assassination of Mir-Hossein Mousavi Khameneh by "parties unknown" had hurt the Iranian economy badly, and the régime blamed it (and similar Western pressures) for the subsequent upsurge of street protests. There was probably some logic on their side this time around, Sanders admitted, although their decision to have Mousavi murdered—or at least to refuse to hold anyone accountable for it (except, of course, for the agents of the Greater Satan, which had undoubtedly ordered the crime specifically to implicate *them*)—damned well had a lot more to do with it. And even if the embargo was making things still worse, *he* wasn't going to shed any tears over their fury and what had to be a steadily growing inner sense of desperation. Their response, however, had included dropping the charade of "peaceful nuclear power" and openly announcing their intention to acquire nuclear weapons as rapidly as possible.

Along, of course, with the renewed observation that the "Zionist entity" had no right to exist and had to be eradicated as soon as possible. Then there was that minor matter of the continued call for the universal caliphate which, for some odd reason, didn't fill the non-Muslim world with joyous anticipation. For that matter, most of the *Muslims* of Sanders' acquaintance weren't particularly enamored of the notion of an *Iranian*-style caliphate.

Despite all of that, Russia (which had worked hard to build influence in Iran for over thirty years, since the fall of the shah) had continued to supply Tehran with nonnuclear military technology up until about eight months ago. At that point, the Russian government had finally given in to Western pressure. Moscow had retreated from the military relationship with ill-concealed resentment, but the parlous state of its own economy had meant it couldn't afford too open a confrontation with its Western trading partners, especially when the combination of new drilling in the U.S., the unfortunate coup which had overtaken Hugo Chávez in Venezuela, general global conservation, and the current (relative) tranquility in the Sunni Middle East had conspired to drive down the price of their own oil so dramatically. So, as of six months ago, Russia had officially suspended all arms and technology shipments to Iran.

Intelligence suggested that China was now sniffing around the opportunities presented by the Russian withdrawal, but it didn't look as if there was going to be much upsurge in Chinese influence in Tehran. For one reason, Sanders suspected darkly, because Russia hadn't really disengaged as fully as the Kremlin claimed it had. And, for another, because China was currently much more interested in the possibilities in Pakistan's oil- and gas-rich but penniless Baluchestan Province.

In the meantime, Iran had stepped up its efforts to supply weapons—and increasingly capable ones—to its proxy forces like Hamas. There'd been a significant upsurge in terrorist attacks in Israel and Iraq, as well, and there wasn't much doubt that Iranian intelligence had been deeply involved in them. Add in the normal vituperation of its lunatic president (who would have believed they could have found someone *worse* than Ahmadinejad?) and the increased fervency of the mullahs' calls for jihad against both the Greater and Lesser Satans, and there was a lot of room for anxiety. In fact, Sanders rather suspected antacid makers were doing land office business in Wonderland on the Potomac.

The hard part was trying to figure out how much of the anxiety was justified, and recent Iranian "military exercises" had added to the ambiguity. There was a lot of discussion about the West's avenues for bringing even more pressure to bear on the régime, and the possibility of a complete naval blockade had been coming up more and more frequently of late. Personally, Sanders didn't think the Palmer Administration had any serious intention of doing it, but the US Navy clearly had the capability, and enough of that navy was forward deployed to the Red Sea and Western Med to make the mullahs understandably nervous.

Whatever the reason, their public belligerence had grown even more vitriolic of late, and Iran had recently reinforced its positions along its eastern frontier with Iraq despite its nominally friendly relationship with Iraq's majority-Shiite government. No one took too much stock in the "friendliness" of that particular relationship, however, given Iraq's continuing relationship with the United States and the last few months' sudden spate of assassinations of Sunni government ministers, governors, and mayors. Even the Shiite Interior Minister, who'd apparently made the mistake of seeming too willing to conciliate his Sunni fellows, had been mysteriously assassinated, and fear that Iran was likely to try something genuinely irrational had risen accordingly.

In addition, Tehran had stationed a corps consisting of an armored division and a mechanized infantry division at Tayyebat in Razavi Khorasan Province, less than ninety miles east of Herat. It was unlikely that a single Iranian division of long-in-the-tooth T-55s and T-72s was going to jump off on an invasion of Afghanistan, especially given all the air power available in-country to knock it on its ass if it tried. Despite that, the Powers That Were had decided that presenting a régime as . . . radically energetic as the current one in Tehran with something a little more noticeable than out-of-sight, out-of-mind F-35s might be a good idea.

Thus Sanders' orders to go and be noticeable.

Of course, this was only the warning order, giving him time to hand over his battalion's present responsibilities to its designated relief and organize the move. It was always possible the actual move would be canceled. In fact, Sanders wished he had a nickel—well, maybe a dollar, given inflation—for every time he'd seen orders canceled or changed at the last minute. He didn't think that was going to happen this time, though. There was too much tension in the air. By this time, tension was actually feeding upon tension in an accelerating feedback loop on both sides of the confrontation.

Given the current circumstances, his presence might simply exacerbate the situation. How much of the Iranians' apparently irrational rhetoric was genuine and how much represented the actual intentions of the régime had always been one of the really fun guessing games where Iran was concerned, and it had turned into even more of a case of paying your money and taking your choice over the last couple of years. So his orders were to *deter* Iranian adventurism without *provoking* Iranian adventurism, and to *defeat* any Iranian adventurism which occurred anyway.

Presumably it all made sense to someone in the Pentagon or, at least, in the Administration. In the meantime, his was not to question why.

And while he was busy not questioning, he supposed it was time to sit down with his S-3 and start planning to move.

. VII .

"So, Ground Base Commander. You wanted to see me?"

"Yes, Fleet Commander." Shairez's ears moved in a subtle expression which mingled agreement and respect, and Fleet Commander Thikair waved her into one of the empty chairs around the briefing-room table.

"Should I assume this means you have that interim report for me?" he asked as she obeyed the unspoken command and seated herself.

"Yes, Sir. I'm afraid it's a bit more 'interim' than I'd hoped, however."

"Oh?" Thikair's ears lifted interrogatively.

"Yes, Sir." Shairez sighed. "Certain generalities are clear enough by now, but these creatures—these humans—are . . . confusing. Or perhaps perplexing would be a better word."

"How so?"

"To be perfectly honest, it may be that one reason I find them that way is because of my own preconceived ideas of what they *ought* to be," the ground base commander confessed. "Their technology level is high enough for my preconceptions to persist in trying to think of them as a single, unified worldwide civilization. Which, manifestly, they are not. We're simply not accustomed to seeing something as archaic as competing nation-states persisting at this level of technology. Our own people were slower than almost all of the Hegemony's other species to create a planetary state, and even we had completed that process well before we reached the level of technology these humans possess. I find it difficult to resist the temptation to hammer my observations of so many disparate cultures into a single, cohesive interpretation."

"I see," Thikair said, although, if he was going to be honest with himself, he suspected the ground base commander was overly concerned by those "preconceptions" of hers. Admittedly, the humans were more advanced technologically than anyone could possibly have expected, but they were still a planet-bound civilization, and the fact that they still had all of those competing nation-states she'd just mentioned only underscored their societal immaturity, as well. In the long run, it didn't really matter if Shairez missed some of the finer nuances. The humans were simply and completely outclassed by the capabilities of his fleet and its ground combat elements and bombardment capability. And whether they had a unified culture or not at the moment, they'd damned well have one after he got done hammering them flat and explaining their new status as clients of the Shongair Empire to them!

"Having said that, however," Shairez continued, "I have reached certain conclusions. I've written all of them up in my formal report, which you'll find in your in-box. There are a few points, though, which I wanted to discuss with you before you read the entire report."

"Such as?" Thikair tilted his chair back comfortably and began idly grooming the tip of his tail.

"Most of the human nation-states, at least the more developed ones, have significant military capability," Shairez said. "I'm speaking in terms of their own known threat environment, of course, not in comparison to *our* capabilities. Three of them stand out as preeminent, however one of them, the one known as the 'United States,' is in a class of its own. Its total military forces are smaller than those of the ones known as the 'People's Republic of China,' and the 'Russian Federation,' but it has by far the largest navy on KU-197-20, and its general combat capabilities appear to be far greater than anyone else's. Technically speaking, at least." She wiggled her ears in a grimace of distaste. "It obviously has no clue how to properly employ those capabilities, however. If it did, it would have settled matters in the region called 'Afghanistan' long ago. Nor would it be tolerating the present state of tension between it and 'Iran,' whose capabilities are laughable in comparison with its own.

"The other two major military powers are 'Russia' and 'China.' All three of them possess sizable fleets of aircraft in addition to large numbers of armored vehicles and foot soldiers. There are several second-rank powers, as well. Not primarily because of any inherent technological inferiority to the major powers, but simply because they lack the numbers of the United States, Russia, and China. And then there are the other nation-states, most with lower indigenous technology bases than the major and secondary powers, whose capabilities range all the way from moderate to negligible. All of them, of course, are technologically inferior to *us*, but given their cumulative numbers they might well prove capable of inflicting significant casualties on our own ground combat forces. A large enough mob armed with nothing but sharp rocks could endanger a rifle-armed soldier, after all, and these creatures have rather more sophisticated weapons than rocks."

"Ground Force Commander Thairys and I have already accepted that we'll probably need a more extensive prelanding bombardment than usual," Thikair said. He shrugged. "We can always expand on our current plans. Kinetic weapons are cheap, when all's said."

"Agreed, Sir. I simply wanted to draw the point to your attention. In addition, though, I'm somewhat concerned over what sort of contingency plans these creatures may have. The sheer number of nation-states and the levels of tension between them suggest to me that their leaders have probably made at least some emergency plans against attacks by their fellows. Shongairi in their position certainly would have, and while their planners couldn't possibly have allowed for the threat our arrival represents, it's still possible they could have a few potentially nasty surprises tucked away. I'm concerned, in particular, about the United States. Given its general greater level of military capability, it's my opinion that contingency planning on its part would be most likely to pose a potential threat to us. I think we need to remember that however crude their technology, these creatures *do* have nuclear weapons, for example, and the United States clearly has the most sophisticated means of delivering them. According to what we've been able to pick up from their news media the major powers—or, at least, the United States and Russia—are supposed to be keeping one another fully informed about their nuclear arsenals." Her ears cocked in an expression of contemptuous disbelief. "I don't understand that particular level of lunacy on their part, but I think we need to assume they aren't really stupid enough to give their enemies completely accurate information on a subject like that."

"No, I don't suppose they are," Thikair agreed slowly. And the ground base commander had a point, he thought. Despite the manifest incompetence demonstrated by the absurd way they'd chosen to handicap themselves in dealing with their primitively equipped adversaries, it would never do to assume that even "Americans" were *that* stupid.

Although it's certainly possible they really are *judging by some of their other actions . . . or inactions,* he reflected, thinking about what could have been accomplished by simply bombarding their adversaries' positions with sufficient concentrations of a suitable neurotoxin.

"Another point, and one which relates to my concerns over their possible contingency planning," Shairez continued, "is their computer networks' resistance to our penetration." She wrinkled her muzzle. "Their cyber technology, especially in their 'First World' nations, is even further advanced than other aspects of their technology. Gaining access to their 'Internet' is absurdly easy, and it's difficult for me to believe, even now, how little thought they appear to have given to genuine security measures. Or, rather, I find it hard to understand how they could have failed to recognize the necessity of restricting certain types of information, rather than making it generally available.

"It's become apparent to me and to my teams, however, that it really is blindness to the importance of securing information, not the absence of the *ability* to secure their systems. Indeed, despite the foolish manner in which they make so much vital information public, they also maintain a large number of truly secure databases, both government and private. Apparently, there's a lively, ongoing background level of cyber war, as well. Some of those involved are clearly competing nation-states, trying to compromise one another's secure systems. Other participants appear to be financial entities, attempting to ferret out one another's secrets or, in some cases, to penetrate the nation-states' systems in order to obtain what they call 'inside information' on financial regulatory decisions and processes. Still others appear to be groups of individuals unaffiliated with any nation-state or financial entity. Indeed, some of them—possibly even the majority of them—appear to be *single* individuals bent on penetrating various systems for reasons of their own."

"And the reason you mention this is—?" Thikair asked when she paused.

"My teams believe they can penetrate virtually all of the cyber defenses we've so far identified, Fleet Commander, but they're limited by their instructions to remain covert. Those defenses and intrusion detection systems are much more capable than we'd originally hoped—presumably as a direct result of the humans' own ongoing cyber warfare—and it's unlikely we could break into their systems without being detected."

"How likely would they be to realize the attack was coming from someone other than another human group?"

"That's impossible to say, Sir. Obviously, their security people are well versed in other human techniques, and if we were to attack them directly using our own technology, I think it's quite possible they'd realize they were looking at something entirely new. On the other hand, they don't know about us and we've gained quite a lot of familiarity with their own technology. We could probably disguise any penetration of their secure systems by using their own techniques, and in that case the natural reaction for them would be to assume it was, in fact, one of those other human groups rather than leap to the conclusion that 'aliens' were trying to invade their systems."

Thikair flexed his ears slowly, grooming his tail more thoughtfully as he considered what she'd just said. She was right that they needed to discover anything they could about "contingency plans." It was unlikely that anything the humans might have come up with could constitute a serious threat to his own operations, but even primitive nuclear weapons could inflict stinging casualties if he got careless. And while he himself was inclined to discount the possibility that anyone as manifestly stupid as humans would realize they were under cyber attack by "aliens," it wasn't outright *impossible.*

Of course, even if they realized the truth there was precious little they'd be able to do about it, unless Shairez's teams discovered something truly startling.

Stop right there, Thikair, he told himself. *Remember, however stupid these creatures are and however crude their technology may be, they aren't* weed-eaters, *and you're talking about a planet with* billions *of them crawling around on its surface. And the last time anyone in the entire Hegemony actually fought anyone much more sophisticated than these humans were when the Barthoni first visited them was—what? Close to a standard millennium ago—over two thousand of KU-197-20's local years. In fact, it was* us, *fighting each other before we ever* encountered *the Dainthar-damned Hegemony. So even though Shairez probably* is *being overly cautious, a little excess caution in a situation like this is unlikely to hurt anything, whereas too blithe an assumption of superiority might well get hundreds of your warriors killed. So you do need to find out what their "contingency plans" are, and you need to do it in a way which will let you spend a few days considering what you discover before you have to attack. But how to do that?*

He thought about it for several moments, then looked back across the briefing-room table at Shairez.

"I strongly suspect, Ground Base Commander, that you've already considered possible solutions to your problem." His ears rose in a half smile. "You're not the sort to simply tell a superior you can't do something."

"I try not to be, at any rate, Sir," she acknowledged with a smile of her own.

"So, tell me, would your solution to this one happen to be launching your attack through one of their own groups?"

"Yes, Sir. It would."

"And which of their groups did you have in mind?"

"I've been considering the nation-state called 'Iran,' Sir. Its relations with most of the First World nation-states are extremely tense and strained. In fact, according to what I've been able to discover, those relations have become progressively much worse over the last few local years. Apparently, internal unrest has been a problem for the current régime, and its opponents haven't approved of the techniques it's used to control that unrest." Her ears twitched derisively. "These creatures' insistence on forms and proper procedures is ridiculous, yet even allowing for that it seems apparent the régime has singularly failed to identify the true leaders of the unrest. Either that or, despite its opponents' condemnation of its 'extremism,' it's failed for some reason known only to itself to act effectively against those leaders and compel their submission.

"In the meantime, however, the hostility existing between it—and especially between it and the United States—could well be made to serve our purposes. Iran's technical capabilities are generally much inferior to those of the United States, but there are specific areas in which those capabilities are rather more sophisticated. Given its relations with the United States and the 'West' in general, a cyber attack coming out of Iran would surprise very few of the human governments. The *sophistication* of the attack might well surprise them, but I believe they would automatically assign responsibility for it to Iran and simply order investigations into how Iran might have acquired the capability to launch it. And given the régime's apparent propensity for routinely misrepresenting inconvenient truths, no one is likely to believe any denial it might issue in the wake of our attack."

"I see."

Thikair thought about it briefly, then flipped his ears in agreement.

"I think all of your points are well taken, Ground Base Commander," he said approvingly. "And I quite agree that it would be well to discover everything we can about any 'contingency plans' the humans might have in place. For that matter, it's probable that there's quite a bit of generally useful information in those secure systems of theirs, and it would be wise of us to acquire as much as possible of it while the computers in which it's housed still exist. One never knows when that sort of data might become useful.

"As for the possibility of using this 'Iran' as a mask, I approve entirely. Meet with your team leaders and come up with a plan to implement your suggestion as soon as possible."

. VIII .

A human hacker would have called it a "man-in-the-middle" attack.

Ground Base Commander Shairez's carefully built remote was deposited on the roof of a coffeehouse in downtown Tehran. Despite the Iranian régime's paranoia and perpetual state of heightened military alert, slipping the remote through its airspace defenses was child's play for the Shongairi. Concealing it once it was down wasn't a lot more difficult, either, since it was little larger than a baseball. The heavily stealthed, unmanned platform which deposited it found a convenient location, hidden in the shadow of an air-conditioning compressor, then departed through the moonless night air as swiftly and unobtrusively as it had arrived.

The location had been selected in advance after a previous platform's incursion had "driven around" at high altitude listening for a suitable portal through which to enter the local WiFi system. The 802.11 standard wireless connection of the coffeeshop which had been chosen offered broad frequency wireless connections to interact with potential victims. Even better, it was completely unprotected, without even the standard WAP's 64-hexadecimal key. It wouldn't have mattered very much if it had been protected—despite the remote's small size, its processing power would have sufficed to break even a substantially more challenging key with a brute-force approach—but it was convenient.

Now the remote inserted itself into the coffeeshop's network and attempted to access the router. In this case, it was a common retail Linksys SOHO, and the coffeeshop's owner had never bothered to replace the default password. The remote got in easily and looked around, checking carefully for intrusion detection systems. There was no sign of one, and it quickly established access and began modifying settings.

The first thing it did was to change the password and wipe out any logs which might have been recorded on the router. Then it modified the gateway—making the router send the traffic of any coffeeshop users through itself. Once it was able to view all the unencrypted traffic of all users of the coffeeshop's connections, it began monitoring and recording. For two days, that was all it did—listen, record, and compress, then retransmit daily dumps of all communications in and out of the coffeeshop to the stealthed Shongair ship which had deployed it.

. . . . .

HIS NAME WAS Rasul Teymourtash, and he was a taxi driver. In a nation where political activism had become a dangerous, high-stakes game, Rasul was about as apolitical as a man could get. He went to mosque on Friday, accepted the five principles of the *Usūl al-Dīn,* performed the ten duties of the *Furū al-Dīn,* and concentrated on keeping himself and his family fed. One of his brothers had been arrested, savagely beaten, and sentenced to fifteen years in prison last year for alleged activity in the outlawed Green Movement. Another had simply disappeared some months before that, which might have been one of the reasons for Rasul's tendency to emulate an ostrich where politics were concerned.

He was also, however, a patron of the coffeehouse Shairez had chosen as her entry point into the Internet. On this particular day, Rasul dropped by the coffeehouse and connected his laptop to its router . . . by way of the Shongair remote. He browsed, he checked his e-mail, and then he decided to download an MP3 music file.

The authorities would not have approved of his choice of music, since Lady Gaga was not high on the list of acceptable musicians. She was, admittedly, rather longer in the tooth than once she had been, and she'd undoubtedly mellowed somewhat over the years, but no one could have mellowed enough—not from *her* original starting point!—to satisfy Iran's leaders. Rasul was well aware of that, of course, yet he also knew he was scarcely alone in pushing that particular set of limits.

What he was unaware of, however, was that the Shongair cyber techs aboard Shairez's starship had made good use of all the data their remote had transmitted to them. Which was why, along with his music video, Rasul had installed and run a Trojan Horse.

The virus turned his laptop into a slaved "bot"—the first of many—which began searching for computers to attack in the United States. Another Trojan, in a second laptop, launched a similar search against computers in the Russian Federation. Another began spying on China, and others reached out to Europe, Israel, and India.

By the end of the day, over six hundred Iranian bots were obediently working the problem of the United States, alone, and as they reached out to still more computers, their numbers continued to grow. They made no move (yet) against their primary targets. Instead, they started with e-commerce sites, looking for vulnerabilities they could exploit in order to worm their way up to the systems in which they were truly interested. They concentrated on the people who used the machines rather than the machines themselves, searching for weak passwords—capitalizing on the fact that human beings may have many online needs but tend to use the limited number of passwords of which their merely organic memories can keep track. They were particularly interested in members of the United States military, and with so many industrious little bots looking, they were bound to find something.

They did.

The first opening was an Air Force E-6, a technical sergeant stationed at Nellis Air Force Base in Nevada. Technical Sergeant James was an Airsoft enthusiast who had decided to order a GR25 SPR—a BB-firing electric version of the M25 sniper rifle.

He placed his order online, through a Website using a 1024 bit SSL/TLS key, a secure socket layer impossible for current human technology to defeat. In fact, even Shongair technology would have found it a challenge, but the bots had never been looking at breaking its encryption in the first place. They'd been looking for human mistakes, vulnerabilities, and they'd found one in the form of a default script left in place when the system was set up. Once through that open door, they were able to access the site's data, looking specifically for military users like Technical Sergeant James. And in that data, they found James' e-mail address and the password he'd used in placing his order . . . which, unfortunately, was also the password he used when accessing the Air Force's logistical tracking system. Which, in turn, offered access to even more data and even more sensitive systems.

It took time, of course. Sergeant James was only one of many gaps the steadily growing army of automated intruders managed to turn up. But computers are patient. They don't care how long an assignment takes, and they don't get bored. They simply keep grinding steadily away at the problem . . . and they also don't care who they are grinding away *for*.

And so, just under a week after Rasul had downloaded Lady Gaga, Ground Base Commander Shairez found the access points she needed.

.IX.

Excuse me, Sir, but I think you'd better see this."

General Thomas Sutcliffe, Commanding Officer, United States Strategic Command, looked up with a quizzical expression as Major General Yolanda O'Higgins stepped into his office. O'Higgins was a Marine, and under normal circumstances, she took the Marines' institutional fetish for sharpness of personal appearance to unparalleled heights. It helped in that regard that she was a naturally precise, organized person—the sort who seldom had to scramble dealing with problems because she usually saw them coming well in advance. It also helped that she was probably one of the three or four smartest people Sutcliffe (who held multiple doctorates of his own) had ever met. She'd established her bona fides in Marine aviation when that wasn't the sort of duty women normally drew, and played a major role in formulating the Corps' input into the F-35 joint strike fighter, but her true strength lay in an incisive intellect and a pronounced ability to think "outside the box." She was also widely acknowledged as one of the US military's foremost experts on cybernetics and information warfare, which was why she currently headed the Joint Functional Component Command-Network Warfare.

JFCC-NW, one of four joint functional component commands over which USSTRATCOM exercised command authority, was responsible for "facilitating cooperative engagement with other national entities" in computer network defense and offensive information warfare. Sutcliffe, despite his own impressive technical education, recognized that he wasn't in O'Higgins' stratospheric league when it came to issues of cyber warfare. In fact, he tended to think of her as the übergeek of übergeeks, and he accorded her all the respect to which an inscrutable wizard was entitled.

Despite which, he was surprised to see her in his office this morning. She was normally punctilious about scheduling meetings, and even if that hadn't been the case, getting past Major Jeff Bradley, Sutcliffe's aide, unannounced wasn't exactly the easiest thing to do.

"And good morning to you, Yolanda," he said mildly. "Excuse me, but did Jeff forget to tell me we had a meeting scheduled for today?"

"No, Sir, I'm afraid he didn't."

"I didn't think so." Sutcliffe cocked his head to one side. "On the other hand, you're not exactly the sort to come bursting in unannounced on a whim. So what *does* bring you here this morning?"

"Sir, we got hit—hard—about twenty-seven minutes ago," O'Higgins said flatly.

"Hit?" Sutcliffe's chair came fully upright as he leaned forward over his desk. "You mean a cyber attack?"

"Sir, I mean a fucking cyber *massacre,*" O'Higgins said even more flatly, and Sutcliffe's eyes narrowed. The major general's mahogany complexion wasn't exactly suited to paling, but Yolanda O'Higgins very, very seldom used that kind of language.

"How bad?" he asked tersely.

"We're really only starting to sort out the details, Sir. It'll be a while before we know how deep they actually got, but they blew right through our perimeter firewalls without even slowing down. And it was across the board. DIA, Homeland Security, CIA, FBI—they hit *all* of us simultaneously, Sir."

O'Higgins might not be equipped to blanch, but Sutcliffe felt the color draining out of his own face. He stared at her for a long, frozen moment, then reached for the phone.

. . . . .

"SO HOW BAD is it? That's the bottom-line question," President Harriet Palmer said, letting her gaze circle the faces of the men and women seated around the table.

There was silence for a moment, then General Koslow, the Chief of the Joint Chiefs of Staff, cleared his throat.

"I think General Sutcliffe's probably the best person to answer that question, Madam President. His people at StratCom were the first to realize what was happening."

Koslow nodded across the table to Sutcliffe, and the president turned to him.

"Well, General Sutcliffe?"

"Madam President, the short answer to your question is that it's pretty damn bad," he said frankly. "I assume you don't want the technical details?"

"You assume correctly, General." Palmer showed her teeth in a tight smile. If Sutcliffe's language bothered her, she showed no sign of it. Of course, she'd been known to let slip the occasional "pithy phrase" herself upon occasion. "I came up through state government, not MIT."

"Yes, Ma'am." Sutcliffe nodded. "In that case, the best way to put it is that as nearly as we can tell someone penetrated somewhere around eighty percent of our secure databases before we managed to cut off access and isolate ourselves from the net."

"*Eighty* percent?" Palmer stared at him in disbelief.

"Yes, Ma'am," he said unflinchingly. "Somewhere around that."

"How?" Palmer demanded. She shook her head. "I may have come up through government, not computer science, but I was under the impression we had the best security systems in the world!"

"So far as we know, Madam President, we do. But no security is perfect, and this apparently used a Trojan of an entirely novel design. We don't have any idea where it came from, and the penetration itself was an incredibly sophisticated, coordinated attack which included some brute-force key crunching that . . . well, let's just say no one on our side ever saw it coming. Or even thought it was *possible* for that matter! And it came at every one of our systems simultaneously—timed to the second—through better than a thousand lower-level systems." He shook his head. "In that respect, all I can say is that it's light-years beyond anything we've ever seen before. Our people are still backtracking, trying to figure out exactly what they did to us. At this moment, though, nobody's got a clue how this could have been put together—how so many lower-level systems could have been penetrated—without *anybody's* intrusion detection software seeing it coming."

"Who did it?" Palmer asked flatly. "Do we at least know *that* much?"

"At this time," Sutcliffe said in the tone of the man who'd rather be facing a firing squad, "all indications are that it came out of Iran, Madam President."

"*Iran?*" If Palmer had been shocked by the degree of penetration, that was nothing compared to her shock at learning the source of the attack. "You mean those lunatics in *Tehran* managed this? Is *that* what you're telling me, General Sutcliffe?"

"We've backtracked the attack to a coffeehouse not far from the Iranian Ministry of Defense's central office in Tehran, Madam President. As far as we can tell, that's where it originated."

"Sweet Jesus," the president said softly, and it was a prayer, not a blasphemy. She sat looking at Sutcliffe for several seconds, then swiveled her head to where the Secretary of Homeland Security sat flanked by the directors of the CIA and FBI and facing the Secretary of Defense across the table.

"Frank?" she said.

"Harriet," Frank Gutierrez said, "we don't know." Gutierrez, the only person present who habitually addressed the president by her first name, had known Palmer for the better part of thirty years, which was how he'd come to be picked to head Homeland Security. "Our own computer people tell us the same thing General Sutcliffe's people are telling him. Hell, for that matter, most of 'our' computer people are also *'his'* computer people! None of them have ever seen anything like this, and all of them agree—*all* of them, Harriet—that it came out of Tehran."

Palmer nodded slowly, her face ashen. No one had to tell her how disastrous this could prove. The sheer amount of information which had been compromised was horrifying to contemplate. Having that information in the hands of what were probably the United States' most bitter enemies only made it still worse. Just thinking about what the Iranian régime could do with that sort of look inside the United States' intelligence networks, that kind of fix on CIA's chains of agents all around the world, was enough to make her physically ill. And that didn't even consider. . . .

"Do you think this had anything to do with Sunflower?" she asked.

"There's no way to be certain either way," Gutierrez said. "On the other hand, given the source of the attack, I don't think we can afford to assume it didn't. In addition. . . ."

It was Gutierrez's turn to pause and draw a deep breath.

"In addition," he resumed a moment later, "we have some indications—they're very preliminary, and none have been confirmed as yet, you understand—that we're not the only ones who got hit. Everyone seems to be playing it close to his or her vest at the moment, but I've had some strange inquiries from my French and British counterparts. We're stonewalling for right now—I told my people we *might* have something to say, to our friends, at least, after this meeting—but from what they're asking, either they got hit themselves or else they know *we* got hit and want to know how badly."

Palmer's nostrils flared. "Sunflower" was the innocuous computer-generated code name Homeland Security's analysts had assigned to a rumored Iranian operation. The various intelligence services had all been catching hints about it over the last couple of years, although they'd managed to keep anyone outside the intelligence community from getting wind of them . . . so far, at least.

Unfortunately, the president had a sick feeling that might be about to change.

The increasingly isolated Iranian hardliners had never wavered in their hatred for all things Western and, in particular, for the United States of America and the State of Israel. And it would appear that Western estimates of how long it would take them to produce nuclear weapons had been overly optimistic. In fact, they'd officially scheduled their first stationary nuclear weapons test for "year's end." That was elastic enough to give them some wiggle room in the face of unexpected problems, and most experts expected their first weapons to be relatively low in yield and large in size, which would make delivering them difficult. According to the experts, making one small enough to fit into a missile with their current technology would be a challenge, and judging by their ongoing missile tests, their accuracy would probably be less than pinpoint even after they did. On the other hand, the "experts" had been wrong before, and once any capability existed, it could always be improved upon.

That was bad enough; worse were the persistent rumors that they'd managed to "acquire" a handful of ex-Soviet tactical warheads from rogue elements within the Russian Federation before it reluctantly cut its ties with Tehran. The Russians, predictably, denied that it could possibly have happened, but Moscow's assurances had been remarkably cold comfort to the West under the circumstances. Especially since the Iranian Supreme Leader had openly stated that it was past time the "Great Satan" received another blow like the September 11 attacks or the 2012 Chicago subway sarin attack.

There was no way to be certain whether or not he meant it, but the Iranians had made no real effort to conceal the upsurge in the quantities of military hardware being provided to the insurgents in Afghanistan. Or, for that matter, their redoubled efforts to destabilize Iraq or the increasing sophistication of the weapons they were providing to Hamas for use against Israel. They routinely denied they were doing anything of the sort, of course, but it was the sort of denial intended to be recognized as a lie when it was issued. Under the circumstances, "Sunflower"—the delivery to a major American airport of one of those ex-Soviet tactical devices the Iranians didn't have aboard a third-party commercial airliner—had to be taken seriously. And now this. . . .

"All right," Palmer said. "We're going to operate on the assumption that it was the Iranians. And we're further going to assume that they launched this attack in order to gain information to facilitate Sunflower. That they were looking for vulnerabilities—and possibly not just on *our* side of the pond—they could exploit to slip Sunflower through our defenses. I'm not saying we should absolutely close our minds to the possibility that it could have been someone else. In fact, I want that possibility explored aggressively. But at this moment, assuming it *wasn't* Iran if it actually was could be disastrous."

She looked around at her advisers once more, aware as never before that they were just that—*advisers*—and that the ultimate decision, and responsibility, was hers. Then her eyes focused on Harrison Li, the Secretary of Defense.

"Harry, you, Frank, and General Koslow will operate on the assumption that Sunflower is a reality and the clock is ticking. For all we know, there's a nuke already airborne right this moment, headed for New York or Atlanta or Los Angeles. We need to find it and stop it, and we need to do it in a way that doesn't create a national panic. God only knows what would happen—how many people might get trampled in the crush—if we ordered an immediate evacuation of every possible target!"

The stillness in the conference room was very nearly absolute.

"I know we've got cover plans in place to ramp up aircraft inspections without telling anyone we're looking for an actual nuclear device," she continued. "I want those plans activated, and I think it's time we had an 'unscheduled' drill here in the States to test our terrorist response plans. Get that laid on immediately . . . and figure out a way to extend our 'drill's' duration. Let's get as many of our first responders mobilized and keep them there as long as we can without going public about Sunflower.

"In the meantime, we need to find out if our allies did get hit, or if it was just us. I'll personally call the British and Canadian prime ministers and the French president, tell them what's happened, and ask them frankly if the same thing's happened to one or more of them. General Sutcliffe, I'll want you and your people available to talk to their people about the technical aspects, but if this is a prelude to Sunflower, we might not be the only targets, and that means we have to bring the others onboard about this ASAP, for their own protection as well as our own.

"For obvious reasons, though, we'll operate on the assumption that we're the target—or at least the *primary* target—and act accordingly. In addition to our Homeland Security exercises, I want all CONUS air defenses on high alert, too. And I want our air defense plans modified on the assumption that the people coming after us have now gained access to our existing plans. I know there's a limit to how they can be adjusted, but I can't believe anyone would go after this kind of information without some plan to use it. From what your tech experts seem to be saying, the people who launched this attack have to have been pretty damned confident they'd get through—that they'd take us by surprise, the first time at least—but they have to have realized we'll beef up our defenses to keep them from doing it again. So if this is the first step in an active attack on one of our cities, they wouldn't have gone after our computers any sooner than they figured they had to. They wouldn't want to give us any more time to react and adjust than they absolutely had to."

Heads nodded around the table and she drew a deep, deep breath.

"All right. Get started. I want a progress report in two hours."

.X.

It was unfortunate that international restrictions on the treatment of POWs didn't also apply to what could be done to someone's own personnel, Stephen Buchevsky reflected as he failed—again—to find a comfortable way to sit in the mil-spec "seat" in the big C-17 Globemaster's spartan belly. The hell with waterboarding! If *he'd* been a jihadi, he'd have spilled his guts within an hour if they strapped him into one of these!

Actually, he supposed a lot of the problem stemmed from his six feet and four inches of height and the fact that he was built more like an offensive lineman than a basketball player. Nothing short of a first-class commercial seat was really going to fit someone his size, and expecting the US military to fly an E-8 commercial first-class would have been about as realistic as his expecting to be drafted as a presidential nominee. Or perhaps even a bit *less* realistic. And if he wanted to be honest (which he didn't), he should also admit that what he disliked even more was the absence of windows. There was something about spending hours sealed in an alloy tube while it vibrated its noisy way through the sky that made him feel not just enclosed, but trapped.

Well, Stevie, he told himself, *if you're* that *unhappy, you could always ask the pilot to let you off to* swim *the rest of the way!*

The thought made him chuckle, and he checked his watch. Kandahar to Aviano, Italy, was roughly three thousand miles, which exceeded the C-17's normal range by a couple of hundred miles. Fortunately—although that might not be *exactly* the right word for it—he'd caught a rare flight returning to the States almost empty. The Air Force needed the big bird badly somewhere, so they wanted it home in the shortest possible time, and with additional fuel and a payload of only thirty or forty people, it could make the entire Kandahar-to-Aviano leg without refueling. Which meant he could look forward to a six-hour flight, assuming they didn't hit any unfavorable winds.

He would have preferred to make the trip with the rest of his people, but he'd ended up dealing with the final paperwork for the return of Bravo Company's equipment. Just another of those happy little chores that fell the way of its senior noncom. On the other hand, and despite the less than luxurious accommodations aboard his aerial chariot, his total transit time would be considerably shorter thanks to this flight's fortuitous availability. And one thing he'd learned to do during his years of service was to sleep anywhere, anytime.

Even here, he thought, squirming into what he could convince himself was a marginally more comfortable position and closing his eyes. *Even here.*

. . . . .

"DADDY!" FOUR-YEAR-OLD SHANIA held out her arms, smiling hugely, as she flung herself from five steps up the staircase into her father's arms with the absolutely fearless confidence that Daddy would catch her. "You're home—*you're home!*"

"Of course I am, Punkin!"

Buchevsky's voice sounded odd to his own ears, somehow, but he laughed as he scooped the small, hurtling body out of the air. He hugged the sturdy yet delicate little girl to his chest, tucking one arm under her bottom for her to sit on while the other arm went around her back so he could tickle her. She squealed in delight, ducking her head, trying to squeeze her arms against her sides and capture his tickling fingers. Her small hands caught his single big one, one fist clenching around his thumb, another around his index finger, and her feet drummed against his rib cage.

"Stop that!" she laughed. "*Stop* that, Daddy!"

"Oh, sure, that's what you *say!*" he chuckled, pressing his lips against the nape of her neck and blowing hard. She squealed again at the fluttering sound, and he straightened enough to press a kiss to the top of her head, instead.

"Me, too, Daddy!" another voice demanded indignantly. "Me, too!"

He looked down, and when he saw a five-year-old Yvonne, he realized why his own voice had sounded a little odd. Shania was three years older than Yvonne, so the only way they could both be four—which he knew had been his favorite age for both of them—was in a dream. He was hearing his own voice, as if it had been recorded and played back to him, and everyone knew that always sounded just a little "off."

His sleeping mind recognized the dream, and some small corner of him realized he was probably dreaming it because of the divorce. Because he knew he was going to see even less of his girls, no matter how hard Trish and he both tried. Because he loved them so much that no matter where he was, his arms still ached for those slender, agile, wigglesome little bodies and the feel of those small, loving arms around his own neck.

And because he knew those things, because he longed for them with such aching intensity, his mind turned away from the awareness that he was dreaming. Turned away from the noise and vibration of the transport plane and burrowed deep, deep into that loving memory of a moment in time which could not ever really have occurred.

"Of course you, too, Honey Bug!" the dream Stephen Buchevsky laughed, bending and sweeping one arm around Yvonne, lifting her up into his embrace. He held both of his little girls—one in the crook of his right arm, one in the crook of his left—and smothered them with daddy kisses.

. . . . .

THE SUDDEN, VIOLENT turn to starboard yanked Buchevsky up out of the dream, and he started to shove himself upright in his uncomfortable seat as the turn turned even steeper. The redoubled, rumbling whine from the big transport's engines told him the pilot had increased power radically, as well, and every one of his instincts told him he wouldn't have liked the reason for all of that if he'd known what it was.

Which didn't keep him from wanting to know anyway. In fact—

"Listen up, everybody!" a harsh, strain-flattened voice rasped over the aircraft's intercom. "We've got a little problem, and we're diverting from Aviano, 'cause Aviano isn't *there* anymore."

Buchevsky's eyes widened. Surely whoever it was on the other end of the intercom had to be joking, his mind tried to insist. But he knew better. There was too much stark shock—and fear—in that voice.

"I don't know what the fuck is going on," the pilot continued. "We've lost our long-ranged comms, but we're getting reports on the civilian bands about low-yield nukes going off all over the goddamned place. From what we're picking up, someone's kicking the shit out of Italy, Austria, Spain, and every NATO base in the entire Med, and—"

The voice broke off for a moment, and Buchevsky heard the harsh sound of an explosively cleared throat. Then—

"And we've got an unconfirmed report that Washington is gone, people. Just fucking *gone*."

Someone kicked Buchevsky in the belly and his hand automatically sought the hard-edged shape under his shirt. Not Washington. Washington *couldn't* be gone. Not with Trish and—

"I don't have a goddamned clue who's doing this, or why," the pilot said, "but we need someplace to set down, fast. We're about eighty miles north-northwest of Podgorica in Montenegro, so I'm diverting inland. Let's hope to hell I can find someplace to put this bird down in one piece . . . and that nobody on the ground thinks *we* had anything to do with this shit!"

. XI .

One more cannonball while I'm trying to cook here, and *someone* isn't getting any hamburgers!" Dave Dvorak said ominously, turning to look over his shoulder at the water-plastered head of dark hair which had just bobbed back to the surface of the swimming pool.

His outsized stainless-steel gas grill was parked on the wooden deck at the deep end of the pool. The deck was separated from the pool itself by a four-foot flagstoned surround, and one wouldn't normally have thought a slender, nine-year-old female could have produced sufficient spray to reach him. His daughter, however, had risen to new heights—not to mention new elevations off the diving board—and the brisk breeze sweeping across the pool had carried him a hefty dollop of chlorine-scented rain.

"Sorry, Daddy!"

Morgana Dvorak's contrition didn't sound especially sincere, her male parental unit noted. She was the smaller of the twins—although there wasn't a lot to choose, height-wise, between her and her sister Maighread—which seemed to have imbued her with an automatic need to test the limits more than either of her two siblings. Maighread was just as capable of working her way towards a desired objective by any means necessary, but she preferred indirection (not to say sneakiness) rather than head-on confrontation. Their younger brother, Malachai, was even more . . . straightforward than Morgana, of course. He didn't so much "test the limits" as charge straight at them. Morgana undoubtedly pushed *more* rules than he did, but nobody could have pushed the ones he did any harder. Probably because he shared his mother's red hair. That was Dvorak's explanation, at any rate. Sharon, on the other hand, was fonder of the explanation which had been offered by one of their friends who also happened to be a child psychologist. Malachai, she'd said, was physically a clone of his mother . . . but *psychologically* he was his father in miniature.

An explanation which was patent nonsense in Dvorak's considered opinion, thank you. And one which made him contemplate a thirteen-year-old Malachai with a distinct sense of dread.

"Yeah, *sure* you're sorry!" he told his errant daughter as she trod water, and she giggled. Unmistakably, she giggled. "You just bear in mind what I said, young lady." He shook his spatula in her direction. "And if you're not careful, I'll cook your burger all the way through, too—turn it into one of those hockey pucks your uncle likes!"

"Hey, now!" Rob Wilson objected from where he reclined, beer in hand, in a folding chaise lounge strategically located upwind of the grill. "Cooking is good. Just because *you* like your food raw doesn't mean *smart* people do."

"There's a difference between cooked and charcoal, you Philistine," Dvorak retorted. "I'm just grateful I managed to rescue my children from your unnatural fascination with things that go crunch."

"Rescue them? Is that what you call brainwashing them into eating sushi?" Wilson demanded.

"Sushi? Did someone say sushi? *Yum!*" Maighread Dvorak put in. She'd just come out of the house, carrying a platter of buns. Her younger brother and her cousin Keelan came behind her, carrying potato salad, pickles, lettuce, and sliced tomatoes and onion rings. Morgana had deposited the mayonnaise, mustard, and ketchup on the picnic table before launching herself into the pool, and Sharon and Veronica Wilson brought up the rear with iced tea, soft drinks, and what looked like a wheelbarrow load of potato chips.

"Unnatural, that's what it is," Wilson said, smiling at his niece. "Fish isn't food to begin with, even when it's cooked. But *raw?*" He shook his head. "Next thing, you'll be expecting me to eat *vegetables!*"

"*Potatoes* are vegetables," Dvorak pointed out, "and you eat—what? nine or ten pounds? twenty?—of them a week!"

"While I always hate coming to Rob's defense, potatoes *aren't* vegetables," his wife corrected him. He cocked an eyebrow at her, and she shrugged. "Potatoes," she explained, "are a traditional Irish delicacy whose ancient pedigree and lineage place them in a unique category, transcending the limitation of mere 'vegetables.' Besides, they have very little of that chlorophyll stuff that gives all those other vegetables such a strange taste. Or that's what I've been told causes it, anyway. I don't eat enough of them to know, myself."

"You shouldn't encourage him, you know," Dvorak said. "Vegetables are good for you."

"Vegetables," his brother-in-law riposted, "are what food eats before it becomes food."

"Carnivore!" Dvorak snorted.

"Me, too! Me, too!" Morgana put in from the pool. "I agree with Uncle Rob! But keep mine pink in the middle, Daddy."

"Of course I will," Dvorak assured her. He slid the current crop of sizzling meat patties to one end of the grill, over a lower flame, and began flipping fresh burgers onto the high-temperature end. "We'll just let your mother's and your uncle's sit down here and cure into proper jerky while ours cook properly."

"Don't let *mine* get dried out," Alec Wilson, Rob's grown son, put in.

"Yeah? Well, in that case, you'd better come down here and start building your burger now," Dvorak invited. "Certain lazy people—I mention no spouses or brothers-in-law in particular, you understand—are going to lie about until the overworked cook gets around to building theirs for them, so they'll just have to take theirs the way they get them."

"Nonsense, I'm sure my wife will look after me just fine, thank you," Wilson said.

"I hate to break this to you," Veronica told him, "but I'm afraid I'm going to be too busy swimming to take care of that for you." She smiled sweetly at him. "Sorry about that."

"Wait a minute," Wilson protested, sitting up in the chaise lounge, "you know I can't cook! You're supposed to—"

The side door onto the pool deck slammed suddenly open, so violently every head turned towards it. Jessica Wilson, Alec's wife, stood staring out of it, and her eyes were wide.

"Jessica?" Sharon's tone was sharpened by sudden concern. "What's wrong, honey?"

"The TV." There was something odd about Jessica's voice. It sounded . . . flattened. Almost crushed. "The TV just said—" She paused and drew a deep breath. "Somebody's *attacking* us!"

. . . . .

THE ENTIRE DVORAK-WILSON clan clustered around the big-screen TV. Dave Dvorak sat in his La-Z-Boy recliner with his daughters in his lap and Sharon perched on the chair arm. Malachai was in his mother's lap, and Dave's right arm was around both of them. Rob Wilson stood beside the coffee table, quivering with too much anger and intensity to sit, and Veronica, Keelan, Alec, and Jessica sat huddled together on the long couch.

". . . still coming in," the ashen-faced reporter on the screen was saying. "Repeating what we already know, many American cities have been attacked. The exact extent of damage is impossible to estimate at this point, but we've lost all communications with our affiliates in Washington, DC, Los Angeles, San Diego, Atlanta, and several smaller cities. Indications are that the continental United States has been attacked with *nuclear* weapons. I repeat, with nuclear—"

His image disappeared abruptly, replaced by the insignia of the Department of Homeland Security.

"This is an emergency broadcast," a flat, mechanical voice said. "A nationwide state of emergency is now in effect. All active duty and reserve military personnel are instructed to report to—"

Dvorak pressed the button on the remote, and the TV went dead.

"What the *fuck* do you thin—?!" his brother-in-law snarled, turning on him with atypical fury.

"Shut up, Rob," Dvorak said flatly. Wilson gaped at him, red-faced with anger, but Dvorak continued in that same flat voice. "I don't know what's happening," he said, "but just from what we've already heard, it's pretty damn obvious somebody's kicked the shit out of the United States. God knows who it is, but if they've managed to hit that many cities simultaneously, then it sure as hell isn't the Iranians! And whoever it is, and whatever they're after, things are going to go to hell in a handbasket pretty damn quick. So instead of sitting around watching TV and hoping somebody will tell us what's happening, we need to get our asses in gear. This is *exactly* what you and I have been working on the cabin for for the last three years!"

Wilson closed his mouth with a click. Then he shook himself, like a dog shaking off water, and made himself draw a deep breath.

"You're right," he said. "How do you want to handle it?"

"Well, we're lucky as hell we're all here in one spot," Dvorak said. He stood, easing his frightened daughters out of his lap and settling them in the chair he'd vacated. Then he reached out and cupped the side of Sharon's face in his right hand. "The fact that we *are* all here means we don't have to go start collecting people, at least."

He let his eyes circle the faces of the adult members of the family, then looked down at the children and smiled as reassuringly as he could before he returned his gaze to his wife's face.

"Sharon, Rob and I will get the Outback hitched to the van. While we're doing that, you and Ronnie get organized to clean out the pantry and the gun safe. Then shove anything else you can think of that might be useful in on top of that. Keep your PSN90 and a couple of the twelve-gauges out and loaded." His expression was grim. "I hope you won't need them, but if you do, I want you to have something heftier than your Taurus."

She looked at him silently for a moment, then nodded, and he turned to Alec.

"Alec, I need you to stay here and help Ronnie and Sharon get that organized. Most people're probably going to be sitting around, too shocked and too busy wondering what the hell's happening to make trouble for anyone else—for a while yet, at least—but we can't be sure of that. So keep an eye out. And get my Browning auto out of the gun safe. I don't want anybody shot if we can help it, and it may be silly and chauvinistic, but a lot of the kind of people who'd make trouble are less likely to push it if they see a *man* with a twelve-gauge standing in front of them than if they see an armed woman even if she's got a Ma Deuce. Stupid of them, but stupid people can kill you just as dead as *smart* people."

Alec nodded, and Dvorak gazed into his eyes for another moment, then drew a deep breath.

"And, Alec," he said, his voice much softer, "if somebody does make trouble, don't hesitate. Warn them off if you can, but if you can't . . ."

"Understood." Alec's voice was equally quiet, and Dvorak turned to Wilson's daughter-in-law, who worked with him and his brother-in-law at the shooting range.

"Jess, I want you to come with me and Rob. We'll hitch the big trailer to my truck and go clean out the range before someone else gets any bright ideas about helping themselves to the stock."

She nodded. Her color was stronger than it had been, although it was obvious she was still more than a little frightened.

"What about the dogs, Daddy?" Maighread asked. Her voice quivered around the edges from the obvious tension and fear of the adults around her, but she was trying hard to be brave, and Dvorak's heart melted inside him as he looked down at her.

"Don't worry, honey," he said, managing—somehow—to keep his own voice steady as he ran his hand lightly over her hair. "They're covered under the plan, too. But speaking of the dogs," he went on, turning to his wife again, "don't forget to break down their crates and stack them in the trailer somehow."

"Anything else you'd like to suggest?" Sharon Dvorak retorted with something like her usual spirit. "Like maybe that I should remember to bring along my hiking boots? Or pack along all the stuff in the medicine cabinets? Stick my Swiss Army knife in my pocket?"

"Actually," he put his arms around her, letting his chin rest on the top of her head, "all of those sound like really good ideas. Be kind to them—they're in a strange place."

He "oofed" as she poked him—hard—in the pit of the stomach, then stood back and looked at all the others again.

"Go ahead and switch the TV back on while you work, if you want, but don't let yourself get mesmerized watching it. We need to *move*—move quickly—and there'll be time to figure out what's going on after we get ourselves safely to the cabin. Clear?"

Heads nodded, and he nodded back, then looked at Wilson and Jessica.

"Let's go get those trailers hitched," he said.

. XII .

Major Dan Torino, call sign "Longbow," loved the F-22 Raptor.

At 5'8" he was no towering giant (few fighter pilots were) but he had a compact, squared-off frame, a solid, hard-trained muscularity, heavy black eyebrows, a proud nose, and intense gray-green eyes. In many ways, he was an easygoing sort of fellow, but those eyes told the true tale, for the killer instinct of the born fighter pilot ran deep in his blood and bone, as well. Even his dark *hair* seemed to bristle aggressively when he thought about flying. Well, to be honest, it bristled *most* of the time, if he ever let his usual "high-and-tight" get out of hand. In fact, it was just plain unruly, and his wife Helen loved to run her fingers through it and tease it into tufts and laugh whenever he let it get a mite long. She called it his "crabgrass tiger look."

But crabgrass or not, he *loved* the F-22.

He knew the party line was that the F-35 Lightning II was the way to go, and he was willing to admit that the Joint Strike Fighter Program had (finally) produced a capable medium-range ground support aircraft—which, after all, was what "strike" fighter was all about, wasn't it? But the sacrifices and trade-offs in the F-35 left the "fighter" part of its designation sucking wind in Torino's opinion. It wasn't turning out to be all that much cheaper by the time the dust settled and all the cost overruns were in, either. In fact, if the total buy on the F-22 had been as large as the projected total buy on the F-35, its fly-away price tag per aircraft would actually have been *lower.*

By any measure he could come up with, the Raptor was still *the* best air-superiority fighter in the world. It had the lowest radar signature, it had the best airborne intercept radar, its new infrared detection system had taken the lead in IR detection and targeting away from the Russians, and in "supercruise" it was capable of "dry" supersonic flight, without the enormous fuel penalties of afterburner operation. It was seventy-five percent faster than the F-35 in "dry" flight, which gave it a far greater operating radius; in afterburner it could break Mach 2.0 without raising a sweat; *and* it was just as capable of hitting ground targets—and even better at penetrating defended airspace in the strike role—than the F-35.

Not to mention the fact that the F-22 had been fully operational since 2005 and the F-35 was still lagging behind (badly) on its projected deployment rates. And likewise not to mention the interesting news stories that Congress was now thinking about capping *its* total production numbers because of cost concerns, as well. In Torino's opinion, there was a certain bittersweet, ironic justice in that possibility, although anyone who was really surprised by the final outcome of this particular little morality play probably liked to buy bridges and magic beans of questionable provenance, as well.

The truth was that the real reason *Raptor* production had been capped at less than two hundred aircraft was that no one had expected to be going up against other fifth-generation fighter operators anytime soon. They *had* expected to be dropping bombs and precision-guided munitions on ground targets in lower-intensity conflicts in places like Afghanistan, however—thus the emphasis on the Lightning and its ability to defeat ground defense systems, like SAMs and antiaircraft fire, rather than other fighters. Besides, with only so many dollars in the till, not even the US military could afford to buy everything it wanted, and the F-35 had a lot more "jointness" going for it. The Navy and Marines badly needed a replacement for the A-6, F/A-18, and Harrier, and this way they got to buy at least some of their aircraft on the Air Force's nickel. Then there were all of the other nations which had been brought into the procurement program, helping to spread the cost burden, whereas Congress had specifically prohibited the overseas sale of the F-22.

All of which explained why "Longbow" Torino had felt incredibly lucky when he found out he was going to be one of the pilots who actually got to fly the aircraft. He'd taken Helen and the kids out and blown the better part of two hundred bucks on a celebratory dinner when he found out he'd been assigned to the First Air Wing's 27th Fighter Squadron. After his wedding and the days his children were born, it had been the greatest day of his life.

A life which suddenly felt unspeakably empty as he sat in the uncomfortable plastic chair, staring down at his hands, trying to wrap his mind around the impossible.

He and three other pilots had been unceremoniously turfed out of their billets at Langley Air Force Base three days earlier. Colonel Ainsborough, the First's CO, claimed he'd chosen Torino to lead the four-ship detachment because the major was the best man for the job. Personally, Torino had been inclined to take that with a grain of salt, but he hadn't complained, even though it did mean he was going to miss his older son's birthday. In the wake of what was rumored to have been a truly massive penetration of DoD's secure databases (and, if the even more quietly whispered rumors were accurate, almost all of their *allies*' databases, as well), it made sense to deploy at least some of their air defense assets to bases that weren't in any of the upper-tier contingency plans, and somebody had to take the duty.

Which was how Torino, Captain "Killer" Cunningham, his wingman, two other 27th Squadron pilots, and a maintenance section had found themselves "stationed" at the Plattsburgh International Airport. Once upon a time, Plattsburgh International had been Plattsburgh Air Force Base. Most of the Air Force buildings were still there, although they'd been converted to civilian use, and its twelve-thousand-foot concrete runway was more than adequate to the needs of an F-22.

And because it was, Torino and his fellow pilots were still alive . . . for now, at least.

Funny how that seemed so much less important than it would have been three days ago.

He raised his head, looking around the improvised ready room. The other three pilots sat equally silent, equally wrapped in their own grim thoughts. None of them knew how bad it really was, but they knew enough. They knew Langley and the rest of the wing—and their families—were gone. They knew Washington had been destroyed, and that neither the president nor the vice president had gotten out. They knew Shaw Air Force Base, the Ninth Air Force's home base, had been destroyed, taking with it the command-and-control element of the eastern seaboard's air defenses. They knew Vandenberg, Nellis, and at least another dozen Air Force bases were gone. They knew Fort Bragg was gone, along with Fort Jackson, Fort Hood, Fort Rucker, Navy Air Station Oceana, NAS Patuxent River, Marine Corps Air Station Cherry Point, MCAS Beaufort. . . .

The list went on forever. In one cataclysmic afternoon of deadly accurate, pinpoint strikes, the United States of America had been annihilated as a military power, and God only knew how many millions of American citizens had died in the process. Against that, what could a single woman and three children matter . . . even if their last name had been Torino?

He looked back down at his hands. As far as he knew, he and his three pilots were all that was left of Air Combat Command. They were it, and against whoever had done this, four fighters—even four Raptors—weren't going to stop them when they followed up their attack.

But who *had* done it? And how? There was no *way* it had been the Iranians, no matter what the rumor mill had said! So who—?

The door to what had been the Direct Air pilots' lounge flew open. The racket as it slammed abruptly into the doorstop brought Torino's head up, and he frowned as he recognized the man standing in the open doorway. He couldn't remember the fellow's name, but he was the senior man from the local Homeland Security office located here at the airport.

"Major Torino!" the newcomer half shouted.

"What?"

"Here!" The man was holding out a cell phone. "He needs to talk to you!"

Torino accepted the phone and raised it to his ear.

"Who is this?" he asked suspiciously.

"Torino? *Major* Torino, US Air Force?" a hoarse voice replied.

"Yes. Who the hell are you?"

"Thank God." The voice paused for a moment, as if its owner were drawing a deep breath, then resumed. "This is Rear Admiral James Robinson, Naval Network and Space Operations Command. I've been hunting for someone—*anyone*—who's still got some air defense capability for the last three hours, and so far you're all I've been able to find."

Torino's eyes narrowed. These days, NAVSPACECOM was primarily a centralized data processing node for USSTRATCOM's Joint Functional Command Component for Space, which had been stood up in 2006 to bring all United States space surveillance systems together under one roof. But JFCC SPACE was—or had been, at least—headquartered at Vandenberg. He knew that was gone, but until 2004, NAVSPACECOM had been the primary headquarters for what had originally been the Navy's Naval Space Command Surveillance, and it continued to function as the backup Space Command Center. If he remembered correctly, it was located at Dahlgren, Virginia, a hundred miles north of Norfolk, and he supposed that whoever had smashed the American military might have overlooked it. There wasn't much to attract the eye, aside from the Naval Surface Warfare Center's airstrip.

"I don't suppose there's any point trying to authenticate to each other, is there, Sir?" Torino's biting irony could have evaporated Lake Champlain, and the man at the other end of the cell phone gave a harsh, ugly bark of laughter.

"No, there isn't. We've still got some comms, but the entire system's been shot full of holes. I don't know why *we* didn't get hit—everybody else in our line of business sure as hell did! But I've been going down the list, trying to find somebody with shooters who's still online. As far as I can tell, you're it for CONUS air defense, although there's supposed to be a couple of other detachments scattered around bases in the Carolinas. I'm trying to get hold of them, too, but as bad as communications are, I don't think I'm going to reach anyone else in time to do any good."

"Forgive me, Admiral, but just how is talking to *me* supposed to do any good?" Torino demanded bitterly. "We're fucked, Sir. That's the short and ugly truth."

"Yes, we are, Major," Robinson said. "But National Command Authority hasn't told us to stand down yet."

"No," Torino admitted. "On the other hand, what the hell can we do?"

"Listen to me, Major. Whoever did this didn't—I repeat, *did not*—use nukes. These were kinetic strikes, delivered from space. In fact, they were delivered from a point approximately thirty thousand miles out. Are you following me? This was not an attack by any other nation. It was an attack from someone else—someone from completely outside our *solar system*!"

"Aliens?" Torino heard the incredulity in his own voice. "You're telling me *aliens* did this? Like some bad outtake from *Independence Day*?"

"I know it sounds crazy, but the tracking data's solid. They were launched in sequenced waves, Major, emanating from seven distinct point sources. They started moving east across North America while simultaneously laying another pattern across the Med, headed west. They took out all of our major bases, and as nearly as I can tell, they've killed every surface unit the Navy had. I imagine they hit our bases in Afghanistan and Iraq, as well, though I don't have any way to confirm that yet—I'm still looking for a comm link to anybody over there. But think about it. It makes sense out of that cyber attack, doesn't it? They were pulling out information for targeting purposes."

Torino wanted to throw the phone away, sit down, and bury his face in his hands. It was ridiculous. Preposterous. Yet if Robinson was who he said he was—and Torino had no reason to doubt him—he was in a better position than almost anyone else on the entire planet to know if aliens were dropping rocks on them.

"Say you're right, Sir," he said after a moment. "Why tell me? Not even a Raptor can intercept meteorites!"

"No, you can't," Robinson agreed grimly. "But I've still got optical tracking and detection available, and the bastards who did this are sending in what look like shuttles."

"*Shuttles?*" Torino said sharply, gray-green eyes suddenly narrow.

"That's what it looks like. You may not realize the optical resolution we can get, but we're getting good detail, and I'm having it set up to dump to the Internet as it comes in. Hopefully enough of the Net's still up for people to see it and realize what we're up against, but what matters right now is that these things have to be way too small to be any kind of interstellar craft. Our people make them to be maybe three times the size of a C-5, and they've got an air-breathing planeform. They've got to be landing vehicles of some sort, and it looks like we've got at least two or three dozen of them heading for someplace in western Pennsylvania or central Virginia."

• • • • •

DAN TORINO'S RAPTOR bored through the thin, frigid air fifty thousand feet above the state of Pennsylvania at just over twelve hundred miles per hour. He tried not to think about the roaring infernos sweeping out from the impact sites he and his detachment had overflown to get here. He tried not to think about the fact that, one way or the other, this was going to be his final combat sortie. And he especially tried not to think about the fact that with the United States of America facing its first foreign invasion in two centuries, all she had to defend herself were four lonely fighter planes.

I wonder how outclassed we're really going to be? he wondered. As a sixteen-year-old, he'd loved the movie *Independence Day,* although he'd realized even then that he was watching the most gloriously overdone, cliché-ridden Grade-B movie in history. As an older and (arguably) more mature fighter pilot and commissioned officer of the United States Air Force, rewatching the movie with his kids on video had caused him a certain degree of physical pain, not to mention leaving him to explain to his offspring where the Air Force had been while the Marine Corps single-handedly defended the world. Still, he couldn't forget the force field which had protected all of the alien vessels in that movie.

Look, stop sweating it, he told himself sternly. *Whatever's going to happen is going to happen, and you sure as hell aren't Will Smith. Hell, you're not even* Bruce Willis, *and at least* he's *the right color! Even if his hair is even worse than yours.*

To his amazement, that actually startled a laugh out of him.

He shook the thought aside and looked out through the superb vision of his one-piece bubble canopy. The F-22 had been designed for stealth from the ground up, and external fuel tanks were about as unstealthy as aircraft got. Nonetheless, they'd left Plattsburgh carrying four of them each, extending their operational range. They'd dropped them over Randolph, New York, three hundred and twenty miles from takeoff, which gave them roughly another thousand miles on internal fuel. If Robinson's prediction was on the money, that would be all the range they'd ever need.

Now, looking out, he could see the other three fighters holding formation on him, and he found himself wishing they had AWACS support. They didn't, but at least they did have the F-22's AN/APG-77 active electronically scanned array radar, which was the next best thing. With a range of two hundred fifty miles in the current upgrade, it offered superb threat detection and identification capabilities. It was capable of tracking multiple targets simultaneously and allowing its pilot to "manage" the battle space as no previous fighter aircraft had ever allowed, and it was a low probability of intercept system, practically impossible for conventional radar warning receivers to detect. Unfortunately, he had no idea whether that would hold true for aliens capable of interstellar flight. Somehow, he wasn't filled with optimism.

They were on their own now, although he'd managed to set up a data link with Robinson. He hadn't brought it online yet, but the people who'd been so busy blowing up cities and air bases hadn't bothered with taking out any of the communication and GPS satellites . . . yet, at least. It was loss of ground stations—the physical destruction of bases—which had torn such holes in the communications net, so he was confident Robinson would be there whenever he brought the link online.

Assuming, of course, that he survived long enough to do anything of the sort. Then again—

He stiffened as a spray of icons appeared suddenly on his heads-up display.

"Flight, Longbow," he said over the multifunction advanced data link, using the call sign he'd been assigned when his flight school instructors discovered he'd been on his high school archery team. "Acquisition. We go as planned."

Brief acknowledgments came back. The MADL had been specifically designed to allow stealth aircraft to communicate and share data without compromising their stealthiness. It combined latency and frequency-hopping through array antenna assemblies that sent tightly directed radio signals between platforms. Hopefully, the bad guys—whoever or whatever the hell they were—weren't going to pick it up. Or, looked at another way, Torino supposed, if the bad guys *were* going to pick it up, then his four fighters were already toast.

He looked out at the other planes. They were spreading farther apart, settling into their preplanned approach, and he returned his attention to the HUD's icons.

There were thirty-six of them, each indicating an airborne target moving at just under six hundred miles per hour, two hundred miles in front of his fighters. Their targets were moving roughly southeast, crossing their range, and he watched the displays projecting the target envelope of the six AIM-120-D AMRAAM "Slammers" nestled in his aircraft's internal weapons bays. The geometry meant he and his flight were closing the range at a shade better than seven hundred miles per hour—call it twelve miles per minute—with a range basket for the Slammers of better than a hundred miles. Of course, the closer he got, the higher his probability of kill became, which made it a trade-off between launch point and the point at which his aircraft could be detected, and he didn't know damn-all about the systems which might do that detecting. . . .

He thought about that for a few moments, trying to weigh and balance factors when he knew nothing at all about the opposition's capabilities. Then he decided.

"Flight, Longbow. Launch in ten mikes from . . . mark."

His left hand was busy, and target designations appeared on his HUD as his onboard computers handed them off to the rest of the flight. They continued arrowing straight towards their targets . . . who ambled along, apparently without a care in the world even as the range dropped to less than a hundred miles. The alien shuttles simply flew onward in their neat formation, stacked in twelve triangular flights of three, and Torino found himself shaking his head.

Well, he thought, *that answers one question. They* can't *pick up our radar.*

· · · · ·

SHUTTLE COMMANDER FARDAHM checked his instruments and flexed his ears in satisfaction.

Fardahm had always secretly envied his fellow pilots who'd been assigned to command the Deathwing assault shuttles. They were the ones who saw all the excitement, got to deliver the troops close to the action, even got to join the hunt when air support was called in. Pilots like Fardahm didn't. Most of the time, at least; there *were* exceptions. This was his third deployment, and his Starlander-class shuttle had been tasked to deliver an entire infantry battalion behind an enemy position to cut off retreat as part of a major attack on his second one.

Normally, though, that wasn't what Starlanders were for. They were the heavy-lift shuttles, designed to transport armored vehicles, construction equipment, large numbers of passengers, and general supplies rather than the combat infantry the Deathwings normally hauled around. They were also unarmed and a good twenty percent slower than the supersonic assault shuttles which were designed to provide ground support for their troops. "Trash haulers," the Deathwing pilots called them, and Fardahm had to admit that sometimes it rankled. Not that he intended ever to admit it to a living soul.

Well, they can call us what they like, but they'd play hell getting anything bigger than a foot-slogger down on this ball of dirt without us! Yeah, and who hauls most of the ammunition those hotshots get to shoot off? Not to mention the food they stuff into their faces!

His ears twitched in derisive amusement, but he had to confess—to himself, at least—that he was more nervous than usual about this op. A Level Two civilization was a hell of a lot more advanced than the primitives they'd been up against in his previous two deployments. He'd watched the long-range imagery of the kinetic strikes going in, taking out the locals' military infrastructure, and been frankly delighted to see it. The night-side strikes had been especially impressive, but what had most impressed *Fardahm* was the knowledge that each of those pinprick boils of light had been blotting away creatures with far better ability to kill Shongair infantry troopers than any other species the Empire had ever conquered. Personally, though he hadn't mentioned it to anyone, he didn't envy the foot-sloggers, this time around. Usually, they got to have all the fun—not to mention the choicer cuts of any local prey—but *this* time they might just find themselves up against adversaries with real firearms, and that could be nasty.

On the other hand, these critters do have a fairly advanced communications ability, he reflected. *That means all of them are going to know we've already kicked Cainharn's own hells out of them. We're not going to have to physically march all over the entire damned planet to get that message across to every isolated little group of primitives. So it's probably actually going to be* easier *for the grunts this time, now that I think about it.*

Well, either way, it wasn't going to be his problem. The infantry might usually get to have the fun dirt-side, but at least shuttle pilots got to sleep in nice, clean bunks every night. And they had access to hot showers, too, for that matter. Of course, he was going to be too busy to be enjoying *his* bunk or any hot showers anytime soon. There were never enough Starlanders, especially during the initial phases of a landing. At the moment, he and the rest of the 9th Heavy Transport Group's triple-twelve of shuttles—almost a full twelfth-part of the fleet's heavy lift landing capability—were headed for a preselected landing zone west of what had once been the capital of something called the United States. They were bringing in the first half of Ground Base Two, tasked with establishing control of the eastern seacoast of this continent. Ground Base One, with overall responsibility for the entire continent, was being landed by the 11th Heavy Transport, much farther west. In something called the "state of Iowa," by the locals.

Fardahm grimaced at the bizarre-sounding words. He was glad *he* wasn't going to have to learn "English." Even if his vocal apparatus had been designed for making such peculiar sounds, it seemed to him that it was a very strange language. For that matter, if these creatures—these "humans"—were going to have planet-wide communications, why in Dainthar's name couldn't they have settled on a *single* language? Was that really asking too much? Just one language, and one that didn't have so many sounds that sounded just like other sounds. It was a good thing their personal comps were going to be able to handle the translation for anyone who actually had to communicate with them. Which, praise Dainthar, *he* wasn't!

He checked his position again. About another tenth of a segment. Of course, he was sixteenth in the landing queue, so—

Shuttle Commander Fardahm's thoughts were interrupted with shocking suddenness as an AIM-120-D Advanced-Medium Range Air-to-Air Missile's forty-pound blast-fragmentation warhead detonated less than five feet from his shuttle's fuselage.

Alarm systems howled, onboard fire alarms shrieked, lights began to flash all over his cockpit, and crimson danger signals appeared on his cornea-projected HUD.

None of them did Fardahm any good at all. He was already reaching for the ejection button when the entire shuttle blew up in midair.

. . . . .

EAT YOUR HEART *out, Will Smith!*

Despite everything, "Longbow" Torino felt his lips curling up in an enormous smile. *These* alien shuttles obviously *didn't* have any force fields protecting them. Not only that, but they clearly hadn't had a clue what was heading for them. His four fighters had launched twenty-four Slammers, and their missiles' performance had done Raytheon proud. Twenty of them had scored clean hits or detonated within lethal distance of their targets, and each of them was a hard kill.

He heard someone else—"Killer" Cunningham, he thought—howling in triumph. The same savage, vengeful satisfaction flamed through his own veins, but it was a cold, burning fire, not hot, and his brain ticked like an icy machine.

The range was down to fifty miles, still dropping at better than ten miles a minute, and there was no sign of any defensive fire. For that matter, there weren't even any decoys or flares.

"Flight, Longbow," he said flatly. "Sidewinders."

· · · · ·

THE SHONGAIR FORMATION disintegrated in confusion and wild panic. No Shongair shuttle had *ever* been downed by hostile fire—not even a Deathwing, which routinely provided close support, far less one of the Starlanders!—and the pilots had no idea what to do. They'd never been trained in combat techniques, because there'd never been any need for them. They were *transport* pilots, and their shuttles were transport vehicles, optimized for maximum cargo capacity. The Starlander was better than six hundred and forty feet long, a variable geometry design capable of relatively high Mach numbers on a reentry profile but designed for economic, subsonic flight in atmosphere. It was capable of vertical takeoff and landing operation on counter-grav but used conventional air-breathing engines in actual flight, and its designers had never intended for it to stray into reach of any armed opponent. And for all its size, it was fragile. Tough-skinned enough to resist muscle-powered projectiles, perhaps, it didn't respond well when the warheads of vastly more sophisticated weapons tore holes in that same skin or white-hot fragments of those same warheads were thrown into its completely unarmored fuel system.

The survivors watched in horrified shock as twenty of their fellows plunged down to catastrophic rendezvous with the ground below, and they didn't even know who was shooting at them! Lockheed Martin had described the F-22's radar cross-section as "the size of a steel marble," which was a remarkable achievement, but this time it didn't really matter. Not as far as the Starlanders were concerned. Their air-to-air radar was designed primarily to avoid aerial collisions between aircraft with transponders—aircraft which *wanted* to be seen—not to locate highly stealthy, heavily armed fighters less than a tenth their own size. Nor had it ever occurred to anyone to fit rear-area cargo-haulers intended for operations against crossbow-armed adversaries with radar warning devices. They were literally blind, totally unable to see Torino's small flight as the four Raptors streaked in behind them.

. . . . .

"FOX TWO! FOX Two!" Major Torino snapped as the two AIM-9X all-aspect Sidewinders popped out of their briefly opened weapons bay doors. The shorter-ranged heat-seeking weapons streaked away, guiding on the brilliant thermal beacons of the alien shuttles' engines, and he watched them racing in on their targets.

All four F-22s launched within seconds of one another, sending eight more missiles into the chaos of the disintegrating Shongair formation. Two of them were targeted on the same victim; within minutes, four more of the big shuttles were plunging to the earth in flames while another three staggered onward with heavy damage. One of the wounded craft trailed a broad ribbon of smoke, and even as Torino looked in its direction, he saw a river of fire joining the smoke.

"Flight, go guns!" he snarled.

. . . . .

IT WAS A nightmare.

Of the thirty-six Starlanders transporting Ground Base Two, twenty-four had been destroyed and three more were going down. The pilots of the nine undamaged survivors had only a single thought: escape. Unfortunately, they'd never been trained for this situation. It wasn't supposed to arise. They were on their own, with no evasive doctrine or tactics to call upon, and almost in unison, they swept their wings and went to full power, accelerating to just over the speed of sound and bolting straight ahead.

. . . . .

THE RAPTORS WERE out of missiles.

Each of them mounted a single twenty-millimeter M61A2 Vulcan Gatling gun in its starboard wing root, normally concealed by a carefully faired popout door to preserve the smoothness stealth required. It was intended solely as a last-ditch weapon, with only four hundred and eighty rounds of ammunition—enough for no more than five seconds of sustained maximum rate fire. Neither Torino nor any of his other pilots had ever really expected to go guns in air-to-air combat, but now that the opportunity was here. . . .

. . . . .

THE STARLANDERS NEVER had a chance.

At their best air-breathing speed, they were barely half as fast as the Raptors in dry thrust. Worse, they were huge targets, unarmored, unarmed, and little more maneuverable—even with counter-grav—than a human-designed heavy transport aircraft. The vectored-thrust F-22s, on the other hand, had been designed for high-gravity agility second to none, and they slashed in on their huge targets like barracuda attacking whales. They fired in short, mercilessly accurate bursts, ripping the shuttles' fuselages open, butchering the construction troops and base admin personnel in their passenger bays, spilling heavy construction equipment over the Virginia countryside.

It was over in less than six minutes.

. . . . .

"FLIGHT, LONGBOW." TORINO'S voice sounded drained, even to him. "Go home."

The acknowledgments came back again, and the four Raptors turned away from the funeral pyres of their victims. Now if only Plattsburgh would still be there when they got there.

. XIII .

Fleet Commander Thikair stood on *Star of Empire*'s flag bridge, studying the gigantic image of the planet below. Glowing icons indicated cities and military bases his kinetic bombardment had removed from existence. There were a lot of them—more than he'd really counted on when he decided to go ahead with the conquest—and he clasped his hands behind him and concentrated on radiating satisfaction.

And you damned well ought *to be satisfied, Thikair. Taking down an entire Level Two civilization in less than two local days has to be some sort of galactic record!*

Which, another little voice reminded him, was because doing anything of the sort directly violated the Hegemony Constitution.

And you didn't plan on taking that sort of losses the very first day, either, another little voice asked pointedly. *In fact, you didn't plan on taking losses like that* at all, *did you?*

No, he hadn't. He admitted it, if only to himself and Thairys. He still wasn't positive exactly what had happened, but if the humans were to be believed an entire heavy transport group of Starlander-class shuttles had been destroyed by only four—only *four!*—"American" aircraft. The whole notion was ridiculous, of course . . . except that he didn't have any better explanation for what had happened.

Shairez and her teams had been horribly enough overloaded going through "just" the massive amount of information they'd managed to extract from the humans' secure databases. They'd been able to give his bombardment planning teams priceless information—the locations of the humans' nuclear missile bases, for example—but she'd warned him there might be holes in their analysis. That might be what had happened in the case of his shuttles, although from the small number of aircraft allegedly involved, it might also be that they'd come from some small detachment which simply hadn't been in her databases to begin with.

Nonetheless, it had been obvious that she hadn't had time to fully digest the take from their cyber attack. No one could have. And it was even worse now, because an amazing amount of the human Internet was still up. The system was obviously much more robust than he'd originally assumed, which might make sense, since according to Shairez's findings, it had been created originally as a dispersed communications network to function in the wake of a human nuclear exchange. At any rate, it was still inundating them with data. With *too much* data, in point of fact. For the first time, a fleet commander's problem wasn't gaining access to information; it was *processing* it. Someone still had to go through it, looking for the nuggets that were truly important, and its sheer volume was creating unanticipated problems. No Shongair commander in history had ever had such an overwhelming mountain of data on his adversaries, and even the redoubtable ground base commander was overwhelmed trying to assimilate it.

Nevertheless, after what had happened to the 9th Transport Group, she'd undertaken a priority search for any references to the "F-22s" which the human Internet reports credited with its destruction. She'd copied the pertinent information to Thikair, and despite himself, he'd been shaken by some of the implications as he'd studied the aircraft's claimed capabilities. He wasn't certain he believed some of them even now. What had happened to his shuttles suggested he should take it seriously, however, and that was an . . . unpleasant possibility to contemplate. It was one thing to know the humans were effectively a Class Two civilization. It was quite another thing, he'd discovered, to recognize some of the nastier possibilities that raised.

The truth is, he thought, *we've never fought anyone with a Class Two tech base. Not even amongst ourselves, before we joined the Hegemony. We were only a Class Three—well, maybe a Class 3.5—by the time we unified the planet under Emperor Ramarth. And all of our research since we joined the Hegemony has really been centered on* naval *weaponry. After all, once you control a planet's orbitals, who cares what they've got on the dirt below you? Either the planetary government surrenders, or you drop KEWs on it until it does. That's the way it has to be, right?*

That had always been the assumption, at any rate. And not just for the Shongairi. The Garm and the Howsanth, two of the Hegemony's more belligerent omnivores, had fought three wars over the past four thousand standard years, and that was the way it had always worked out for them, as well. Certainly no one had wasted any time and effort designing heavy combat equipment to use at the bottom of a gravity well!

But when you and all of your opponents are trapped at the bottom of that same gravity well, you don't have a lot of choice, do you? he reflected. *So it's probably no wonder these creatures' military technology is better than any other Class Two civilization we've ever encountered. It's still not good enough—it can't be, in the long run—but they* have *demonstrated that under exactly the wrong circumstances, they can hurt us badly.*

He managed not to grimace at the thought, but it wasn't easy. When his brilliant notion occurred to him, he hadn't fully digested just how big and thoroughly inhabited this planet, this . . . "Earth" truly was. Again, it was a factor of technology. None of the other planets the Empire had assimilated had possessed the technological capability to simply *feed* this many people. Nor, for that matter, the medical technology to keep them alive in such preposterous numbers. The most densely populated planet previously conquered by the Shongairi had boasted no more than five hundred million sentients, which was barely forty percent more than the population of this world's "United States" alone . . . and less than half the *individual* populations of the nation-states of "India" and "China." The notion that there really were *billions* of them down there was something he'd discovered he hadn't truly grasped even while he threw it around in planning sessions with his staff. Nor had he really considered the difficulty in getting the local authorities to submit in some sort of timely fashion when there were so Dainthar-damned many different nation-states and each of them had its own government!

He wondered now if he hadn't allowed himself to fully digest it because he'd known that if he had, he would have changed his mind.

Oh, stop it! *So there were more of them on the damned planet than you'd figured on. And so you've already killed—what? Two billion of them, wasn't it? And given the fact that their technology seems to have been a little better than you allowed for, you may well end up having to kill a few more of them, as well. So what's the problem? There're plenty more where* they *came from—according to their own statistics, they breed like damned* garshu*! And you told Ahzmer and the others you're willing to kill off the entire species if it doesn't work out. So fretting about a little extra breakage along the way is pretty pointless, wouldn't you say?*

Of course it was. In fact, he admitted, his biggest concern was how many major engineering works these humans had created. There was no doubt that he could exterminate them if he had to, but he was beginning to question whether it would be possible to eliminate the physical evidence of the level their culture had attained after all.

Well, we'll just have to keep it from coming to that, won't we?

"Pass the word to Ground Force Commander Thairys," he told Ship Commander Ahzmer quietly, never taking his eyes from those glowing icons. "Expedite his landings. I want his troops on the ground as quickly as possible, especially around the ground base sites. And make sure they have all the fire support they need."

"Yes, Sir."

"And tell Ground Base Commander Shairez I want her to pull together a more complete précis on the military technology of this 'United States.' I know she's buried under a mountain of data at the moment, but if what happened to the Ninth Transport Group is any indication, we may have to pay a little more attention to making certain that particular *hasthar*'s completely dead before we move on to other priorities."

· · · · ·

"SO WHAT DO you make of it?" Dave Dvorak asked quietly, looking over his brother-in-law's shoulder.

The two of them stood behind Sharon Dvorak's chair as she sat at her computer keyboard, and all three of them were watching the YouTube video streaming on her flat screen. It had been posted by someone who claimed to be a US Navy rear admiral, and it was pretty spectacular stuff, a skillfully edited montage of footage from orbital surveillance systems and the gun cameras (or whatever the hell they were called these days) of US Air Force fighters.

"Looks to me like this squid—Robinson—is right," Rob Wilson said grimly. "Trust me, those fuckers"—a blunt index finger tapped the image of a flaming Starlander shuttle—"didn't come out of any air force *I* ever heard of! Just look at the size of the bastards—they're big as goddamned *missile cruisers*!" He shook his head. "Uh-uh. I think he's right. They've gotta come from someplace else, and I don't have any better idea about 'someplace else' than he's serving up."

"I think he's right, Dave," Sharon said quietly, and managed to give her husband a grin when she looked up over her shoulder at him. "Besides, you're the big science-fiction reader. You ought to be jumping right on top of this!"

"Somebody once said that an 'adventure' was someone *else* being cold, hungry, tired, and scared far, far away from *you*," Dvorak replied wryly. "At the moment, I'm feeling a little too close to this to be very adventurous. In fact," he met her eyes levelly, then looked at his brother-in-law, "I'm scared to death."

"You think maybe the rest of us aren't?" Sharon asked gently, reaching one hand up to him. He caught it and held it, then looked back at the flat screen as the video played itself out again.

There was plenty of panicky confusion, desperation, and (inevitably) conspiracy-mongering paranoia on the net, but there was a lot of what looked like solid information still coming in, as well, and he was glad Sharon was monitoring it. On the other hand, he had to wonder just how thoroughly the Internet had been penetrated. It would have been the best way to keep track of what humanity was telling itself . . . and to insert things Earth's attackers *wanted* humanity to know or believe were true. That kind of information warfare would have been his very first priority if *he'd* been setting out to invade a planet, and he had to assume the other side was at least as smart as he was. In fact, he'd damned well better assume they were a hell of a lot *smarter* than he was!

The good news was that, for the moment at least, his family was probably as safe as anyone on the entire globe. The sprawling old cabin on the back side of Cold Mountain, above the headwaters of Little Green Creek in Jackson County, North Carolina, was in the Nantahala National Forest. It had been built (and then added onto . . . repeatedly) in the 1890s by one of Sharon and Rob's more peculiar—and reclusive—great-great-granduncles, and it had remained in the family ever since. It was less than a mile from the nearest road (although, in Dvorak's opinion, calling Cold Mountain Road a "road" was a bit of a stretch), but its mile and a half or so of twisting "driveway" was hardly inviting—a narrow ribbon of dirt with occasional patches of gravel and other patches of bare bedrock that threaded its way under the interlaced branches of overhanging trees while it climbed over sixteen hundred feet to cross the saddle between Cold Mountain and Panthertail Mountain. Even knowing exactly where it was, he'd never been able to find it on Google Earth even at maximum zoom, and the cabin itself was almost equally invisible.

The family had been coming up to the cabin summers ever since Rob and Sharon had been teenagers, although no one had actually lived in it year round for at least fifty years. Describing its amenities as "primitive" would have constituted aggravated assault on a perfectly serviceable adjective, but that hadn't been a problem, since the family expeditions had been more in the nature of camping trips than anything else.

There'd always been a risk of vandalism, of course, but there was little traffic in that particular part of the national forest, aside from a handful of hard-core hikers, and most hikers and hunters were actually pretty considerate of other people's property. More recently, one of the Wilsons' cousins who was a National Park Service ranger had accrued enough seniority to request—and get—assignment to the Highlands Ranger District a few years back. He'd kept an eye on the place for them since then . . . and especially over the last three years.

That was when Dvorak and Wilson (who, according to at least some of their friends, were both politically somewhere to the right of Attila the Hun, although *possibly* still to the left of Genghis Khan) had decided to take Homeland Security's advice to organize their own plan in case of a national disaster or major terrorist incident. The Chicago subway attack, which had killed three of Dvorak's cousins, had helped the notion gel.

So they'd decided to turn the cabin into their bolthole. It was certainly big enough, since Old Mountain Man Wilson had been the father of a sizable brood. In fact, there were proud-of-his-oddities-though-we'd-never-admit-it family rumors that one reason he'd lived so far back in the hills was to avoid neighbors who might have figured out he was a bigamist . . . and that most of the add-ons to the original structure had been for additional wives. Of course, there had been that lack of amenities and modern conveniences, but they'd been talking about remodeling the cabin to modernize it and make it more comfortable for over ten years. Once they finally decided to think in terms of refuges rather than vacations, that talk had turned into action. In fact, Dvorak had to admit, the two of them had gotten carried away and put far more effort (and money) into the "renovations" than they'd ever really intended to.

His loving wife *had* occasionally accused him of being OCD. At times, he was forced to concede she might actually have a point.

The old stone-and-log cabin had been completely reroofed (and *that* had been a nightmare project for just the two of them and Alec), thoroughly weatherproofed, insulated, and sheetrocked. They'd also considered other requirements, like water and electricity. Fortunately, the headwaters of Little Green Creek lay on the cabin property, so (with Alec once more "volunteered" to assist), they'd built themselves a solid masonry dam to impound a reservoir that was over twelve feet deep at the deepest point. Designing a dam that ambitious had turned out to be more than either of them could handle, but they'd discussed the problem with a friend of theirs who happened to be a licensed (although retired) civil engineer. He'd very carefully failed to ask them about little things like permits, and they hadn't officially paid him a thing for his "suggestions" (accompanied by detailed blueprints) . . . although he'd wound up, somehow, with a life membership and free shooting privileges in the indoor range.

There hadn't been any tearing rush to fill their new holding pond overnight, so they'd installed a base-mounted sluice in the form of four large-diameter, independently valved pipes. The stream's normal outflow would have driven three of those pipes at full capacity; at high levels after heavy rains, all four of them together couldn't have carried the full flow, of course, which was why their engineer friend had also included a standard overflow sluice plus a "hundred-year storm" emergency sluice. But leaving two pipes open and two pipes closed had allowed them to gradually fill their reservoir without seriously impacting the stream's flow to join the Tuckasegee River roughly one mile downstream.

By that time, they'd been seriously bitten by the "Gee! Wonder how we can make it even better?" bug, and their various children had been urging them on gleefully, since they regarded the entire pond as their own personal, private (and very, *very* cold) swimming hole. So they'd installed two separate but parallel PVC penstocks to deliver water to a pair of in-line Francis turbines, each coupled to an independent generator. The creek fell over six hundred feet in its run to the Tuckasegee, and the penstocks extended in a straight line for almost five hundred feet down its steep bed from their intakes, two feet below the top of the dam. That gave them a total vertical fall of just over eighty feet to the powerhouse, where each seven-horsepower turbine drove a separate micro-generator before the water was returned to the streambed. Water flow in the stream was generally constant and reliable, and each generator produced around a hundred and twenty kilowatt hours daily. Even one of them would have been a pretty serious case of overkill for a single household, but that only meant they could let one generator stand idle at any given moment. Besides, it was always better to realize you had more power than you *wanted* rather than discovering you had less power than you *needed*, and both of them figured redundancy was a beautiful thing.

The entire project had cost them several thousand dollars, more barked knuckles and calluses than either of them cared to remember, and far too many hours standing in ice-cold water wrestling with mortar and river rocks while their loving families enjoyed picnic lunches and kibitzed cheerfully. In fact, after a particularly lively offering of "advice," Jessica had ended up unceremoniously dunked by her husband one memorable afternoon.

And somehow—no one knew how to this very day, honest!—Sharon and Veronica had likewise tumbled into the water when their loving husbands sought to help them rescue Jessica.

They'd finished the task—eventually—and they'd also installed a standby emergency generator in a prefab utility building behind the cabin, just in case. ("Redundancy!" Dvorak had said. "*Toujours la* redundancy!" At which point Wilson had clocked him over the head with a three-foot length of plastic pipe.) Then they'd managed (not without more than a few profanity-laced moments) to truck in three polyethylene four-feet-by-eleven-feet thousand-gallon tanks to provide it with fuel (and act as a reservoir for vehicles, if it should come to that).

They'd been surprised by how cheaply tanks that size could be purchased. For that matter, they'd been surprised by how cheaply a lot of the things they needed could be purchased—not that the entire undertaking hadn't ended up costing considerably more than they'd projected when they first launched themselves on it anyway. They'd wound up putting well over fifty thousand dollars into it by the time all was said and done, but relying on their own labor had let them hold costs down remarkably.

Of course, installing the actual generators and wiring the cabin (with low-power demand, long-life fluorescents instead of incandescent bulbs) had been another interesting task . . . but Joel Skinner, a professional electrician and crony, had also mysteriously ended up with a range life membership and shooting privileges before it was done.

With electricity in plentiful supply, they'd built a new pump house over the original spring-fed well and installed a new electric pump and pressure tank. Then they'd added a second pump—and another hundred yards or so of buried PVC pipe—from the dam to establish a backup gravity-fed reservoir for the cabin. They'd hauled in *another* thousand-gallon tank to serve as a cistern above the cabin and installed a primitive water heater by running several courses of pipe (*not* PVC, this time) through the back of the cabin's main fireplace and into a holding tank. They probably could have simply settled for an electric water heater and been done with it, but both of them had discovered they'd been deeply bitten by the "belt and suspenders" approach to the project. They'd gone ahead and invested in demand water heater units for the cabin's bathroom and kitchen, but it was nice to know they had an electricity-independent fallback.

After the fuel and water tanks, the preplumbed eight-foot-by-five-foot poly septic tank had seemed ridiculously easy to get up that never to be sufficiently damned "driveway," but *burying* the thing (and building the leaching field . . . after finding a place they were positive wasn't going to affect the local groundwater) had been an even worse nightmare than the roof. And, mysteriously, the shooting range had ended up hemorrhaging still more potential cash flow when Ken Lehman, a plumber who attended Dvorak's church, had acquired life membership shooting privileges, as well.

In the meantime, Sharon and Veronica had gotten bitten by the same bug and, with the assistance of their offspring (or, perhaps, *despite* the assistance of their offspring), they'd replaced every square inch of flooring in the cabin and completely refurbished the old root cellar buried under it. The grout lines in the kitchen weren't all ruler-straight, perhaps, but the colorful goldenrod-and-white tiles made it a much brighter and more cheerful place to cook.

Dennis Vardry, the Wilson cousin and ranger, had almost suffered apoplexy when he discovered everything they'd done, but even with the penstocks and the cistern drawing off the creek, water flow below the dam wasn't significantly impacted. All of the changes and improvements were on property Rob and Sharon jointly owned, so he'd decided he knew nothing—nothing!—about any of it. Besides, he and his wife got to use the cabin whenever no Dvoraks or Wilsons were actively in residence, and they weren't going to turn their noses up at electrical conveniences, thank you very much.

The cabin also had a well-stocked pantry to go with the root cellar, but Dvorak and Wilson had decided that since so many of their friends had teased them over their paranoia, they might as well go ahead and *be* paranoid. Although actually, if Dvorak was going to be completely fair, the suggestion had been made—to his own subsequent regret—by *Alec* Wilson.

Alec was the one who'd stumbled across the cave on the north side of the mountain two or three hundred feet above the cabin. In fact, he'd literally tripped and fallen into it, although he continued to stoutly insist he'd *intended* to go spelunking the whole time.

It was a good-sized cave, running back over ninety feet into the mountainside, sixty feet wide at its widest, and close to twelve feet high at its highest point. The entrance itself was no more than five feet tall and only twenty feet across, and it was obvious that more than one of Nantahala's bears had made its quarters there in the past. It was also dry inside and a long way above the local water table, however.

"Okay," Alec had said, grinning at his father and uncle-in-law. "You two are so gung ho to go about making us a hidey hole up here in the hills. Doesn't this just shout 'bunker' to you?"

His grin had gotten even broader, then faded when he saw the matching speculative gleams as Dvorak and Wilson looked at one another.

"Hey!" There'd been an edge of alarm in his own eyes. "I was just kidding! You two aren't really thinking—?"

Alas, they had been. It had taken them (and a grumbling Alec) the better part of another year, but they'd leveled the floor (mostly) and then enlarged the cave opening and closed it off with a timber-and-earth wall four feet thick with a sturdy security door in the middle of it. The outer face of the wall was dirt, shaped to fit the contour of the slope around it and covered in mountain laurel (transplanted from the thickets nature had already provided on the hill above the cave), and the security door was masked by a carefully camouflaged earth-covered panel which had to be lifted out of the way to gain access. They'd provided concealed ventilation, as well, put in lighting and a dehumidifier wired through their own switchboard, and installed a second gasoline-powered backup generator and two three hundred and fifty gallon tanks for fuel.

That was where the majority of their food supplies were actually parked. The cave was so naturally dry that they probably really didn't need the dehumidifier, but it was a relatively modest unit without a lot of power demand. It wasn't that much trouble, and it couldn't hurt, especially when they'd turned the cave into their primary storage facility. They'd calculated that they had enough canned and freeze-dried food tucked away inside the "bunker" to supply a group of ten people for a year and enough stored vegetable seed for at least three years' worth of gardens. Even if someone happened along and vandalized the cabin after all, they'd have a fallback position in case of an emergency.

And it was also where they'd stashed away a complete backup set of all twelve Foxfire books and almost all of their medical and first-aid supplies. Not to mention where they'd now parked the full inventory from The D & W Indoor Shooting Range, plus most of the contents of two serious gun nuts' gun safes. Not to mention Dvorak's home loading bench (and supplies) and Wilson's gunsmithing tools. Taken all together, it would have been enough to make certain federal law enforcement professionals reach for the "dangerous-right-wing-militia-nut" panic button on sight, although possibly not under current conditions, Dvorak thought now, grimly.

So, yes, the good news was that they had their heads down someplace no one was going to bother them and, for the moment at least, it looked like they'd be able to keep them there.

The bad news was that their world had been invaded by aliens who didn't seem to give a single damn how many humans got killed in the process. And at the moment, the Internet was their only way to form any idea at all of how many humans had *already* been killed.

When Dvorak and Wilson had first started work on the cabin, they'd put in a satellite dish and bought satellite phones. At that point, they hadn't been especially worried about things like radio location—largely because they'd been thinking in terms of purely terrestrial threats and, friends' political opinions aside, neither of them had really mistrusted their own government to the extent that they'd actually given much consideration to hiding from it. They'd both been Boy Scouts in their youth, however. They still took that "Be Prepared" business seriously, so "not much consideration" wasn't exactly the same as saying they'd given *no* thought to the proposition, and Alec, as their family computer geek, had been given a homework assignment of figuring out how they could maintain Internet access without betraying radio signatures if, for some reason, that should seem like a good thing to do.

Alec, who normally regarded his father and uncle with the sort of fond exasperation reserved for lovable lunatics, had decided to take this assignment seriously, and solved it by locating a microwave relay tower a little over a mile from the cabin. He'd pointed out that it would be relatively simple to take a laptop to the base of the tower, plug in, and ride the tower's signal. His fond father and doting uncle had pointed out in return that hiking a mile—most of which was vertical, although by no means all in the same direction—through cold rain or (worse) snow was not something they looked forward to doing. So Alec, in the spirit of cheerful cooperation, had laid in a couple of miles worth of fiber-optic cable . . . and handed them the bill for it with a smile.

None of them were feeling particularly cheerful at the moment, and all of them had things like radio location finding very much on their minds under the circumstances, so Alec and his uncle had spent most of yesterday afternoon stringing the fiber optic between the cabin and the tower. They'd laid it along the ground and covered it carefully with deep mountain leaf mold. Dvorak, whose paranoia had shifted into steroids mode over the last couple of days, would really have preferred not to establish any "breadcrumb" trail some ill-intentioned person could backtrack to the cabin, but after some consideration, he and Wilson had agreed that that minor risk was far outweighed by their need to keep track of what was happening in the world as long as the Internet lasted.

Not that it was proving particularly pleasant knowledge.

"It'd be nice to at least know what these people want," he said now, shaking his head as he glowered at Sharon's display. "I mean, did they just dial in on that idiot Sagan's 'Eat at Carl's' broadcasts and decide to check the menu? Or did we *do* something to piss them off? I assume they'll get around to talking to us sooner or later, but until they do, we don't have a clue what's going to happen."

"Maybe not," Wilson said harshly, "but we sure as hell know what's *already* happened. Or enough of it, anyway." He jabbed a finger at the monitor. "God knows the net's been full enough of it!"

Which it had, Dvorak thought. Which it had.

He didn't know if the list of destroyed cities was complete yet. He was pretty sure the *worldwide* list wasn't, but he hoped—prayed—that the list of murdered US populations had been completed. Washington, Los Angeles, San Francisco, Denver, Spokane . . . Closer to home, Columbia (apparently because of its proximity to Fort Jackson); Sumter (that would have been Shaw Air Force Base); Charleston (because of the Naval Nuclear Power Training Command?); and Atlanta (he didn't have a clue about that one, unless it had simply been a population center to be taken out). It went on seemingly forever, although—thank God—whoever it was hadn't hit some of the other major population centers. New York City was still there, even if the panicked exodus of its citizens was busy turning it into a nightmare zone of confusion and looting. Chicago was still intact, and remarkably calm (so far, at least) compared to New York. Boston, Philadelphia, Pittsburgh, Cincinnati, Indianapolis, Houston . . . they were all still there, although they were busily emptying of population as people tried to get away from what might be the next ground zero.

No one had an estimate of total casualties yet, but it was already brutally evident that the United States of America had suffered more dead—civilian and military—than ever before in its entire history. And it was obvious from the conversation on the Internet that the sheer, incredulous shock of the initial attack was still rippling outward, still gaining strength. It was as if no one, particularly Americans, could believe something like this could truly happen.

And what happens when the shock begins to dissipate? he wondered.

What happens when we find out exactly the same thing happened everywhere else? And what happens when the bastards who did this finally communicate and tell us what the hell it is they want?

"I guess the good news is that they don't simply want to go ahead and kill us all off . . . yet, at least," he said out loud. Wilson looked at him, and he shrugged. "If that was what they wanted to do, I figure they'd still be dropping rocks," he pointed out.

"Nothing to say they can't go ahead and start doing it again anytime they want to," Wilson responded, and he nodded.

"Absolutely. But you know, whoever these bastards are, they aren't Superman. Hell, they're not even Clark Kent! Look what the Air Force did to those transports, or shuttles, or whatever. Their technology's obviously better than ours, or they wouldn't be here, but how *much* better is it? Judging by Robinson's YouTube post, we're at least in shouting range."

"Except for the fact that they can drop those fucking rocks on our heads and we *can't* drop rocks on theirs," Wilson growled.

"Agreed. But I've got to wonder what their logistics look like." Both of Wilson's eyebrows rose, and Dvorak snorted. "Hey, *you* were the Marine, so think about it. Is this Eisenhower getting ready to invade Normandy? Or Holland Smith and Marc Mitscher invading Iwo Jima? Or is it just Cortés going after the Aztecs on a frigging shoestring? From what we're seeing over the Internet, they seem to be landing in a fairly small number of spots, and they have to have lost a bunch of people and equipment when all those transports went down. How much manpower can they actually have if they've come all the way from another star system? Do they have millions of troops stacked up in cryogenic sleep like cordwood? Or do they have only a few hundred thousand? Maybe even less?"

"However many they've got, they've still got the rock-droppers, too," Wilson said.

"Agreed," Dvorak repeated with a nod. "I'm only saying that if their technology isn't *that* much better than ours, and if they don't have one hell of a lot of manpower up there in orbit, then they're probably going to find out that an entire planet's a damned big mouthful."

There was an ugly light in his eyes, and Sharon looked up quickly.

"David Dvorak—!" she began.

"Oh, don't worry, honey." He patted her on the shoulder. "Rob and I didn't put all that time into Operation Hidey Hole just so we could do something stupid. We're not going to forget about the kids, either." He shrugged.

"For that matter, we're probably about as thoroughly out of their way as anybody could get right at the moment. And if it's all the same with you, I think we'll just stay there."

"Damned right it's 'all the same' to me!"

"I know. But I'm willing to bet you it's not going to be very long at all before these people—or whatever they are—run into somebody who *is* prepared to do something stupid. Somebody who just doesn't care anymore, for example. And when that happens, I don't think they'll enjoy the experience."

. XIV .

Stephen Buchevsky stood by the road and wondered—again—just what the hell to do next.

Their pilot hadn't managed to find any friendly airfields, after all. He'd done his best, but all but out of fuel, with his communications out and high-kiloton-range explosions dotting the face of Europe (and after dodging warning shots from an ancient Yugoslav Air Force MIG-21 which seemed convinced *his* aircraft had had something to do with the general mayhem), his options had been limited. He'd tried to make it into Romanian airspace—he'd actually managed to establish contact with the Romanian Air Force helicopter base at Caransebeş and been cleared for approach—but he'd run out of time and gas. Despite the unpromising terrain over which he'd found himself when the tanks finally ran dry, he'd managed to find a stretch of road that would almost do, and he'd set the big plane down with his last few gallons of fuel.

The C-17 had been designed for rough-field landings, but its designers hadn't had anything quite that rough in mind. Worse, The Book called for a minimum thirty-five-hundred-foot runway, and he hadn't had anywhere near that much space to work with. At least the aircraft had been about as light as it was going to get, having burned off so much fuel, and he'd thrown all four F117-PW-100 turbofans into full reverse thrust. Unfortunately, it hadn't been enough. Buchevsky thought it might still have worked if the road hadn't crossed a culvert the pilot hadn't been able to see from the air. He'd lost both main gear when it collapsed under the plane's hundred-and-forty-ton weight. Worse, he hadn't lost the gear simultaneously, and the sudden, asymmetrical drag had thrown the aircraft totally out of control. It had crashed down on its belly, then spun madly as it left the road and plowed into heavy tree cover like some sort of demented Frisbee. When it had finally stopped careening through the trees, both wings were gone and the entire forward third of its fuselage had been crushed and tangled wreckage.

At least it hadn't burned or exploded, but neither pilot had survived, and the only other two officers aboard were among the six passengers who'd been killed, which left Buchevsky the ranking member of their small group. Two more passengers were brutally injured, and he'd gotten them out of the wreckage into the best shelter he could contrive, but they didn't have anything resembling a doctor.

Nor did they have much in the way of equipment. Buchevsky had his personal weapons, as did six of the others, but that was it, and none of them had very much ammunition. Not surprisingly, he supposed, since they weren't supposed to have had *any* onboard the aircraft. Fortunately (in this case, at least) it was extraordinarily difficult to separate troops returning from a combat zone from at least *some* ammo.

There were also at least some first-aid supplies—enough to set the broken arms three of the passengers had suffered and make at least a token attempt at patching up the worst injured. But that was about it, and he really, really wished he could at least talk to somebody higher up the command hierarchy than he was. Unfortunately, he was it.

Which, he thought mordantly, *at least gives me something to keep me busy.*

And it also gave him something besides Washington to worry about. He'd argued with Trish when she decided to take Shania and Yvonne to live with her mother, but that had been because of the crime rate and the cost of living in DC. Well, that and how far it was from *his* parents. He'd never, *ever* worried about—

He touched his chest, feeling the silver cross against his skin, under his tee-shirt. The cross a proud Shania had given him last Christmas, engraved with his initials plus her own and her younger sister's. She'd bought it with her very own money (though he suspected his father, who'd helped her find it, had understated the price to her just a bit when he placed the order for her and arranged the engraving), and she'd solemnly promised him that it would keep him safe and bring him back to them.

Safe. She'd wanted to keep *him* safe, but when she'd really needed him, when it had been his job to keep *her* safe—

He pushed that thought aside yet again, just as he pushed aside thoughts of a small Methodist rectory in South Carolina, fleeing almost gratefully back to the contemplation of the cluster-fuck he had to deal with somehow.

Gunnery Sergeant Calvin Meyers was their group's second-ranking member, which made him Buchevsky's XO . . . to the obvious disgruntlement of Sergeant Francisco Ramirez, the senior Army noncom. But if Ramirez resented the fact that they'd just become a Marine-run show, he was keeping his mouth shut. Probably because he recognized what an unmitigated pain in the ass Buchevsky's job had just become.

They had a limited quantity of food, courtesy of the aircraft's overwater survival package, but none of them had any idea of their position. Or, rather, they knew exactly where they were, thanks to his Marine-issue DAGR handheld GPS—they just didn't have any idea of what that meant in terms of the local geography.

Or in terms of the local population . . . if any.

Their latitude and longitude put them just on the Serbian side of the Romanian border, and a bit over ten miles southwest of the Danube. The area was mountainous and heavily forested, although the road threaded through occasional cleared sections—like this one—where farmland stretched for a hundred yards or so on either side. But either there weren't very many civilians in the area or else the locals had decided that with nuclear weapons dropping all over the landscape it might be wiser to keep their heads down and stay away from any crashed aircraft.

There were two farmhouses within five miles of their location, but there'd been no sign of any inhabitants when Meyers took a two-man team to look for help for their injured. Buchevsky suspected the farm families had taken themselves elsewhere when obviously foreign military personnel arrived on their doorsteps. Given what had just happened, he couldn't really blame them. In fact, he'd just about come to the conclusion that avoiding contact with the locals would probably be a pretty good idea from his perspective, as well. At least until things had settled down and he—and, hopefully, they—had been able to figure out what the hell was happening.

People in this neck of the woods probably aren't feeling all that friendly towards the good old United States of America, anyway, in light of little things like their relations with Bosnia-Herzegovina and the Republic of Croatia, he reflected. *And even if they were, they'd have to be suspicious as hell if foreigners come waltzing onto their land at a moment like this. Not to mention the fact that the first thing that's going to occur to a lot of them is that they're likely to be inundated by hungry people. The notion of having hungry soldiers—especially hungry* foreign *soldiers—"requisitioning" what they have isn't going to appeal to them, and they might just figure that shooting first and using their visitors for really good fertilizer later would be the best way to avoid any unpleasantness.*

But even assuming that kind of caution might be a good idea, what did it mean for his two really badly injured survivors? One thing they couldn't do was move them—not without a medevac, and the chance of getting a helicopter in here to pick them up was nonexistent. If they could find someone who could call them an ambulance, or at least provide *some* sort of vehicle, or just call the local country doctor, it might mean those people would survive after all. On the other hand, maybe it wouldn't, either. Buchevsky had seen a lot of badly wounded people over the years, and neither of their seriously injured people looked like they were going to make it. One of them had a brutal head injury—the entire right side of her skull was depressed and . . . spongy feeling—while the other obviously had major internal bleeding. Neither of them was conscious, for which Buchevsky could only be grateful, given the nature of their injuries.

In the meantime, he had to decide what to do in light of the fact that not one of them spoke Serbian, they were totally out of communication with anyone, and the last they'd heard, the entire planet seemed to be succumbing to spontaneous insanity.

So where's the problem? he asked himself sardonically. *Hell, it ought to be a piece of cake for a hardened senior Marine noncom such as yourself! Of course—*

"I think you'd better listen to this, Top," a voice said, and Buchevsky turned towards the speaker.

"Listen to what, Gunny?"

"We're getting something really weird on the radio, Top."

Buchevsky's eyes narrowed. He'd never actually met Meyers before this flight, but the sandy-haired, compact, strongly built, slow-talking Marine from the Appalachian coalfields had struck him as a solid, unflappable sort. At the moment, however, Meyers was pasty-pale, and his hands shook as he extended the emergency radio they'd recovered from the wrecked fuselage.

Meyers turned the volume back up, and Buchevsky's eyes narrowed even farther. The voice coming from the radio sounded . . . mechanical. Artificial. It carried absolutely no emotions or tonal emphasis.

That was the first thing that struck him. Then he jerked back half a step, as if he'd just been punched, as what the voice was *saying* registered.

"—am Fleet Commander Thikair of the Shongair Empire, and I am addressing your entire planet on all frequencies. Your world lies helpless before us. Our kinetic energy weapons have destroyed your major national capitals, your military bases, and your warships. We can, and will, conduct additional kinetic strikes wherever necessary. You will now submit and become productive and obedient subjects of the Empire, or you will be destroyed, as your governments and military forces have already been destroyed."

Buchevsky stared at the radio, his mind cowering back from the black, bottomless pit which yawned suddenly where his family once had been as the mechanical voice confirmed what he'd desperately told himself was no more than a rumor. His intellect had known better, yet his emotions had refused to accept that Washington was truly gone. But now—

Trish . . . despite the divorce, she'd still been an almost physical part of him. And Shania . . . Yvonne. . . . Shannie was only eight, for God's sake! Yvonne was only *five!* It wasn't possible. It couldn't have happened. *It couldn't!*

The mechanical-sounding English ceased. There was a brief surge of something that sounded like Chinese, and then it switched to Spanish.

"It's saying the same thing it just said in English," Sergeant Ramirez said flatly, and Buchevsky shook himself. He realized his hand was pressed almost convulsively against his chest, against Shania's cross, and he closed his eyes tightly, squeezing them against the tears he would not—could not—shed. That dreadful abyss yawned inside him, trying to suck him under, and part of him wanted nothing else in the world but to let the undertow take him. Yet he couldn't. He had responsibilities. The job.

"Do you *believe* this shit, Top?" Meyers asked hoarsely.

"I don't know." Buchevsky's own voice came out sounding broken and rusty, and he made himself lower his hand, opened his eyes upon a suddenly hateful world. Then he cleared his throat harshly. "I don't know," he managed in a more normal-sounding tone. "Or, at least, I know I don't *want* to believe it, Gunny."

"Me neither," another voice said. This one was a soprano, and it belonged to Staff Sergeant Michelle Truman, the Air Force's senior surviving representative. Buchevsky raised an eyebrow at her, grateful for the additional distraction from the pain trying to tear the heart right out of him, and the auburn-haired staff sergeant grimaced.

"I don't want to believe it, Top," she said, "but think about it. We already knew somebody seems to've been blowing the shit out of just about everybody, and who the hell had that many nukes? Or enough delivery vehicles to hit that many targets?" She shook her head. "I'm no expert on kinetic weapons, either, but I've read a little science fiction, and I'd say an orbital kinetic strike would probably look just like a nuke to the naked eye. So, yeah, probably if this bastard is telling the truth, nukes are exactly what any survivors would've been reporting."

"Oh, shit," Meyers muttered, then looked back at Buchevsky. He didn't say another word, but he didn't have to, and Buchevsky drew a deep breath.

"I don't know, Gunny," he said again. "I just don't know."

. . . . .

HE STILL DIDN'T know—not really—the next morning, but one thing they *couldn't* do was simply huddle here. They'd seen no sign of traffic along the road the C-17 had destroyed, and so far as they could tell, neither of the local farm families had returned home overnight. Roads normally went somewhere, though, so if they followed this one long enough, "somewhere" was where they'd eventually wind up. On the other hand, there was that little uncertainty factor where getting embroiled with the local civilians was concerned.

At least his decision tree had been rather brutally simplified in one respect when both the badly injured passengers died during the night. He'd tried hard not to feel grateful for that, but he was guiltily aware that it would have been dishonest of him, even if he'd managed to succeed.

Come on. You're not grateful they're dead, *Stevie,* he told himself grimly. *You're just grateful they won't be slowing the rest of you down. There's a difference.*

He even knew it was true . . . which didn't make him feel any better. And neither did the fact that he'd put his wife's and daughters' faces into a small mental box, along with his desperate worry about his parents, and locked them away, buried the pain deep enough to let him deal with his responsibilities to the living. Someday, he knew, he would have to reopen that box. Endure the pain, admit the loss. But this wasn't someday. Not yet. For now he could tell himself others depended upon him, that he had to put aside his own pain while he dealt with *their* needs, and he wondered if that made him a coward.

In the meantime, he'd simply dug two more graves and recited as much of the funeral service as he could remember.

Now he stood in the coolness just before dawn, rifle slung, ruck adjusted, the dog tags of all their dead in his pocket, looking at the sky as it turned pale above the forested, sixteen-hundred-foot ridge east of the road.

Another thing the overnight deaths had done for him was obviate the necessity of finding medical assistance. Which meant he could afford to stay away from population centers, at least for a while. He'd sent Meyers,

Ramirez, and Lance Corporal Ignacio Gutierrez back to the closer farmhouse, to gather up as much canned goods as they could comfortably carry. He'd felt bad about that—the farmers were going to need food soon enough themselves—but at least they had their crops already in and growing, and he'd told Meyers he could take no more than half of whatever the farmhouse pantry held. They'd also stacked all of the currency any of them had on the kitchen table. God only knew if it was ever going to be worth anything again, but if it was, it ought to be ample compensation for the value of the food.

Yeah, sure. You go right on thinking that, a little corner of his mind told him. *You know damned well how the people that food belonged to are going to react when they find out you guys have already started looting. Or are you going to call it "living off the land"?*

Shut up, the rest of his mind told that little corner.

"Ready to move out, Top," Meyers' voice said behind him, and he looked over his shoulder.

"All right," he said out loud, trying hard to radiate a confidence he was far from feeling, and waved one arm in the general direction of Romania. "In that case, I guess we should be going."

Now if I only had some damned idea where *we're going.*

.XV.

Platoon Commander Yirku stood in the open hatch of his command ground effect vehicle as his armored platoon sped down the long, broad roadway that stabbed straight through the mountains. The bridges which crossed the main roadbed at intervals, especially as the platoon approached what were (or had been) towns or cities, forced his column to squeeze in on itself, but overall Yirku was delighted. His tanks' grav-cushions could care less what surface lay under them, but that didn't protect their crews from seasickness if they had to move rapidly across rough ground, and this was his second "colony expedition." When they first began briefing for the mission, he'd rather glumly anticipated operating across wilderness terrain which might be crossed here and there by "roads" which were little more than random animal tracks when they first began briefing for the mission. That, after all, had been his experience last time around, and his heart had sunk as he'd studied the initial survey reports and realized what kind of mountains his platoon was going to be dropped into. But that was before they'd actually hit dirt and he'd gotten his first experience of the local road net and realized how good it actually was.

Yet despite his relief at avoiding *harku*-trails through soggy forests, Yirku admitted (very privately) that he found the humans' infrastructure . . . unsettling. There was so *much* of it, especially in areas which had belonged to nations like this "United States." And crude though its construction might appear—none of it used proper ceramacrete, for example, and the bridges he'd passed under probably wouldn't last more than a local century or so without requiring replacement—most of it was well laid out. The fact that they'd managed to construct so much of it, so well suited to their current technology level's requirements, was sobering, too.

And then—his mood darkened—there were the *other* implications of this planet's level of civilization. Having decent road networks was all very well, and he wasn't going to pretend he wasn't suitably grateful, but if the rumor mill was accurate, there was a downside to the locals' technology. He wasn't prepared to accept the more preposterous stories, yet he was confident they wouldn't have been so persistent or arisen so quickly if there hadn't been at least *some* truth to them. It seemed unlikely on the face of it, of course. If these creatures had managed to knock down even a single heavy-lift shuttle, they'd already inflicted more aircraft losses than any other indigenous species the Empire had engulfed! As for the ridiculous, panic-monger rumors that they'd brought down *half a twelve* of them—!

His ears flattened in dismissal. Nonsense! Sheer hysteria, that was what it was. And he was letting himself be pushed into jumping at shadows even worrying about it. Oh, there were enough "humans" on this planet that at least some of them were probably going to fight back, at least initially, and they might land a few lucky blows in the process. But as soon as they figured out that they'd been utterly defeated, they'd see reason and submit decently. And when that happened—

Platoon Commander Yirku's thoughts broke off abruptly as he emerged from under the latest bridge and the fifteen-pound round from the M136/AT-4 light antiarmor weapon struck the side of his vehicle's turret at a velocity of three hundred and sixty feet per second. Its High Penetration HEAT warhead produced a hypervelocity gas jet capable of penetrating up to six hundred millimeters of rolled homogenous steel armor, and it carved through the GEV's light armor like an incandescent dagger.

The resultant internal explosion disemboweled the tank effortlessly, killed every member of the crew, and launched the upper half of Yirku's body in a graceful, flaming arc.

Ten more rockets stabbed down into the embankment-enclosed cut of Interstate 81 virtually simultaneously, and eight of them found their targets, exploding like thunderbolts. Each of them killed another GEV, and the humans who'd launched them had deliberately concentrated on the front and back edges of the platoon's neat road column. Despite their grav-cushions, the four survivors of Yirku's platoon were temporarily trapped behind the blazing, exploding carcasses of their fellows. They were still there—perfect stationary targets—when the next quartet of rockets came sizzling in.

The ambushers—a scratch-built pickup team of Tennessee National Guardsmen, all of them veterans of deployments to Iraq or Afghanistan—were on the move, filtering back into the trees, almost before the final Shongair tank had exploded.

· · · · ·

COLONEL NICOLAE BASESCU sat in the commander's hatch of his T-72M1, his mind wrapped around a curiously empty, singing silence, and waited.

The first prototype of his tank—the export model of the Russian T-72A—had been completed in 1970, seven years before Basescu's own birth, and it had become sadly outclassed by more modern, more deadly designs. It was still superior to the Romanian Army's home-built T-85s, based on the even more venerable T-55, but that wasn't saying much compared to designs like the Russians' T-80s and T-90s, the Americans' M1A2, or the French Leclerc.

And it's certainly *not saying much compared to aliens who can actually travel between the stars,* Basescu thought.

Unfortunately, it was all he had. Now if he only knew what he was supposed to be doing with the seven tanks of his scraped-up command.

Stop that, he told himself sternly. *You're an officer of the Romanian Army. You know* exactly *what you're supposed to be doing. And if that American Internet video is accurate, these creatures, these . . . Shongairi, aren't really superhuman. We* can *kill them. Or,* he corrected himself, *at least the* Americans *can kill their* aircraft. *So. . . .*

He gazed through the opening a few minutes' work with an ax had created. His tanks were as carefully concealed as he could manage inside the industrial buildings across the frontage road from the hundred-meter-wide Mureș River. The two lanes of the E-81 highway crossed the river on a double-span cantilever bridge, flanked on the east by a rail bridge, two kilometers southwest of Alba Iulia, the capital of Alba *județ*. The city of eighty thousand—the city where Michael the Brave had achieved the first union of the three great provinces of Romania in 1599—was two-thirds empty, and Basescu didn't like to think about what those fleeing civilians were going to do when they started running out of whatever supplies they'd managed to snatch up in their flight. But he didn't blame them for running. Not when their city was barely two hundred and seventy kilometers northwest of where Bucharest had been three days ago.

He wished he dared to use his radios, but the broadcasts from the alien commander suggested that any transmissions would be unwise in light of the invaders' penetration of the airwaves. Fortunately at least the landlines were still up. He doubted they would be for much longer, but for now they sufficed for him to know about the alien column speeding up the highway towards him . . . and Alba Iulia.

. . . . .

COMPANY COMMANDER BARMIT punched up his navigation systems, but they were being cantankerous again, and he muttered a quiet yet heartfelt curse as he jabbed at the control panel a second time.

As far as he was concerned, the town ahead of him was scarcely large enough to merit the attention of two entire companies of infantry, even if Ground Base Commander Shairez's prebombardment analysis *had* identified it as some sort of administrative subcenter. Its proximity to what had been a national capital suggested to Barmit's superiors that it had probably been sufficiently important to prove useful as a headquarters for the local occupation forces. Personally, Barmit suspected the reverse was more likely true. An administrative center this close to something the size of that other city—"Bucharest," or something equally outlandish—was more likely to be lost in the capital's shadow than functioning as any sort of important secondary brain.

Too bad Ground Force Commander Thairys didn't ask for my opinion, he thought dryly, still jabbing at the recalcitrant display.

The imagery finally came up and stabilized, and his ears flicked in a grimace as it confirmed his memory. He keyed his com.

"All right," he said. "We're coming up on another river, and our objective's just beyond that. The column will cross the bridge in standard road formation, but let's not take chances."

He started to mention the rumors about what had happened to the 9th Transport Group. His littermate Barmiat was a Navy maintenance tech aboard *Star of Empire,* and according to his brief e-mail, the 9th had lost at least a quarter of its shuttles to the locals' aircraft. That level of losses struck Barmit as unlikely, to say the least, but Barmiat was usually a levelheaded sort, which suggested there might be at least something behind the story this time. On the other hand, Battalion Commander Rathia had already cautioned him against spreading "alarmist rumors."

"Remember that we haven't actually seen these creatures' weapons," he contented himself with, instead. "Red Section, you spread left. White Section, we'll spread right."

. . . . .

COLONEL BASESCU TWITCHED upright as the alien vehicles came into sight. He focused his binoculars, snapping the approaching vehicles into much sharper clarity, and a part of him was almost disappointed by how unremarkable they appeared. How . . . mundane.

Most of them were some sort of wheeled transport vehicles, with a boxy sort of look that made him think of armored personnel carriers. There were around thirty of those, and it was obvious they were being escorted by five other vehicles.

He shifted his attention to those escorts and stiffened as he realized just how unmundane *they* were. They sped along, low-slung and dark, hovering perhaps a meter or two above the ground, and some sort of long, slender gun barrels projected from their squared-off, slab-sided turrets. Either they had enormous faith in the stopping ability of their armor, or else their designers hadn't been very worried about kinetic-impact weapons, he thought.

The approaching formation slowed as the things which were probably APCs began forming into a column of twos under the watchful eye of the things which were probably tanks, and he lowered the binoculars and picked up the handset for the field telephone he'd had strung between the tanks once they'd been maneuvered into their hides.

"Mihai," he told his second section commander, "we'll take the tanks. Radu, I want you and Matthius to concentrate on the transports. Don't fire until Mihai and I do—then try to jam them up on the bridge."

. . . . .

BARMIT FELT HIS ears relaxing in satisfaction as the wheeled vehicles settled into a narrower road column in the approaches to the bridge and his GEVs headed across the river, watching its flanks. The sharp drop from the roadbed to the surface of the water provided the usual "stomach-left-behind" sensation, but once they were actually out over the water, their motion became glassy-smooth. He rotated his turret to the left, keeping an eye on the bridge as he led White Section's other two GEVs between the small islands in the center of the river, idling along to keep pace with the transports.

. . . . .

THEY MAY HAVE *magic tanks, but they don't have very good doctrine, do they?* a corner of Basescu's brain reflected. They hadn't so much as bothered to send any scouts across, or even to leave one of their tanks on the far bank in an overwatch position. Not that he intended to complain.

The tank turret slewed slowly to the right as his gunner tracked his assigned target, but Basescu was watching the wheeled vehicles. The entire bridge was barely a hundred and fifty meters long, and he wanted all of them actually onto it if he could arrange it.

. . . . .

COMPANY COMMANDER BARMIT sighed as his GEV approached the far bank. Climbing up out of the riverbed again was going to be rather less pleasant, and he slowed, deliberately prolonging the smoothness as he watched the transports heading across the bridge.

Kind of the "humans" to build us all these nice highways, he reflected, thinking about this region's heavily forested mountains. *It would be a real pain to—*

. . . . .

***"FIRE!"* NICOLAE BASESCU** barked, and Company Commander Barmit's ruminations were terminated abruptly by the arrival of a nineteen-kilogram 3BK29 HEAT round capable of penetrating three hundred millimeters of armor at a range of two kilometers.

. . . . .

BASESCU FELT A stab of exhilaration as the tank bucked, the outer wall of its concealing building disappeared in the fierce muzzle blast of its 2A46 120-millimeter main gun, and his target exploded. Three of the other four escort tanks were first-round kills, as well. They crashed into the river in eruptions of orange fire, white spray, and smoke, and the stub of the semi-combustible cartridge case ejected from the gun. The automatic loader's carousel picked up the next round, feeding the separate projectile and cartridge into the breech, and his carefully briefed commanders were engaging targets without any additional orders from him.

The surviving alien tank swerved crazily sideways, turret swiveling madly, and then Basescu winced as it fired.

He didn't know what it was armed with, but it wasn't like any cannon *he'd* ever seen. A bar of solid light spat from the end of its "gun," and the building concealing his number three tank exploded as the T-72's fuel and ammunition detonated thunderously. But even as the alien tank fired, two more 120-millimeter rounds slammed into it almost simultaneously.

It died as spectacularly as its fellows had, and Radu and Matthias hadn't been sitting on their hands. They'd done exactly what he wanted, nailing both the leading and rearmost of the wheeled transports only after they were well out onto the bridge. The others were trapped there, sitting ducks, unable to maneuver, and his surviving tanks walked their fire steadily along their column.

At least some of the aliens managed to bail out of their vehicles, but it was less than three hundred meters to the far side of the river, and the coaxial 7.62-millimeter machine guns and the heavier 12.7-millimeter cupola-mounted weapons at the tank commanders' stations were waiting for them. At such short range, it was a massacre.

. . . . .

"CEASE FIRE!" BASESCU barked. "Fall back!"

His crews responded almost instantly, and the tanks' powerful V-12 engines snorted black smoke as the T-72s backed out of their hiding places and sped down the highway at sixty kilometers per hour. What the aliens had already accomplished with their "kinetic weapons" suggested that staying in one place would be a very bad idea, and Basescu had picked out his next fighting position before he ever settled into this one. It would take them barely fifteen minutes to reach it, and only another fifteen to twenty minutes to maneuver the tanks back into hiding.

. . . . .

PRECISELY SEVENTEEN MINUTES later, incandescent streaks of light came sizzling out of the cloudless heavens to eliminate every one of Nicolae Basescu's tanks—and half the city of Alba Iulia—in a blast of fury that shook the Carpathian Mountains.

. . . . .

COMPANY COMMANDER KIRTHA'S column of transports rumbled along steadily. The local weather had obviously been dry, and the clouds of dust his column had thrown up when they'd had to cut across country had made him grateful his GEV command vehicle was sealed against it. Now if only he'd been assigned to one of the major bases on the continent called "America." Or at least the western fringes of *this* one!

His ears flicked in derisive amusement at his own thoughts. This world had the best road net Kirtha had ever seen. Even here, it was incomparably better than anything he'd ever campaigned across before, so it was pretty silly of him to be bitching—even if only to himself—because someone else had gotten an even *better* road net than he had!

Could be game trails through triple-canopy jungle, like Rishu, he reminded himself. *Or what about those miserable, endless swamps in southern Bahshi?*

Well, that was probably true. But he supposed it was simply Shongair nature to always want something a *little* better than one had.

The dusty, broken pavement of the stretch of roadbed his column was currently approaching was a case in point, he decided glumly. Obviously, the "humans" had been engaged in construction or repair work—it was scarcely the first time he'd seen *that* since landing!—and a fresh, smothering fog of dust was already rising from the wheeled vehicles' passage.

It wouldn't be so bad if they were all grav-cushion, he told himself, but GEVs were expensive, and the counter-grav generators used up precious internal volume not even troop carriers, much less freight-haulers, could afford to give away. Imperial wheeled vehicles had excellent off-road capability with their all-wheel drive and variable tire pressures, of course, so they could almost always get through, whatever the terrain. And in this instance, even a miserable road like this stretch allowed them to move much more efficiently than on the vast majority of planets the Empire had occupied.

And at least we're out in the middle of nice, flat ground as far as the eye can see, Kirtha reminded himself.

He didn't like the rumors about what had happened to some of the first-wave landing shuttles. Of course, that was the concern of the shuttle pukes, not the ground forces, but still. . . . And the even more fragmentary rumors about ambushes on isolated detachments were even more . . . bothersome. That wasn't supposed to happen, especially from someone as effortlessly and utterly defeated as these creatures had been. And even if it did happen, it wasn't supposed to be *effective*—not against armored vehicles and crack Imperial infantry! And the ones responsible for it were supposed to be destroyed.

Which, if the rumors were accurate, wasn't happening the way it was supposed to. *Some* of the attackers were being spotted and destroyed, but with Hegemony technology, *all* of them should have been wiped out, and the rumor mill suggested some of them *weren't* being. Still, there were no convenient mountainsides or thick belts of forest to hide attackers out here in the midst of these endless, flat fields of grain, and—

. . . . .

CAPTAIN PIETER STEFANOVICH Ushakov watched through his binoculars with pitiless satisfaction as the entire alien convoy and its escort of tanks disappeared in a fiery wave of destruction two kilometers long. The scores of 120-millimeter mortar rounds buried in the stretch of the M-03 motorway between Valky and Nova Vodolaga as his own version of the "improvised explosive devices" which had given the Americans such grief in Iraq and Afghanistan had proved quite successful, he thought coldly.

Now, he thought, *to see exactly how these weasels respond.*

He was fully aware of the risks in remaining in the vicinity, but he needed some understanding of the aliens' capabilities and doctrine, and the only way to get that was to see what they did. He was confident he'd piled enough earth on top of his position to conceal any thermal signature, and aside from the radio-controlled detonator, he was completely unarmed, with no ferrous metal on his person, which would hopefully defeat any magnetic detectors. So unless they used some sort of deep-scan radar, he ought to be *relatively* safe from detection.

And even if it turned out he wasn't, Vladislava, Daria, Nikolai, and Grigori had been visiting his parents in Kiev when the kinetic strikes hit.

. XVI .

It was hot. It was also dry, and his battalion was no longer in a position to keep itself properly hydrated. "If you don't need to piss, you aren't drinking enough." That was the mantra of the US forces in the Middle East, but the distribution and maintenance platoons the brigade support battalion had been supposed to detach to him had been delayed by last-minute paperwork. They hadn't made it out of the FOB in time, the single purification plant he had with him was intended to supply only a single company, there weren't going to be any more water trucks or trailers any-time soon, and the Harirud River's levels were low thanks to the current drought and the water quality was . . . questionable. What each unit had already stored and what was available from the river's meager flow and that single purification plant was all they had, and it wasn't enough.

Which probably won't be a problem all that much longer, if Traynor and Strang are right, Lieutenant Colonel Alastair Sanders thought grimly. *And they probably are.*

Captain Mark Traynor was his S-2, the officer tasked with responsibility for the battalion's intelligence and security, and Lieutenant Christine Strang was his S-5, responsible for the battalion's signal operations. For the last couple of days, it had been their grim duty to try to make some kind of sense out of what had happened to the rest of the world.

For the first twenty-four hours or so, all they'd had was confusion, speculation, and shock. Sanders' battalion had been in transit to Herat when the attacks came screaming in out of nowhere. He suspected that was the only thing which had saved them when the rest of the brigade was wiped out behind them, but it also meant they were completely isolated, totally out of the loop and with no support units anywhere in sight.

At first, from the garbled messages they'd gotten, they'd assumed the disaster was purely local. But then other reports had started coming in—reports of strikes on carrier groups at sea, on NATO bases scattered across

Europe, on Israel. Nor had they been limited to US allies. If the last they'd heard from national command authority was accurate, Tehran was gone, too. And so was Moscow. Beijing.

And, of course, Washington.

As far as Alastair Sanders knew, his battalion was the last organized military formation of the entire United States Army.

He tried, again, to wrap his mind around that concept as he stared unseeingly into the incandescent band where the setting sun hovered on the western horizon. And, again, he failed. It simply wasn't something he was equipped to envision or imagine. It wasn't something that could *happen*. Yet it had, and if the broadcast from this "Fleet Commander Thikair" was to be believed, this was only the beginning of the nightmare.

Maybe it is, he told himself harshly, *but whatever demands "Thikair" may be throwing around, nobody's ordered* me *to stand down.*

With Tehran (among other places) gone, he'd seen no point in continuing his movement to Herat. Which, apparently, had been a good thing, since the reconnaissance troop he'd deployed forward had reported the city's total destruction just before midnight last night. He hadn't really needed the cavalry scouts' reports, given the incredible brilliance of the fireballs which had illuminated the heavens. His current position in the rugged semimountainous foothills twelve kilometers west of the town of Chesht-e sharif was a hundred and thirty kilometers—eighty miles—from Herat, but he'd been able to see the towering incandescence of the explosions just fine.

The local Afghan citizens had seen the same dreadful sight. The majority of them had already refugeed out, showing a degree of common sense of which Sanders could only approve. Some, however, had stayed, and an impressive array of personal weapons had turned up among them. Given the number of rocket-propelled grenades which had also turned up, Sanders was inclined to think quite a few of the stay-behinds probably had affiliations with the Taliban or one of the other officially outlawed militias. On the other hand, they might simply have been affiliated with the local poppy-growing industry—not that the two possibilities were mutually exclusive by any means.

Wherever they'd come from, however, none of them seemed to have any problem at the moment with the infidel Americans' presence in their midst. They might not care much for "crusaders" under normal circumstances, but these weren't normal, and they'd helped enthusiastically when Sanders started preparing his positions. In fact, some of them had obeyed his orders to scatter and disperse into the hills around them only with obvious reluctance. In some ways, he would have liked to let them stay and fight, but they'd be far more useful in the long run as an in-place guerrilla force (God knew Sanders had had plenty of experience of what a pain in the ass *mujahedin* in mountains could be!) than getting underfoot during the kind of defense he planned to mount if any bad guys came his way. And, perhaps even more to the point, dispersal was the only pretense of "protection" he could offer them against a threat which could destroy every national capital in the world literally overnight.

With no way to know what to expect from the aliens who had attacked his homeworld, he hadn't truly anticipated any sort of attack on his present, isolated position even after the destruction of Herat. After all, why should anyone want to capture a place like Chesht-e sharif when there were so many far more valuable prizes lying about?

At the same time, every bone in his body had cried out to find, attack, and destroy the creatures who had wreaked such destruction upon his world, but he hadn't known *where* to find them. He was far too short on fuel for any sort of maneuvering campaign, anyway, with no hope of more, and even if that hadn't been true, he would have been up against someone with starships in orbit. They had to have reconnaissance capabilities out the ying-yang, and he was damned if he'd put his units into motion in broad daylight so the same people who'd taken out Washington with a kinetic bombardment could do the same thing to them.

He'd had no intention of being caught napping if there *was* an attack, however, so he'd dispersed his troops into defensive positions and gone to rigorous emissions control, and his reconnaissance troops had set out remote sensors (using fiber optics rather than radio to report back, this time). They'd also been instructed to launch UAVs for a closer look if their remotes detected movement, but the ground control teams had been very firmly ordered to preprogram the UAVs' flight paths and keep their own transmitters completely shut down until and unless there was actual hard contact with the enemy.

At the same time, Lieutenant Strang had continued her efforts, along with Lieutenant Bradshaw's signal/network support platoon, to contact some higher authority, but Sanders had ordered her to displace her directional antenna to a point ten miles north of his main formation in the rugged hills above the Harirud. And she'd been further instructed to dismount the antenna and locate it as far away from her own vehicle as the available cable would permit. He didn't know if any of that would do any good, but it had seemed worth trying.

She'd finally managed to establish contact with an Admiral Robinson at something called NAVSPACECOM. She'd had to look it up to identify it as the Naval Network and Space Operations Command in far-off Dahlgren, Virginia, and there was no way for her to authenticate his identity, but it seemed unlikely anyone would be playing silly games at a time like this. And according to Admiral Robinson, at least some of whose satellites were apparently still operational, the aliens had landed a substantial force in what had once been Iran.

Sanders couldn't think of anything in Iran worth occupying—or not in comparison to a hell of a lot of other places around the planet, at least—but Robinson was insistent. And given the quality of the raw video Strang had downloaded from him, Sanders was inclined to take the admiral's word for it.

God bless the US Air Force, he thought, then shook his head with a harsh, humorless chuckle. *Never thought I'd be saying* that, *but I guess we don't have to worry about funding turf battles anymore. And,* damn, *but those fighter jocks ripped those bastards a new one!*

They'd done something else, too. They'd shown Alastair Sanders these bastards—these Shongairi—weren't invincible. Those transport aircraft or shuttles or whatever they'd been had gone down like sitting ducks, and it was obvious they hadn't had even a clue that the Air Force was coming for them. That suggested that whatever advanced capabilities the invaders might have, their units' situational awareness was limited, at best, and their higher command evidently did a piss poor job of maintaining any sort of oversight. Admittedly, from what little he knew about the F-22, those fighters would have probably been extraordinarily difficult even for US systems to pick up, but aliens capable of traveling interstellar distances should also be capable of things like that.

Unless, of course, they've never developed *the capability for some reason,* he thought again. *It seems ridiculous, but that's the only answer that suggests itself. Maybe they're just not used to attacking advanced—relatively speaking, at least—races?*

He wasn't going to invest any huge amount of optimism in that sort of assumption, but he also reminded himself not to overlook the consequences of military complacency and lack of imagination. There was that little matter of how the US military had been caught looking in the wrong direction in Vietnam, for example, when they suddenly found themselves fighting guerrillas in the jungle instead of Soviet tanks in the Fulda Gap. It hadn't been as bad in Desert Storm or Iraqi Freedom—not from a purely military perspective, anyway—but there'd still been a painful learning curve following the destruction of Saddam Hussein's conventional forces. The experience in both of those operations had led (among other things) to the Army's reorganization into its current modular brigade format, and it had also stood the U.S. in good stead during the ongoing operations in Afghanistan. Yet there was no denying that military organizations were also bureaucratic ones, and bureaucracies tended to get caught on the wrong foot by changing circumstances, especially if they'd been too successful for too long. Military machines which faced no significant challenge saw little reason to change or adapt. After a long enough period of supremacy, they—or factions within them, at least—got far too focused on guarding their own rice bowls to consider the preposterous possibility that someone might actually pose a threat to *them*.

Which was why the poor bastards who served such militaries had so often found themselves bringing knives to a gunfight.

Was it possible the aliens—the Shongairi—were in an analogous situation? The problem in more recent U.S. experience had been getting too caught up in advanced, heavy combat capabilities. They'd been slow to appreciate the realities of "asymmetric warfare," in no small part because of their duty to plan for worst-case scenarios. They'd had too much sophistication for the task at hand—or, rather, their sophistication had been pointed in the wrong directions—because it had been designed to defeat the most capable *possible* foe rather than addressing the far more limited capabilities of the ones they'd actually ended up fighting. He would have expected the same sort of thinking to afflict a species with interstellar flight, since it would have seemed logical that anyone capable of putting up a fight would have had comparable levels of technology.

But if that were true, it certainly hadn't been in evidence when the Air Force caught up with them. So did that mean they'd gone the other way? Had their military been doing the equivalent of fighting in Vietnam's jungles so long it was no longer prepared for the Fulda Gap when it came along? There was no way for him to tell, and he wasn't going to *rely* on it, but deep inside, he hoped—prayed—that was the case. Because if it was, then his battalion might just have a chance when it caught up with them, as well.

Which looked like it was probably going to happen pretty damned soon.

"All right," he said, letting his eyes sweep across the faces of his absurdly young-looking company and platoon commanders. "It looks like Robinson was right. They're on the ground in Iran, and they're coming this way. The bastards probably took out Herat last night just to clear their route, and the reconnaissance troops say they're headed our way along A77. Best strength estimate is one hundred and fifty of those floating bastards we've tentatively classified as 'tanks' and in the vicinity of three hundred wheeled vehicles. Still no sign of missile launchers on any of their vehicles, but don't get too cocky about that. We've got no idea what kind of guns these . . . people might have, and they could have pop-up launchers carried under armor, where we just haven't seen them. Their current approach speed is sixty-three kilometers an hour—that's a hard number from the remote sensors and the UAVs—which puts them here almost exactly ninety minutes after sunset."

And, he thought, *the fact that they haven't even noticed the UAVs have been keeping an eye on them for almost an hour—and transmitting to us the whole time—says interesting things, too. Assuming they* really *haven't noticed them, at any rate. I suppose they could simply be ignoring them for some reason. Like to lull you into overconfidence, Alastair?*

"You all know as much about what's happened as I do," he continued, letting no sign of that particular thought color his expression or tone. "And you've seen the footage of what the Air Force managed to do to them. I figure we've got a good chance of getting in the first licks. After that, damned if I know what's going to happen, but I don't expect it to be outstandingly good."

He bared his teeth in a humorless grin, and almost to his surprise, two or three of his subordinates actually chuckled.

"I don't have a clue why these people are heading into Afghanistan, of all places," he went on, "but I think we owe it to a lot of other people to get some of our own back. Remember your briefings. No one engages until I give the word. All radios on receive-only until I give the word. Do *not* bring up your JBCPs until and unless I instruct you to. And when I say it's time to bug out, we rendezvous *immediately* and boogie as planned. Clear?"

Heads nodded grimly, one at a time.

"All right, people. Let's get back to our units. But first"—he raised one hand, holding them a moment longer—"let me just say I'm proud, *damned* proud, of all of you and all your people. I always have been, but never more than I am right this minute. I know how every one of you has to be worrying about what's been going on back home. I've been worrying about it, too. But for right now, it's time for us to go on doing our jobs as well as all of you and all of them always have before. As far as we know, we're all the United States has left. I hope and pray that's not the case, but if it is, then we are by *God* going to give these murderous bastards the frigging boot, and I want our toes so far up their asses the only thing they can taste is made-in-the-U.S.-of-A. shoe leather! I want them to frigging *choke* on it!"

As historically memorable prebattle speeches went, it probably left a little something to be desired, he thought. Yet as he looked around the silent faces for a moment longer he saw the hardness in the eyes, the tightness of the jaw muscles, the anger crackling just under the surface, and he was content. He looked back at them, letting them see his own eyes, the promise of his own anger, then nodded back to them.

"Go," he said.

. . . . .

BRIGADE COMMANDER HARSHAIR grumbled to himself—but quietly, quietly!—as his long, ungainly column (three separate columns of wheeled vehicles traveling abreast, actually, with one battalion of the armored regiment's more heavily protected GEVs strung out protectively along the flanks) drove along the "human" road.

Truth to tell, the road was better than he'd expected in such a sparsely populated region, although with so much traffic spread out on either side of it the dust was a literally choking fog. Fortunately, his command vehicle was hermetically sealed, yet he still had to open the hatch occasionally, and every time he did more of the infernal dust filtered inside. And, inevitably, into the electronics' Cainharn-taken cooling fans.

The better part of a thousand standard years since we got into space, and we still *can't design dust filters that work!* His ears waggled in a grimace of disgust. *Or, at least, none of our vaunted researchers can tear himself away from the Fleet's precious needs long enough to run down that particular prey for us poor grunts in the field.* They *get new sensor suites every forty years or so, and* we *can't even get something to keep dust out of the . . . less than capable systems we've already got! Why am I not surprised?*

Still and all, he had to admit he'd faced worse conditions on more than one world in the Emperor's service. And it was a good (if unaccustomed) feeling to have his entire brigade assembled in one place for a change, instead of parceled out into tiny company- or platoon-sized—or even *squad*-sized—packets, each squatting somewhere in a firebase keeping an eye on the local primitives. Brigade commanders—for that matter, *regiment* commanders—tended to become administrators, more than anything else, in a typical colonizing expedition, and it was nice to be a hands-on commander for a change.

Even if his present orders did strike him as a bit foolish.

He knew about the disaster which had overtaken the shuttles transporting Ground Base Two's lead echelon, and he'd heard other reports about APCs and even a few GEVs being ambushed. Obviously certain commanders hadn't been paying enough attention if they'd let themselves be surprised that way. And he supposed that, to give Cainharn his due, these "humans'" weapons might be somewhat more effective than their prelanding intelligence had projected. But even so, allowing an entire brigade—an armored regiment with no fewer than twelve twelves of GEVs and two full regiments of infantry, plus support echelons—to be diverted into the arid, Dainthar-forsaken mountains towards which he was headed seemed . . . excessive. The kinetic bombardment had taken out every known military base in the areas the locals called Iraq, Afghanistan, and Iran. Certainly he'd personally confirmed that every single base in Iran had been blasted into rubble, and whatever might have happened to Ground Base Two, the shuttles which had landed his own forces had encountered no resistance worth mentioning. Surely the same thing had happened in Afghanistan and Iraq, but Fleet Command had decided it was imperative to make sure of that.

Harshair had been given his orders directly by Ground Force Commander Thairys, so there was no doubt they came from the very top. Thairys hadn't explained the thinking behind those orders, yet it sounded to Harshair that his superiors had been badly surprised—even frightened—by what had happened to the Starlanders transporting Ground Base Two. They wanted to make certain *all* of the military forces of the "United States" were thoroughly neutralized, and Harshair was supposed to do just that by tidying up any pieces the KEWs might have somehow miraculously missed in Afghanistan. He supposed other ground forces were going to find themselves tasked with similarly ridiculous objectives, since if he remembered correctly from the briefings, the United States had maintained bases in a great many parts of this world.

Well, he thought, studying the panoramic view provided by the three reconnaissance and communication drones heading the column, *at least it shouldn't take too long. And don't turn up your nose at the opportunity to play with your entire command, Harshair! It hasn't come your way very often, now has it?*

. . . . .

ALASTAIR SANDERS SAT very still, feeling the sweat under his headset. It was unnaturally dark inside the command vehicle, with all of its displays down. He especially missed the "Blue Tracker" map displays of his JBCP (the Joint Battle Command Platform system which had succeeded the original FBCB2), which normally showed him the exact positions of his individual units. Without them, he felt as if ninety percent of his situational awareness had disappeared, but JBCP relied on a unit's individual satellite uplink to locate it, and he wasn't going to give any orbiting recon platform that kind of a beacon. In fact, he wasn't allowing *any* emissions—not even his command track's engine was running at the moment—as he sat leaning back, eyes closed, listening to the very young-sounding voice coming over the headset via the optical fiber cable. His signals platoon had set up two alternate, well-separated remote transmitters against the moment when he finally had to begin using radio to control his units, but for now he was relying solely on the landline network those units had established over the last twenty hours.

It's like going back to the Dark Age days of field telephones, plotting board overlays, and grease pencils, a corner of his hindbrain whispered. *Next thing you know, you'll be using carrier pigeons!*

At the moment, all of his subunit commanders were listening to the feed from one of his advanced reconnaissance troops right along with him. He wanted to be absolutely certain every one of them knew everything *he* knew when the moment came. Smart officers who were kept in the loop and encouraged to exercise initiative had always been the true secret to success, that same corner of his mind reflected.

". . . another two klicks or so," the voice to which the rest of his mind listened was saying. "We're picking up pretty broadband transmissions. They don't seem to be encrypted. And there's some kind of really weird . . . vibration, or sound, or *something*."

"Raven One, Five Actual," Sanders said. "Can you expand on that last? What kind of 'something'?"

"Five, Raven One," the junior noncom monitoring the remotes replied, "negative. Not really, Sir. It's almost like we're *hearing* something, but we aren't."

"Do you have any idea of what's producing it, Raven One?"

"We can't be certain, Five, but if I had to guess, I'd say it's coming from those UAVs or whatever they're using. It seems to get . . . louder when one of them comes our way, and when one of them passed overhead a few minutes ago it really set our teeth on edge. I know that doesn't really *explain* anything, Sir, but it's the best I can do. And we're getting some really weird emissions from them, in addition to a lot of recognizable radio transmissions. Maybe it's whatever's holding them up. We got a good visual on one of them, and there's no sign of propellers or turbines, anyway. They do show really high-temperature signatures on the thermals, though."

"Okay, Raven One. Thanks."

Sanders glanced at his watch. Another kilometer, the scout had said. At thirty miles an hour, they'd be covering a kilometer every forty-eight seconds or so, which meant—

"All units, Five Actual," he said clearly over the hardwired communications net. "Start engines. Archer Five, your Avengers are cleared to take down any aircraft or drones as soon as Hammer engages."

. . . . .

CAPTAIN EMILIANO GUTIERREZ'S massive M1A2—named "Peggy" in his wife's honor—shuddered as the fifteen-hundred-horsepower Honeywell AGT turbine snarled angrily to life. His sixty-eight-ton tank (about the size of—and immeasurably more lethal than—the dreaded World War II Royal Tiger tank) was carefully hidden, turret-down, in the bed of the Harirud between the river's lowered water and a steep ridge. The A77 roadbed made a sharp hairpin bend directly west of his position, hugging the crest of the ten-meter ridge to keep it safely above water level when the river flooded. The slope up to the road was covered in low-growing trees and shrubbery, brown-edged and tired-looking from the drought, and east of the river lay the startling green of irrigated, cultivated fields.

The other eleven tanks of his own Delta Company and the twelve M2A3 Bradley infantry fighting vehicles of Captain Aldo Altabani's Alpha Company were spread along the foot of that slope, noses angled up towards its top, hidden under tarps, nettings, and cut branches and bundles of standing wheat harvested from the farmland behind them.

Gutierrez was uncomfortably aware that the traditional U.S. ability to call on superior air assets was on the other side this time around. That had implications he'd spent quite a bit of time trying not to think about too hard. He also knew the other side's reconnaissance assets had to be a lot better than the battalion's, too, but he could at least hope the Old Man had gotten them under cover in time. And at least his vehicles—unlike those of Captain Adamakos' Force Anvil—hadn't ended up covered in dirt!

Now displays flickered as Peggy's systems came online. They were comfortingly familiar, yet he knew this was going to be the strangest engagement he'd ever heard of, and not just because they were going up against bug-eyed aliens from another star system. The intricate electronic web which normally bound the battalion's units together into a single whole was down. Aside from Colonel Sanders himself, they were all on radio silence until and unless he told them differently. The JBCP links which let unit commanders plot their individual tracks' positions were also down. Even the tanks' Quick Kill active missile defense system's scanning radar was down. Nobody was radiating anything they didn't absolutely have to. In fact, that was the reason their engines had been down. Sure, it had saved fuel, but it also turned each vehicle into an inert hunk of metal. They could probably be picked up by magnetometers, or spotted by ground-mapping radar, but be damned if they were going to give away any more signature than they absolutely had to!

Even Alpha Company's three attached M106A4 self-propelled mortars, dug in five hundred meters behind the rest of his vehicles, were in receive-only mode, which meant they couldn't take full advantage of their digitalized mortar fire control system. The MFCS' *full* capabilities required GPS input, and as part of their EMCON procedures, Colonel Sanders had ordered all GPS transmissions disabled. Still, the commander's interface functioned just fine as a ballistic computer in stand-alone mode, and they'd put out the old-fashioned aiming posts. They were receiving download from the UAVs for the fire support platoon's plotting boards, as well, and Gutierrez figured the track-mounted 120-millimeter mortars would probably give a good account of themselves . . . as long as they lasted, at any rate.

Still, it would be nice to have the displays up, he thought, gluing his eyes to his commander's passive sighting system. He had it in low-light imaging, and at the moment all it showed him were stubby trees, bushes, and tranquil, cobalt-black night sky, touched with pearl behind him to the east as the moon began to rise. Of course, that was going to change.

He felt or heard or . . . sensed the odd vibration or sound Raven One had tried to describe to Lieutenant Colonel Sanders. It was very faint—apparently Peggy's armor was sufficient to damp it, and he'd probably never have noticed it if he hadn't been waiting for it—but it was still the most peculiar sensation he'd ever felt. On the other hand, he was far too keyed up to worry about that at the moment.

. . . . .

BRIGADE COMMANDER HARSHAIR frowned thoughtfully, studying the display from his lead RC drone. One of the Empire's greatest advantages had always been its night-vision equipment. Quite a few of the savages he'd helped pacify in the Emperor's service had come to the conclusion that the Shongairi must all be wizards who could see in total blackness. That was why he'd timed his penetration of these mountains for the hours of darkness.

Still, the imagery wasn't as clear as it might have been in daylight, even with the out-sized local moon beginning to rise, and he grimaced and leaned forward, using the heel of one six-fingered hand to wipe dust off the flat screen display. He'd thought for years that they ought to provide at least higher-level commanders with holographic displays that would give them a better feel for the actual terrain elevations, but he didn't expect to see it anytime soon. That would have *cost* more than the flat displays, after all, and squeezing the imager in might have been a problem, but still. . . .

Easy enough for those idiots sitting safe at home to think in terms of cost instead of effectiveness, he reflected grumpily. *After all,* they *aren't out here hunting abos all over Cainharn's backyard! Do them good to spend a year or two on the ground with the rest of us, damned if it wouldn't. But—*

He paused in mid-thought. That was odd. Why hadn't he noticed that angular shape before? Of course, it was probably only a trick of the shadows cast by the rising moon, but still. . . .

"Switch RC Two to thermal," he directed.

. . . . .

"HAMMER FIVE, FIVE Actual," Alastair Sanders said crisply, simultaneously nodding to the noncom who commanded his M2 command track to bring up the single display linked to the take from the UAV circling steadily above the enemy column. "Engage."

"Five Actual, Hammer Five. Wilco. All Hammers, Five. Advance and engage!"

. . . . .

BRIGADE COMMANDER HARSHAIR'S eyes flew wide in astonishment as the display he'd been watching shifted over to thermal mode and bright, glaring beacons of heat appeared on it.

Impossible! Those had to be high-output internal combustion engines! Where in Cainharn's hells had they *been* until this moment? Why hadn't any of the fleet's reconnaissance officers mentioned them to him?! *And what were they?!*

. . . . .

FORCE HAMMER'S ABRAMS snorted up the incline in a sudden bellow of acceleration. For all its massive size, the M1A2 was capable of almost seventy kilometers per hour—forty-five miles per hour—on a road and almost fifty kilometers per hour even cross-country. In point of fact, with the engine governor (which had been installed primarily for crew safety reasons) removed, it was capable of over *sixty* miles per hour on an improved surface, and it had a power-to-weight ratio of 24.5 horsepower per metric ton. That might not sound like much compared to the typical family sedan, but it was forty percent higher than the ratio the speedy World War II T34 had enjoyed, and that gave it an astonishing acceleration rate and nimbleness—not to mention power to spare, even on a sharp grade. Now Gutierrez's tanks ripped clear of their overhead concealment, shedding their cocoons of tarps and cut greenery like water. The camouflage went spinning away on the hurricane breath of their turbine exhausts, their broad tracks ground through the dry soil, smashing trees and shrubbery contemptuously aside, throwing up rooster tails of dirt and crushed vegetation, and they rose, like Leviathan sounding from the depths, until their turrets just topped the ridgeline.

The Old Man's timing had been impeccable, a corner of Gutierrez's mind noted. He might not have had his displays up, but it was obvious he still had his instincts.

"Target. APC. One o'clock. Sabot," he announced, designating the target with his own sight.

"Target!" the tank's gunner replied as he acquired the target and his laser rangefinder registered on it.

"Sabot up!" the loader announced. It was a confirmation this time, actually. There was no need to load; they'd started with a sabot round up the pipe.

"On the way!"

The entire massive vehicle lurched to the recoil of the 120-millimeter M256 Rheinmetal smoothbore. An incredible geyser of flame and propellant gases ripped the night apart, totally destroying the night vision of anyone looking at it. The muzzle blast of the M256 was violent enough to create a blast and over-pressure danger zone for exposed personnel a hundred and sixty-five feet *behind* the tank when it was fired, and a fan-shaped swath of dried leaves and drought-browned grass burst into flame along the ridge crest in its path. A fragment of a second later, the subcaliber M829A3 long-rod spent-uranium penetrator, carbon fiber sabot shed, impacted less than two inches from the gunner's point of aim at a velocity of over eighteen hundred meters per second, twice the muzzle velocity of the enormously lighter bullet from an M16.

Armor that would have stopped arrows from any longbow ever made never had a chance against a round designed to disembowel the latest Russian main battle tank. The same penetrator continued onward to rip into the APC directly *beyond* it, and as both of them erupted in a blinding orange and white gush of flaming fuel, Emiliano Gutierrez made a mental note that he could save the sabot rounds for *heavy* targets. HEAT would work just fine, at least on the wheeled vehicles.

Then the other eleven tanks opened fire, as well.

. . . . .

"TAKE THEM DOWN!" Sergeant First Class Eduardo Hidalgo snapped, and three FIM92F Stinger antiair missiles launched from the two AN/TWQ-1 Avengers of his air defense section.

The Stinger had first been fielded over thirty years earlier, but in its current upgrade it was still one of the best MANPAD—Man-Portable Air-Defense—missiles in the world. The Avenger was a Humvee-mounted system with a gyro-stabilized air defense turret which carried two four-missile Stinger pods. The Up-Gun Avenger had replaced the right-hand missile pod with an MP3 .50-caliber machine gun, and a further upgrade had substituted the same M242 Bushmaster 25-millimeter cannon the Bradley mounted for the .50 caliber. Hidalgo had been pissed off when the Up-Gun version was disallowed for Second Brigade and they'd been ordered to remount the second missile pod, because he'd really wanted the additional ground firepower for battery defense in a war where air attack was unlikely, to say the least. Now, though. . . .

All three Stingers slashed straight towards targets hovering at an altitude of less than seven hundred feet, and those targets never even bobbled in midair, far less tried to evade. Two of his three birds scored direct hits, their targets disappearing in brilliant bubbles of light, like lightning in the darkness. The third Stinger passed within inches of *its* target, its proximity fuse activated, and the Shongair drone tumbled out of the sky.

. . . . .

HARSHAIR STARED AT his displays in horrified disbelief.

The carnage exploding across his direct-view displays was terrible enough, but the ones tied to his forward RC drones had gone suddenly and abruptly blank. In all his years campaigning for the Empire, no enemy had ever managed to destroy one of his drones. He'd had them break down on occasion—not even imperial equipment was perfect—but he'd *never* had one simply knocked out of the sky!

And he still hadn't had *one* knocked out of the sky, the tiny corner of his brain which wasn't paralyzed in shock told him in a preposterously calm mental tone. No, he'd had *three* of them knocked out of the sky—simultaneously.

One of his assistants, responding to bone-deep training despite her own shock, started punching in commands to transfer the command vehicle's viewpoint to other drones, but she didn't seem to be having a lot of success, that same tiny corner of Harshair's awareness noted.

. . . . .

THERE WAS A reason the Shongair sensor tech was having trouble finding another drone.

At almost the same instant SFC Hidalgo's Avengers had taken down the three lead drones, a second section of Avengers, three kilometers farther west, hidden in the fields behind Force Furnace, blew four more drones which had been covering Harshair's column's southern flank out of the night. And moments after that, individually deployed Stinger teams hidden in the rugged mountains *north* of the A77 roadbed with the original, shoulder-fired launchers had opened fire on the drones on *that* side of the column.

In the space of barely twenty-five seconds, Alastair Sanders' battalion had put out every one of Brigade Commander Harshair's aerial eyes.

. . . . .

WILD EXULTATION, TINGED with more than a little awe, flared through Captain Gutierrez. The vista before him was unbelievable.

At least thirty vehicles gushed flame and smoke in a solid sea of fire, and that sea spread wider every moment as tendrils of blazing fuel snaked out from the central carnage. Bodies—some of them already on fire, as well—vomited out of the hatches of demolished vehicles, and strings of 25-millimeter tracer streaked out from the infantry's Bradleys' Bushmasters. Whenever one of those strings touched an alien vehicle, that vehicle exploded, and what his Abrams' main guns did was far, far worse.

"Hammer Five, Five Actual," an impossibly calm voice said in his helmet earphones. "Advance. Give them the boot!"

"Five Actual, Hammer Five. Wilco, Sir!"

The landlines had disintegrated when his vehicles advanced; he was on the radio now, and he hoped like hell no orbiting starships were listening in. But there was no time to worry about that.

"All Hammers, Hammer Five. Advance!"

The massive Abrams tanks and smaller, lighter Bradleys crossed the crest of the road and drove straight into the madness.

. . . . .

THE SHONGAIR VEHICLE crews had never imagined anything like it.

They'd never confronted anyone with weapons capable of matching their own. Once in a while an arrow or thrown spear managed to find an open viewport and sneak inside. And they'd lost vehicles occasionally to improvised ambushes, when the local aborigines managed to surprise them at close range, swarm over them, pry open hatches and get at their hapless crews with hand-to-hand weapons. Some of those aborigines had been clever enough to arrange pits or other traps which had disabled or immobilized their vehicles. And some of their vehicles had been destroyed when they were forced to abandon them in the field because of breakdown or when one of their firebases had been temporarily overrun and the local aborigines had known to set their fuel tanks on fire. They'd even—on very rare occasions—encountered aborigines clever enough to manufacture what humans would have called "Molotov cocktails" out of captured Shongair fuel.

But they'd never met anyone with vehicles as combat capable as their own. Never. And as the holocaust which had enveloped the head of their column lapped back around its flanks, some of them lived long enough to realize that they still hadn't. That the despised humans' vehicles were far *more* combat capable than their own.

It wasn't really their fault. This wasn't the kind of battle they'd been trained to fight. Not the kind of combat their vehicles had been built to survive or their doctrine had been framed to confront.

Eight of the armored regiment's GEVs battled their way out of the wild confusion of APCs trying to flee in every direction. Five of them took direct hits from 120-millimeter guns and promptly disintegrated. Two more were threshed into flaming wreckage by the jackhammer fire of Alpha Company's Bradleys.

The eighth lasted long enough to fire its own turreted laser at "Ferdinand," Gutierrez's number five Abrams.

The Shongairi had no way to realize it (yet), but their energy weapons were actually shorter-ranged in atmosphere than the human tanks' main guns. That wasn't a factor in this case—both combatants were well inside their opponent's range envelope. But whereas Ferdinand's spent-uranium penetrator punched cleanly through the GEV's frontal armor, igniting a fierce conflagration which blew the alien vehicle apart moments later, the GEV's laser wasn't powerful enough to blast its way through the depleted uranium-augmented Chobham armor of the tank's glacis. It would have been more than sufficient to breach Ferdinand's thinner *side* armor, and its transfer energy managed to shatter a sizable area of the frontal plate's surface area, but it didn't have the power or the pulse duration to actually breach it.

Now the horrifying, thundering monsters came straight for the rest of the Shongairi in Harshair's column, grinding contemptuously through or over the flaming carcasses of their dead comrades' vehicles, trampling the wreckage underfoot, and the entire brigade began to come apart.

. . . . .

OVER THE LAST four or five years, the Army's entire fleet of Abrams had been upgraded to TUSK status by the installation of the Tank Urban Survival Kit developed after Iraqi Freedom. Their side armor had been fitted with additional reactive armor, and slat armor had been fitted to protect them against rocket-propelled grenades and other shaped charge weapons fired from behind them. Neither of those features were particularly critical at the present moment, but TUSK also included a remote weapons turret armed with a .50-caliber machine gun in place of the original open-mount, exposed .50 at the commander's hatch. Now, as the tanks ground forward, those heavy machine guns thundered, spitting their hate even as the main guns continued to seek out and destroy vehicles and the 7.62-millimeter machine guns mounted coaxially with those main guns stitched fist-sized exit wounds through individual Shongairi, whose body armor was approximately as effective as so much straw against them.

Yet dreadful as the tanks' harvest was, the far lighter Bradleys were almost as bad. And even as they advanced, the mortar vehicles behind them—guided by the continuous overhead surveillance of the UAVs the Shongairi still didn't realize were there—began to pound the middle and rear of the column, as well. The M298 mortar, adapted from the Israeli Army, had a maximum range of almost four and a half miles. In the first minute, it could fire sixteen thirty-pound rounds, each with a lethal radius of over seventy feet. Thereafter, as barrel heat became a factor, it had a sustained rate of four rounds per minute.

. . . . .

ONCE MORE, THE Shongairi had never experienced anything like it. They had mobile mortars of their own, the heaviest of which had almost half again the range of the weapons firing at them, and they'd used those weapons with devastating effect against opponents in the past. But no one else had ever dropped mortar bombs on *them,* and troopers who were veterans of a score of past skirmishes fled in screaming panic as the incandescent bubbles of high explosive and white-hot steel fragments marched through their ranks.

. . . . .

"FURNACE FIVE, FIVE Actual. Engage. Anvil Five, Five Actual, advance to Point Carson and engage at will."

"Five Actual, Furnace Five. Wilco."

"Five Actual, Anvil Five. Rolling."

The responses came back over the landline net, and Captain Michael Wallace's Force Furnace—four more Abrams from his own Charlie Company's first platoon, and the four Bradleys of Captain Achilles Adamakos' Bravo Company's second platoon—opened fire from camouflaged positions three and a half miles west of Force Hammer in the neat, irrigated fields south of the river. They were barely three hundred meters from the roadway, and the camouflage with which they'd been draped flew away, flaming, on their muzzle flashes as they opened a merciless fire on the previously unengaged flank of Harshair's column. At that range, even a .50-caliber machine gun was fully capable of penetrating the armor of a Shongair personnel carrier, and the heavier weapons picked off the larger, more heavily armored GEVs with dreadful precision.

The carnage was incredible, and at the same moment, dismounted infantry teams armed with Javelin antitank launchers opened up from the mountains north of Force Furnace, reaping a dreadful harvest as still more of Harshair's armored regiment's GEVs exploded in fountains of flame.

Another mile west from Force Furnace's position, still on the south side of the river, Captain Adamakos' Force Anvil snorted its way up out of the dust wallows of its half-buried hides, shedding the dirt-covered tarps which had been spread across its units' positions. The other two platoons of Captain Wallace's armored company and the first and third platoons of Adamakos' own mech infantry company had been hidden on either side of a dirt track that branched off from the main road another mile west of Wallace's position and ran south across a bridge. That bridge wasn't remotely strong enough to support an Abrams, or even a Bradley, but the water level was comfortably within the vehicles' fording depth and the engineers had carefully surveyed the riverbed, locating the only two potholes which might have mired one of them.

Now the eight tanks and eight infantry Bradleys, accompanied by four of the six M3A3 cavalry Bradleys of the two reconnaissance troops which had been attached to the battalion, charged along the dusty track at almost fifty miles per hour. Huge billows of dust spurted up from their spinning tracks, silver and black in the light of the rising moon, but none of the terrified, stunned Shongairi already trapped in the battalion's fire sack even noticed. They were too busy writhing and dying under the fire of the battalion's other two combat teams.

. . . . .

ALASTAIR SANDERS WATCHED from the circling UAV as Force Anvil smashed into the tail of the Shongair column, and his eyes were bleak. Adamakos' guns were trained to his left, towards the column's westernmost end, belching their hate in fiery lines of tracer from the Bradleys and enormous muzzle flashes from the tanks as they raced for the river. Both the Abrams and the Bradley had fully stabilized main gun systems, capable of scoring first-round hits while traveling at full speed in rough terrain, and no more than a handful of Shongair vehicles at the very rear of the column escaped into the night.

Then Force Anvil crashed across the river without even slowing, hurling up immense sheets of muddy water. The tanks and Bradleys churned up the farther bank, swung sharply to their right, and advanced to meet Force Hammer as Gutierrez's command ground into the Shongairi from the east.

The night was no longer dark. It was illuminated with hideous brilliance by the flames spewing from his battalion's victims, and vicious bursts of machine-gun fire cut down desperately fleeing Shongairi. Some of the aliens scuttled towards the beckoning shelter of the rugged hillsides north of the road, only to encounter his deployed, dismounted infantry in fire teams built around machine guns and riflemen who cut them down with lethal precision. There was no mercy in the battalion's personnel, no hesitation, and this was a veteran unit. It knew exactly what it was doing, and Alastair Sanders felt a fierce, cold, exultant pride in his personnel.

"All force commanders, Five Actual," he said. "Lantern. I say again, Lantern."

Acknowledgments came back, and his "Blue Tracker" displays came to life, showing him—and them—the positions of every friendly unit. Perhaps some orbiting starship *would* pick them up . . . but it seemed unlikely what was already going on down here could be missed forever, and he wanted no blue-on-blue "friendly fire" incidents.

. . . . .

BRIGADE COMMANDER HARSHAIR was frantic. Every time he deployed one of his RC drones, the infernal humans shot it right out of the air, depriving him not simply of reconnaissance but of any communication with higher authority. He was on his own, and it was impossible to make any sense out of the garbled, gabbled scraps of frantic combat chatter he was picking up. The only thing he knew was that he and his brigade had rolled straight into Cainharn's own hell.

They're primitives*! Barbarians!* his brain gibbered. *They don't even have* interplanetary *spacecraft, far less supralight capability! They can't be* doing *this! It can't be* happening*!*

Yet it was. The direct vision displays showed him those terrible "primitive" behemoths driving straight towards him from the east like Cainharn's demons, and his blood ran cold as the blinding lightning bolts of muzzle flashes stabbed through his shattering brigade. They were grinding disabled vehicles—and *troopers*, alive or dead—under those broad "primitive" treads of theirs, and their accuracy was impossible to credit. They were firing—on the move!—*at least* as accurately as his own GEVs could have, and his vehicles had never been designed to resist *that* kind of fire. They might as well not have been armored at all, he thought sickly, as he watched wheeled APCs trying to climb the hills north of the road in desperate futility.

Then one of those "primitive" cannon swiveled in his direction, a laser pulse established the exact range, an M830A1 High Explosive Armored Tearing shaped-charge projectile impacted on the frontal armor of his command vehicle, and the final fate of his brigade became a moot point, so far as he was concerned.

. . . . .

LIEUTENANT COLONEL ALASTAIR Sanders watched carefully as Force Anvil met Force Hammer. Friendly fire casualties were a CO's worst nightmare in the middle of a roaring holocaust of destroyed vehicles like this even with the best datalink and electronic IFF gear in the world. But he'd trained his people hard in maneuver warfare—especially night attacks—ever since he'd first assumed command of the battalion, and tonight that was paying off hugely.

Despite all of that, though, he was astounded that they hadn't already been wiped out. There was no way the commander of the force his battalion had just spent twenty-five cataclysmic minutes reducing to wreckage could have failed to get out a situation report! And surely if the Shongairi could take out carrier battle groups at sea, they could take out land-bound vehicles! Yet they hadn't. Were the alien starships simply holding their fire in hopes of not killing any of their own surviving personnel? Hoping they could still recover survivors from the massacre?

Well, if that's what they're hoping, they're going to be disappointed, he thought grimly, surveying the thickly heaped, mostly smoldering and charred alien bodies strewn along the roadway. Occasional shots continued to ring out as here and there one of those bodies stirred, and he bared his teeth at the sight. *On the other hand, if they've just been holding their fire until we clear the area, we're about to find that out.*

"All units, Five Actual," he said. "Execute Bug-Out."

All along that hellish, blazing stretch of road, Abrams tanks pulled to the shoulder. Their crews bailed out, leaving the JBCP links up and switching on every other bit of electronic gear which had been shut down throughout the battle to keep them company. They climbed into or on top of the Bradleys which came grinding through the flame-wracked wreckage to collect them . . . and which had just shut all of *their* emissions down. Infantry teams streamed down out of their hillside positions, and every Bradley and MRAP of the battalion went hurtling along the A77 roadway deeper into Afghanistan.

Sanders hated leaving those tanks and their combat capability behind, but he had no illusions about what the sort of kinetic bombardment that took out entire capital cities could do if they ever locked on to him. Besides, difficult as it was to believe, they'd shot out virtually their entire main gun ammunition supply killing Shongairi, and he had no idea where he might find replacement ammo. So he turned the tanks into the most powerfully radiating decoys he could come up with and left them at the site of destruction while all of his other vehicles, radios completely shut down, raced for safety.

. . . . .

THEY GOT ALMOST a hundred kilometers farther into Afghanistan, and they'd split into a dozen different groups as planned, dropping off parties on foot to scatter and go to ground in the best concealment they could find, before the bombardment Sanders had feared found them.

Three Bradleys and thirty-two percent of his personnel survived the vengeful follow-up strikes.

Lieutenant Colonel Alastair Sanders was not among them.

. XVII .

Rob Wilson's head came up as he heard the crunch of tires on gravel and the sound of an engine working hard in four-wheel drive mode. Once upon a time, that wouldn't have concerned him, but this was no longer once upon a time, and he casually checked the .40 caliber HK USP in the ballistic nylon holster on his right hip as he stepped to the front door of the cabin.

Both of the coal-black German shepherds who'd been drowsing in the patches of sunlight coming in the front windows raised their heads, ears pricking, and Dave Dvorak looked up from the book he'd been reading to the four children in a sort of fallback to more normal times. His own head cocked, eyes going momentarily distant as he listened, and then he handed the book to Maighread and stood up. He crossed to the window to the right of the cabin door and quietly took down the AR-10 rifle from the rack above it. He pulled back the bolt to check the chamber, then let it come forward again, feeding a .308 round, and set the safety.

The shepherds came to their feet and headed for the door, beginning to growl softly as they sensed the tension of their humans. Merlin—the male and the larger of the two at a hundred and two pounds—started to push by Wilson's legs onto the porch, but a quiet command from Dvorak stopped him. The big dog stood with his head at Wilson's knee, his slightly smaller mate Nimue on the human's other side, while both of them listened as intently as the two men.

The kids got very quiet, their eyes going huge, and Sharon and Veronica went over and sat down with them, gathering them into their arms while the men looked out to where the driveway came out of the trees.

Neither of them said anything, but the heavy-duty gate closing off the driveway had been chained and padlocked shut, and they hadn't issued any invitations. . . .

An SUV poked its nose out of the dense shadows of the tree-enclosed driveway, and Dave felt himself relaxing at least a little. The vehicle wore the colors of the National Park Service, and the red-haired man behind the wheel bore a pronounced family resemblance to Sharon and Rob.

He glanced at Wilson and saw his brother-in-law's physical tension ease a bit. Then Wilson glanced at him, twitched his own head at the doorway, and stepped out to greet their visitor. Dvorak watched him go . . . but he didn't put down his rifle.

"Rob." The driver had climbed out of his vehicle. He held up his right hand, showing a padlock key, then pocketed the key and extended the now empty hand to Wilson. "I swear, that damned 'driveway' of yours gets steeper every time I drive up it!"

"Dennis," Wilson said, stepping close enough to take the proffered hand . . . which happened to put him close enough to unobtrusively make sure the driver had been alone in his car. He gripped the hand firmly, then glanced over his shoulder at the cabin with a slight nod. "Wondered when you were going to drop by. Are you and Millie okay? You need to be thinking about moving in up here?"

"Things aren't that bad . . . yet, anyway," Dennis Vardry told his third cousin. He reclaimed his hand and used it to push his hat onto the back of his head, then looked around and grimaced. "You know, I thought you and Dave were just plain nuts when you started working on this place. Mind you, Millie and I've enjoyed ourselves up here more'n once, specially since you seeded that pond of yours with trout and put in the picnic shelter. Now, though. . . ."

"Yeah," Dvorak agreed, stepping out onto the cabin's front porch. The two shepherds pushed past him, no longer growling, and bounded up to Vardry to demand he pet them. "*We* thought we were nuts, too. In fact, I wish we had been."

"You and me, both," Vardry said, reaching down to cuff Merlin gently and affectionately before Nimue stood up with her feet on his shoulders so he could scratch her chest. He noted the rifle in Dvorak's hands, just as he'd already noticed the automatic on his cousin's hip, but he didn't mention either weapon.

And just as they didn't mention the fact that *he* was wearing a sidearm . . . and had a Ruger Mini-14 racked in his SUV.

"You sure you and Millie are okay?" Dvorak asked. Dennis and Mildred Vardry had no children, and Mildred was wheelchair-bound from an early adolescent spinal injury. She was about as indomitable as people came, but he knew her disability had to be worrying Dennis a lot more than it ever had before. "You know," he went on, "Rob and I always figured the two of you should count on having a roof over your head here if the wheels ever came off. Not just because you've been keeping an eye on the place for us, either. Family's family, Dennis."

"I know." Vardry nodded, although from his tone it was obvious he'd been touched by the offer. "I know, and if it gets bad enough, believe me, we'll come a-running. In fact, I may dump Millie up here whether she wants to come or not if it starts looking really ugly. And it may. Boy *howdy,* it may."

"You've been watching the Internet, too?" Dvorak asked.

"Yep." Vardry shook his head. "Sounds like things are going bad to worse. You heard about Charlotte?"

"We heard," Wilson confirmed grimly.

Nobody was positive what had provoked it, but the Internet consensus was that it had probably been another of the local ambushes the "Shongairi" seemed to have been stumbling into. Apparently "Fleet Commander Thikair" hadn't been kidding when he said he was prepared to launch as many additional kinetic strikes as it took to make humanity yield. Whether he'd thought he was getting the guilty parties or had simply decided to issue a terrifying example to discourage future attacks had mattered very little to the portion of the North Carolina city's people who hadn't evacuated. No one knew how many of those 1.7 million people in the city's metro area had still been there at the time, but however many had, the aliens had made a clean sweep. According to a witness from Mecklenburg County who'd been far enough (barely) outside the blast zone to survive, there'd been eleven separate impacts, and the JPEGs of the ruins he'd posted the next day looked like something from the far side of the moon.

"Well, I just heard from a friend of mine in the State Highway Patrol that this 'Thikair' bastard's been in direct contact with the Governor. Him or one of his flunkies, anyway. Seems like he's telling the Governor what happened to Charlotte could happen to Raleigh if he doesn't make all of his people 'submit' to this damned empire."

"I can't say I'm surprised to hear it," Dvorak said after a moment. "It's part of the pattern, as far as I can see." Vardry looked at him, and he shrugged. "It doesn't seem like he's had a lot of success figuring out who's left on the national level." Dvorak bared his teeth for a moment. "The son-of-a-bitch has even been posting open messages on the Internet, trying to get somebody to come forward. But it looks like he did too good a job of killing off the government—either that or whoever's left is too smart to come out into the open and talk to him. He can't find anybody to make them formally surrender to him, anyway. So now it looks like he's reaching down to the state level." He laughed harshly. "I don't think he's going to have a lot of luck in *South* Carolina, given the way the bastard took out Columbia in the first wave."

"I think you're right about that," Vardry said after a moment. "And according to my friend, Governor Howell doesn't think he's got any choice but to do whatever he's told."

"I can see where it might be a little hard to argue with someone who's just killed off twenty percent or so of your citizens," Wilson said grimly.

"Me, too." Vardry nodded, then shrugged. "Haven't heard anything about 'submitting' through my own 'chain of command' yet. I figure it's coming, as soon as these bastards do find somebody they think can give the order. In the meantime, though, something's come up."

His tone had changed with the final sentence, and Dvorak felt his mental ears pricking.

"What kind of 'something'?" he asked.

"This fellow knocked on my door last night," Vardry said. "Never saw him before in my life, but he said he'd been looking for me. Or, rather, looking for *you*, Rob."

"Me?" Wilson's surprise was evident, and Vardry shrugged.

"Says he's a friend of yours. Says his name's Mitchell."

"Mitchell?" Wilson repeated. "*Sam* Mitchell?"

"That's what he says. What his ID says, too, for that matter. Big fella, black hair going gray, two, three inches taller even than Dave here, shoulders like a damned wall."

"That sure sounds like him," Wilson agreed. "Everybody calls him 'Big Sam' for a reason. He's a cop from the Greenville PD."

"Yeah, it does sound like him," Dvorak agreed with a nod. "He's one of the regulars at the range, Dennis. Wins a hell of a lot of pizza from people who don't think he can punch out an X-ring holding a handgun upside down and firing with his little finger."

"Well, he sure sounded like he knew you two," Vardry acknowledged.

"You say he's looking for me?"

"Yep. He says you mentioned something about a cabin up here in Nantahala, and something else about having a cousin who was a ranger. So apparently he's spent the last couple of weeks putting two and two together until he finally came up with me. He wanted me to put him in touch with you, but I figured before I gave anyone directions to your little hidey-hole, I'd best come make sure you'd be happy to see him."

Dvorak looked at Wilson.

"Is there any reason we shouldn't be happy to see him, Rob?"

"I can't think of one right offhand," Wilson replied slowly. "Sam's all right. You know that. Hell, I've known him for—what? Going on twelve years now." He looked back at his cousin. "He's a good cop, Dennis."

"He may be a cop," Vardry said, "but he's wearing desert camo right now."

"Well, he's South Carolina Guard, too," Wilson said. "Military police unit—132nd Military Police Company, I think." He grinned. "We always gave each other grief about that. Him being Army and me being Marines, I mean."

"Do you think it means anything that he's in camo right now?" Dvorak asked thoughtfully.

"Hell, Dave, I don't know!"

"Actually," Vardry said dryly, "I think it means quite a bit."

"Why?" Dvorak's eyes had narrowed, and the ranger shrugged.

"Because according to him, the reason he's looking for you—or for Rob, at least—is because my loose-lipped cousin appears to've mentioned that the two of you were building your own version of the Ark up here in the mountains."

"He wants to join us?" Dvorak couldn't quite keep the dismay out of his voice. He and Rob had never made any particular secret—among their friends, at least—about what they were doing, although they'd seldom gone into any great detail. Now he suddenly found himself wondering how many more of those friends might be thinking in the direction of the North Carolina mountains.

"In a manner of speaking," Vardry said. "It's more a case of his looking for someplace to drop something off, though."

"Drop *what* off?" Wilson demanded in the tone of someone who was heading towards exasperation. His thoughts were obviously moving along the same line as Dvorak's.

"You guys remember that Homeland Security 'drill' that just happened to get called right before everything went to hell, right?" Vardry looked back and forth between the brothers-in-law, and both of them nodded with more than a hint of impatience. "Well, his unit got called up for it. Most of them were in Columbia when the Shongairi hit it, but he and four of his buddies had been sent on some kind of errand. I'm not sure how it all worked out, but the bottom line is that he's got a couple of deuce-and-a-halfs loaded with stuff these floppy-eared bastards really wouldn't like him to have. And he's looking for someplace to stash some of it."

. XVIII .

Stephen Buchevsky felt his body trying to ooze out even flatter as the grinding, tooth-rattling vibration grew louder on the far side of the ridgeline. He *hated* the sensation, yet at the same time he was grateful for it—just as he hated having exactly zero ammunition for the 40-millimeter M203 grenade launcher that was usually attached to his M16A4 yet felt unspeakably grateful that at least he had plenty of ammo for the rifle itself.

His attention remained fixed on the "sound" of the alien recon drone, but a corner of his mind went wandering back over the last week and a half.

He'd managed to avoid any contact with Serbian civilians and gotten his small party of Americans across the Danube and into Romania. That had taken them the better part of three days . . . and no sooner had they reached the far side of the river than they'd come across the remains of a couple of platoons of Romanian infantry who had been caught in column on the road. It was obvious they'd been surprised by an air attack—presumably from the Shongair equivalent of helicopter gunships of some sort. It was the first chance he'd had to see the effect of Shongair weapons, and it had been something of a relief to discover that most of the Romanians had been killed by what looked like standard bullet wounds rather than some sort of death ray, but there'd also been a handful of craters with oddly glassy interiors from obviously heavier weapons.

They'd found no survivors, and from the distribution of the bodies, it was clear their attackers had pursued and picked off everyone who'd lived through the initial strike as they'd tried to scatter into the cover of the nearby forest.

It had been a grim discovery, yet the Romanians' disaster had represented unlooked-for good fortune for Buchevsky's ill-assorted command. There'd been plenty of personal weapons to salvage, as well as hand grenades, more light antiarmor weapons, and MANPAD SAMs—the

Russian-designed SA 14 "Gremlin" varient—than they could possibly have carried. They'd even been able to supply themselves with canteens and a couple of weeks of rations. Best of all, in a lot of ways (as far as Buchevsky was concerned, anyway), was that the current Romanian-produced version of the Soviet bloc AK-74 had been chambered to 5.56-millimeter NATO after Romania joined the alliance. He'd been afraid he'd have to give up his M16, but the Romanian troops had been well supplied with ammo which suited his own weapon just fine. Now every member of his party of refugees had at least his or her own rifle, and most of them were equipped with Makarov 9-millimeter semiauto pistols, as well. There'd also been a mortar section attached to one of the platoons, but he'd passed (not without some regret) on taking any of their weapons along. They'd been equipped with 82-millimeter weapons, each of which weighed upward of forty pounds, and each mortar bomb weighed close to eight pounds. Given everything they already had to carry, their total lack of transport, and the fact that the *last* thing he wanted to do was to get into some sort of sustained firefight with the Shongairi, he couldn't possibly have justified the encumbrance. Besides, it made a lot more sense to him to use what weight-carrying capability they had on MANPADs and LAWs.

On the other hand, if they *did* find themselves forced to fight—whether against the aliens or against belligerent locals—they were far better equipped than he'd ever really hoped they might be.

That was the good news. The bad news was that there'd clearly been a major exodus from most of the towns and cities following the aliens' ruthless bombardment. They'd spotted several large groups—hundreds of people, in some cases. Most of them had been accompanied by at least some armed men, and they hadn't seemed inclined to take chances. Probably most of them were already aware of how ugly it was going to get when their particular group of civilians' supplies started running out (if they hadn't already), and whatever else they might have been thinking, none of them had been happy to see thirty-three armed strangers in desert camo.

Foreign desert camo.

A few warning shots had been fired, one of them with sufficiently serious intent to notch the top of PFC Lyman Curry's left ear, and Buchevsky had taken the hint. Still, he had to at least find someplace where his own people could establish a modicum of security while they went about the day-to-day business of surviving.

That was what he'd been hunting for today, moving through the thickly wooded mountains, staying well upslope from the roads running through the valleys despite the harder going. Some of his people, including Sergeant Ramirez, had been inclined to bitch about that at first. Buchevsky hadn't really minded if they complained about it as long as they *did* it, however, and even the strongest objections had disappeared quickly when they'd discovered the massacred Romanian platoons and realized just how important overhead concealment was.

Especially after they'd encountered the alien recon drones for themselves.

From the odd, dark-colored flying objects' behavior, Buchevsky figured they were something like the US military's Predators and other UAVs: small, unmanned aircraft used for reconnaissance. What he didn't know was whether or not they were *armed*—a question which possessed a certain urgency, given those glassy-looking craters. It was always possible it had been drones just like them—or their more warlike cousins, perhaps; even today, only a minority of US drones were armed, after all—who'd caught those Romanians on the road. Nor did he have any idea whether or not his salvaged shoulder-fired SAMs would work against them, and he had no pressing desire to explore the possibility unless it was absolutely a matter of life or death.

Fortunately, although the odd-looking, bulbous little flyers were fast, they weren't the least bit stealthy. Whatever propelled them produced a heavy, persistent, tooth-grating vibration. That wasn't really the right word for it, and he knew it, but he couldn't come up with a better term for a sensation that was felt, not heard. And whatever it was, it was detectable from beyond visual range.

He'd discussed it with Staff Sergeant Truman and PO/3 Jasmine Sherman, their sole Navy noncom. Truman was an electronics specialist, and Sherman wore the guided missile and electronic wave rating mark of a missile technician. Between them, they formed what Buchevsky thought of as his "brain trust," but neither woman had a clue what the aliens used for propulsion. What they did agree on was that humans were probably more sensitive to the "vibration" it produced than the aliens were, since it wouldn't have made a lot of sense for anyone to produce a reconnaissance platform they *knew* people could hear from beyond visual range.

Buchevsky wasn't going to bet the farm on the belief that his people *could* "hear" the drones before the drones could see them, however. Which was why he'd waved his entire group to ground when the telltale vibration came burring through the fillings in his teeth from the ridgeline to his immediate north. Now if only—

That was when he heard the firing . . . and the screams.

It shouldn't have mattered. His responsibility was to his own people. To keeping them alive until he somehow got them home . . . assuming there was any "home" *for* them. But when he heard the shouts, when he heard the screams—when he recognized the shrieks of terrified children—he found himself back on his feet.

He turned his head, saw Calvin Meyers watching him, and then he swung his hand in a wide arc and pointed to the right.

A dozen of his people stayed right where they were—not out of cowardice, but because they were too confused and surprised by his sudden change of plans to realize what he was doing—and he didn't blame them. Even as he started forward, he knew it was insane. The majority of the C-17's passengers had been support personnel, not combat troops. Less than half his people had actual combat experience, and five of *them* had been tankers, not infantry. No wonder they didn't understand what he was doing!

Meyers had understood, though, and so had Ramirez—even if he was an Army puke—and Lance Corporal Gutierrez, Corporal Alice Macomb, and half a dozen others.

Buchevsky started forward, and they followed him in a crouching run.

. . . . .

PLATOON COMMANDER RAYZHAR bared his canines as his troopers advanced up the valley. He'd been on this accursed planet for less than seven local days, and already he'd come to hate its inhabitants as he'd never hated before in his life. They had no sense of decency, no sense of honor! They'd been *defeated,* Cainharn take them! The Shongairi had proven they were the mightier, yet instead of submitting and acknowledging their inferiority like any rational sentient, they persisted in their insane attacks!

Rayzhar had lost two litter-brothers in the ambush of Company Commander Barmit's column. Litter-brothers who'd been shot down like weed-eaters for the pot, as if *they'd* been the inferiors. That was something Rayzhar had no intention of forgetting—or forgiving—until he'd collected enough "humans'" souls to serve both of them in Dainthar's realm for all eternity.

He really had no business making this attack, but the RC drone slaved to his command transport had shown him the ragged band cowering in the mountainside cul-de-sac. There were no more than fifty or sixty of them, but half a dozen wore the same uniforms as the humans who'd massacred his litter-brothers. That was enough for him. Besides, HQ would never see the take from the drone—he'd make sure of that before he reactivated its transmitter—and he expected no questions when he reported he'd taken fire from the humans and simply responded to it.

He looked up from the holographic display board linked to the drone and barked an order at Gersa, the commander of his second squad.

"Swing right! Get around their flank!"

Gersa acknowledged, and Rayzhar bared his canines again—this time in satisfaction—as two of the renegade human warriors were cut down. A mortar round from one of the transports exploded farther up the cul-de-sac, among the humans cowering in the trees, and a savage sense of pleasure filled him as he listened to their shrieks of agony.

• • • • •

BUCHEVSKY FOUND HIMSELF on the ridgeline, looking down into a scene straight out of hell. More than fifty civilians, over half of them children, were hunkered down in the fragile cover of evergreens and hardwoods while a handful of Romanian soldiers tried frantically to protect them from at least twenty-five or thirty of the aliens. There were also three wheeled vehicles on the road below, and one of them mounted a turret with some sort of mortarlike support weapon. Even as Buchevsky watched, it fired, and an eye-tearing burst of brilliance erupted near the top of the cul-de-sac. He heard the shrieks of seared, dying children, and below the surface of his racing thoughts, he realized what had really happened. Why he'd changed his plans completely—put all the people he was responsible for at risk instead of simply lying low.

Civilians. *Children.* They were what he was supposed to *protect,* and deep at the heart of him was the bleeding wound of his own daughters, the children he would never see again. The Shongairi had taken his girls from him, and he would rip out their throats with his teeth, strangle them with his bare hands, drown them in his own life's blood, before he let them take another single child.

"Gunny, get the vehicles!" he snapped, his curt voice showing no sign of his own self-recognition.

"On it, Top!" Meyers acknowledged, and waved to Gutierrez and Robert Szu, one of their army privates. Gutierrez and Szu—like Meyers—carried RBR-M60s. The Romanian single-shot antiarmor weapons had been derived from the US M72 LAW, which obviated any problems Meyers and the others might have experienced figuring out how the things operated. They also had a theoretical range of over a thousand meters and the power to take out most older main battle tanks, and Meyers, Gutierrez, and Szu went skittering through the woods towards the road with them.

Buchevsky left that in the gunny's competent hands as he reached out and grabbed Corporal Macomb by the shoulder. She carried one of the salvaged SAM launchers, and Buchevsky jabbed a nod at the drone hovering motionless overhead, watching the massacre unfold.

"When the Gunny fires, take that damned thing out," he said flatly.

"Right, Top." Macomb's voice was higher-pitched than usual, her expression frightened, but her hands were steady as she lifted the SAM's tube to her shoulder.

"The rest of you, with me!" Buchevsky barked. It wasn't much in the way of detailed instructions, but four of the eight people still with him were Marines, and three of the others were Army riflemen. Eleven Bravo was pretty much the same MOS for Army pukes and the Green Machine alike, when you came down to it.

Besides, the tactical situation was brutally simple.

. . . . .

RAYZHAR SAW ANOTHER uniformed human die. Then he snarled in fury as one of his own troopers screamed, rose on his toes, and went down in a spray of blood. The Shongairi were unaccustomed to facing enemies whose missile weapons could penetrate their body armor. In fact, Rayzhar had never actually seen that happen before—not straight *through* the armor, instead of simply hitting something it didn't cover—and he felt a chill spike of fear even through his rage. But he wasn't about to let it stop him. Their superiors had warned them these creatures' infantry weapons were more powerful than the muscle-powered bows, or even the crossbows, the Shongairi had faced in their previous conquests. It wasn't as if he hadn't realized—intellectually, at least—that it could happen. Of course he hadn't *expected* it, not really, whatever he might have thought he was prepared for, but there were only three armed humans left. Only three, and then—

. . . . .

BUCHEVSKY HEARD THE explosions as the alien vehicles vomited flame and smoke. At almost the same instant the SA-14 streaked towards the rock-steady alien drone, trailing a tail of fire, and two things became clear. One, whatever held the drones up, they radiated enough heat signature for the Gremlin to see them. Two, whatever the drones were made of, it wasn't tough enough to survive the one-kilo warhead's impact.

He laid the glowing dot of his rifle sight on the weird, slender, doglike alien whose waving hands suggested he was in command and squeezed the trigger.

. . . . .

A THREE-ROUND BURST of 5.56-millimeter slugs punched through the back of Rayzhar's body armor. They kept right on going until they punched out his breastplate in a spray of red, as well, and the squad commander heard someone's gurgling scream. He realized vaguely that it was his own, and then he crashed facedown into the dirt of an alien planet.

He wasn't alone. There were only nine riflemen up on his flank, but all of them were combat veterans, they had perfect fields of fire, and every single one of them had heard Fleet Commander Thikair's broadcast. They knew why Rayzhar and his troopers had come to their world, what had happened to their cities and homes. There was no mercy in them, and their fire was deadly accurate.

The Shongairi recoiled in shock as more of them died or collapsed in agony—shock that became terror as they realized their vehicles had just been destroyed behind them, as well. They had no idea how many attackers they faced, but they recognized defeat when they saw it, and they turned towards the new attack, raising their weapons over their heads in surrender, flattening their ears in token of honorable submission.

. . . . .

STEPHEN BUCHEVSKY SAW the aliens turning towards his people, raising their weapons to charge up the ridge, and behind his granite eyes he saw the children they had just killed and maimed . . . and his daughters.

"*Kill them!*" he rasped.

. XIX .

"I want an explanation."

Fleet Commander Thikair glowered around the conference table. None of his senior officers needed to ask what it was he wanted explained, and more than one set of eyes slid sideways to Ground Force Commander Thairys. His casualty rate to date was over—*well* over—ten times his most pessimistic prelanding estimate . . . and climbing.

"I have no excuse, Fleet Commander."

Thairys flattened his ears in submission to Thikair's authority, and there was silence for a second or two. But then Ground Base Commander Shairez raised one diffident hand.

"If I may, Fleet Commander?"

Thikair turned his attention to her. Up until a day-twelfth or so ago, Shairez had been down on the accursed planet, supervising the construction of Ground Base Seven in the flat, fertile farmland on the western side of what the humans called the Black Sea. He had no idea why they called it "black," but he was coming to the conclusion that the only thing he could logically expect out of these creatures was *illogic*.

Shairez looked as tired as he could remember ever having seen her. She'd originally been supposed to command Ground Base Two, and it was only by the grace of Dainthar he hadn't lost her when those accursed humans massacred forty percent of Ground Base Two's personnel—and destroyed thirty percent of the base's infrastructure and *all* of its construction personnel—on the very first day. That had been a devastating blow, but it was far from the only one Thikair's fleet had suffered. In fact, the reason Shairez was now in command of Ground Base Seven was that Ground Base Commander Ermath, who'd been supposed to command that base, had gotten too close to a human with a ground-launched antiaircraft rocket of some sort in the nation-state of "Turkey." It probably spoke well of Ermath that he'd wanted a firsthand look at the opposition his troopers were facing, but the confirmation that the humans actually had individual *human-portable* weapons capable of knocking down even Deathwing assault shuttles had been an unpleasant shock.

And speaking of "unpleasant shocks," there was always what had happened to Brigade Commander Harshair, wasn't there?

Thikair knew Shairez had been continuing her analysis of the masses of data she'd pulled from the humans' Internet even as she oversaw her new base's completion. She'd not only managed to get Ground Base Seven's construction back on schedule while simultaneously supervising her analysis teams, but actually moved the base *ahead* of schedule, despite all the fleet's unanticipated casualties and logistic headaches.

No wonder she looked fatigued.

"If you have any explanation, Base Commander," he told her, his voice losing some of its flat anger, "I would be delighted to hear it."

"I doubt there is any *single* explanation, Sir." Her ears were half lowered in respect, although not so flat to her head as Thairys', and her tone was calm. "Instead, I think we're looking at a combination of factors."

"Which are?" Thikair leaned back, his immediate ire further dampened by her demeanor.

"The first, Sir, is simply that this is the first Level Two culture we've ever—that *anyone* has ever—attempted to subdue. We knew that going in, but I'm afraid we have to face the fact that we made insufficient allowance for what that meant. While their technology is inherently inferior to our own, it's far less *relatively* inferior than anything we've ever encountered. Worse, although our base technology is superior, they've done a better job than we have of applying the capabilities they *have* to their weaponry.

"As a case in point, our troopers have never before confronted any primitive species which possessed armored fighting vehicles, cartridge-firing firearms, or combat aircraft. None of our models took that sort of capability into consideration, and because we've never fought any *non*primitive species with such capabilities we failed—*I*, for one, failed badly—when it came to evaluating the lethality of the humans' equipment. In addition, we've never before—the entire Hegemony has never before—encountered a species which had attained this level of technology without effectively creating a single worldwide state." She flipped her ears in a shrug. "There have been other species which failed to do so, but none of them survived to attain hypertravel and thus qualify for membership in the Hegemony. And, of course, the entire Hegemony's interaction with such . . . divided societies at this level is nonexistent because of their protected status once they attain Level Two technology. All of that means we had no comparable civilizations to use as measuring sticks when we began evaluating this one's threat potential.

"It's become painfully evident, however, that no doubt as a consequence of this species' history, because of the ongoing competition between their nation-states, their weaponry is actually considerably more advanced than our own was at a comparable level of technology. Their armored vehicles, for example, while much slower, clumsier, shorter-legged, and tactically cumbersome than ours, mount weapons capable of destroying our heaviest units and are actually better protected than our own. Indeed, from the fragmentary data we've recovered from Brigade Commander Harshair's units, some of their main battle tanks are even capable of sustaining direct hits from our GEVs' main weapons, as long as our fire impacts on their frontal armor, and remaining in action. Worse, even their *infantry* have weapons—individually portable weapons, not simply crew-served ones—capable of destroying our most heavily armored vehicles. We could have produced equally capable or even more capable weapons—for example, I suspect it would prove fairly straightforward to build a vehicle-mounted railgun with performance better even than their 'tanks' 'main weapons—but it never occurred to us to do so because we've never *needed* them. That means that, despite the basic tech imbalance, the weapons they have are actually superior to the ones *our* troopers have, and that's skewed Ground Force Commander Thairys' original calculations badly."

Thikair bared one canine in frustration, but she had a point. In fact, it was one *he* ought to have borne in mind and insisted be far more thoroughly factored into the prelanding planning.

But that's not really totally fair, he told himself after a moment. *You* did *allow for a much higher than usual level of capability on their part—that's why you and Thairys planned such an extensive bombardment. Why you destroyed every major human army and navy. Why you hit them hard enough that* any *species would have to recognize how massively superior your capabilities were and submit. And even if they have the ability to hurt us, they* do *have to recognize they can't ultimately win, so why haven't they* submitted?

"A second factor," Shairez continued, "may be that our initial bombardment was too successful. Although their Internet continues to operate, it's evident that there's enormous confusion on their part. There are no clear messages from their authorities at anything except a very local level. I believe we may have so thoroughly disrupted their national governments' communications and command structures that there may be no way for individual units to be ordered to stand down."

"'Stand *down*'?" Squadron Commander Jainfar repeated incredulously. "They're *defeated,* Base Commander! I don't care if they've managed to hurt us here and there, *nothing* is going to change that. And I don't care how stupid they are, or how disrupted their 'command structures' may be, either! As you say, they're still communicating with one another over their 'Internet,' so they *have* to know that!"

"Perhaps so, Squadron Commander." Shairez faced the old space dog squarely. "Unfortunately, as yet we know very little about this species' psychology. We do know there's something significantly different about them, given their incredible rate of advancement, but that's really all we know. It could be that they simply don't *care* that we've defeated them."

Jainfar started to say something else, but then visibly restrained himself. It was obvious he couldn't imagine any nominally intelligent species thinking in such a bizarre fashion, but Shairez *was* the expedition's expert on non-Shongairi sapients.

"Even if that's true, Ground Base Commander," Thikair's tone was closer to normal, "it doesn't change our problem." He looked at Thairys. "What sort of loss rates are we looking at, assuming these creatures' behavior doesn't change?"

"Potentially disastrous ones, Sir," Thairys acknowledged grimly. "We've already written off over eleven percent of our armored vehicles. Worse, we never expected to need that many GEVs in the first place against the opposition we anticipated, which means we have nowhere near the vehicles and crews it looks like we're going to need. We've actually lost a higher absolute number of troop and cargo transports, but we had many times as many of those to begin with. Infantry losses are another matter, and I'm not at all sure our present casualty rates are sustainable. And I must point out that we have barely eight local days of ground combat experience. It's entirely possible for projections based on what we've seen so far to be almost as badly flawed as our initial estimates."

The ground force commander clearly didn't like adding that caveat. Which was fair enough. Thikair didn't much like *hearing* it.

"I believe the Ground Force Commander may be unduly pessimistic, Sir." All eyes switched to Shairez once more, and the ground base commander flicked her ears in a shrug. "I realize that may sound odd after what I just said, yet I believe it may be true nonetheless. My own analysis suggests we're looking at two basic types of incidents, both of which appear to be the work of scattered, usually relatively small units acting independently of any higher command or coordination.

"On one hand, we have units making use of the humans' heavy weapons and employing what I suspect is their standard doctrine. Examples of this would be what happened to Brigade Commander Harshair or the destruction of Company Commander Barmit's command in my own ground base's area of responsibility. On the other, we have what seem to be primarily infantry forces equipped with light weapons or using what appear to be improvised explosives and weapons.

"In the case of the former, they've frequently inflicted severe losses—again as in Harshair's and, to a lesser degree, Barmit's cases. In fact, more often than not, they've inflicted grossly disproportionate casualties. However, in *those* instances, our space-to-surface interdiction systems are normally able to locate and destroy them. In short, humans who attack us in that fashion seldom survive to attack a second time, and they already have few heavy weapons left. Logically, losses to that sort of attack should begin to taper off quite rapidly. Indeed, from the most recent combat reports I've viewed that would appear to be happening already.

"In the case of the second type of attack, however, the attackers have proved far more elusive. Our orbital reconnaissance systems are all biased towards locating heavier, more technologically advanced weapons. In fact, they're really oriented primarily for *fleet* combat, not for planetary operations at all. Our air-breathing reconnaissance systems, on the other hand, while specifically designed for planetary operations, are all oriented towards locating and tracking primitive opponents with no understanding of their capabilities. Our orbital systems look for electronic emissions, the sort of high-intensity thermal signatures we might find from operating power plants, and things of that nature. As far as the ability to track the natives is concerned, they're at least reasonably well suited to locating and following *large* thermal signatures—the sort associated with cities or towns, or with organized bodies of troops in the field. They're far less well equipped to pick out individual humans or small groups of individuals, however. We've always relied upon our air-breathing systems to provide our ground commanders with that sort of short-range tactical information.

"But *these* creatures obviously have similar sorts of sensor capabilities. Not as advanced as ours, perhaps," Thikair would have been happier if she hadn't added the qualifier, "but sufficiently advanced for them to understand the sorts of precautions needed to defeat or at least minimize our normal advantage in sensor reach. As a consequence, we're severely handicapped in dealing with the smaller, pure infantry forces whose attacks are beginning to significantly outnumber those of forces with heavy weapons.

"The good news is that although their infantry-portable weapons are far more powerful than we ever anticipated, they're far *less* dangerous than their heavy armored vehicles or artillery. This means, among other things, that they can engage only smaller forces of our own warriors with any real prospect of success."

"I believe that's substantially accurate," Thairys said after a moment. "One of the implications, however, is that in order to deter attacks by these infantry forces, we would still find ourselves obliged to operate using larger forces of our own. But we have a strictly limited supply of personnel, so the larger our individual forces become, the fewer we can deploy at any given moment. In order to deter attack, we would be forced to severely reduce the coverage of the entire planet which we can hope to maintain."

"I take your point, Thairys," Thikair said, and bared all his upper canines in a wintry smile. "I must confess that a planet with any sort of technology begins to look significantly larger when one begins to consider the need to actually picket its entire surface out of the resources of a single colonization fleet!"

He'd considered saying something a bit stronger, but that was as close as he cared to come to even suggesting that he might have bitten off more than his fleet could chew.

"Very well," he continued after a moment, "I believe the time has come to shift our approach. In respect to that consideration, however, Ground Base Commander Shairez, could you tell us the state of these creatures' 'Internet'?"

"Of course, Fleet Commander," Shairez said, although she was perfectly well aware that he'd already read her report. That she was delivering it not for his ears but for those of his staff and senior officers.

"The humans' cyber net is not only more extensive than we had assumed before we actually invaded it, but considerably more robust. I realize you were already aware of those facts before we attacked the planet, but I believe we've all been somewhat surprised by the implications of that fact for human coordination and dissemination of information. I confess that my own staff was slow to grasp them, although in their defense I must point out that they've been dealing with an extraordinary information overload.

"The general distribution of the imagery of the destruction of so much of Ground Base Two's infrastructure and personnel has had particularly grave implications. I believe many of the humans have interpreted that . . . unfortunate episode as an indication that we have not, in fact, fully secured our control of their planet. Even Shongairi in that position might consider that they weren't in honor bound to submit at this stage. Certainly prisoner interrogation indicates a great many *humans* appear to have interpreted it in that fashion.

"Perhaps worse, however, the humans continue to distribute information about our deployments and force movements, and also about the strengths and weaknesses of our combat equipment. We've discovered some evidence—strong evidence, actually—to suggest that the human 'Robinson' was directly responsible for what happened to Brigade Commander Harshair's forces because he was able to use the humans' intact communications to alert an 'American' force to Harshair's approach."

Tactful of her not to mention that the "American force" in question was only one of their battalions, *not even a full regiment*, Thikair thought sourly behind his expressionless ears. *Dainthar only knows what would have happened if Harshair had run his muzzle into something* they *called a brigade! On the other hand, I don't suppose it could have been a* lot *worse, given that less than eight percent of his personnel—and only a single twelve of personnel transports and cargo vehicles—survived the experience as it was.*

"Other information is also being passed," Shairez continued. "Some of it is of little consequence to our operations but still useful to the humans in terms of guiding them to sources of shelter, food, that sort of thing. Some of the messages being passed may actually be of benefit to us. Messages of that sort would include exaggerated reports of our strength, speculation as to capabilities and 'super weapons' we may simply have chosen so far not to employ, and speculation that all which has so far befallen their planet is actually the result of collusion with us on the part of their governments or some cabal of their own kind." Her ears shrugged briefly up and down in an expression of mingled bafflement and amusement. "There's something almost Shongair about some of the rumors and speculation, although I can't quite imagine any of our people entertaining such bizarre speculations about our leaders.

"There is very little evidence of any ability, or even any organized effort, on the part of nation-state governments to reassert control via the Internet, however. Calls for such an effort have been posted repeatedly, but without evoking any response. Or, at least, any response which the majority of humans appear to consider genuine rather than the work of what humans call 'crackpots'—the term would appear normally to be reserved for the weak-minded and/or charlatans, Fleet Commander—or something emanating from us. Apparently humans have had experience in the past with outsiders exerting control through a theoretically legitimate government. Indeed, they have several terms for that sort of arrangement and the humans who support it. 'Puppet government,' 'façade democracy,' 'collaborators,' 'quislings,' 'capitalist running dogs,' 'fellow travelers' . . . the list is a long one, and it would appear humans do not feel duty or honor bound, when such arrangements are resorted to, in submitting to the local government's authority."

Ears went to half-cock all around the table in bafflement as Thikair's officers tried to wrap their minds around such a bizarre psychology. It was obvious from their body language that they'd been no more successful at it than *he* had, the fleet commander reflected dryly.

"And the security aspects of the current situation, Ground Base Commander?" he inquired aloud.

"To this point, Fleet Commander, my staff and I aren't particularly concerned over the security of our own systems. While the humans' computer technology is in many ways surprisingly advanced and innovative, it's far from the equal of our own. They do show an amazing degree of . . . 'ingenuity' is probably the best word for it. Their efforts to penetrate our security measures have become increasingly sophisticated much more rapidly than we initially projected, but that may not be as surprising as it seems, in light of their general rate of technological advancement. Efforts to break into our systems are also increasing in number and frequency, as well. I have no fear that those efforts will succeed in the immediate future, yet I must concede that if they are allowed to continue, the odds that they will *ultimately* succeed become significantly higher."

She hadn't mentioned that so far as she and her analysts could tell virtually all of the attempts to penetrate the fleet's computer nets had been what humans called "freelance," Thikair reflected. Assuming the local government entities had possessed greater cybernetic resources than individual citizens, that suggested a degree of widely distributed capability and self-motivation he really preferred not to consider too closely.

"So far," he said out loud, speaking to all of them now, "we've allowed these creatures' navigational and communications satellites to remain functional. Now that we have our entire fleet in orbit around the planet, the human navigational satellites have lost their immediate postlanding utility for us. I see no reason to permit *them* to continue to use that capability, and I suspect that denying it to these small parties of infantry of theirs may make their lives more difficult in the future, as well.

"By the same token, we left their communications satellites intact for the same reason we left their Internet in operation—so that they could communicate news of their defeat to one another and submit, and so that we would have a sophisticated communications interface when they had the decency to do so. Obviously, that isn't going to happen anytime soon, and I've come to the conclusion that the negative consequences of leaving the 'Internet' intact outweigh any positive ones, particularly in light of what Ground Base Commander Shairez has just reported. I believe she's correct about the fashion in which 'Robinson' has so impeded our efforts, and I would not be astonished to discover that other humans continue to utilize this capability to coordinate their small combat groups. I realize our cyber techs are searching for indications of precisely that, but it's become painfully evident that these creatures are far more capable of communicating through indirection than we are. Ground Base Commander Shairez tells me they actually have a term for the practice—they call it 'double meaning.'"

He raised one ear and half bared a canine in grim humor at the baffled expressions of some of his officers. He'd had to spend some time thinking about the term himself before he realized how applicable it appeared to be to human "psychology"—assuming such a neat and tidy term had any particular relationship to whatever it was which really served humans in the place of logic and reason.

"In light of those considerations," he continued, "beginning today, I want their 'GPS' destroyed and their communications disrupted. Take out their satellites and seek out and destroy as many of their ground-based communications systems as possible. We'll still be able to establish direct contact with anyone with whom we choose to communicate; I will no longer allow them to communicate with one another in order to coordinate their actions against us. At such time as they recognize reality and submit, we may restore that communication."

"If I may point out, Sir," Shairez said respectfully, "there will be serious secondary consequences to your proposed actions." Thikair looked at her, and her ears moved in an expression of profound respect. "There's already been massive disruption of the humans' societies, especially in the more technically advanced nation-states, Sir. I would estimate for example that no more than thirty percent of their remaining power generation stations are operational. There's been a massive exodus of population from their urban centers, as well. Even some of those who had begun to filter back into their surviving cities have fled once more, following our kinetic strikes on cities where our forces have met resistance. Transportation systems are breaking down, especially as fuel distribution is interrupted. That means urban populations are unable to feed themselves, which is further accelerating the rate at which their cities are emptying."

"Your point, Ground Base Commander?" Ground Force Commander Thairys prompted when she paused.

"My point, Ground Force Commander," she replied, "is that they've been relying heavily on their communications to coordinate such central services as have continued to function at all. Cutting off those communications as the Fleet Commander proposes can only accelerate the disintegration of those societies. The death rate among the humans will soar as that occurs. Of more immediate concern, however, is that as their society disintegrates, the possibility of our being able to locate some central authority with both the sanity and the capability to submit will decrease still further."

"As always, your points are well taken, Ground Base Commander," Thikair said after a moment. "Nonetheless, I think we have no choice but to proceed as I've already indicated. To be perfectly honest, I will shed no tears if the fatality rate among these creatures rises to a level which finally compels them to recognize reality and submit. And encouraging the disintegration of their more advanced nation-states strikes me as rather more of a plus than a minus at this time. We've been trying for almost two of their weeks to get them to submit and end the destruction. They've either steadfastly refused, or else they lack the ability. In either case, we've gone far enough to meet them in that respect.

"At the same time, these more advanced nation-states are the ones most likely to continue to provide significant opposition. As you yourself pointed out, our troops are already reporting encounters with improvised weaponry, and the more technically advanced societies are those most capable of producing *effective* improvised weaponry. Moreover, I suspect our standard techniques for neutralizing conquered populations will ultimately prove more effective against the less advanced humans, whose capabilities are closer to those of the species we've already conquered."

He looked at Shairez. The ground base commander met his eyes levelly but respectfully, then bent her head and flattened her ears in recognition of his authority.

"In light of what I've just said, Thairys," Thikair resumed, turning back to the ground force commander, "I want you to revise your deployment stance. For the immediate future, I want to concentrate on these creatures' more heavily developed and advanced societies. That's where we're encountering the most significant threats, so let's start by establishing fully secured enclaves from which we can operate in greater strength as we spread out to consolidate. And if we can push along the disintegration of organized resistance in the process, so much the better."

"Yes, Sir," Thairys acknowledged. "That may take some time, however. In particular, we have infantry forces deployed for the purpose of hunting down and destroying known groups of human attackers. They're operating in widely separated locations, and pulling them out to combine elsewhere is going to stretch our troop lift capacity, especially given the transport losses we've already suffered."

"Would those forces be necessary to meet the objectives I just described?"

"No, Sir. Some additional infantry will be needed, but we can land the additional troops directly from space. And, in addition, we need more actual combat experience against these roving attack groups. We need to refine our tactics, and as Ground Base Commander Shairez has just pointed out, even our most experienced combat veterans have never faced *this* level of threat in the past. I'd really prefer to keep at least some of our own infantry out in the hinterland, where we can continue to blood more junior officers in a lower threat level environment. And honor, as well as prudence, dictates that we allow our warriors to seek out and destroy the enemies who have killed their comrades when they ought to have submitted."

"As long as you're capable of carrying out the concentrations I've just directed, I have no objection," Thikair told him.

And as long as we're able to somehow get a tourniquet on this steady flow of casualties, the fleet commander added to himself.

. XX .

"Well, *that's* unpleasant news." Dave Dvorak grimaced. "On the other hand, I wondered how much longer they'd wait before they got around to taking it out."

Alec Wilson had just poked his head into the kitchen to inform them that their link to the Internet was down. Given the fact that they knew the relay tower into which they'd tapped was still functional, that suggested the Shongairi had finally decided to knock the net itself out from under humanity, probably starting with the telecommunications satellites which had somehow survived so far.

"Yeah." Rob Wilson shook his head as Alec withdrew his head to rejoin Jessica in the effort to make certain the problem wasn't at their end. "Assuming the net's really down, that is, and it's not just at our end. Not exactly the *smartest* thing they could've done, though."

"I never thought it was very smart of them to leave it up in the first place," Veronica Wilson said, pouring herself another cup of coffee.

She and her husband were coffee drinkers; Dvorak and Sharon weren't, and coffee wasn't something they were likely to be seeing a lot more of anytime soon. That was why she and Wilson had agreed to ration themselves to only two cups each at breakfast. He was already working on tapering off, however, and he shook his head with a virtuous expression when she waved the pot in his direction.

"Sure, Mr. Slim Jim," she told him, shaking her head, then looked back at Dvorak, sitting at the head of the breakfast table. "Letting us talk to each other—letting Robinson put up that video of what happened to their shuttles in Virginia, for instance—always struck me as pretty stupid," she said.

"It had its upsides from our perspective," Wilson agreed. "The biggest one was Robinson, though. What he posted proved we could take down their shuttles, that their hardware was vulnerable. Without that, I think a lot of people would've been a lot more hesitant about pulling the trigger when they saw them coming. But what they should've done—hell, what they may've been *doing* for all we know!—was use the net to spread disinformation. Think about it, Ronnie. Done right, they could've sucked us into one mousetrap after another. And that doesn't even consider the propaganda possibilities! You think a steady diet of real or CGI footage of our side getting the shit blown out of it wouldn't've gone a long way to undoing the consequences of what Robinson and those fighter jocks pulled off?"

"You've got a point," Dvorak agreed. "On the other hand, my impression's been that these critters don't have anything like a solid handle on human psychology. They keep talking about 'submitting' like it's the only reasonable thing for us to do. And"—he shook his head—"from a purely logical perspective, they're probably right. They've sure as hell proved they can hammer the shit out of any target they want to once they find it! And"—he shook his head again, his expression going grimmer—"they've probably already killed a third or so of the human race. That doesn't even count the number of people who haven't starved yet but will, either. Or the number of people who're going to get killed by other *humans* trying to protect their own food supplies and housing."

There was a moment of silence as they looked down at their breakfast plates. They'd established a tight series of meal plans as one of their very first priorities, stretching food carefully. Yet they also knew they had a year's worth of canned and preserved supplies, plus the garden they'd put in right after arriving and a huge supply of home-canning equipment. That garden (planted with heritage seeds, despite the higher yield and greater disease resistance of genetically modified seeds) had been carefully located to conceal the traffic marks they hadn't been able to avoid leaving behind when they'd moved all of their more recent supplies—and firearms—into the cave. Disguising the area where they'd flattened the mountain grasses and pounded down the dead leaves had seemed like a good idea at the time, and putting in the garden had given them the perfect "obvious reason" to till up all that evidence.

And now that the exodus from America's cities had been given time to sweep out over the countryside, it seemed like a *really* good idea.

For the first time in modern history, starvation was a serious threat—indeed, a grim certainty—for large percentages of the American population. Flight from the remaining urban centers had redoubled when the Shongairi started simply destroying towns and cities—like Charlotte—where their ground forces met serious resistance. Chicago had probably been the real motivator, though, Dvorak thought grimly. Charlotte had been bad enough, but people outside the Carolinas hadn't really thought of Charlotte as a "big" city. Chicago, though . . . *that* had been seen as a major hit, and Fleet Commander Thikair's message—posted, of course, on the Internet immediately after Chicago's destruction—that other cities would receive the same treatment if his troops were fired on in them had only accelerated the process.

Which was leading inevitably to the disintegration of the country's social and technical infrastructures. Which, in turn, might well be exactly what the Shongairi had wanted.

Frankly, Dvorak was astonished the transportation system and power grid had remained operational—to some extent, at least—as long as they had. It helped a lot, locally anyway, that North and South Carolina had both been home to numerous nuclear power plants. At least interruptions in fuel deliveries hadn't automatically shut them down. Of course, the Shongairi had taken out both of the McGwire reactors when they destroyed Charlotte, and the Summer plant in South Carolina had shut down when Columbia was destroyed. As far as Dvorak could make out from the fragmentary reports which had come over the Internet, that reactor hadn't actually been destroyed when the state capital was, but it was still off-line. Possibly because of shock damage. More probably because the people who would have been operating it were either dead or fled after the Columbia strike.

How much longer any of those generating stations were going to stay up was problematical, of course. Local government was doing its best to protect them, along with other critical services, but throughout much of the country those authorities were being steadily overwhelmed by the influx of desperate, hungry refugees. Dvorak knew damned well that he would have done *anything* it took to keep his kids fed. He couldn't blame other parents for feeling exactly the same way, and that didn't even consider what people would do to keep their *own* bellies filled. So he wasn't surprised "looting" and other crimes of violence—and reactive vigilantism—had become commonplace. By the same token, he wasn't about to let anyone take away what he and his family had built for themselves against this very day.

He wasn't too concerned about being inundated by refugees. Although they were less than five miles west of NC-281, that was scarcely a major interstate, and the intervening distance was all trees and mountains. US-64, which looped as near as three and a half miles to the south, was both closer and more likely to see heavy refugee traffic, but the terrain between them and the highway was just as bad—or worse—and no side roads split off from it in their direction. There were a few homes scattered through the area, but it wasn't farm country, and it wasn't going to look very appealing to city folks who didn't have a clue about how to survive in the woods. Anybody who got far enough out into the boonies to actually spot the point at which their "driveway" left Cold Mountain Road (and it was pretty damned unlikely any refugees *would* get that far) *might* notice there'd been a fair amount of traffic up it. It was unlikely, though, since they'd spent several hours spreading dead leaves and pine needles—collected from much higher up the mountain—over the first couple of hundred yards of the roadbed. Alec had waxed especially artistic and dragged down a couple of dead hemlocks and arranged them in what Dvorak had to admit was a realistic-looking snag of naturally fallen deadwood across the roadbed. All in all, that driveway looked as if no one had driven up it in years, so as long as no one happened along when they were actually using it. . . .

What he was considerably more concerned about was the possibility that one of those local government entities, trying desperately to feed its own citizens—and whatever refugees had been dumped upon it—might decide to take it upon itself to collect supplies from "hoarders" for redistribution. Which was one reason the garden was where it was. If someone with official—or even quasi-official—status turned up, they'd find a substantial but not enormous store of canned and preserved foods in the cabin pantry, and they'd find a garden large enough to provide a fairly comfortable cushion for a family of ten. What they *wouldn't* find, and what none of his family was going to point out to them, was what was tucked away in the cave.

"Like I say," he continued out loud, "they really don't seem to understand the way humans tick. Of course the only reasonable thing to do is give up, but we aren't always all that reasonable a bunch. And while I'm sure there's a heap of people who're prepared to do just that anyway—who'd *love* to surrender—if the Shongairi would only feed them and their kids, they aren't offering to do that, are they?" He shook his head. "Seems like the only thing they understand is the stick. Apparently nobody's told them that if you want humans to cooperate, you've got to use a carrot, too. And they don't seem to understand that pushing people into a corner where they figure they haven't got anything left to lose is only going to make them even more likely to fight back. Or, for that matter, just how bloody-minded, ornery, and stubborn humans can be when you really piss them off by doing little things like, oh, blowing up the occasional city with a couple of million people living in it."

"Are they just too stupid to figure that out?" Sharon Dvorak wondered out loud. "Or is it something about the way *they* think? Are they being blinded by, I don't know . . . by their own preconceptions or assumptions, do you think?"

"I don't know," her husband admitted. "On the one hand, God knows there've been plenty of humans who did really stupid things even without the excuse of being an entirely separate species, or even a separate country or culture. Heck, for that matter, we've seen U.S. *politicians* do that often enough! I don't suppose you want me to catalog them for you?"

He grinned as he asked the question, and the others around the table laughed when Sharon shook her head vigorously. Dave Dvorak had originally intended to teach college-level history, and his love for the subject had never abated. Asking him *anything* that could lead to historical examples was a risky proposition.

"All right, *be* that way," he said. "The point stands, though. And, on the other hand, I could also—if I were permitted to—give you an even longer list of historical examples of human beings screwing up because they totally misread a *different* human culture. That stupid 'Everyone must be just like me' blindness has bitten people on the butt more times than I could count. I'd think any bunch of successful interstellar conquerors would have to learn to take that into consideration, but that could very well be my own cultural and 'humanocentric' biases talking." He shrugged. "Whether it's because they're stupid or some other reason, though, the outcome's going to be pretty much the same. Except, of course, that if it's because of 'some other reason' rather than inherent stupidity, they may eventually figure out which way is up after all."

"Well, they're taking their own fucking time about it," Wilson growled.

"Rob," his sister said in a level, ominous tone, cutting her eyes towards the four children sitting around the other breakfast table a few feet away. He looked at her, opened his mouth, noted the subtle but pronounced hardening of her blue eyes, thought about it for a moment, then visibly changed his mind about what he'd been about to say.

"Sorry," he said instead, then gave himself a little shake. "What I was going to say," he continued, "was that they're taking their . . . sweet time about figuring out how humans work. They should've been feeding us what *they* wanted us to see over the net. And they should've been encouraging us to use it to talk with each other as a way to figure out what we're up to."

"You're right." Dvorak nodded. "But nobody who was going to be able to put anything effective together in the first place was very likely to talk about it openly on the net, anyway."

"Especially after what happened to Robinson," Sharon said sadly.

"We still don't *know* that they got him when they took out Dahlgren," Dvorak replied.

His tone, however, said clearly that he doubted the admiral who'd organized the destruction of the Shongair shuttles had gotten out before his command post was destroyed from orbit. Obviously the aliens had figured out how to find *that,* at any rate. And while the people sitting around Dvorak's table knew the F-22s which had carried out the attack had made it back to base, that was *all* they knew about them. On the other hand, according to Robinson's postings, those pilots had been operating from improvised facilities at a dispersed location. Even assuming the aliens hadn't been able to track them back to base and take them out on the ground, the aircrew had to realize they couldn't continue to mount successful sorties without Robinson's target guidance and someone to resupply them with ammunition. So the only sane thing for them to have done would have been to abandon their aircraft, get the hell out of Dodge, and maybe see if they couldn't find some other way to make the Shongairi miserable.

I sure as hell hope *that's what they did, anyway. We need people like that. And anybody with the sheer balls to do what they did deserves a hell of a lot better than getting swatted out of the air while they grope around for targets without ground control. And he for* damn *sure deserves better than just going up in a fireball along with his air base when he can't even fight back!*

Which brought him to another consideration, and he glanced across the table at his brother-in-law, wondering if Wilson was thinking the same thing he was. When he looked back at his wife, he *knew* Sharon was.

"Kids," he said, turning his head to address the youngsters over his shoulder, "why don't you guys go ahead and get the tomatoes and squash weeded while it's still cool and shady? If you can get done with your chores before lunch, your moms will take you over to the dam this afternoon and let you swim for an hour or so. Okay?"

Youthful faces turned to him with predictable "why do you expect such slave labor out of us" expressions, but they were all good kids. They always had been. And even if they didn't understand everything that was going on, they understood enough to be growing up heartbreakingly quickly. In fact, there weren't even token protests. He was a bit surprised by that, until they'd disappeared out the door and Sharon snorted.

"You do realize you just let them out of washing the morning's dishes, don't you, Einstein?"

"Oops." He grinned at her, then shrugged. "Sorry about that."

"Not as sorry as you're *going* to be," she assured him. "Ronnie and I will wash, but guess who's drying?"

"Fair enough, I guess," he acknowledged, standing and carrying his own plate towards the sink. "In fact, why don't we go ahead and get started on that while we talk."

"What's to talk about?" Sharon's tone was considerably grimmer than it had been. "You two told Sam you'd meet him. There's no way you can tell him you won't be there at this late date."

"I know." She'd carried her own plate across to the sink while she was talking, and he wrapped an arm around her and gave her an apologetic hug. "We wouldn't have gotten involved if we didn't think it was important, though, honey."

"Oh, yes, you would have," she retorted. "You and Rob both." She shook her head. "I know how it sticks in your craw to be hiding out up here in the hills instead of fighting back . . . even if you *are* smart enough to realize you can't shoot down starships with rifles, however good your scope is! You'd be dancing like a little boy who needs to pee if Ronnie and I had told you you couldn't go."

"Not Rob," Ronnie disagreed, carrying two of the kids' plates over to them. Sharon looked at her, and her sister-in-law shrugged. "He wouldn't be dancing anywhere . . . because I'd have had to hit him over the head with a hammer to keep him from going!"

"Probably true, in his case," Dvorak allowed reflectively. "Once that Marine stuff gets into your DNA some of your mental circuitry just seems to shut down."

"Hey, *I* wasn't the one who let him put that stuff in the bunker!" Wilson retorted. Dvorak gave him a very level look, and he shrugged. "Okay, so I *would've* let him. Only I didn't have to, because *you* opened your mouth and agreed before I could. So there."

Which, Dvorak reflected, was true enough.

He took his niece's breakfast plate from Veronica and began scraping it into the compost bag, then paused as a cold, damp nose pressed against his leg and whuffled. He looked down and saw Nimue sitting neatly beside him, head cocked and eyes hopeful.

"David Dvorak—!" Sharon said warningly, and he looked back up at her. "Don't you *dare* give her table scraps," his wife told him in an ominous tone. "It's hard enough keeping the *kids* from sneaking her things without you getting started!"

Dvorak looked back down at the big dog. Sharon was right that the rule had always been no scraps for the dogs, but it was also true that their supply of dried dog food wasn't going to last forever, too. And Nimue and Merlin had obviously decided little things like alien invasions shouldn't interfere with their love life. By Dvorak's estimate, Nimue was a couple of weeks into her two-month gestation period, and her scrounging instincts seemed to have kicked up another notch or three.

"She's eating for five or six now, you know," he said wheedlingly to his wife.

"And doing just fine on dry food, as long as we've got it," Sharon replied uncompromisingly, and he shrugged.

"You're right, of course, honey," he said, turning back to the compost bag. He scraped carefully, and—

"Oops!"

Nimue pounced on the piece of biscuit and the half sausage Keelan had left behind almost before they hit the floor. Her tongue flashed, and the scraps disappeared in a single swipe.

"*David!*" Sharon exploded.

"It was an *accident*, honey," he said, looking at her with guileless brown eyes. "Honest! You don't think I would have done that on purpose, do you?"

"Oh, *no!*" she agreed with awful irony. "Not any more than you and Rob would've let somebody stash all those guns and things in your precious cave! You are just *so* lucky none of the kids were here to see you do that."

He chuckled and shook his head at her, then finished scraping the plate and stacked it in the sink with the others, and his memory replayed the conversation with "Big Sam" Mitchell.

He still didn't have all the details, but Mitchell's military police unit had indeed been called up under the Homeland Security "training exercise." Which meant it had been at Fort Jackson when the huge base was completely obliterated from orbit. Mitchell hadn't been there at that deadly moment, however, although exactly how he'd come to be part of the detail moving two trucks loaded with military ordnance still wasn't entirely clear. Apparently, however, Mitchell hadn't been able to find anyone left in South Carolina after the initial attack with the authority to tell him what to do with his cargo, so he'd had to make up his mind on his own.

Personally, Dvorak was a little surprised he hadn't simply driven up to North Carolina, where the state government had taken a far less severe beating, and handed his trucks over to whatever was left of the North Carolina National Guard. He didn't know how much of the North Carolina Guard *was* left, of course, since it, too, had been called up as part of the Homeland Security exercise, and the major bases in North Carolina—from Fort Bragg's enormous reservation to Cherry Point—had been just as thoroughly destroyed. But Mitchell hadn't been thinking that way. In fact, he'd already been thinking in terms of long-term guerrilla resistance, since he hadn't seen any way the invasion itself could be defeated. What he wanted was to distribute his weapons and ammunition into separate, well-concealed caches where it would be available *after* the invasion.

"If it's good enough for the jihadies, it's damned well good enough for *me*," he'd said harshly. "And these bastards may've taken out the main bases, but there's a lot more hardware lying around in depots and National Guard armories than they probably realize. Once they start pulling up inventories, though, they're going to figure that out. So I wanna get this stuff—and anything else I can scrounge up—distributed out, first."

It made sense to Dvorak. Well, as much sense as anything could, at any rate. There was no way to tell at this point whether any sort of guerrilla resistance would ultimately be practical or simply suicidal, but without the wherewithal to *do* the resisting, the question would have been moot, anyway. So he'd agreed to let Mitchell store a couple of dozen M136 antiarmor launchers, a half-dozen M249 squad machine guns, a pair of heavier M240 *medium* machine guns, two cases of M16 rifles, and a sizable supply of ammunition in the cave.

That was only a part of Mitchell's initial haul, however, and once Dvorak and Wilson had vouched for him, he'd been able to establish cautious contact with several of Dennis Vardry's friends and acquaintances among his fellow rangers and North Carolina law enforcement personnel. All of them had agreed to keep Mitchell's deliveries "off the books" as far as their own superiors were concerned, and he'd been quietly delivering his original load—plus quite a few other weapons he'd managed to scrounge up—to them for storage and concealment.

Dvorak and Wilson had agreed to help with deliveries in their area, which accounted for Sharon's and Ronnie's current unhappiness. Neither of them was going to argue, but that didn't mean they liked it.

"Either way," Sharon said, "there's no damn way either one of you is staying home this evening. Ronnie and I already know that much. But don't either of you take any stupid chances, either!" She looked up at her much taller husband, blue eyes dark, and jabbed him in the chest—hard—with a rigid forefinger. "I'll go ahead and take care of the toothbrushing and the bedtime prayers tonight, David Malachai Dvorak, but don't you *dare* leave me to explain why Daddy won't be coming home."

. . . . .

THE LATE AFTERNOON was uncomfortably warm—hot, actually, for the North Carolina mountains—despite the approach of evening and the dense shadow of the tree cover which met almost solidly overhead. Probably because the trees providing that self-same shade meant there was no breeze, Dave Dvorak thought grumpily. He'd always had a tendency to sweat heavily, and he blotted irritably at the perspiration coating his forehead and stinging the corners of his eyes.

At least the repellant was still keeping the gnats at bay . . . for now, anyway.

At the moment, he, Wilson, and four others—one North Carolina state trooper, a Transylvania County sheriff's deputy, and two local civilians—were spread out to cover a section of Diamond Creek Road, a half mile up from State Road 215, a mile or so northwest of Rosman, North Carolina. An ex–South Carolina National Guard deuce-and-a-half—more formally, an M35-A3 two-and-a-half-ton medium truck—was parked off the road under the overhanging trees, with its driver sitting on the bumper-mounted winch while he awaited the arrival of the half-dozen other men and three pickup trucks which were supposed to relieve him of his cargo.

Dvorak's own Dodge Ram was parked in Rosman, with Alec Wilson (and a twelve-gauge shotgun) making certain it stayed there. Rosman was one of the towns which had done a better job than most of maintaining public order, but it was still possible someone might find a relatively new, powerful, four-wheel drive long-bed pickup with the heavy towing package too attractive to pass up. Or, for that matter, might decide to siphon a little gas out of its tank. He and his brother-in-law had decided to park it in town anyway, on the basis that the exercise of a little hike would do them good . . . and that they didn't want *their* wheels to go out from under them if anything happened to go wrong at this evening's drop-off.

Not that anything's gone wrong with any of Sam's other drops, he reminded himself now. *On the other hand, it was pretty clear before the net went out from under us that the puppies had decided to step up their efforts here in the States. If they really are concentrating on putting us down for the count before they deal with the rest of the world, then it's likely they're going to be keeping a closer eye out for this sort of thing.*

He grimaced, then snorted silently in amusement as he thought about how much what he was doing at this very moment resembled what must have been going on in the hills and mountains of Iraq, Afghanistan, and Pakistan for so long. Except, of course, that the tech-advantage shoe was pretty firmly on the other foot, this time around, and pinching like hell! It wasn't really funny, he guessed, but it was . . . ironic.

Of course, there was always—

His thoughts chopped off abruptly as he felt a strange grating, vibrating sensation. He'd never felt anything like it, and he couldn't have come up with a good way to describe it to someone else, but he knew instantly what it had to be. Mitchell and some of Vardry's contacts had tried to describe it to him, and he felt his belly muscles tighten convulsively as his head came up, eyes searching.

Almost simultaneously, he saw Mitchell standing up and heard the rumble of heavy engines from the south. He looked across at Wilson quickly, and saw his brother-in-law lifting his binoculars. Wilson wasn't looking in the direction of the road, though; he was looking up, instead, towards a break in the tree cover.

From his own position, Dvorak couldn't even see the sky. He darted another look down the road, but there was nothing in sight yet, so he drew a deep breath, gathered up his heavy rifle, rose into a crouch, and dashed across to Wilson's position.

He flopped down behind the rocky outcrop Wilson had selected for cover when they first arrived, sweating a lot harder than heat alone could have explained, just as the first alien vehicle came grumbling around the bend.

It didn't look like one of the armored personnel carriers Mitchell had described to them. Nobody knew exactly how *well* armored those APCs were, but they were clearly proof against most small arms fire, and according to the descriptions, all of them carried at least one turreted weapon. This, however, was one of the aliens' unarmored cargo carriers, which actually looked pretty much like a standard canvas (well, fabric) covered stakebed human truck. They'd been seeing more of those lately, according to reports, which had suggested to Dvorak that this really was more a case of Cortés and Mexico than of Eisenhower and Normandy. *He* damned well wouldn't have been using cargo trucks as troop transports instead of the aliens' equivalent of Bradleys or Strykers if he'd had a choice!

Unfortunately, even if this particular "truck" wasn't armored, it did have some sort of machine gun on a ring mount on the roof of its cab. And there were a dozen Shongair infantry in the flat, open bed.

It was the first time Dvorak had actually seen one of the aliens, and he was struck by how apt the nickname "puppies" really was. They were slender, built very much on the model of his own Merlin and Nimue, with deep but narrow chests, and it looked like they were toe-walkers, with odd, backward-bending knees. Their heads—what he could see of them under the oddly elongated helmets they were wearing—looked more like a coyote's than a shepherd's, though, with long muzzles and sharp, obviously carnivore teeth, and they had brushy, foxlike tails. They wore body armor, as well as the helmets, but from the reports he'd heard, their armor wasn't as good as what was normally issued to the US military. (Or had been, when there'd *been* a US military, at least, he thought grimly.) The shape of their chests *might* account for some of that, though, since it forced the armor to assume a sort of flat-sided, prowlike configuration that didn't look well suited to antiballistic considerations.

There was a second, identical truck behind the first one, and he watched Mitchell turning to face both vehicles as the first truck's infantry unloaded. The second truckload stayed where it was, and he sensed Wilson shaking his head beside him.

"What?" he asked softly, and Wilson snorted.

"Their field manuals must've been written by their version of George Armstrong Custer," the ex-Marine (who'd clearly been feeling considerably less *ex-* over the last few weeks) growled under his breath. "Hell—*Air Farce* pussies'd know not to stand around scratching their asses like that!"

Dvorak raised an eyebrow, then looked back down at the road. What looked like it was probably an officer or a noncom was climbing down from the lead truck's cab and walking towards Mitchell. The alien had a sidearm in what looked like the Shongair equivalent of a shoulder holster, but other than that he seemed unarmed. His troopers carried slender-barreled rifles of some sort. From here, it looked like they had simple iron sights, which struck him as a bit bizarre. Surely interstellar travelers should be able to at least match the optical and electronic sights humans had developed! On the other hand, he reminded himself, humans had been killing one another quite handily for centuries without fancy sights. Those weapons looked fully adequate to perform the same task, especially at this relatively short range.

The good news, though, was that only the dismounted troops had their rifles ready for use. The ones still in the second truck were too busy craning their necks and gawking to unsling their own weapons. On the other hand, both machine gunners had swung their weapons to cover Mitchell and the deuce-and-a-half, so they presumably thought they had the situation thoroughly under control.

Which probably is *pretty stupid of them,* he realized suddenly. *They ought to be watching the* woods*—looking for nasty surprises like the* rest *of us—instead of concentrating all their attention on the one guy they've already located.*

His thought broke off abruptly as Wilson punched him in the shoulder.

"Up there!" his brother-in-law hissed, and pointed.

Dvorak followed the pointing finger and saw a peculiar, dark-bronze-colored object. It was roughly ovoid in shape, perhaps three feet in its longer axis and two feet in the shorter one, and the ugly, unpleasant "vibration" he was "hearing" clearly came from it. As he watched, it darted quickly to one side, then stopped and hovered, almost like a hummingbird or a dragonfly. It was trying to find a clear line of sight to the parked human truck, he realized, and it wasn't having much luck. They hadn't exactly picked that parking spot at random.

"Think you can kill that damned thing?" Wilson asked softly, cutting his eyes at Dvorak's rifle.

Dvorak glanced at him, then back up at the hovering probe. It was holding rock steady, about two hundred and fifty yards from his present position. Normally, that would have been an easy shot. In fact, he wasn't worried about whether or not he could *hit* it right now. The problem was that he didn't know if he could destroy it.

If that had been a human-built UAV up there, he wouldn't have had any doubts. The semiautomatic rifle he'd brought along with him was a heavy damned thing—it weighed almost thirty pounds even unloaded—but that was because it was a Barrett .50 XM500. It had cost him several thousand dollars (as Sharon had rather acidly pointed out at the time). That wasn't too surprising, given that each round of ammunition cost over five bucks . . . or that he'd paid better than two thousand for the sight equipped with the Barrett Optical Ranging System. He'd brought the weapon along in case really long-range fire was required . . . and also because the big .50-caliber slugs were ideal for disabling light vehicles. Light vehicles like the cargo trucks the Shongairi had arrived in. And, maybe—*maybe!*—"light vehicles" like the hovering, spying remote.

"Of course I can *hit* the damned thing, you idiot," he whispered out of the side of his mouth now, rolling into position and settling the bipod on one end of Wilson's outcrop. He dialed the BORS' adjustment turret to two hundred and fifty yards, wishing he dared to use his laser range finder to confirm his range estimate. He couldn't be certain his guesstimate of the drone's dimensions were accurate, either, which meant the Mil-Dot range finder built into the BORS wasn't necessarily reliable, either.

Close enough, he thought, nestling the rifle's customized butt into his shoulder. The BORS had been monitoring temperature and barometric pressure ever since he switched it on, and it was already programmed for his ammunition's ballistic performance. As the sight settled on the drone, it compensated for the angle to the target, as well. There was no crosswind at all, as far as he could tell looking at the motionless leaves, so even if he was off a bit on the range estimate it wasn't going to be enough to make a lot of difference.

"Hitting it's the *easy* part," he growled as he captured the sight picture and settled into complete stillness. "Your guess is as good as mine whether or not I can *kill* it, though!"

"Well, I think we're gonna have to find out," Wilson replied grimly. He had his own weapon leveled across the other end of the downhill end of the same outcrop. "If I say shoot, kill the fucker. Then get onto those trucks. You worry about the gunners, then the drivers; the rest of us'll worry about the grunts."

. . . . .

SQUAD COMMANDER GUNSHAIL was in a foul mood as he approached the single human. He had a great many better things he could be doing with his time than wandering around these Dainthar-forsaken woods! And he was scarcely amused to find out that he'd been sent all the way up here on a wild-*malkar* hunt only to find a single human at the end of it.

Still, he reminded himself, *don't get too carried away. There's only one of it, but that is one of the cargo vehicles their armed forces used. And you can't see into its cargo bed.*

On the other hand, he had two light auto-cannon covering it at the moment, not to mention two twelves of infantry. Even if there was something in there that shouldn't be, it wasn't going to be surprising anyone. Besides, the human he *could* see wasn't armed, and it was regarding him with what certainly looked like proper submissiveness.

Assuming that anything *they've briefed us on for this entire misbegotten planet is accurate, at any rate,* he thought grumpily, and brought his personal computer's translating software online.

. . . . .

SAM MITCHELL WATCHED the alien carefully, wondering how the hell he was going to get out of this one.

The doglike creature paused a few yards from him, and he heard a curious, sibilant snarling sound. Then—

"What are you doing out here, human?" a mechanical voice asked from a small device on the alien's belt.

"Waiting for a friend," Mitchell replied after a moment, speaking slowly and carefully.

"Indeed?" It was impossible to read any emphasis or emotion from the translator's artificial voice, and Mitchell had no idea how to interpret Shongair body language, but he wouldn't have been a bit surprised if the question had been sarcastic. "And why would you be waiting for a friend up here in the forest, human?"

"Because we're going hunting," Mitchell said. "Food's been short since you . . . people arrived. We're hoping to get a couple of deer to feed our families."

. . . . .

***AH! FOR THE** first time on this accursed planet, I'm dealing with something I* understand *for a change,* Gunshail thought. Indeed, he felt something almost like a surge of sympathy, possibly even companionship, for the repulsively hairless alien in front of him.

At least the creatures giving us so much grief aren't weed-eaters, he told himself. *That's something, I suppose. Of course, the fact that this one* says *he's out here to hunt doesn't mean he really is.*

. . . . .

"YOUR VEHICLE APPEARS somewhat large for only two hunters," the mechanical voice observed.

"Rob doesn't have a truck, only a car—a passenger vehicle without much cargo space, I mean," Mitchell replied. He shrugged, deliberately overdoing the gesture in hopes the alien would recognize its meaning. "I admit this is a lot of truck to haul around just a couple of deer, but it's what I could get my hands on. All that was available to me, I mean."

. . . . .

THAT WAS POSSIBLE, Gunshail reflected. He wasn't exactly certain what a "deer" was, so he had no measuring stick for how large a vehicle would be required to transport the carcasses of two or three of them. And the Shongairi had already observed that these creatures appeared to have a bewildering variety of vehicles. Indeed, here in this "United States" it sometimes seemed they had more vehicles than humans! And they'd already encountered several instances of individual humans or local authorities using ex-military equipment. Still. . . .

. . . . .

"I SHALL HAVE to check the vehicle," the mechanical voice said. "Do not do anything to alarm my warriors."

"Wouldn't dream of it," Mitchell said with every ounce of sincerity he could summon.

. . . . .

GUNSHAIL LOOKED OVER at his dismounted troops, then flicked his ears in the direction of the human's vehicle. His troopers had heard his side of the conversation in their own language, so they already knew what he wanted, and Section Commander Brasik lowered his own ears in response to the unspoken order.

Gunshail knew Brasik was one of those who had come to deeply and sincerely hate all humans for their bloody-minded perversity and lack of civilized morals. For that matter, Gunshail wasn't all that fond of them himself. Unlike the section commander, however, who would have vastly preferred to simply shoot every human he encountered and let Dainthar and Cainharn sort out who (if anyone) got its soul, Gunshail understood that sooner or later they were going to have to start interacting with these creatures without simply killing them out of hand. That was, after all, the reason for conquering them in the first place.

His superiors had made that very point rather firmly to him after that unfortunate business with the human female and its offspring. He still thought his battalion commander had been a bit unreasonable about the whole thing. How was Gunshail supposed to know it had half a twelve of cubs in its backseat? Or that it was unarmed? It hadn't stopped when he'd waved its vehicle to a halt. Instead, it had actually *accelerated,* so of course his squad had opened fire on it! Anyone would have. In fact, he still wasn't so sure his superiors' argument that it had simply panicked and tried to flee to protect its young was accurate. Not that any of them had survived in the end anyway, of course.

All right, it had been wasteful. He admitted it. And apparently these "humans" really didn't understand that any honorable hunters ate their kill—that it would have been an insult to the prey if they *hadn't* eaten it! They'd certainly carried on hysterically enough about it, anyway. He still didn't think he'd been all *that* far out of line, and he suspected his immediate superiors hadn't thought so, either. They would have reprimanded him a lot more firmly if they had.

Still, they'd been firm enough to satisfy their own superiors. And they'd also pointed out that Ground Base Commander Teraik, commanding the rather jury-rigged Ground Base Two Alpha being built just outside the human city of "Greensboro" as a make-do substitute for the original, destroyed Ground Base Two, would really prefer to convince the local humans to submit without killing them all off in the process. So he was prepared to give *this* human the benefit of the doubt and assume it was capable of at least the rudiments of honorable behavior.

For now, at least; he could always change his mind if he decided to.

• • • • •

"SHIT," ROB WILSON muttered softly but intensely as two of the aliens started trotting towards the rear of Mitchell's truck. The minute they looked in there, they were going to know exactly what they were seeing. At which point, things were going to get ugly.

"Still got a shot?" he whispered, his own eyes on Mitchell as he settled more firmly into position behind his fiberglass-stocked Springfield Armory MA9827 M1A.

Unlike his wife and his sister, who were perfectly happy with the 5.56- and 5.7-millimeter rounds, respectively, in a rifle, Wilson had enormous faith in the stopping power of the .308 Winchester (also known, in certain quarters, as the 7.62 NATO). He'd been a squad-designated marksman in his time, using a specially modified and accurized version of the old M14, the original of his present M1A. That weapon had always been his first and greatest love (well, where firearms were concerned, anyway), and he'd been less surprised than many when the M4's shorter effective range turned around and bit US troops in the ass in longer-ranged engagements in the mountains of Afghanistan. The M16A4, which retained the barrel of the old A2, had better range than the shorter-barreled M4, but even it came up short at extended ranges, and the Springfield's custom stock felt like an extension of his own body as he nestled into it.

He wasn't his brother-in-law's equal for the *really* long-range shot, but he came damned close, and he knew he was actually better than Dvorak at laying down long-range *rapid* fire. For which, of course, the .308 was vastly superior to any wimpy souped-up .22, whatever his loving wife or sister might have to say. It was a simple matter of ballistics, really. The 147-grain bullet of the standard NATO load weighed better than twice as much as the 5.65's 62-grain slug, and at extended range it transferred three times the energy—the real measure of a bullet's power—to the target. And, of course, he wasn't limited to military specs. His M1A launched a substantially *heavier* round than the standard NATO load at a slightly higher velocity . . . and delivered twenty-four percent more energy than even the 7.62 at five hundred yards.

So what if he couldn't carry as many rounds for the same weight? So what if the weapon weighed ten pounds unloaded? When he needed to reach out and touch someone, none of that mattered to him at all. Besides, as he'd pointed out rather complacently to Veronica on more than one occasion, if you hit what you were aiming at in the first place, especially with a bullet that was all grown up, how many rounds did you *need*?

Of course, Veronica had whacked him on more than one of those occasions, as well.

"The son-of-a-bitch's just *sitting* there," Dvorak muttered back. "Of *course* I've got a shot! Didn't these dumb bastards ever hear of 'evasive action'?"

"Don't complain." Wilson laid the glowing dot of his sight on the back of the alien commander's neck, below the bottom rim of his helmet, and took up the slack on the national-match-grade two-stage trigger. "You just take it down the instant I fire. Got it?"

"Got it," Dvorak confirmed tautly.

. . . . .

MITCHELL MADE HIMSELF stand very still, outwardly relaxed. He knew approximately where Rob Wilson was, and he also knew exactly what Wilson was going to do. Mitchell might have worried about someone else's having decided to bug out when the bad guys turned up, but not Wilson. Or Dvorak, for that matter. And because he knew where Wilson was, he knew he was out of the ex-Marine's line of fire to the Shongair CO. That being the case, he also knew who Wilson's first target would be, and he gazed at the other dismounted infantry from the corner of one eye, thinking about his own target selection.

. . . . .

GUNSHAIL TURNED HIS head, glancing at the troopers Brasik had picked to check the back of the human's vehicle. Given the fact that the human in question was standing there perfectly calmly, it was extraordinarily unlikely they were going to find anything incriminating or dangerous. Which was just as well with Gunshail. If he got back to base in time, he could still get in on the *chranshar* game his litter-brother Gunshara had organized, and—

The 168-grain .308 round, traveling at just over twenty-seven hundred feet per second, delivered 1.3 foot-*tons* of energy to a point one half inch behind the left eye on the profile the squad commander had just obligingly presented to Rob Wilson. It drilled straight through the brain the Shongairi kept in approximately the same place humans did, hit the inner liner of his helmet, and blew it off the ruins of his head in a grisly spray of red and gray.

. . . . .

DVORAK TWITCHED AS Wilson opened fire, but only internally. His sight picture never even wavered, and he squeezed his own trigger.

The muzzle blast from a muzzle brake–equipped .50-caliber rifle was almost impossible to describe adequately. So was the recoil. But any concerns he might have had about the toughness of the Shongair remote disappeared as the 647-grain bullet punched entirely through it. There was no spectacular explosion, no streamer of smoke, no sudden flash of flame—nothing except for a sudden twitch . . . and the equally sudden disappearance of that teeth-grating "vibration." The remote dropped straight down, crashing through tree branches as it thudded to the ground, but Dvorak had already switched targets, and the second shot from his ten-round magazine punched effortlessly through the body armor of the gunner on the lead cargo vehicle. The Shongair's torso literally disintegrated in a spray of crimson, and Dvorak's third shot sprayed the same truck's driver over the cab's interior.

He heard—and felt—more shots from Wilson and at least two other rifles from other spots on the hillside, but that wasn't his affair. He had his own job to do, and he traversed smoothly to the second truck, whose gunner was just starting to react, swinging his ring-mounted automatic weapon wildly around towards the hillside from which the totally unexpected rifle fire was coming.

Before the alien ever found his assailants, Dave Dvorak came on target again, and his finger squeezed.

· · · · ·

SAM MITCHELL SAW the talkative Shongair's head disintegrate.

Unlike the members of Gunshail's patrol, he'd been actively expecting exactly what had just happened. And, also unlike the members of Gunshail's patrol, he knew about the small-of-the-back holster under his light civilian jacket and the Para-Ordnance P14 .45 APC semiauto in it.

Mitchell had been a qualified concealed-carry instructor for over fifteen years. Over those years, and during his career as a police officer, he'd spent literally uncounted hours on tactical shooting ranges, and he'd given as much attention to the best way to get a concealed-carry handgun into action as he had to doing the same thing with an open-carry service holster.

His right hand swept back, with an odd little muscle-memory quarter-turn of the wrist that used the side of his palm to lift the jacket away from his side and out of its way. It kept going, settling on the pistol's grip even as he threw himself to his left, towards the front end of his truck.

The Shongair infantry were still turning towards their crumpling officer as his weapon cleared the holster. The 1911-style safety came off under his right thumb just as Wilson's second shot drilled straight through Section Commander Brasik's backplate and the Shongair dropped without a word. An instant later, the second thunderous report from Dvorak's .50 caliber roared, and other rifles opened up from the concealing tree trunks upslope from the road.

Mitchell's pistol came up automatically, without conscious thought. The sight picture leapt into focus, and a Shongair trooper's head exploded as a 200-grain jacketed hollow point +P .45-caliber round punched into its forehead at a thousand feet per second. Sam Mitchell had won a lot of pizza on his friends' shooting range; the stakes were rather more important at the moment, however, and his brown eyes were merciless as he took down his second target.

· · · · ·

DVORAK KILLED THE driver of the second vehicle, and the other Shongair who'd been in the cab with him. That left him with four rounds in the magazine, and he rather suspected that anything he might contribute to the firefight would be superfluous. That being the case, he transferred his attention to the instrument panels of the two trucks, punching two rounds diagonally through each of them in hopes of taking out any radios they might contain.

There was no way for him to realize that Squad Commander Gunshail's sole communications link to his headquarters had been through the overhead remote he'd already killed. But even if he'd known, he would have shot up the trucks anyway, just to make sure.

. . . . .

THE SHONGAIRI STILL in the second truck never had a chance.

Mitchell was now completely shielded from them by his own vehicle, and they had three invisible riflemen on the hill behind them. That would have been bad enough, but the *fourth* man behind them was bellied down behind an M249 PIP. The product-improved variant of the standard light machine gun of the US military fired the same 5.56-millimeter round as the M16A4 and its shorter, lighter sibling the M4, but unlike the rifles (which were limited to three-round bursts of automatic fire), it fired full auto at a maximum rate of almost a thousand rounds per minute. And unlike the riflemen, the machine gunner didn't have to worry about Mitchell's being in his line of fire. He also had a two-hundred-round belt clipped to the underside of his weapon in a plastic box, and five seconds after he squeezed the trigger, every Shongairi in the back of that vehicle was dead or dying.

. . . . .

MITCHELL HAD NEVER consciously realized he was crouching until the shooting stopped and he felt himself coming fully back upright.

Two of the dismounted Shongairi were still moving, and his expression never flinched as he finished them off. He heard three spaced, careful rifle shots almost simultaneously and knew Wilson was doing the same thing to any survivors from the second truck.

He stepped around the front of the deuce-and-a-half into the middle of the road, ejected the partially used magazine, and replaced it with a fully loaded one, all on autopilot. Then he reset the safety, reached back to tuck the pistol back into its holster, and looked up, faintly surprised to discover his hands weren't shaking, as Wilson and Dvorak came down the slope towards him.

"Christ, what a cluster-fuck!" Wilson said. Mitchell's ears weren't working all that well in the wake of so much gunfire, but he heard the ex-Marine clearly enough. Besides, he would've known what Wilson was saying even if he'd been totally deaf.

Dvorak, on the other hand, had actually worn ear protectors. Mitchell knew how mercilessly Wilson had ribbed his brother-in-law over those in the past when he wore them on deer hunts, but Dvorak had always pointed out that the sensitivity of the electronic shooting muffs he favored could actually be turned up to improve his hearing while still being available to *protect* his hearing. And given the cannon he'd decided to bring with him, Mitchell wasn't at all surprised to see them this time.

"I've *gotta* get me a pair of those," he told Dvorak now, digging the tip of one index finger into a loudly ringing ear.

"I've got an extra pair you can have, assuming we get out of this in one piece," Dvorak said tartly.

"I'll drink to that," Mitchell agreed, turning around as the other men who'd been scattered around the hillside came slithering down towards them.

He took a quick look at his own truck, which appeared undamaged, then turned back to the others.

"Either these bastards' HQ already knows what happened, or else nobody's going to get nervous until they don't turn up on schedule," he said then. "In either case, we've got to make tracks. The question is, who wants to ride back to Rosman with me and who wants to travel on foot? If they do know what happened, they're going to have someone else on the way pretty damn quick, and a moving truck isn't going to be hard for them to spot. On the other hand, if they *don't* already know, it'll get us all back to town and out of the area quicker. And we don't know how good those damned flying eyes of theirs are at spotting the thermal signatures of individual people or something like that through tree cover, for that matter."

Wilson and Dvorak looked at each other. They'd discovered on the way out that the vertical nature of much of the local terrain added quite a bit to the straight-line distance they'd had to travel, and neither of them was getting any younger. Besides, Mitchell was right about their ignorance of the aliens' UAVs' sensor capabilities.

"I think this is a time for speed, not pooping and snooping in the woods," Wilson said, and Dvorak nodded. The county deputy looked as if he was tempted to dispute that, but he didn't, and Mitchell tossed his head at the truck.

"Let's get saddled up, then," he said.

"Just a sec," Dvorak responded, and passed the Barrett to his brother-in-law. He stepped over to the dead Shongairi and quickly collected Gunshail's sidearm and a couple of the Shongair rifles, along with one dead trooper's combat harness and clamshell upper-body armor. He peeled off and tossed away anything that looked remotely electronic but kept the ammo pouches. He'd been wanting to get some kind of feel for these critters' individual weapons and equipment, and he wasn't passing up the chance now.

"Let's go," he said.

. XXI .

An insect scuttled across the back of Stephen Buchevsky's sweating neck. He ignored it, keeping his eyes on the aliens as they set about bivouacking.

The insect on his neck went elsewhere, and he checked the RDG-5 hand grenade. He wouldn't have dared to use a radio, even if he'd had one, but the grenade's detonation would work just fine as an attack signal.

He really would have preferred leaving this patrol alone, but he couldn't. He had no idea what they were doing in the area, and it really didn't matter. Whatever else they might do, every Shongair unit appeared to be on its own permanent seek-and-destroy mission, and he couldn't allow that when the civilians he and his people had become responsible for were in this patrol's way.

His reaction to the Shongairi's attack on the Romanian civilians had landed him with yet another mission—one he would vastly have preferred to avoid. Or that was what he told himself, anyway. The rest of his people—with the possible exception of Ramirez—seemed to cherish none of the reservations he himself felt. In fact, he often thought the only reason *he* felt them was because he was in command. It was his *job* to feel them. But however it happened, he and his marooned Americans had become the protectors of a slowly but steadily growing band of Romanians.

Fortunately, one of the Romanians in question—Elizabeth Cantacuzène—had been a university teacher. Her English was heavily accented, but her grammar (and, Buchevsky suspected, her vocabulary) was considerably better than his, and just acquiring a local translator had been worth almost all of the headaches which come with it. Several of the others spoke at least passable English—a hell of a lot better than *his* Romanian, anyway!—as well.

By now, he had just under sixty armed men and women under his command. His Americans formed the core of his force, but their numbers were almost equaled by a handful of Romanian soldiers and the much larger number of civilians who were in the process of receiving a crash course in military survival from him, Gunny Meyers, and Sergeant Alexander Jonescu of the Romanian Army. He'd organized them into four roughly equal-sized "squads": one commanded by Meyers, one by Ramirez, one by Jonescu, and one by Alice Macomb. Michelle Truman was senior to Macomb, but she and Sherman were still too valuable as his "brain trust" for him to "waste her" in a shooter's slot. Besides, she was learning Romanian from Cantacuzène.

Fortunately, Sergeant Jonescu already spoke English (British style, not *real* English, but beggars couldn't be choosers), and Buchevsky had managed to get at least one English speaker into each of his squads. It was clumsy, but it worked, and they'd spent hours in camp each night drilling on hand signals that required no spoken language. And at least the parameters of their situation were painfully clear to everyone.

Evade. *Hide.* Do whatever it took to keep the civilians—now close to two hundred of them—safe. Stay on the move. Avoid roads and towns. Look out constantly for any source of food. It turned out Calvin Meyers was an accomplished deer hunter, and he and two like-minded souls who had been members of the Romanian forestry service were contributing significantly to keeping their people fed. Still, summer was sliding slowly but steadily towards fall, and all too soon cold and starvation would become deadly threats.

But for that to happen, first we have to survive *the summer, don't we?* he thought harshly. *Which means these bastards have to be stopped before they figure out the civilians are out here to be killed. And we've got to do it without their getting a message back to base.*

He didn't like it. He didn't like it at all. But he didn't see any choice, either. These aliens couldn't possibly have enough troops down here to be sending entire squads of them rummaging around every patch of woods on the damned planet, yet for some frigging reason they seemed *determined* to use however many of them it took to run down his own band of refugees. He was beginning to think they must have killed the wrong guy's brother or some damned thing!

Whatever the reason, he had no option but to deal with the current batch of flop-eared bastards to catch up with them, and with Cantacuzène's assistance, he'd interrogated every single person who'd seen the Shongairi in action, hunting information on the aliens' tactics and doctrine.

It was obvious they were sudden death on large bodies of troops or units equipped with heavy weapons. Some of that was probably because crewmen inside tanks couldn't "hear" approaching recon drones the way infantry in the open could, he thought. It might also be an indication that the aliens' sensors were better designed to detect mechanized forces, or at least units with heavy emission signatures, which was one reason he'd gotten rid of all of his radios. He'd dumped his GPS, as well—although not without severe regrets—for the same reason, which hadn't helped his sense of isolation one bit. At least he'd been able to come up with some Romanian road maps, which helped, but he felt one hell of a long way from home whenever he looked at the Romanian legends printed on them.

From both his questioning and his own observations, it appeared the infantry patrols had less sensor coverage than those floating tanks or their road convoys. And in the handful of additional brushes he'd had with their infantry, it had become evident that the invaders weren't in any sort of free-flow communications net that extended beyond their immediate unit. If they had been, he felt sure, by now one of the patrols they'd attacked would have managed to call in one of their kinetic strikes, or at least an air attack.

Which is why we've got to hit them fast, make sure we take out their vehicles with the first strike . . . and that nobody who might be packing a personal radio lives long enough to use it.

It looked like they were beginning to settle down. Obviously, they had no idea Buchevsky or his people were out here, which suited him just fine.

Go ahead, he thought grimly. *Get comfortable. Drop off. I've got your sleeping pill right here. In about another five—*

"Excuse me, Sergeant, but is this really wise?"

Stephen Buchevsky twitched as if someone had just applied a high-voltage charge to a particularly sensitive portion of his anatomy, and his head whipped around towards the whispered question.

The question which had just been asked in his very ear in almost unaccented English . . . by a voice he'd never heard in his life.

. . . . .

"NOW SUPPOSE YOU just tell me who you are and where the *hell* you came from?" Buchevsky demanded ten minutes later.

He stood facing a perfect stranger, two hundred meters from the Shongair bivouac, and he wished the light were better. Not that he was even tempted to strike a match.

The stranger looked like he was about five-nine or maybe five-ten—slightly above average height for a Romanian, anyway, although still well short of Buchevsky's towering inches. He had a sharp-prowed nose, large, deep-set green eyes, and dark hair. That was about all Buchevsky could tell, aside from the fact that his smile seemed faintly amused.

"Excuse me," the other man said. "I had no desire to . . . startle you, Sergeant. However, I knew something which you do not. There is a second patrol just under a kilometer away in that direction."

He pointed back up the narrow road along which the Shongairi had approached, and an icy finger stroked suddenly down Buchevsky's spine.

"How do you know that?"

"My men and I have been watching them," the stranger said. "And it is a formation we have seen before—one they have adopted in the last few days. I believe they are experimenting with new tactics, sending out pairs of infantry teams in support of one another."

"Damn. I was hoping they'd take longer to think of that," Buchevsky muttered. "Looks like they may be smarter than I'd assumed from their original tactics."

"I do not know how intelligent they may be, Sergeant. But I do suspect that if you were to attack *this* patrol, the other one would probably call up heavy support quickly."

"That's exactly what they'd do," Buchevsky agreed, then frowned.

"Not that I'm not grateful for the warning, or anything," he said, "but you still haven't told me who you are, where you came from, or how you got here."

"Surely"—this time the amusement in the Romanian's voice was unmistakable—"those would be more reasonable questions for *me* to be asking of an American Marine here in the heart of Wallachia?"

Buchevsky's jaw clenched, but the other man chuckled and shook his head.

"Forgive me, Sergeant. I have been told I have a questionable sense of humor. My name is Basarab, Mircea Basarab. And my men and I have been doing much what I suspect you have—attempting to protect my people from these 'Shongair' butchers." He grimaced. "Protecting civilians from invaders is, alas, something of a national pastime in these parts. It would appear that the only thing which truly changes are the names and motives of the invaders." He shrugged, then twitched his head in a generally northerly direction. "As for where I have come from, the villages my men and I have taken under our protection are up near Lake Vidraru, fifty or sixty kilometers north of here."

"I see. . . ." Buchevsky said slowly, and white teeth glinted at him in the dimness.

"I believe you do, Sergeant. And, yes, I also believe our villagers could absorb the civilians *you* have been protecting. These are typical mountain villages, largely self-sufficient, with few 'modern amenities,' of course. They grow their own food, and feeding this many additional mouths will strain their resources severely. I doubt anyone will grow fat over the winter! But they will do their best, and the additional hands will be welcome as they prepare for the snows. And from what I have seen of you and your band, you would be a most welcome addition to their defenses."

Buchevsky cocked his head, straining to see the other's expression. It was all coming at him far too quickly. He knew he ought to be standing back, considering the stranger's offer coldly and rationally. Yet what he actually felt was a wave of unspeakable relief as the men, women, and children—always the children—for whom he'd become responsible were offered at least a reprieve from starvation and frostbite.

"And how would we get there with these puppies sitting in our lap?" he asked.

"Obviously, Sergeant, we must first *remove* them from 'our lap.' Since my men are already in position to deal with the second patrol, and yours are already in position to deal with *this* patrol, I would suggest we both get back to work. I presume you intended to use that grenade to signal the start of your own attack?"

Buchevsky nodded, and Basarab shrugged.

"I see no reason why you should change your plans in that regard. Allow me fifteen minutes—no, perhaps twenty would be better—to return to my own men and tell them to listen for your attack. After that"—those white teeth glittered again, and this time, Buchevsky knew, that smile was cold and cruel—"feel free to announce your presence to these vermin. Loudly."

.XXII.

"Longbow" Torino crouched in the heavy woods where Interstate 89 crossed the power right-of-way, five miles to the west of what had once been Concord, New Hampshire.

He wasn't sure what had happened to Concord—or, rather, he wasn't sure *why* it happened. *What* had happened had been painfully clear when he and his gaunt, grim-faced band of orphaned military personnel, equally orphaned survivors of half a dozen police and sheriffs departments (they even had one somewhat battered FBI agent who'd turned up from somewhere), and armed civilians reached the outskirts of the devastated city. The most logical explanation was that it had been taken out by the Shongairi on the very first day because of its status as New Hampshire's capital. On the other hand, Concord's population had been under forty-five thousand. State capital or no, that seemed like a small target for the aliens to have taken out that early.

Another possibility was that something unpleasant had happened to the Shongairi in the vicinity. In fact, he thought that was a much more likely explanation. From what he'd seen of the surviving New Hampshirites he'd met so far, John Stark's inheritors seemed inclined to take their state motto of "Live Free or Die" as seriously as *he* had, and it had cost them in Shongair retaliations.

Well, at least that's not going to happen tonight, he thought grimly. *There's nothing left around here big enough to retaliate* against. *Those fucking floppy-eared bastards've seen to* that*!*

He looked around, considering his men's (and women's) positions, and tried to remember how he'd gotten here. Maybe someday, if there ever was a "someday," he could sort it out. For now, it was a blur.

He could remember Admiral Robinson ordering him to abandon his F-22s at Plattsburgh and get out using ground transport. He could remember wanting to argue about that, too, but the admiral had been right. Without the wherewithal to rearm and support his aircraft, the expensive, highly capable fighters were useless, and it could only be a matter of time before the Shongairi managed to figure out where they'd come from or—even worse—where they'd gone again.

On the other hand, as he'd pointed out to Robinson, if they left the aircraft where they were it would inevitably invite a kinetic strike on Plattsburgh. So he and his pilots had refueled, taken off again, programmed their fighters to head straight east across the Atlantic Ocean, then punched out over New Hampshire.

The ejection seat's reality had been worse than anything he'd experienced in training, even though he'd been traveling at a relatively low speed (well, low for an F-22, anyway), but he and his pilots had reached the ground more or less uninjured. From there, they'd headed south.

He'd lost "Killer" Cunningham a week or so after that, when his quartet of Air Force officers joined a hodgepodge of New York and New Hampshire National Guardsmen, the members of two local police forces, and four regular Army noncoms who'd turned up out of nowhere in an attack on a Shongair troop convoy. They'd taken out the floating "tanks" at the head of the column with M136s, then shot up the unarmored trucks behind it. They'd missed spotting a pair of armed APCs, unfortunately, and one of them had blown Cunningham apart, along with the rest of the six-man section he'd been leading. One of the Army types had gotten the APC a fraction of a second later, and the other APC had been destroyed, as well, but they'd lost almost a quarter of their own force in the attack.

Torino had learned from that. He'd learned that stand-up fights against the aliens were a bad idea. He'd learned they were perfectly willing to use their kinetic bombardment capability against even relatively small targets—and perfectly happy to resort to reprisals against civilians—when they'd gotten a quarter of his surviving men while they tried to get out of the area. The Shongairi had used what had to have been blind fire that time, saturating the area from which they'd attacked with KEWs, and then destroyed three small towns within a couple of miles of the attack itself for good measure. He'd learned the advantage of being able to get the hell out of Dodge in a hurry from that experience, and in subsequent raids he'd learned that the aliens' hovering remotes had to be taken out early in any engagement. The learning curve had been steep and littered with human bodies, but by *God,* he'd learned!

All of which explained why he'd chosen his present position.

According to the scattered bands of survivors he'd encountered on his way towards Concord, the Shongairi were using I-89 heavily. He'd been surprised at first that an interstellar invasion force was so roadbound, but he was perfectly happy to take advantage of it, so he'd gotten out his road maps and started looking for a suitable spot.

The fact that the Shongairi had already destroyed Concord was a factor in his planning. He'd made it a point since his second raid to conduct operations as far away as possible from any city or town in order to deprive the Shongairi of a handy target for retaliation. He'd had passing contact with three other groups of guerrillas, and from the limited accounts he'd been able to compare, it sounded like the Shongair policy was to destroy any human town within three or four miles of an attack. Beyond that, they seemed to ignore the local population . . . so far, at least. Torino had decided to take four miles as his minimum limit whenever possible, but that was sometimes surprisingly difficult to manage, despite the rural nature of so much of upper New York and New England.

That wasn't a problem in this case, though, since the aliens had already taken Concord out and every nearby town had promptly emptied in the aftermath. On the other hand, he'd scouted the ruins on the fringe of the onetime state capital and found a deep basement sublevel under what was left of one of Concord Hospital's main buildings. The hospital had been outside the primary zone of destruction, but not by far, and it had taken massive blast and fire damage. Some of its bigger, more substantial buildings were still at least partially intact, however, and there were still intact abandoned vehicles in several of the parking lots which had been in those buildings' blast shadows, as well. He'd picked up half a dozen additional vans and SUVs from those parking lots. More to the point, if he and his raiders could get to the hospital quickly enough after their strike—it was barely four miles from his current location—they could hide their vehicles in the lower story of a more or less intact parking garage and themselves in the basement.

It all depended on how quickly they could get there, and he figured the odds were probably in their favor . . . assuming they could take out any of those damned drones quickly enough. And that the Shongairi still hadn't figured out how to reduce the lag in their response loop. He didn't understand why the aliens hadn't adapted that way already, but it was evident from their response patterns that their various forces had nowhere near the degree of netcentric awareness the US military had developed. They were *slow*. In fact, it seemed to Torino that their units weren't routinely in communication with higher echelons. If they had been, then surely they could have gotten air support to the units he'd attacked far more quickly than they had. From the way the convoys and detachments he'd hit had reacted, they seemed to have pretty good *intra*-unit communications, but it was almost as if higher command wasn't keeping an eye on them at all. And they didn't seem to call their situation in very quickly, either. Except that once . . . the time they'd missed the recon drone. *That* time he'd lost almost thirty men and women to the ground-attack aircraft—or more probably shuttles, he'd decided—that had come screaming in out of the night.

In fact, he'd come to suspect that the "recon" drones he'd been downing were actually the Shongairi's primary communications platforms. That they carried Shongair ground units' uplinks to their communications net as well as served as reconnaissance platforms. In some ways, that might actually make sense, although putting so many eggs into a single basket that way seemed a questionable decision to him.

Of course, a lot probably depended on the threat environments they'd faced before. He could think of a few situations in which it might have made reasonably good sense to combine platforms that way. For one thing, it would have reduced the amount of equipment they had to schlep around—and service—in the field. It might let them economize on specialist personnel, as well, by putting the same . . . people in charge of both functions. So if they thought those platforms were safe from enemy action, then, yeah, it wouldn't have been totally insane for them to piggyback functions that way.

But even if the Shongairi had made the decision for reasons that made sense at the time, they had to be dumber than rocks not to have . . . revisited their choice in light of what had been happening to them since arriving on Earth. Or not to have figured out how to reduce their vulnerabilities, at least! Although the drones were relatively fast and surprisingly maneuverable, they made no *use* of that maneuverability. They simply parked themselves above the unit to which they were assigned and moved steadily along at that unit's pace. Even in a combat situation, instead of dodging or taking any sort of evasive action, they only *sat* there, looking down. The closest he'd seen any of them come to trying to avoid ground fire had been to ascend to around five hundred feet and hover there.

That was high enough to make them extremely difficult targets for most riflemen, but they were sitting ducks for the FIM-92 Stingers he'd been able to salvage from a New York National Guard Armory. The Stinger had a maximum range of over five thousand yards and—even more importantly—could reach a maximum altitude of over *twelve* thousand feet. Of course, he was starting to run low on Stingers, and God only knew where he was going to lay hands on more of them, but it still seemed incredibly stupid to operate what were apparently such vital links in their communications system in such a vulnerable fashion. Especially when it was painfully evident they didn't *have* to do it.

Not that he intended to complain, and he had three of his remaining dozen or so Stingers deployed in the woods on the north side of the interstate. Unless this was a much larger convoy than he expected, it would have only two of the drones deployed above it, and they'd be easy kills for the Stingers.

As soon as the drones went down, his infantry—also deployed in the trees north of the highway—would open up with M136s to kill the APCs at either end of the convoy while his three machine guns ripped hell out of the unarmored trucks themselves. He had a total of forty riflemen, as well, all with M16s, and a dozen of them had under-barrel 40-millimeter grenade launchers. They wouldn't have a lot of time to work with—he'd impressed on all of them that they had thirty seconds, max, from the time the first APC blew up until they boogied for the vehicles waiting on State Road 202 to take them straight to the hospital. They needed to get out and get hidden quickly—preferably before any of those orbital sensors he was sure were up there, however inefficiently they might seem to be used, got the word to start tracking vehicles fleeing the area.

Thirty seconds might not sound like much, but in combat, he'd discovered, it could seem like an eternity. It ought to be long enough, at any rate. With that many rifles to support the machine guns they should be able to kill almost all the Shongairi in the convoy before they boogied. And so far, at least, he'd seen no sign that the aliens were even close to adjusting their response patterns enough to close that window on him.

Of course, if they *did* adjust properly, he'd probably only get to find out about it once, now wouldn't he?

He snorted at the thought, yet it was true, and he wondered sometimes if their failure to change their doctrine quickly indicated that they were simply inherently bad at improvising or adapting for some reason. One of his instructors at the Air Force Academy had insisted that one major reason the Japanese had lost World War II so decisively was that the Japanese language was much more poorly suited to improvisation, to changing plans on the fly, than English was. After all, she'd pointed out, cognitive thought was bound up in the syntax of the thinker's native speech, and so was the ability to quickly and clearly communicate changes in plan to subordinates. That, she had argued, was a primary reason Japanese units had persisted in trying to drive through even a broken plan rather than stopping what wasn't working and coming up with a new approach on the fly . . . something US Marine units had been very *good* at doing. Was it possible the Shongairi had something like the same problem on steroids?

It was an intriguing possibility, but in his bleaker moments he knew it wasn't really going to matter in the end. The aliens were still at the top of the gravity well, still able to drop rocks on anybody who pissed them off. Ultimately, Dan Torino and other people like him—people who no longer had anything to lose—could kill a lot of them, but they couldn't *stop* them. He was pretty sure this invasion had already cost them a lot more heavily than they'd expected, yet in the end, they could literally blast the human race back into the Stone Age anytime they chose.

There's probably some point on a graph somewhere, he thought now. *Some point where the cost of* subjugating *the Earth crosses the value of* conquering *the Earth more or less intact. The point where they decide to just go ahead and take out all of our infrastructure, kill however many of us it takes to make us give up, rather than try to preserve it for whatever value it may generate for them down the road. And if there is, then probably what I'm doing is the worst damn thing I could possibly do. I'm one of the people pushing that "cost" line higher and higher, when any rational person should probably be thinking about ways to convince them not to kill any more of us than they have to. But I guess I'm just not rational that way anymore. And neither are a hell of a lot of other human beings, from what I've heard. Not so far, at least.*

He grimaced, but he didn't change his mind. He knew he wasn't going to, either. Maybe it was the wrong thing to do, and maybe ultimately it was only going to get the human race hurt even worse than it already had been, but he simply couldn't *not* do it. He'd kill every single Shongair he could, and he'd go right on doing it until he was out of ammunition and he ripped out his last kill's throat with his bare teeth and fingernails. That was just the way it was.

"Hsssst! I hear them coming!" his second in command hissed softly, and he nodded.

"Good," Longbow Torino said quietly, chambering a round in his own M16. "Good."

. XXIII .

Platoon Commander Dirak didn't like this one bit, but orders were orders.

He moved slowly at the center of his second squad, ears up and straining for the slightest sound as he followed the double-twelve troopers of his first squad along the narrow road. The trail, really, because calling the narrow lane of roughly graded dirt a "road" was being far too generous. It was better than many he'd seen on other conquered worlds, but compared to *this* world's usual road net. . . .

Unfortunately, it was all he had at the moment, and his people had been civilized for a thousand standard years. Much of the acuity of hearing and scent which had once marked the margin between death and survival had slipped away, and he felt more than half blind in this heavily shadowed, massive forest.

There were no longer any forests like this on his homeworld—not with this towering primeval canopy and tree trunks which could be half as broad as a Shongair's height at the base—yet the woodland around him was surprisingly free of brush and undergrowth. According to the expedition's botanists that was only to be expected in a mature forest where so little direct sunlight reached the ground. No doubt they knew what they were talking about, but it still seemed . . . wrong to Dirak. And, perversely, he liked the saplings and underbrush which did grow along the verge of this narrow trail even less. They probably confirmed the botanists' theories, since some sun did get through along the line the trail broke in the overhead canopy, but they also formed a dense, leafy wall along the trail's borders which left him feeling cramped and shut in.

Actually, a lot of his anxiety was probably due to the fact that he'd been expressly ordered to leave his assigned recon and communications relay drone well behind his point, anchored to the wheeled transports snorting laboriously along the same trail far behind him. Analysis of what had happened to the last three patrols into this area suggested that the "humans" had somehow managed to destroy the drones before they ever engaged the infantry those drones were supporting with surveillance and secure communications. No one had any idea how the primitives—only, of course, they weren't really primitives, were they?—might have been able to detect and target them so effectively, but no one could be permitted to get away with inflicting that sort of losses. Something clearly had to be done to bring these attackers to heel, and the lack of honor they'd shown in not only refusing to submit when they'd so clearly been defeated but actually ambushing Shongair patrols like assassins had to be punished.

Unfortunately, standard tactics to accomplish those laudable ends didn't appear to be working, so HQ had decided to try a more stealthy approach . . . and chosen Dirak to carry out the experiment.

As it happened, Dirak had begun to formulate a theory of his own, not that anyone seemed particularly interested in hearing about it. Nor that he was especially eager to offer it, for that matter. The ancient, ancestral pack had not looked kindly upon beta and gamma members who jostled the pack alphas' elbows. Originality might have been valuable in a *leader,* but it had been dangerous in an undermember. In order to become a leader, an alpha had required the ability to think problems through, to adjust and recognize opportunities for advancement . . . which, of course, was the very thing which had made those qualities dangerous to an *established* pack leader when they manifested in one of his betas. And since one of the things at which effective pack leaders were supposed to excel was the elimination of threats to the pack—or to its leader—betas who seemed *too* smart had tended to suffer accidents . . . among other things. At the best of times, they'd been kept firmly in their places, even at the cost of completely ignoring good suggestions from them, lest *their* competence seem to undermine their *pack leader's* competence. Which, Dirak had occasionally thought, had not been a very consistent attitude even then . . . and certainly wasn't one *now.* Unfortunately, it seemed to be programmed into his people at an almost genetic level, despite the inherent inefficiency it represented.

It never occurred even to Dirak that his ability to recognize that problem even in the privacy of his own mind made him significantly different from the majority of his kind. On the other hand, it *did* occur to him that—as a human might have put it—the brightest and tallest flowers got picked (or cut) first.

We ought to figure out a way to get past that, he thought . . . very cautiously, with no intention of ever sharing the thought with another soul. *The Empire's going to need the best, sharpest thinkers we can find when the time comes to deal with the weed-eaters and their sycophants. Yet we're systematically depriving ourselves of that very quality. Or, at least, we're certainly not* encouraging *it!*

Well, no one had ever suggested every aspect of Shongair nature was perfect, he supposed. Still, he was tempted to suggest—to his immediate superior, at least—that part of the problem might be that their operational doctrine was still constrained by their experience against primitive foes. A reconnaissance and communication remote at three hundred *marshag* was effectively beyond the reach of any bow or crossbow the Shongairi had ever encountered. There was no need for them to be particularly evasive targets when no one had the range to knock them down anyway. *These* creatures' weapons, however, *did* have the range to knock them down, so might it not make a modicum of sense to think about programming the remotes to at least . . . move around some? Dodge? Be something besides a motionless target?

In the meantime, though, he had his orders. He *had* done a little modification of his own, without mentioning it to his company commander, and *his* remote was in constant motion, circling and turning in midair. Of course, that presented a few problems of its own, given that no one had ever considered the desirability of designing hardware to stabilize the view from drones that didn't dodge around a lot, anyway. He couldn't simply lock his drone's pickup on a single point and let a turreted lens and onboard software keep his area of interest centered while the vehicle circled the area, the way a human operator might have done in similar circumstances. It was making him a little dizzy when he surveyed his tactical board, since he wasn't accustomed to having his aerial viewpoint moving around that way, but if it helped keep the RC undestroyed, he'd put up with a little vertigo.

Oh, how the gods must have smiled upon me for me to draw this duty, he reflected morosely. *I understand the need to gain experience against these . . . creatures, the need to blood our inexperienced troops, get a better idea of their tactical capabilities. And of course they can't be permitted to dishonorably massacre our warriors and then get away unpunished! But why did* I *get chosen to poke* my *head into the* hasthar*'s den? It wasn't like—*

He heard an explosion behind him, the display board linked to his remote went abruptly dead, and he wheeled towards the thunderous sound. He couldn't see through the overhead canopy, but he didn't need to see it to know the explosion had been his RC drone. Apparently its evasions hadn't been evasive enough, but how had they even *seen* it through these damnable leaves and branches?!

The question was still ripping through his brain when he heard more explosions—this time on the ground . . . where his two reserve squads were following along in their APCs.

He hadn't yet had time to realize what *those* explosions were before the assault rifles hidden behind trees and under drifts of leaves all along the southern flank of the trail opened fire.

And, unfortunately for Platoon Commander Dirak's future as a Shongair innovator, the men and women behind those assault rifles had figured out how to recognize a Shongair infantry formation's commanding officer.

· · · · ·

"CEASE FIRE! *CEASE* fire!" Stephen Buchevsky bellowed, and the bark and chatter of automatic weapons fire faded abruptly.

He held his own position, M16 still ready, while he surveyed the kill zone and the tumbled, grotesquely sprawled drift of Shongair bodies. One or two were still writhing, although it didn't look like they would be for long.

"Good," a voice said behind him with fierce, obvious satisfaction, and he looked over his shoulder. Mircea Basarab stood in the dense forest shadows, looking out over the ambushed patrol. "Well done, my Stephen."

"Maybe so, but we better be moving," Buchevsky replied, safeing his weapon and rising from his firing position.

His own expression, he knew, was more anxious than Basarab's. This was the third hard contact with the Shongairi in the six days since he'd placed his people under Basarab's command, and from what the Romanian had said, they were getting close to the enclave he'd established in the mountains around Lake Vidraru. Which meant they really needed to shake this persistent—if inept—pursuit.

"I think we have a short while," Basarab disagreed, glancing farther down the trail to the columns of smoke rising from what had been armored vehicles until Jonescu's squad and half of Basarab's original men dealt with them. "It seems unlikely they got a message out this time, either."

"Maybe not," Buchevsky conceded. "But their superiors have to know at least roughly where they are. When they don't check in on schedule, someone's going to come looking for them. Again."

He might have sounded as if he were disagreeing, but he wasn't, really. First, because Basarab was probably correct. But secondly, because over the course of the last week or so, he'd come to realize Mircea Basarab was one of the best officers he'd ever served under. Which, he reflected, was high praise for any foreign officer from any Marine . . . and didn't keep the Romanian from being one of the scariest men Buchevsky had ever met.

A lot of people might not have realized that. In better light, Basarab's face had a bony, foxlike handsomeness and his smile was frequently warm. Buchevsky was convinced the warmth in that smile was genuine, too, but there were also dark, still places behind those brilliant green eyes. Still places which were no stranger to all too many people from the post-Ceausescu Balkans or the Afghan mountains where Buchevsky had spent so much time. Dark places Master Sergeant Stephen Buchevsky recognized because he'd met so many other scary men in his life . . . and because there was now a dark, still place labeled "Washington, DC" inside him, as well.

Yet whatever lay in Basarab's past, the man was almost frighteningly competent, and he radiated a sort of effortless charisma Buchevsky had seldom encountered. The sort of charisma which could win the loyalty of even a Stephen Buchevsky, and even on such relatively short acquaintance.

"Your point is well taken, my Stephen," Basarab said now, smiling almost as if he'd read Buchevsky's mind and reaching up to place one hand on the towering American's shoulder. Like the almost possessive way he said "my Stephen," it could have been patronizing. It wasn't.

"However," he continued, his smile fading, "I believe it may be time to send these vermin elsewhere."

"Sounds great to me." A trace of skepticism edged Buchevsky's voice, and Basarab chuckled. It was not a particularly pleasant sound.

"I believe we can accomplish it," he said, and whistled shrilly.

Moments later, Take Bratianu, a dark-haired, broad-shouldered Romanian in a leather jerkin festooned with knives, hand grenades, and extra rifle magazines, blended out of the forest.

Buchevsky was picking up Romanian quickly, thanks to Elizabeth Cantacuzène, but the exchange which followed was far too rapid for his still rudimentary grasp of the language to sort out. It lasted for a few moments, then Bratianu nodded and Basarab turned back to Buchevsky.

"Take speaks no English, I fear," he said.

That *was obvious,* Buchevsky thought dryly. On the other hand, Bratianu didn't *need* to speak English to communicate the fact that he was one seriously bad-assed individual. None of Basarab's men did.

There were only twenty of them, but they moved like ghosts. Buchevsky was no slouch in the field, yet he knew when he was outclassed at pooping and snooping in the shrubbery. These men were far better at it than he'd ever been, and in addition to rifles, pistols, and hand grenades, most of them—like Bratianu himself—were liberally equipped with a ferocious assortment of knives, hatchets, and machetelike blades that would have served perfectly well as short swords like the old Roman *gladius*. Indeed, Buchevsky suspected they would have preferred using cold steel instead of any namby-pamby assault rifles.

Now, as Bratianu and his fellows moved along the trail, knives flashed and the handful of Shongair wounded stopped writhing.

Buchevsky had no problem with that. Indeed, his eyes were bleakly satisfied. But when some of the Romanians began stripping the alien bodies while others began cutting down several stout young saplings growing along the edge of the trail, he frowned and glanced at Basarab with one eyebrow raised.

The Romanian only shook his head.

"Wait," he said, and Buchevsky turned back to the others.

They worked briskly, wielding their hatchets and machetes with practiced efficiency as they cut the saplings into roughly ten-foot lengths, then shaped points at either end. In a surprisingly short period they had over a dozen of them, and Buchevsky's eyes widened in shock as they calmly began picking up dead Shongairi and impaling them.

They worked their way through the entire stack of bodies who'd fallen to Buchevsky's own ambush, cutting more saplings when their original supply ran out. Blood and other body fluids oozed down the crude, rough-barked stakes, but he said nothing as the stakes' other ends were sunk into the soft woodland soil. Twenty-five dead aliens hung there, lining the trail like insects mounted on pins, grotesque in the tree shadows, and he felt Basarab's eyes.

"Are you shocked, my Stephen?" the Romanian asked quietly.

"I . . ." Buchevsky inhaled deeply. "Yeah, I guess I am. Some," he admitted. He turned to face the other man. "I think maybe because it's a little too close to some of the things I've seen jihadies do to make the point that nobody better fuck with them."

"Indeed?" Basarab's eyes were cold. "I suppose I should not be surprised by that. *We* learned the tradition long ago from their Turkish co-religionists, after all, and it would seem some things do not change. But at least these were already dead when they were staked."

"Would it have made a difference?" Buchevsky asked quietly, and Basarab's nostrils flared. But then the other man gave himself a little shake.

"Once?" He shrugged. "No. As I say, the practice has long roots in this area. One of Romania's most famous sons, after all, was known as 'Vlad the Impaler,' was he not?" He smiled thinly. "For that matter, I did not, as you Americans say, have a happy childhood myself, and there was a time when I inflicted cruelty on all those about me. When I *enjoyed* it. In those days, no doubt, I would have preferred them alive."

He shook his head, and his expression saddened as he gazed at the impaled alien bodies.

"I suppose there have been many like me. Men who have been so angered, so hurt, by what was done to them or those they loved that they became monsters themselves. I think, though, that I became . . . more of the monster than many of them. I am not proud of all in my past, my Stephen, but neither am I mad any longer. I have been more fortunate than some of those others, because I have had time to wrestle with my inner demon. I have even been able to travel, to see other lands, visit other places not so soaked in memories of blood and violence. To let some of the voices screaming in my head fall silent, soothed by peace. I remember a doctor I spoke to once—in Austria I think it was. . . ."

His voice trailed off, and his eyes grew distant as he gazed at the impaled bodies. Then they refocused on the present, and he looked back at Buchevsky.

"Even so, I fear it took too many years—years that demanded too high a price from those for whom I cared, and those who cared for me—before I realized at last that all the cruelty in the universe cannot avenge a broken childhood or appease an orphaned young man's rage at what was done to him and to those he loved."

He glanced at the bodies again, then shook himself once more—this time with a brisker, more businesslike expression—and turned his back on them, as if he were turning his back upon that broken childhood, as well.

"But this, my Stephen, has nothing to do with the darkness inside me," he said.

"No?" Buchevsky raised an eyebrow.

"No. It is obvious these vermin will persist in pursuing us. So we will give them something to fix their attention upon—something to make any creature, even one of these, hot with hate. And then we will give them someone besides your civilians to pursue. Take and most of my men will head south, leaving a trail so obvious that even these"—he twitched his head at the slaughtered patrol without looking away from the towering Marine—"could scarcely miss it. He will lead them aside until they are dozens of kilometers away. Then he will slip away and return to us."

"Without their being able to follow him?"

"Do not be so skeptical, my friend!" Basarab chuckled and squeezed Buchevsky's shoulder. "I did not pick these men at random! There are no more skilled woodsmen in all of Romania. Have no fear that they will lead our enemies to us."

"I hope you're right," Buchevsky said, looking back at the impaled bodies and thinking about how *he* would have reacted in the aliens' place. "I hope you're right."

. XXIV .

Water sloshed around Pieter Ushakov's legs as the raft grounded and he waded the last few meters to the eastern bank of the Voronezh River.

He tried not to think too hard about the nature of some of the flotsam and jetsam they'd encountered on the way across. It helped—some—that he'd seen so much carnage by now that he'd been largely anesthetized, but there were still moments. Especially when the bodies were so small they reminded him of—

He chopped that thought off before it could fully form and looked around warily, AK-74 ready. He'd needed it once already today, but no immediate threat presented itself, and he relaxed . . . slightly.

The city of Voronezh, capital of the Russian oblast of the same name, had been the site of savage combat during World War II's Stalingrad campaign. It had been rebuilt after the war, recovering to a population of over eight hundred thousand by 2010. Home to Voronezh State University, it had been one of Russia's more cosmopolitan cities, although the locals sometimes wished it hadn't. Foreign students attending universities in Russia usually went to Voronezh State University for a year first to hone their Russian language skills, and there'd been occasional clashes—some of them nasty—between the native Russians and the influx of foreigners.

That wasn't going to happen anymore, he thought grimly, climbing to the stub of the more southern of the two highway bridges which had once crossed the river and gazing back into the west while he waited for the rest of his men to join him. The destruction the Nazis had visited on Voronezh in the 1940s was nothing compared to the total devastation the Shongairi had inflicted.

He and his thirty-five-man company of partisans were lucky they'd made it across the river alive. Despite the totality with which three-quarters of the city had been literally obliterated, there were still ruins around the periphery, and those ruins were inhabited. If "inhabited" was the right word for half-starved bands of looters fighting over whatever food or other supplies might still be available in the wreckage, at any rate. Thirty-five well-fed (relatively speaking, at least) men with obviously hefty knapsacks had presented a tempting target for ambushes, even if they were all armed. Fortunately, only one band of marauders had been foolish or desperate enough to actually try an attack . . . which had resulted in the elimination of the band in question.

Of course, we haven't made it all *the way across yet, have we, Pieter?* he reminded himself sourly.

They'd crossed the worst of the devastation—and most of what had been the city—but the hinterland in front of them might be even worse. It had been devastated by blast and fire, especially along its western edge, along the river, and from here it looked as if there'd been at least one additional kinetic impact to the northeast, but it had been outside the primary impact zone. The majority of its structures were still more or less standing, and the burned-out sea of shattered walls, roofless ruins, and battered industrial buildings offered all manner of unpleasant possibilities. That was one reason he'd chosen to cross this stretch in daylight, when they'd have a better chance of seeing trouble coming.

Ushakov turned his head as Lieutenant Ivan Anatoliavitch Kolesnikov climbed up the bridge ramp to join him. Kolesnikov had been the senior platoon commander in his own company; now he and Ushakov were the only surviving officers of their entire engineering battalion. For that matter, as far as Ushakov knew, he, Kolesnikov, and Sergeant Fyodor Ivanovich Belov were the battalion's only survivors—period.

"Well, that looks unpleasant," Kolesnikov said, turning to survey the wasteland east of them. "Stinks, too."

Ushakov nodded. Murdered cities, he'd discovered, had a charnel reek all their own—one that persisted well after the people who lived in them had been slaughtered. The heat didn't help, either. He figured it had to be at least fifty degrees—what he supposed he would have had to get used to calling ninety degrees if he'd ever gotten around to taking Aldokim's offer and gone to work somewhere they used the Fahrenheit system. That was pretty damned hot for Voronezh, even at this time of year, and the temperature and humidity combined to produce a sauna.

And to enhance the stench.

"I won't be sorry to get back out into the open countryside myself," Ushakov said now. "And not just because of the stink."

"I know what you mean." Kolesnikov grimaced. "You know, if *I'd* lived here I'd have moved out by now. All the farmland around here, you'd think at least some of these people would be considering the possibility of turning farmer before they starve!"

Ushakov nodded again. The farmland around Voronezh was rich and fertile, even by Ukrainian standards. And Kolesnikov was right—if the people hunkering down in the city's ruins had only been willing to divert their efforts to farming they'd have found themselves far better off in a few months' time, when today's heat would be only a bitterly missed memory.

They're going to starve . . . if they don't freeze to death first, he thought from behind blue eyes which had died with his family. *God only knows what winter's going to be like, but I'd be surprised if twenty-five percent of the preinvasion population survives till spring. Assuming the fucking Shongairi let* anyone *survive.*

He was fairly confident it was going to be a moot point in his own case. And even though he'd never admitted it aloud to anyone—not even Kolesnikov—the aching void inside him was glad it would be so. He'd keep as many of his men alive as long as he could, but when the time came for the pain to finally end. . . .

He wiped sweat from his forehead, turning to watch the rest of his men wade ashore from the raft they'd constructed.

One good thing about engineers, he thought mordantly. *We're good at improvising river crossings.*

They were good at blowing things up, too, he reflected, and that was what they'd been doing for the last five ugly weeks. Or until they'd started running out of targets, at least.

For a while, he'd been able to keep track—generally, at least—of what was happening elsewhere over the Internet. Then, two and a half weeks ago, the Internet had suddenly stopped working. There appeared to be a handful of nodes still in operation, but that handful was shrinking steadily, which suggested that either the Shongairi were systematically destroying them as they found them, or else the power net was finally going completely down.

Either of those was a bad sign. Not that there'd been any *good* signs lately.

The American Admiral Robinson's posting of the destruction of twenty or thirty Shongair landing shuttles had done more than Ushakov would have believed possible for his own morale when he finally viewed it on his Army-issue laptop. It had obviously encouraged quite a few other people with the realization that the aliens weren't truly invincible, as well. A French antiaircraft battery had taken down three more shuttles—the smaller, faster ones the Shongairi apparently used for air-mobile infantry operations—as well, and there were rumors the Shongairi had been savagely bloodied by an American armored battalion the prelanding bombardment had somehow overlooked in Afghanistan.

Aside from that, though, the news had been an unending succession of reports of Shongair landings, devastated cities, collapsing public services, and the onset of disease and starvation as transportation nets and public hygiene began to fail.

Ushakov estimated that he and his "company"—although it would barely have qualified as a platoon before the Shongairi had arrived—had killed well over a thousand of the aliens so far. For that matter, his initial IED attack might have killed that many all by itself. He'd never been able to get a body count on that one, though, since the Shongairi had airlifted out all their dead before he'd ever left his camouflaged hide, so he hadn't added them to his official tally. He was certain they'd gotten at least that many since then, though. The fact that the aliens were astonishingly short on airlift for an interstellar invasion force helped a lot in that respect. They made heavy use of human road networks in their operational areas, and that concentrated targets where humans could get at them. Assuming, of course, that the human attackers knew which roads the targets were using at any given moment.

At first, there'd been quite a few of those targets close to home. Now, though, Shongair convoys were getting thin on the ground. From the last few hints he'd gotten before the Internet went down, Ushakov suspected the Shongairi had realized their initial deployment pattern had been . . . overly ambitious. They'd apparently thought they could use relatively small, widely separated forces to secure control of vast areas of the planet, which seemed uncommonly stupid to Ushakov. Surely they should have realized there were enough human beings and enough guns lying around Earth to turn squad-level detachments into targets too tempting to pass up!

From the sound of things that realization had finally percolated through whatever they used for brains, however. If he was right, they were pulling their forces in, concentrating them in smaller geographical areas in the first step of initiating some sort of pacification program.

Well, "pacification" worked wonderfully as hell for us *when the fucking Soviets dragged us into Afghanistan, didn't it?* he thought sourly, remembering Vladislava's uncles and his own father's cousin Ilarion. *Admittedly, the Americans and their allies had a lot better luck there than we did, but even they found the* mujahedin*—I'm sorry, the* Taliban, *as if there were a frigging difference!—a royal pain in the ass. And they had at least some notion about how to convince the locals they were the good fellows and the other side were the bad fellows, which this Thikair obviously doesn't. Well, the Soviets never quite got the hang of that when it was our turn in Afghanistan, but even* they *came closer to it than this! So unless he miraculously* gets *some notion, I don't imagine friend Thikair's long-eared bastards are going to find it a whole lot easier than* we *did.*

For the moment, though, the Shongairi appeared to be concentrating on North America and letting Europe and the rest of the world stew in its own juices. After all, starvation and disease would do most of their job for them if they were only patient. Ushakov didn't know how badly Asia and China had been hit, but the estimates he'd heard over the Internet were that India alone had probably suffered close to four hundred million dead in just the initial strikes. Other reports suggested China had gotten hammered even harder than that after the Central Committee (or something calling itself that, at any rate) had called for simultaneous uprisings in all of their major cities. He'd never been particularly fond of the Chinese—that much of the old Soviet tradition and its prejudices had carried over—but his stomach tightened every time he thought of what had probably happened to any city which had obeyed *that* order.

There wasn't anything he could do about that, however. In fact, if he was going to be realistic there wasn't anything he could do *effectively* about much of anything. But there had to be a limit to the Shongairi's resources somewhere. Somewhere, at some point, the bastards had to simply run out of manpower. Maybe humanity couldn't kill enough of them to reach that point, but Pieter Ushakov damned well meant to try.

Which was why he and his company were trekking steadily eastward.

The Shongairi had apparently reduced their presence—outside North America, at least—to a series of zones, each no more than two or three hundred kilometers across and centered on the ground bases they'd established immediately after the bombardment. There didn't appear to be any of those bases in what had been Ukraine, but there was supposed to be one near the town of Inzhavino in Tambov oblast, five hundred–odd kilometers southeast of the ruins of Moscow. That was close to eight hundred kilometers from what was left of Kiev, but he was almost halfway there.

Another week to Inzhavino, he thought. *Maybe more like ten days, under the circumstances. But we've only got another hundred kilometers or so to go before we get into their "occupation zone," and we'll start finding targets pretty quickly then.*

He didn't know if it was going to do any good at all in the long run. For his planet and his species, at any rate. But that didn't really matter to him, and it didn't really matter to any of the men with him, either. Because one way or the other, it was going to do one hell of a lot of good for the vengeful hunger blazing inside all of them.

We may not last long, he thought with bleak, bitter satisfaction, *but these fuckers are* damned *well going to know we were here.*

"Come on, Vanya!" he said, slapping Kolesnikov on the shoulder. "If we get a move on, we can be clear of all this wreckage by sunset and find a nice secure spot to bivouac for the night."

. XXV .

Fleet Commander Thikair pressed the admittance stud on his chair arm when the signal chimed, and the briefing-room door hissed open. Ground Base Commander Shairez entered the compartment, crossed to the conference table, and lowered her ears in salute.

"You wished to see me, Fleet Commander?" Shairez said respectfully, and Thikair's ears flicked assent.

"I did, Ground Base Commander," he replied, and gestured at one of the chairs on the far side of the briefing-room table. Ground Force Commander Thairys sat to Thikair's left and Squadron Commander Jainfar sat to his right. Now Shairez sat, facing all three of her superiors calmly, and Thikair leaned forward, folding his six-fingered hands on the table before him.

"We've been engaged on KU-197-20 for one standard month, tomorrow," he said. "That is approximately two and a half local months, better than a double-twelfth of one of their years, and I think that makes this a reasonable time for us to assess our current situation. I wished you to attend this meeting so that you might hear Ground Force Commander Thairys' and Squadron Commander Jainfar's reports and so they might hear yours."

"Of course, Fleet Commander."

"Very well." Thikair turned his head to the left, looking at Thairys. "Ground Force Commander?" he invited.

"The situation remains far from satisfactory, Fleet Commander," Thairys said without flinching. "There have been improvements in some respects; in others, the situation has actually worsened. Our vehicular losses remain painfully high. Although we've had no more fiascoes like Harshair's, we continue to lose them in twelves and double-twelves—two or three here, another two over there, three more trucks and an APC over here. And occasionally, unfortunately, the humans get lucky and take out an entire convoy of as many as a double-twelve or more trucks in a single raid."

His ears shrugged unhappily.

"Infantry losses also remain high, but it's the loss of vehicles which causes me the greatest concern. We have only limited shuttle-lift capability—or, rather, only limited tactical *troop* lift capability. While the humans' supply of what they call 'SAMs' appears to be gradually depleting itself, they retain far too many of them for me to be comfortable operating Starlanders anywhere near an actual scene of combat. We've lost even Deathwings to them, which is bad enough, but at least a Deathwing carries no more than a single platoon of infantry at a time.

"The consequence of restricting Starlander operation only to rear area movements is to severely cramp our tactical flexibility. We simply dare not move our forces around as swiftly and aggressively as our normal doctrine requires. In addition, the need to continually replenish personnel and material in an effort to keep pace with losses, coupled with the destruction of an entire heavy transport group on the very first day of landing operations, means the Starlanders we do have are heavily tasked with 'normal' space-to-surface landing operations. Which, of course, means they are unavailable for rear area logistic requirements, throwing an even greater burden upon our wheeled transport, which we've been losing in significant numbers from the very beginning. That's forced us to even further restrict our operations in the secondary and tertiary occupation zones in order to concentrate on the primary zones on the continent of North America.

"We've attempted to make up some of our transport deficiencies by impressing human equipment. Unfortunately, our people are significantly shorter than humans, and human heavy transport equipment is considerably more primitive than our own. The interiors of human vehicles are not sized for us, and most of their heavy vehicles use something they call 'manual transmissions.' In general, our people find it very difficult to develop any proficiency in operating them. We've resorted to attempting to hire or impress humans to operate that equipment for us, but with only limited success. Many humans simply refuse, even when threatened with reprisals. Others agree, then vanish—despite having honorably submitted, I might add—as soon as our backs are turned. Still others agree, then actually abscond with their cargoes at the first opportunity! Some of my field maintenance units are attempting to convert human vehicles to meet our needs, but the operational pace and the depletion of our own vehicle pool confronts them with monumental internal maintenance requirements. Frankly, Fleet Commander, despite the huge number of human vehicles on the continent, it would require some time—possibly as much as a standard year—to make worthwhile progress in providing our transport needs out of human-built equipment."

"I see." Thikair's ears nodded. "And the operations themselves?"

"We're making some progress." It seemed to Shairez that Thairys was choosing his words with some care. "Our primary operating zones in North America are expanding steadily. Unfortunately, the price in casualties remains high. Even human hunting and recreational weapons are, frankly, frighteningly effective against our infantry, and it would appear that on this continent, and particularly in the United States nation-state, there were more guns than there were *inhabitants* prior to our arrival! Most of those weapons now seem to be being employed against us.

"The good news is that our field grade and junior officers are making progress in adapting to this novel threat environment. I fear we still have quite some way to go before fully adjusting, but I see steady improvement in that regard. The other good news is that the frequency of attacks does seem to be declining, at least somewhat, and as Ground Base Commander Shairez suggested would be the case, we're seeing virtually no heavy weapons at this time. I believe I can confidently report that effectively all of their aircraft, armored units, and field artillery have been destroyed, although we continue to confront their human-portable antiarmor and antiair missiles and mortars."

"I see," Thikair said, and turned his gaze to Jainfar.

"In light of Ground Force Commander Thairys' losses, Squadron Commander, what can you tell us about the status of the industrial ships?"

"As you instructed me, Fleet Commander," Jainfar replied, "I instructed the ship commanders of *Imperial Sword* and *Stellar Dawn* to begin deployment last month. Our progress has been somewhat hampered by the overriding priority of providing enough maintenance techs to our ground forces, which has somewhat reduced the personnel available to me. We've modified our procedures, however, and I believe we've now effectively compensated for those diversions.

"Accordingly, I feel confident *Imperial Sword* can have our first industrial node operational within the next five standard months, which is one month sooner than doctrine and normal operational tempos would suggest. To do that, unfortunately, I'll be forced to divert personnel from *Stellar Dawn,* which will probably push *her* complete activation back by at least two standard months.

"I'm afraid, however, that our initial mission planning never contemplated material losses on the scale we've experienced. As a consequence, none of our industrial modules were programmed or configured to replace, for example, GEVs. The assumption was that we would require a more generalized capability, and both the software and the modules themselves are configured for the initial creation and expansion of a basic industrial presence and infrastructure, not the construction of heavy-combat equipment. I have personnel now working on how best to reconfigure to meet our actual current needs. My best estimate, however, is that it will be a minimum of six standard months before we'll be able to begin replacing Ground Force Commander Thairys' vehicle losses. If we comply with the requests of some of his brigade and division commanders that we upgrade our equipment to match or exceed the capabilities of the humans' combat vehicles, that delay will probably double. It might even be worse than that, which leads me to seriously question the wisdom of the effort, although I do have a team working on possible new design concepts in order to be as ready as we can if the ultimate decision is to upgrade.

"In addition, however, I fear that until *Stellar Dawn* and our full complement of resource-collection vessels come fully online and the solar furnaces can begin smelting resources from the local asteroids in adequate quantities, production levels will be limited. I believe it will be closer to nine standard months before we're in a position to truly begin rebuilding his original table of organization and equipment, even using completely unmodified designs."

Thikair managed not to wince, but only because he'd already known most of what Thairys and Jainfar were going to report. Six standard months would be fifteen human months—more than a full local year for the humans to continue whittling away at his dwindling forces. Thairys was right to focus on their losses in vehicles and shuttles, of course, but even infantry losses were several times the original expeditionary planners' estimates, and *those* couldn't be replaced even after the industrial ships came completely online. Only the fact that he'd been supplied with enough troopers to subdue—and then provide garrisons for—no less than three star systems had given them the depth to meet operational needs (and losses) to date, and Thikair had long since accepted that he'd have to write off the colonization of the other two systems. Indeed, he was beginning to wonder if he could continue to sustain present operational tempos long enough to complete even KU-197-20's conquest in the first place, far less occupy it properly afterward.

Oh, stop being so pessimistic! he scolded himself. *What's that phrase, that human phrase, Shairez shared with you the other day? The one about not getting discouraged just because things seem difficult? Darkest before the dawn, or something like that, wasn't it? Well, if even* these *creatures recognize the need not to give up just because the job looks a little tougher than you expected in the beginning, then certainly a member of any* civilized *race should be able to keep the same thing in mind!*

"Very well, Squadron Commander," he said out loud. "I won't pretend I'm delighted by your report, or by Ground Force Commander Thairys', but all any officer can ask of his warriors is that they do the very best they can under the circumstances and then honestly report the truth of their progress to him, which is what I'm sure you both have done. Having said that, of course, I want to see the expansion of our industrial capacity pressed forward as rapidly as possible. If you or any of your junior officers should see any way in which the process can be accelerated, by all means do so. And if you should discover that any additional resources or personnel could assist you in that regard, inform me immediately and I'll do my very best to get them for you."

"Of course, Fleet Commander," Jainfar replied, and Thikair turned to Shairez.

"And now for you, Ground Base Commander," he said.

"I regret to admit it, Fleet Commander," she began, "but I've been unable to meet the schedule you and I discussed prior to the landing. A great deal of that is due to the sheer mass of data we acquired from the humans' Internet and have had to sift and evaluate, of course. That task is still not completed, but we've reached a point at which I can safely delegate it to my own subordinates, which will free up time for me to deal with my other responsibilities. I hope that will put me in a position to make up some of the lost time, but I can't pretend I'm not considerably behind.

"In particular, I've been forced to defer my efforts to fully evaluate this species' psychology. I'm afraid that's one task I haven't been able to delegate."

Thikair very carefully kept his ears motionless, tending a smile.

"Haven't been able to delegate," indeed, he thought. *Haven't been willing to let anyone else play with that particular fascinating puzzle before* you *do, is what you mean, Ground Base Commander!*

He knew that wasn't completely fair to Shairez. She wasn't the sort to let her personal desires interfere with the performance of her duties or the discharge of her responsibilities. At the same time, she undoubtedly *was* fascinated by the bizarre fashion in which these creatures' brains apparently functioned.

And more to the point, he reflected more soberly, *she's probably the only senior officer I've got who's capable of figuring* out *how their brains work. Assuming they actually* do *work, that is!*

Not for the first time since arriving in this Cainharn of a star system, Thikair found himself wishing that at least a few more Shongairi had ever developed Shairez's interest in xenopsychology. Unfortunately, they hadn't.

"I intend to begin devoting the majority of my attention to that project as soon as possible," Shairez continued. "Hopefully, within the next month or so, I should be able to provide at least a preliminary analysis of their psychology and to determine whether or not they are, indeed, educable via neural educator technology."

Her own ears wiggled in a wry smile.

"Fortunately, my ground base's zone of responsibility is nowhere near as . . . lively as some of the other ground base commanders' zones. Most of the local human cities and towns have been abandoned, and no more than a twelfth-part of their populations have returned. I'm afraid there's been quite a lot of starvation among the humans, and also an upsurge in disease, but the decision to concentrate our primary efforts on North America and our major secondary effort on the western portion of Europe has simplified my own ground force commanders' tasks. In fact, I've been able to provide at least some degree of reinforcement to Base Commander Fursa's, whose ZOR is considerably more . . . active than my own."

"I'm happy to hear it's having a positive effect for someone, Ground Base Commander," Thairys said dryly.

"Well," Thikair said with a bleak ear lift of his own, "at least I'm fairly confident your operations are having consequences for the humans which are even less pleasant than our own experiences, Ground Force Commander."

.XXVI.

"That's the last of them, Longbow."

As Major Torino turned his head and looked over his shoulder at the tall, bearded, dark-skinned man who'd just spoken, it struck him once again just how unlikely anyone once would have considered his choice of second-in-command.

Abu Bakr bin Muhammed el-Hiri was an American-born convert to Islam. Prior to the Shongair invasion, he'd been one of the most vocal—indeed, vociferous—critics of the ongoing American involvement in Iraq and Afghanistan. He'd been accused many times of going further than simple criticism, in fact, and the name he'd chosen when he converted—"Abu Bakr, son of Muhammed, the Wildcat"—hadn't helped convince any of his accusers they were wrong. In fact, Torino was pretty sure they *hadn't* been wrong.

Despite his choice of a military career, and despite his own tendency to lose patience with the people he considered ostriches, Torino had always accepted the legitimacy of debating American foreign policy. He'd thought that people who argued that if America would only leave Islam alone, Islamic extremists would leave America alone were wrong, but he was willing to admit he might be wrong about that. The possibility wasn't going to keep him from doing everything he could to kick the shit out of anyone who messed with America, since he refused to allow himself to be paralyzed by "might have been," but he admitted it existed. And whatever other people might have thought about the subject, he'd never simply lumped all Muslims together any more than he'd lumped all of his fellow Baptists (or, for that matter, Methodists, Episcopalians, Lutherans, Presbyterians, and Catholics) together. Personally, he'd considered extremists of any persuasion—especially those prepared to resort to bombings, assassination, kidnappings, arson, and/or armed insurrection against the laws of legally elected representative governments—lunatics, whatever the basis of their own particular lunacies, and he'd been perfectly prepared to do whatever it took to protect the people and the Constitution of the United States of America against *any* of them. Whether or not he and Abu Bakr might have agreed politically, other people had every right to form their own opinions, however. More than that, it was the responsibility of the American military to protect and defend everyone, not just the portion of "everyone" whose views happened to coincide with those of one Major Daniel Torino, unless they stepped across the bounds of disagreement into actual violation of the law.

Nonetheless, he couldn't escape the suspicion that Abu Bakr would not have found him a congenial dinner companion as recently as two or three months ago.

Of course, he thought grimly, things had changed.

"The Wildcat" might not have been a great admirer of American society or government, but he'd clearly decided the Shongairi were even worse. The fact that his entire family, aside from his younger brother Mus'ad, had been in Washington, DC, when it suddenly ceased to exist would probably have been enough to accomplish that all by itself. Yet over the two or three weeks since Abu Bakr had attached himself to Torino's band of raiders, the major had realized it wouldn't have taken that personal loss. Stereotypes had a tendency to disappear quickly in the crucible, and Torino had come to the realization that whatever Abu Bakr's politics might have been, they'd grown out of a genuine sense of commitment, a true belief in his principles, and a burning desire to do what he believed was right.

Perhaps he had become "a traitor to his country" by going further than simple participation in peaceable debate and legal political activism. Torino didn't know for sure about that, and he wasn't going to ask, because it no longer mattered to him any more than the fact of his own uniform (when he could find one) and "Crusader" heritage mattered to Abu Bakr. What mattered at the moment was that Abu Bakr was smart, tough, determined, disciplined, capable as hell, and just as determined to kill Shongairi as Daniel Marcus Torino himself.

Assuming either one of them had been going to survive (which they damned well weren't), they might well have found themselves in opposing positions once more. For the moment, however, both of them had other things to think about.

"How many made it?" Torino asked now.

"Not as many as we'd hoped," Abu Bakr replied grimly. "Looks like something must've happened to Hammond. There's no sign of his van—or of Clifton or Breyer, either."

Torino nodded, keeping his face expressionless. He'd had lots of practice at that since that eons-ago day he'd been ordered to Plattsburgh.

Despite that, Abu Bakr's report made it harder than it would have been under other circumstances. He'd deliberately broken their band up into smaller groups of no more than two or three vehicles each and sent each subgroup down a separate route, or at least separated them by a day or two if they were using the same route. Each group had been well armed, with leaders who'd survived the same learning curve Torino and Abu Bakr had survived. They ought to have been able to take care of themselves under most circumstances, and he'd judged that traveling that way was less likely to attract the Shongairi's attention than moving in a larger, more noticeable convoy would have. He was still confident he'd been right about that, and Eric Hammond's had been the best-manned and armed of them all. But that didn't change the fact that he hadn't arrived after all . . . or that he'd been transporting four of their remaining Stingers and that Jane Breyer had been the best they had at convincing frightened refugees to risk talking to them, not to mention a near-genius at constructing homemade Claymore mines. In some ways, though, the news that Angie Clifton hadn't made the rendezvous point was even worse. She'd been their only trained physician . . . and the majority of their scavenged medical supplies had been in the trunk of her car.

Well, you all knew it was going to be a risk using the roads, he told himself grimly. *And not just because of the Shongairi, either. That's why you came down through the mountains and followed the Parkway as far as you could to stay off the interstates. You weren't just avoiding the puppies; you were staying as far away as you could from* human *scavengers with guns, too. The truth is, you're damned lucky you got this far without losing even more people, and you know it!*

The fact that that was true was cold comfort at the moment, but he'd gotten used to moments like that over the last two or three months, as well.

He closed his eyes for a moment, squeezing the bridge of his nose between thumb and forefinger while he considered what to do next.

Targets had gotten progressively thinner on the ground in the Northeast, especially after the Shongairi finally lost patience and destroyed New York City and Boston. Not to mention Syracuse, Albany, and Buffalo, in New York State; Springfield and Bridgeport, in Massachusetts; Paterson,

Newark, and Jersey City, in New Jersey; Philadelphia, Pittsburgh, and Harrisburg, in Pennsylvania; and Cleveland and Akron, in eastern Ohio. There'd probably been even more cities and towns than he'd heard about, but that had been enough to make the aliens' attitude towards the swath between Maryland and Canada abundantly clear. The destruction of all of those cities together had probably killed less than another couple of million Americans, given the mass exodus from any conveniently concentrated urban target, but New York, Pennsylvania, and eastern Ohio had already been sinking into complete chaos and anarchy because of that same exodus. Now it looked like the panic the fresh wave of devastation had induced had effectively finished public order off completely.

It hadn't happened because surviving local governments and law enforcement agencies weren't trying their damnedest to prevent it, either. You simply couldn't displace that many members of an urban population with no experience of producing their own food—and no *means* of producing it, even if they'd known how—without mammoth disruptions. Throw in the breakdown of public health systems, the disappearance of gasoline, the steady disintegration of the power grid, the sudden scarcity of medical supplies, and a refugee population with zero experience at maintaining sanitation and hygiene in mass encampments, and the recipe for anarchy was pretty much complete.

Of course, the loss on the very first day of so many of the people who would normally have been available to resist those disruptions hadn't helped. Torino still had no idea why that huge Homeland Security exercise had been called—he didn't *think* he would have been sent off to Plattsburgh without someone at least mentioning the possibility of an outside attack if anyone in Washington had really figured out "aliens" were coming—but one of the consequences had been to concentrate huge numbers of first responders in the very areas the Shongairi had blasted from orbit in the first wave. The survivors of Reserve and Guard units were mostly doing their best to assist whatever local government and law enforcement survived, but others were too busy doing what Torino himself was doing at the moment.

And still others, much as he hated facing the fact, were using their weapons and their own internal cohesion for much less selfless purposes. His own band had encountered two separate groups of onetime National Guardsmen whose leaders were busy setting up as local warlords. One of those leaders had made the mistake of attempting to add Torino's people—and especially their weapons—to his own "protective association." That particular would-be warlord was never going to bother anyone again, and a quarter of the liberated slaves he'd been "protecting" (the majority of whom, oddly enough, had been young, female, and physically attractive) had joined Torino. The ones who'd chosen not to had been given most of the thugs' weapons and directed towards Scranton, which had somehow survived the Shongairi's kinetic broom and where local officials were reported to have done a far better job of maintaining public order in Lackawanna and the surrounding counties. Of course, Torino figured there was a limit to how much longer Scranton would be able to continue absorbing refugees from the rest of the region. Eventually, the authorities would be forced to close their "borders" or go under like the areas around them.

For that matter, they might leave the border closing too late and go under anyway.

It looked to Torino as if the Shongairi were doing everything they could to encourage exactly that kind of disintegration, in which case they might simply be waiting until Scranton had attracted as many refugees as possible before striking *it,* as well. Of course, he could be wrong about that. He could simply be looking at the unintended consequences of a strategy which had completely different objectives. In either case, however, the confusion, anarchy, spreading starvation, and growing disease threat were far too vast for his limited resources to have made any difference. So, given that the Shongairi seemed to have completely withdrawn their ground forces from the area, he'd decided to shift hunting grounds.

It continued to amaze him how the tattered wreckage of a society which had been so totally dependent on cell phones and the Internet still managed to pass news along. It often got distorted in the process, yet he'd discovered it didn't get a lot more garbled than it had been with every yahoo in creation adding his own ten cents' worth of exaggeration when he posted his version of events (or, for that matter, his complete *fabrication* of events) online. And news and rumors spread with remarkable speed even without electronic media and even in a society which was rapidly disintegrating.

Assuming the reports they'd been able to pick up were remotely accurate, the Shongairi had established a base somewhere in North or South Carolina. Apparently, they'd modified their initial strategy from one of a general occupation to establishing what the US military would have called "Forward Operating Bases" and gradually extending perimeters of control from there. It made at least some sense, and from other bits and pieces they'd been able to piece together, the Carolinas—or, at least, *North*

Carolina—had been far less devastated than New England and the mid-Atlantic states. They hadn't been as heavily populated to begin with, and apparently they'd been hit less hard in the initial Shongair bombardment.

Well, that was the story on North Carolina, anyway. From the sound of things, South Carolina had taken a harder initial hit and had most of its state government knocked out on the very first day. At least he'd never heard anyone mention the South Carolina governor by name, whereas Judson Howell, the Governor of North Carolina, apparently continued to head a more or less functional state government.

If Torino had been an alien invader with a functional brain, it would have made sense to *him* to move in on a fairly stable area with a central authority he could compel to obey him, and that seemed to be exactly what the Shongairi had done. Which meant that if he wanted to find Shongair convoys to ambush and Shongair troopers to kill, North Carolina was the place to go looking for them.

If these people have *managed to maintain anything like a degree of public order,* he thought now, eyes still closed, *they probably aren't going to be very happy to see you, Dan. The last thing they or their families need is for you to be turning their state into the kind of disaster area you just left up north. Most of them probably don't like these flop-eared bastards any more than you do, but if you start getting them, or their wives, or their husbands, or their kids killed. . . .*

Well, if that was the way it was, that was the way it was. The Shongairi wouldn't have been pulling in their horns if they hadn't been getting hurt a lot worse than they'd ever counted on. From everything he'd been able to determine—which, admittedly, might not be all that accurate given the limitations on his communications—they were getting thinner and thinner on the ground. Especially in terms of transport. For that much, at least, he had confirmation from the five ex-truckers who'd fled after being drafted by the aliens to drive human trucks for them. All five of them had ended up joining him, and his raiders had been seeing the occasional human-built (and driven) tractor-trailer rig in the Shongair convoys they'd been hitting even before the aliens had shifted their stance.

Which means we're hurting *the fuckers,* he thought fiercely. *However bad it looks from our side,* they're *getting the shit kicked out of them by people just like us, too, or they wouldn't be resorting to using* our *equipment. So if we can just go* on *hurting them, go on bleeding them, hammering their capabilities back. . . .*

He decided—again—not to think about that cost-benefit graph he'd thought about outside Concord. Not to wonder whether or not he and his followers, people like Abu Bakr, had the right to go on killing Shongairi no matter what the aliens might ultimately decide to do about it.

Instead, he opened his eyes, nodded to Abu Bakr, and unfolded one of the North Carolina road maps they'd scavenged from the looted remnants of a gas station in Virginia. He laid it out on the hood of the Honda CRV he'd appropriated as his current "command vehicle" and both of them leaned over to look at it.

"We're about here," Torino said, tapping the line of US Highway 421 a couple of miles west of a small circle marked "Boone, North Carolina," and looked back up at his unlikely lieutenant. "According to everything we've heard, this base of theirs is down around Greensboro, about a hundred miles from here. I still don't want to use the interstate or highways any more than we have to; we're a lot more likely to run into puppy convoys or patrols or simply get spotted by their orbital recon if we try that. So it looks to me like our best bet is to stay on 421 to Wilkesboro, then take State-268 to Ronda and cross I-77 on US-21 and head for Boonville. From there we can take State-67 as far as Winston-Salem. I don't think there's any point planning further ahead than that till we get closer, get a better feel for what's going down hereabouts."

"Makes sense to me," Abu Bakr agreed, craning his neck to study the map. Then he shook his head. "Man, I thought some of those town names in the Pennsylvania boonies were weird! Ronda? Boonville? And what the heck is a 'Yadkinville'? Or a *'Pfafftown'*?"

Even now, Torino had noticed, Abu Bakr never swore, and he shook his own head with a crooked smile.

"Let's not be criticizing Southern naming conventions, Abu Bakr," he said. "*I'm* a Southern boy, you know. Grew up on what used to be the family farm off Snapfinger Road, in Georgia, as a matter of fact. You wanna make fun of *that* name?"

He didn't mention that the onetime family farm in question—and his parents—had been less than eleven miles from downtown Atlanta when the kinetic weapons arrived.

"Wouldn't dream of it!" Abu Bakr responded with a chuckle. "Matter of fact, that one actually makes sense. Sort of, at least. Lot more than 'Pfafftown,' anyway."

"I'm glad you approve. Now let's see about figuring out how we want to split up for the last stage."

. XXVII .

Fleet Commander Thikair pressed the admittance stud, then tipped back in his chair as Ground Base Commander Shairez stepped through the door into his personal quarters. It closed silently behind her, and he quirked his ears at her thoughtfully for a moment before he indicated another chair with the clawed tip of one finger.

"Be seated, Ground Base Commander," he said, deliberately formal because of the irregularity of meeting with her here.

"Thank you, Fleet Commander."

He watched her settle into the chair. She carried herself with almost her usual self-confidence, he thought, yet there was something about the set of her ears. And about her eyes.

She's changed, he thought. *Aged.* He snorted mentally. *Well, we've all* done that, *haven't we? But there's more to it in her case. More than when I last spoke to her over the com, in fact.*

Apprehension prickled through him at that realization, since their last conversation had been less than three of the local days ago. They'd had enough surprises since dropping out of hyper for anything which could affect the imperturbable, always efficient Shairez so obviously—and in such a short time—to make him acutely unhappy.

"What, precisely, did you wish to see me about, Ground Base Commander?" he asked after a moment. *And why,* he did not ask aloud, *did you wish to see me about it in* private?

"I've made substantial progress with my initial psychological profile of these humans, Sir. As I'd said in my last personal report to you, that project had been badly delayed by the more pressing emergencies which had to be dealt with immediately. In fact, I still haven't completed my full analysis of the results, but certain clear differences between Shongair and human psychology have already emerged. On the basis of those differences, unfortunately"—she met his gaze unwaveringly—"I've been forced to the conclusion that our initial hopes for this planet were . . . rather badly misplaced."

Thikair sat very still. It was a testimony to her inner strength that she'd spoken so calmly, he thought. It was clear from her expression and tone that she was *not* referring to any of the manifold problems they'd already experienced, which meant she'd discovered something even more disastrous. Not many subordinates could have brought that word to an imperial colonizing expedition's supreme commander without flinching . . . particularly when the hopes in question had been not "our" initial hopes, but *his* initial hopes.

He drew a deep breath, feeling his ears fold back against his skull, and closed his eyes while he considered how much those hopes had cost his expedition in just three local months. Of course, he reflected grimly, it had cost the humans even more. Yet no matter what he did, the insane creatures *refused* to submit.

Perhaps Shairez was about to explain that obstinacy of theirs to him. Odd to discover that he suddenly had so much less desire to have that riddle solved after all. Yet. . . .

"*How* badly misplaced?" he asked without opening his eyes.

"The problem, Sir," she replied a bit obliquely, "is that we've never before encountered a species like this one. Their psychology is . . . unlike anything in our previous experience."

"That much I'd already surmised," Thikair said with poison-dry humor. "Should I conclude you now have a better grasp of how it differs?"

"Yes, Sir."

Even the redoubtable Shairez hesitated for a moment, however, and it was her turn to inhale deeply before she resumed.

"First, Sir," she began then, "you must understand that there are huge local variations in their psychologies. That's inevitable, of course, given the fashion in which they've retained so many separate nation-states this late into their societal development. I confess, however, that even now I hadn't realized they retained so many bewilderingly different cultural and *societal* templates, as well. I'm afraid the degree to which their planetary communication net—and their entertainment media, in particular—had . . . cross-pollinated thanks to their communications satellites, Internet, and mass dissemination of 'movies' and recorded music helped me to underestimate their . . . profound diversity." Her ears flicked a shrug. "I've attempted throughout to remind myself that these creatures aren't *us,* that their developmental and evolutionary history bears no resemblance to our own. Yet I continue to find my own cultural experiences insisting that anyone with this level of technology must have developed some sort of common, worldwide culture. Except very superficially, however, that most definitely is *not* the case.

"There are, however, certain common *strands*. And one of those, Fleet Commander, is that, essentially, they have no submission mechanism as we understand the term."

"I beg your pardon?" Thikair's eyes popped open. Despite all their experience with this perverse, irrational, illogical species, that *couldn't* be true, could it? The very idea was preposterous!

"No *submission* mechanism?" he repeated, trying to be certain he'd actually understood her correctly. "*None?*"

Shairez seemed unsurprised by his reaction. She simply let her ears droop in an expression of weary, exhausted unhappiness and sighed.

"None, Sir," she confirmed heavily. "There are a few—a very few—other races of the Hegemony which perhaps approach the humans' psychology, but I can think of no more than two or three. All of them, like the humans, are omnivores, but none—not even the Kreptu—come close to this species' . . . level of perversity. Frankly, any Shongair psychologist would pronounce all humans insane, Sir, and in this case even the weedeaters would probably agree with us!"

Of course they would, Thikair thought bleakly. *Trust the Cainharn-cursed humans to be the first species* every *race of the Hegemony would proclaim mad!*

"Unlike herbivores," Shairez continued, using the technical term this time, instead of the customary pejorative, almost as if the precision of her language could protect her from what she was saying, "or even the overwhelming majority of omnivores, for that matter, they have a streak of very Shongair-like ferocity, yet their sense of self is almost invariably greater than their sense of the pack."

She was obviously groping for a way to describe something outside any understood racial psychology, Thikair thought.

"Almost all herbivores have a very strong herd instinct," she said. "While they may, under some circumstances, fight ferociously, their first and overwhelming instinct is to *avoid* conflict, and their basic psychology subordinates the individual's good—even his very survival—to the good of the 'herd.' Most of them now define that 'herd' in terms of entire planetary populations or star nations, but it remains the platform from which all of their decisions and policies proceed.

"Most of the Hegemony's omnivores share that orientation to a greater or a lesser degree, although a handful approach our own psychological stance, which emphasizes not the herd, but the *pack*. None of them approach it very *closely*, however, because for all of them the urge to seek prey is secondary—part of their survival imperatives, yes, but not *primary* to their race's early survival. None of them were at the top of their planetary food chains in their prehistoric, pretechnic periods. Indeed, most of them became tool users and eventually developed civilizations primarily because they were so poorly suited by nature as predators. They required tools and technology to overcome their inherent weakness and to protect themselves against *other* predators, and like the herbivores, flight from danger was more important in their evolutionary history, more central to their development, than the pursuit of prey.

"Our species, however, unlike any of the Hegemony's other member races, evolved primarily as *hunters*, not prey. Prior to our own tool-using period, we *were* at or near the very top of our planetary food chain, and so we evolved a social structure and psychology oriented around that primary function rather than a template designed to protect us from *other* predators. Unlike virtually all herbivores and the vast majority of omnivores, Shongairi's pride in our personal accomplishments—the proof of our ability—all relates to the ancient, primal importance of the individual hunter's prowess as the definer of his status within the pack.

"Yet the pack is still greater than the individual. Our sense of self-worth, of accomplishment, is validated only within the context of the pack. And the submission of the weaker to the stronger, of the follower to the leader—of the beta or the gamma to the alpha—comes from that same context. It isn't simply the basis of our honor code and our philosophy, Fleet Commander; it's bred into our very *genes* to submit to the pack leader. To defer to the individual whose strength dominates all about him. Of course our people, and especially our males, have always *challenged* our leaders, as well, for that was how the ancient pack ensured that its leadership remained strong. Yet within our psychology and culture, there have always been properly defined channels—customs, mores, and traditions—which defined how and when that challenge could be presented. And once a leader has reaffirmed his dominance, his strength—his right to lead—the challenger submits once more. Our entire philosophy, our ethics, our societal expectations and our considerations of honor, all proceed from that fundamental starting point: the weaker and the less capable, for the good of all, *always* submits to his legitimately stronger, more capable superior."

"Of course," Thikair said, just a bit impatiently. "How else could a society such as ours survive? For that matter, we've seen the same response in every other alien species I can think of! Even the weed-eaters—perhaps *especially* the weed-eaters!"

"Sir, while the outcome may *appear* to be the same, the response to which you're referring proceeds from completely different psychological bases. The herbivore or the omnivore submits not out of honor expectations or as an individual submitting to the leader of his pack. Oh, some of the herbivores—and even more of the omnivores—do have superficially similar psychological inclinations, yielding place to those who have demonstrated by whatever standards a given species may apply, which may include ritual combat between individuals, that he or she is better suited to lead. And, for that matter, more entitled on the basis of that demonstrated superiority—once again, for the overall good of the herd—to pass on his or her genetic heritage. Our own psychology incorporates its own shadow of that same thinking. But when an herbivore or omnivore submits to demonstrated strength from *outside* the herd, it's a combination of fear response and the individual's subordination to the well-being of the herd as a whole, not an acknowledgment of natural, demonstrated superiority. He—or she—submits both to prevent his or her own destruction and to avoid provoking attacks from the enemy upon the rest of the herd. That's why in extreme circumstances individuals will allow themselves to be killed—often without even token resistance—in order to deflect threat from the rest of the herd.

"But humans don't think that way. In fact, you're correct; a society such as ours could *not* survive among humans. Their instinct to submit is enormously weaker than our own, and it's far superseded by the individual's drive to defeat threats to his primary loyalty group—which is neither the pack nor the herd."

"What?" Thikair blinked at her, and her ears waved in a grimace.

"A human's primary loyalty is to his *family grouping*, Sir. Not to the herd, of which the family forms only a small part. And not to the pack, where the emphasis is on strength and value *to* the pack. There are exceptions, but that orientation forms the bedrock of human motivation. You might think of them almost as . . . as a herd composed of *individual* packs of predators. Humans are capable of extending that sense of loyalty beyond the family grouping—to organizations, communities, to nation-states or philosophies—but the fundamental motivating mechanism of the individual family is as hardwired into them as submission to the stronger is hardwired into us."

She paused for a moment, looking at him, as if giving him an opportunity to digest that incomprehensible concept, then cleared her throat and continued in a harsher voice.

"That fundamental difference is bad enough, Sir, yet I'm afraid there's worse. Most human cultures I've so far been able to study lack even the same sort of fear-coupled pseudo-submission response we've observed in the vast majority of the Hegemony's herbivores and omnivores. They share the same fight-or-flight auto response, and the majority of them will usually choose to flee from an opponent they believe they cannot defeat or which they believe has the capacity to injure them badly even if they might triumph in the end. Even that response is trumped by that loyalty to the family group, however. Unlike herbivores who will abandon the individual to protect the whole, humans will run enormous risks—even to large numbers of their 'herd' or extra-family societal groupings—to save individuals. Thousands of them will turn out to search for a single lost individual, especially a lost cub, even in conditions which place the searchers themselves at grave risk, and even when the searchers *know* the likelihood of finding the one for whom they search alive is effectively nonexistent. They will send enormous parties of rescuers into collapsing mines in efforts to rescue far smaller numbers of trapped workers who are almost certainly dead before the effort is even mounted.

"Sir, I realize how bizarre this all sounds, yet I've compiled *hundreds* of cases of human beings running into burning buildings or other deadly peril to rescue cubs who have as yet made no demonstrated contribution whatsoever to their society—to their herd or their pack. Indeed, total strangers will voluntarily put their own lives in peril to rescue *other* parents' young. Worse, my research indicates that a very large percentage of humans will attack *any* foe, regardless of its strength or power, in defense of their own mates or young. And they will do it with *no regard whatsoever* for the implications to the rest of their pack or herd. They simply don't care. It never even *occurs* to them to think in those terms. Indeed, these humans are so mad by our standards that they consider other humans who are *not* willing to run such risks for their own mates and young insane, or at least so cowardly as to be beneath the contempt of any 'right-thinking' human."

Thikair felt as if someone had just hit him over the head with a club. He looked at her, trying to wrap his mind around the bizarre psychology she was trying to explain. Intellectually, he could grasp it, at least imperfectly; emotionally, it made no sense at all.

"Fleet Commander," she continued, "I've administered all the standard psychological exams. As you directed, I've also experimented to determine how responsive to neural education techniques humans might be, and I can report that our neural educators work quite well. Indeed, they work better with humans than with the majority of the Hegemony's species. But my opinion, based on the admittedly imperfect and incomplete psychological profile I've so far been able to construct, suggests to me that it would be the height of folly to use humans as a client race.

"They will never understand the natural submission of the weaker to the stronger. It is not, as we had assumed, evidence of knowingly dishonorable conduct on their part, either. It's simply the way their minds work. Instead of submitting *to* the stronger, they will work unceasingly to *become* the stronger, and not for the purpose of assuming leadership of the pack. Some of them, yes, will react very like we Shongairi might. Others may react in fashions which approach the pseudo-submission of a weed-eater. Still others may very well seek to *feign* submission. But most will see the function of strength as the protection of their primary loyalty group. They will focus their energy on destroying any and all threats to it, even when attempting to destroy the threat *in itself* risks destruction of the group, and they will *never* forget or forgive a threat to that which they protect. They will see the infliction of losses, especially within their own primary family loyalty groups, not as a reasonable demonstration of the reasons for submission to their superiors, but as an unforgivable act. As an offense which must be *avenged,* not as a demonstration which must be accepted.

"Sir, we might be able to enforce temporary obedience, and it's possible we could actually convince many of them to accept us as their natural masters. As I say, they have many societal and cultural templates, and some of them may prove more amenable than others. Yet we will never convince *all* of them of that, and my judgment, based on what I've already determined about their fundamental psychology, is that in the fullness of time that same hardwired loyalty to the family above all will reemerge in the children or grandchildren even of those who might themselves genuinely submit to us. And so, even if we ultimately succeed in compelling them to yield, they will never—*can* never—truly surrender. And if we attempt to use whatever quirk in their makeup empowers their insane inventiveness, it will only mean we'll eventually find our 'clients' turning upon us with all the inventiveness and ferocity we've observed out of them here, but with all our own technological capabilities . . . as a *starting* point."

. . . . .

"IT WOULD APPEAR," Thikair told his senior officers, "that my approach to this planet was not the most brilliant accomplishment of my career."

They looked back at him, most still obviously bemused by Shairez's report. None of them, he reflected, had reacted to it any better than *he* had.

"Clearly," he continued, "it's necessary to reevaluate our policy—*my* policy—in light of the Ground Base Commander's discoveries. And, frankly, in light of our already severe operational losses.

"Our efforts to date to compel the humans to submit have killed somewhere over half the original planetary population and cost us massive losses of our own. Ground Force Commander Thairys' current estimate is that if we continue operations for one local year, we will have lost three-quarters of his personnel and in excess of *ninety percent* of his original combat and support ground vehicles. In that same time period, we will have killed over half the *remaining* humans. It seems evident that even if Ground Base Commander Shairez's model is in error, we cannot sustain losses at that level. Nor, assuming her model is as accurate and insightful as her previous work has always been, would we dare risk providing such a . . . recalcitrant species with access to modern technology after killing more than nine in twelve of them first."

There was silence in the conference room as he surveyed their faces.

"The time has come to cut our losses," he said flatly. "I'm not prepared to give up this planet, not after the price we've already paid for it. But at the same time, I've concluded that humans are too dangerous. Indeed, faced with what we've discovered here—which amply confirms the Council's reaction to the initial survey reports—I believe many of the Hegemony's other races would share that conclusion! Certainly it's clear Vice-Speaker Koomaatkia would, and in this instance I feel confident the Kreptu's reaction would be shared fully by the Garm, the Howsanth, the Traighor, and the Cherail. For that matter, even the Barthoni and the Liatu would feel nothing but relief if . . . something were to happen to the humans, whatever their official, sanctimonious position might be."

He looked around the table once more, watching understanding struggle with the aftershocks of Shairez's astounding report, then drew a deep breath.

"I've decided to implement our backup strategy and develop a targeted bioweapon," he said even more flatly. "There are obvious potential consequences to such a decision on my part. Despite the fact that the Barthoni and Liatu are obviously horrified by what they know of humans, the 'progressives' among them already hate and despise *us,* as well. There will be great pressure upon their political leaders to 'take a stand' against this fresh evidence of Shongair 'murderousness.' We've all had enough experience with their enlightened views to know *that* much!"

He half bared a canine in a derisive challenge grin, and one or two of his senior officers actually chuckled.

"At the same time, however," he continued, "those same political leaders will in fact be deeply relieved that someone else has removed the threat these humans might ultimately prove. And I feel confident that if any of them press the Council too hard, the more . . . pragmatic Council members, like Vice-Speaker Koomaatkia, will seek to dissuade them. Especially if the Emperor should hint that he's prepared to make public certain recordings of conversations between Koomaatkia and Minister for Colonization Vairtha. Under the circumstances, I very much doubt our critics—on the Council, at least—would care to have their sanctimonious hypocrisy exposed so long as we can provide them with even the most threadbare of excuses to simply accept whatever happens here.

"Accordingly, I've decided it would be as well for us to establish as clearly as possible that the release of our bioweapon was completely 'accidental' and no part of any deliberate policy to exterminate this pestiferous species. That will provide those hypocrites with the cover they need to avoid asking any inconvenient questions which might inadvertently unmask their own sanctimony in allowing—no, *encouraging*—us to conquer the humans in the first place. Which is why I've determined the research will be conducted in your ground base, Ground Base Commander Teraik."

Thikair turned and looked directly at the officer in command of Ground Base Two Alpha. Teraik looked back alertly, but it was clear he was a bit perplexed by the logic behind Thikair's choice of his base.

"I have three primary reasons for that decision," Thikair explained, still gazing into Teraik's eyes. "First, I have complete faith in your capabilities. Second, your base's ZOR comes closest to any of our zones here in North America to having been suitably pacified. Third, we will be able to point out to any 'impartial investigators' the Council might assign to this case that because we were forced to put your base's facilities together out of whatever was left over from the original Ground Base Two's destruction, your equipment was, perhaps, in less than perfect condition and so more prone to 'accidental failure.'"

Teraik's ears flicked in acknowledgment, but he still looked a little unsure, and Thikair drew an unobtrusive breath.

"I realize your zone isn't truly pacified," he said, managing to keep himself from sounding overly patient with a slightly slow subordinate. "Nonetheless, you've established at least the skeleton of a proper relationship with the local ruler—with 'Governor Howell,' I believe he's called. It ought to be possible with only minor editing of our reports to make it clear that he's been earnestly and loyally cooperating with us for the last two local months.

"Of course, I've reviewed his 'submission' in light of Ground Base Commander Shairez's discoveries, and it now seems clear that his apparent cooperation has in fact been the result of a *feigned* submission. It has undoubtedly given him access to a great deal of information no other human spy could have obtained, not to mention offering him still other advantages. Indeed, several things which had been puzzling me become much clearer looked at from that perspective. For example, I believe I now understand why decisions which worked to the benefit of the humans in his area of authority were always implemented so much more speedily and efficiently than decisions which worked to *our* benefit in the same area." Thikair's ears smiled grimly. "With my vision now cleared by the Ground Base Commander's findings, it seems painfully evident to me that one of the reasons he chose to 'submit' in the first place was to insinuate himself into our confidence, put himself into a position to achieve exactly that sort of manipulation and interference. Indeed, Ground Base Commander Shairez has pointed out to me that there is actually a specific human word—'sabotage'—which undoubtedly sums up his true motivation for appearing so helpful to us."

Several of the officers around the table bared gleaming canines at the thought of such dishonorable behavior, but Thikair raised a restraining hand.

"I share your disgust at such actions," he assured them, "but bear in mind that from his perspective, they were *not* dishonorable. I realize no Shongair will ever truly be able to understand such a warped view of the universe, yet that doesn't make it untrue. Despite that, I naturally share your desire to punish him as fully as his actions deserve under *our* code of honor. Unfortunately, since my objective in selecting Ground Base Two Alpha as the site for our 'accident' is to allow us to argue that we would never intentionally have attacked the one area on the entire planet where our pacification program was clearly working, I can scarcely order the local native ruler executed for treachery and his body parts distributed to our officers' messes, however much he might deserve it. It would undermine too much of our cover story's believability."

Some of his officers still appeared disgruntled, and he didn't blame them a bit. He didn't rebuke them, either. In fact, his ears rose in a slow, gloating smile.

"Oh, no," he told them softly. "It would *never* do to execute him for his treachery. On the other hand, Ground Base Commander Shairez tells us that these creatures' primary loyalty is to their own family groups. That being so, I see no reason our bioweapon couldn't be 'accidentally released' in his home first."

. XXVIII .

"Move it! *Move* it! Damn it, Vanya—*move it*!"

Pieter Ushakov had no idea how he'd found the breath to shout at Ivan Kolesnikov. A corner of his brain reflected that he shouldn't be able to—no one running as hard as *he* was running was supposed to have breath for anything but panting.

Of course, he'd discovered over the past months that enough adrenaline could overcome almost anything.

Another explosion thundered, and that corner of his brain which was still thinking instead of concentrating on dodging the next tree and not falling over his own feet cringed. The explosions were coming closer, and another thing he'd discovered was that whatever their other weaknesses, the Shongairi were no slouches when it came to laying in mortar fire. Their weapons were long-ranged, powerful, and accurate. They seemed to fire a little more slowly than their human counterparts, but they made up for it with an enviable assortment of ammunition. So far he'd encountered or observed at least two different high-explosive variants, incendiary rounds, smoke, one that deployed really *nasty* antipersonnel submunitions, and another which dispensed what looked (judging from the condition of the corpses) like a quick-acting and effective neurotoxin.

Fortunately, they didn't seem to have a lot of the latter. Either that, or they had to get release from higher command authority before they used it. On the other hand, it was obvious they had no shortage of HE.

Another salvo came scorching in, and he heard a cut-off shriek from his left rear. He grabbed a tree trunk, slingshotting himself around to face back the way he'd come and stabbing a look towards the source of the scream. He blinked sweat from his eyes, then grunted and hurled himself back into motion after Kolesnikov. There wasn't enough left of the man who'd screamed for him to be certain who it was, but he thought it was Chashnikov, one of the Russians who'd joined them week before last. It didn't really matter—whoever the poor bastard *had* been, he was dead now—but Ushakov felt a stab of shame as he realized how relieved he was to know he wasn't going to have to go back and try to get a wounded man to safety, after all.

Funny, that observer corner of his mind reflected. So much of him just wanted to let go and die, try to catch up with Vladislava and the children, but another stubborn part of him insisted on going on surviving.

Can't kill the weasels if you're dead, he told himself. *Which is a pretty good reason to run* faster, *you idiot!*

He wanted desperately to look at his watch, check the time, but he was too busy staying on his feet and dodging obstacles to spare any attention for that. Besides, either he'd done his sums correctly, or he hadn't. And if he hadn't, it wasn't going to matter very much.

Behind him, thick black smoke and flames belched from the burning vehicles of the Shongair convoy. They'd blown the bridge after the GEV had crossed but while the trio of APCs leading the cargo vehicles were still on it. All three of those had gone straight to the bottom of the river, and the GEV had immediately turned around, spinning through a full hundred and eighty degrees to come rushing back across the muddy brown water to save its charges.

Unfortunately for the GEV, Ushakov had watched this particular river crossing for three days before he and his company attacked. He'd noted where the GEV left the road and started across the river every single time, and he'd buried ten kilos of plastic explosive to wait for it. He'd have preferred something better—he'd stumbled across a small supply of Russian TM-72 antitank mines a month ago, when he'd scouted the remnants of a Russian Army ordnance depot, and they'd proved highly effective. Unfortunately, he'd expended the last of them in barely a week.

On the other hand, he'd found a rather larger supply of explosives—more than his men had been able to carry, as a matter of fact—at the same time. They'd spent a couple of days backpacking those explosives to a safer location, and he'd discovered that ten kilograms or so of PVV-5A (the Russian equivalent of the American C-4 plastic explosive), formed into a crude shaped charge by molding it around a funnel-shaped form, did a marvelous job of disemboweling one of the weasels' hovering tanks. He'd rather thought it would; he'd taken the opportunity to examine a knocked-out GEV for himself in the first week after the landing and found that Shongair designers seemed never to have heard of the concept of antitank mines or even simple IEDs. The belly armor of their armored vehicles was laughable compared to that of human AFVs, at any rate, and the only question in his mind after his inspection had been whether or not they floated too far above the ground to be effectively attacked.

They didn't. Not if the attack was properly planned and executed, at least. The trick was to detonate the charge at exactly the right moment and in exactly the right spot. Shongair predictability made putting his homemade mine in the right place relatively simple; after that, it was simply a matter of steady nerves, a reliable detonator system, and an eye which had learned to judge the GEVs' speed accurately.

With the GEV and the leading APCs disposed of, the riflemen and the two machine gunners posted along the northern edge of the roadway had laced the unarmored cargo vehicles with deadly accurate fire. Half of the "cargo" vehicles had actually been loaded with Shongair troopers, and Ushakov had taken a cold, burning pleasure from their screams.

The screams had gone higher and shriller as the machine guns' tracers had ignited the vehicles' fuel tanks and the stench of burning alien flesh added itself to the nightmare carnage. Then the trailing APCs had come charging up . . . and the improvised explosive devices he'd buried in the ditches on either side of the road against exactly that moment had taken out two of them, as well.

The third had proven a much uglier proposition. Its commander had been warier than his fellows. Instead of charging in, he'd trailed his companions, which had allowed him to avoid the IED one of them obligingly detonated thirty meters in front of him. And he'd had a well-trained gunner, as well. He'd picked off four of Ushakov's raiders before Ushakov realized he hadn't gotten all three of the rear APCs, after all.

Without any purpose-designed antiarmor weapons (he'd used the last of his scavenged Russian RPGs weeks ago), he hadn't had a good way to take out the APC. Its armor would probably have resisted the fire of his rifles and RPK-74 light machine guns even without upgrades, but this APC's commander had added additional sheets of some sort of composite which Ushakov had been pretty sure would have resisted even *heavy* machine-gun fire.

In the absence of good ways to deal with it, he'd had to settle for *bad* ways, and they'd lost eight more good men before they managed to get most of a Molotov cocktail's flaming contents through one of the infantry firing ports. A poor design feature, that. Probably another indication that the Shongairi weren't really used to fighting people who could fight back.

That still hadn't finished the damned thing off. They'd been able to hear the screams and shrieks of badly burned aliens from inside the troop compartment during lulls in the firing, but the turret-mounted automatic weapon on top of it had maintained a steady barrage of fire. Without troopers manning the firing ports any longer, however, it had been blind to the flanks and rear, and two more of his men had managed to get close alongside and heave a pair of hand grenades in through another of those conveniently large firing ports.

That had finally done for it, and the surviving members of his attack force had devoted a few more moments to tossing individual incendiaries into the half dozen or so trucks which hadn't already gone up in flames before they took to their heels.

The quick-response force the Shongairi kept stationed at the junction ten kilometers farther west of the river had turned up right on schedule, as well. With the bridge down, the mortar trucks hadn't been able to come after them, but they'd started lobbing their mortar bombs quickly enough. And even now he could feel the tooth-grating vibration of one of their damned drones. No wonder their fire was getting more accurate!

I hope Fyodor's ready! Ushakov thought. *Because if he's not. . . .*

The precious hoarded 9K38 Igla SAM—a NATO officer would have called it an SA-18 "Grouse"—streaked up out of the trees somewhere ahead of him. Seconds later, there was an explosion and the vibration stopped abruptly.

Good boy, Fyodor! Now, if the rest *of my brilliant plan works—*

Deprived of their aerial eye, the Shongairi were going to do one of two things, and he hoped he'd correctly estimated which one they'd choose. And that his estimate of their command-response time was accurate. They seemed to be getting ever shorter on equipment, so he figured there was a pretty good chance he'd been right. If he'd guessed wrong, on the other hand, they'd have another drone, and they'd send it after him.

Well, Fyodor has two more Iglas, so as long as they don't have three *more drones, it should still work out. Except, of course, that he's supposed to be running to save his* own *ass by now.*

Well, a man couldn't have everything.

He dodged around another tree, vaulted over a fallen trunk, and sucked in another deep breath as he saw the landmark he'd been looking for. Another two hundred meters and—

"Mama! Mama! *MammaMammaMamma!*"

Pieter Ushakov's heart stopped as he heard the terrified young voice screaming. His head whipped around, blue eyes wide. There weren't any civilians in the area—that was the very reason he'd picked this spot! Where in the name of God—?

Then he saw her, almost directly behind him, head swinging from side to side, eyes darting everywhere in a frantic search for nonexistent safety as the mortar bombs continued to explode. She couldn't have been any older than his own Vladislava, probably younger, and she had the same wheat-colored hair. But this young woman was thin and gaunt with starvation, her clothing tattered and dirty. Even from fifty meters away he could see the desperation, the terror, in her face. Not for herself, but for the baby in her arms and the two white-faced, ragged, half-starved children clinging to their mother's skirts.

He had no idea where she'd come from, how she'd gotten there. It didn't matter, anyway. The world was full of refugees, all trying desperately to survive, and somehow this woman and her children had stumbled into the midst of his attack at the worst possible moment.

He knew what he ought to do, what he *had* to do. But what he had to do was different from what he *could* do. He didn't think about it, didn't consider it, didn't even realize he'd started moving again until he was halfway to them.

She saw him coming, and he saw the sudden flicker of fragile hope as she recognized the Russian forest-pattern camouflage he wore. They'd liberated that from the Army depot, too, that isolated corner of his brain thought.

He didn't say a word. There wasn't time for that . . . nor was there any need. He simply held out his arms and scooped up one of the larger children in each of them. They were so small, so frail, with the delicate bones he remembered from his own children but wasted and thin with hunger and privation, and he felt one of them—a little girl, he thought—twisting in his grip to wrap her arms about his neck and cling to him with desperate strength.

He turned back the way he'd been headed originally, running after his vanished men. The young mother followed him, running as fast as she could, stumbling after him through fallen leaves, tripping and almost falling as she hung her toe on a branch. He could hear her desperate, panting gasps, her frantic effort to live—not for herself, but for her children—and he made himself slow down. She didn't know where he was going. Without him as a guide, she'd never get there . . . but if she slowed him too much, *none* of them would get there in time.

There!

"Left!" he heard himself gasp. *"Left!"*

She heard him and changed direction, stumbling up the slight slope towards the black opening.

"In!" he panted. "Jump in—*now*!"

She didn't hesitate. She plunged straight down into the opening. It was almost two meters to the bottom, but she managed to land upright, and Ushakov was on her heels.

"Don't stop! Keep going!"

Alive so far, he thought. *Now we find out if it's deep enough!*

The tunnel roof was so low he had to bend sharply to keep from striking his head, and it was only feebly illuminated by the lanterns burning far ahead of them, but the young woman struggled forward more quickly than Ushakov would have believed she could.

The passage drove straight into the side of the hill, away from the river. Its floor was almost level, but the hill rose steeply above it, and its walls still breathed a sense of dampness. It was a water main which had once served the small city the Shongairi had destroyed when they first located their base in the vicinity. But the pumping stations had died with the city they'd served, and now Ushakov had another use for it.

"Hang on tight, darling!" he said to the child clinging to him, and felt her thin arms clutch convulsively tighter as his released her and his freed hand reached out, trailing along the cement wall.

His fingers found what they'd been searching for.

"Fire in the hole!" he screamed, and pulled the lanyard.

He just had time to get his arm wrapped back around the terrified little girl, hugging her and her brother tightly, when the chain of explosions thundered behind him.

He was closer to them than he'd expected to be, slowed by the young woman in front of him, and he drew both of the children as close as he could, tucking them against his chest, and curved his body to shield them as the concussion picked him up in hands of fury.

. XXIX .

"So, my Stephen. What do you think?"

Buchevsky finished his salad and took a long swallow of beer. His grandmama had always urged him to eat his vegetables, yet he was still a bit bemused by how sinfully luxurious fresh salad tasted after weeks of scrounging whatever he and his people could find.

Which, unfortunately, was really more or less what Basarab was asking him about.

"I don't know, Mircea," he said. "I mean, I really still don't know all that much about Romania. I'm learning," he grinned and shook his head, "and Elizabeth's finally pounding at least the rudiments of Romanian through my thick skull, but you know a lot more about how other Romanians are going to react than I do."

Then his expression sobered, and this time his headshake was a lot grimmer than its predecessor had been.

"I'm afraid the one thing that comes up front and center for me every time I think about it, though," he said, "is the need to protect what we've got from people who aren't going to have anywhere as much as they need to get through the winter. I don't want to be cold about it, but our primary loyalty has to be to *our* people."

"You are correct, of course," Basarab agreed with a touch of sadness, gazing down at the handwritten note on the table. It was the first of several expected responses to notes of his own, and both he and Buchevsky were acutely aware of the days slipping past.

Those days—like the current night outside the log-walled cabin—were noticeably cooler, and autumn color was creeping across the mountainsides above the Arges River and the enormous blue gem of Lake Vidraru. The lake was less than seventy kilometers north of the ruins of Pitești, the kinetically devastated capital of Argeș *județ*, or the County of Argeș, but it was also in the heart of a wilderness preserve which, like almost half of all forests in Romania, had been managed for watershed rather than timber production. That management philosophy explained why the country had one of the largest areas of undisturbed forest in all of Europe, and the cabin in which they sat lay just below the crest of a fourteen-hundred-meter ridge about two miles west of *Barajul Vidraru*—Vidraru Dam, also known as the Gheorghiu-Dej Dam—at the southern end of the huge lake. From its front door—or, rather, from its roof since he needed the extra height to get clear of the intervening trees—Buchevsky could see all the way down to the lake in daylight. The cabin itself had been built by the forestry service, rather than as part of any of the three villages Basarab had organized into his own little kingdom, but Buchevsky had pressed it into service as a listening and observation post because of its elevation and location.

So far, it hadn't actually been needed in that role, and he hoped things would stay that way.

Despite Lake Vidraru's relative proximity to Pitești, few survivors from the kinetic strike which had destroyed the city had headed up into the lake's vicinity. There hadn't been much farmland to attract hungry survivors, and Buchevsky supposed the mountains and heavy forest had been too forbidding to appeal to urban dwellers. On the other hand, the reasons might have been far simpler and grimmer than any of that. There didn't seem to have *been* all that many Pitești survivors, after all.

Another factor was probably the fact that there were so few roads into the area to begin with, despite its recreational potential, and the DN-7C roadway followed the *eastern* shore of the lake. There were scarcely even any forest tracks leading to Basarab's villages, which were like isolated throwbacks to another age, tucked away in the midst of heavy woodland and mountain ridgelines *west* of the reservoir. Although they were within a few miles of the lake, just *finding* them would have been extraordinarily difficult without a guide, and actually walking into one of them was like stepping into a time machine. In fact, they reminded Buchevsky rather strongly of the village in the musical *Brigadoon.*

Which isn't such a bad thing, under the circumstances, he reflected, looking into the candle on the rough table between him and Basarab and thinking about the total blackness wrapped around the cabin, undisturbed by anything so decadently modern as incandescent lighting. *There sits Lake Vidraru, with its hydroelectric generators, and these people don't even have electricity! Which means they aren't radiating any emissions the Shongairi are likely to pick up on.*

Over the last couple of months, he, his Americans, and their Romanians had been welcomed by the villagers and—as Basarab had warned—been put to work preparing for the onset of winter. One reason his supper's salad had tasted so good was because he knew he wouldn't be having them for much longer. It wasn't as if there'd be fresh produce coming in from California or Florida *this* winter. Which was rather the point of the matter under discussion, when he came down to it.

Damn. No matter how he tried to avoid it, his brain insisted on coming back to Basarab's proposal.

He sighed, sipping beer, brown eyes hooded in the candlelight.

"Whether we like it or not, my Stephen," Basarab said now, "it must be considered. And it must be resolved now, while all concerned are still relatively well provided for. While we can make our arrangements in good faith and amity, without the natural . . . narrowness of perspective, let us say, which starving men bring to such discussions."

"Mircea, I don't see any reason why I *should* like it. After all, I haven't liked one goddamned thing that's happened since those bastards started dropping their fucking rocks on us!"

Basarab arched one eyebrow, and Buchevsky was a little surprised himself by the jagged edge of hatred which had roughened his voice. It took him unawares, sometimes, that hate. When the memory of Trish and the girls came looming up out of the depths once again, fangs bared, to remind him of the loss and the pain and the anguish.

Isn't it one hell *of a note when the best thing I can think of is that the people I loved most in all the world probably died without knowing a thing about it?* he thought.

"They have not endeared themselves to me, either," Basarab said after a moment. "Indeed, is that not rather the point? It has been . . . difficult to remember that we dare not take the fight to them. By the same token, however, if starvation and desperation drive others into actions which draw the aliens' attention to our area, then having swallowed our pride and hidden will have been for naught in the end."

Buchevsky nodded in understanding. Basarab had made it clear from the beginning that avoiding contact with the enemy, lying low, was the best way to protect the civilians for whom they were responsible, and he was right. They might have demonstrated their ability to punish individual patrols, to inflict loss and pain on the Shongairi, but that very experience had made it abundantly clear they dared not openly confront and challenge the invaders. In the final analysis, no matter how much damage they managed to inflict first, anyone who could destroy entire cities with kinetic strikes could certainly destroy three isolated villages in the mountains of Wallachia.

He and Basarab both knew that, but that didn't change the fact that Basarab's natural orientation—like Buchevsky's own—was towards taking the offensive. Towards seeking out and destroying the enemy, not hiding from him.

Buchevsky had always recognized that tendency in himself, and the years he'd spent imbibing the United States Marine Corps' philosophy and doctrine had only intensified it. Yet he suspected that the drive to find and crush anyone or anything which threatened those under his protection might be even stronger in Basarab than it was in him. There were times when he could almost physically taste the other man's burning desire to take the war to the Shongairi, when those green eyes were cold and hungry, filled with hate for his country's rapists. When the fact that Basarab so clearly understood why he dared not feed that hunger, that need to strike back, only made the Romanian's self-control even more impressive.

And he was right. Giving in to that hunger would have come under the heading of a Really Bad Idea.

Basarab's runners had made contact with several other small enclaves across central and southern Romania—even a couple in northern Bulgaria, a hundred and fifty miles to the south—and by now those enclaves were becoming as concerned with defending themselves against other humans as fending off the Shongairi. After the initial bombardments and confused combat of the first several weeks, the invaders had apparently decided to pull back from the unfriendly terrain of the mountains and settle for occupying more open areas. It was hard to be certain of that—or if it represented anything other than a purely local situation—with the collapse of the planetary communications net, but it seemed reasonable. As Buchevsky's brain trust of Truman and Sherman had pointed out, troop lift would almost certainly be a limiting factor for any interstellar expedition, so it would make sense to avoid stretching it any further than necessary by doing things like going up into the hills after dirt-poor, hardscrabble mountain villages.

According to Vasile Costantinescu, the leader of another enclave six or seven miles away, at the northeastern end of the lake, the Shongairi had established an outpost—hell, it sounded like a damned forward operating base to Buchevsky!—near the town of Viziru in Brăila *județ*. To Buchevsky, that was only a dot a hundred and fifty-odd miles to the east on an increasingly worn-out Romanian road map, but Basarab had explained that it lay in the flat, fertile farmland west of the Black Sea. It certainly sounded like terrain which would be far easier to control than rugged, forested mountainsides, but from the sound of things, the Shongairi were being surprisingly passive.

Costantinescu had family in the area, and according to the reports he'd received from them, the aliens had chosen to restrict their presence to an area no more than sixty or seventy miles across, centered on their well-defended, strongly fortified base. Within that area, they reacted quickly (and, it sounded to Buchevsky, far more effectively than they had against him and Basarab during their trek to Lake Vidraru) to any armed resistance. Beyond that, they seemed content to let the surviving Romanians stew in their own juices.

Letting them sit there in lordly disdain for the mere humans about them set Buchevsky's teeth on edge, but that was a purely emotional—and, in his own opinion, remarkably stupid—reaction. Whatever his emotions might think, his intellect knew damned well that the farther away from his people they stayed, and the more passive they were, the better.

Human refugees were an entirely different threat, and one Buchevsky was happy they hadn't had to deal with . . . yet. Starvation, exposure, and disease had probably killed at least half the civilians who'd fled their homes after the initial attacks, and those who remained were becoming increasingly desperate as winter approached. Some of the other enclaves had already been forced to fight, often ruthlessly, against their own kind to preserve the resources their own people were going to need to survive.

In many ways, it was the fact that the aliens' actions had forced humans to kill *each other* in the name of simple survival that fueled Stephen Buchevsky's deepest rage. Which was probably the reason he didn't really want to think too much about Basarab's proposal.

But he's right, the American admitted with a mental sigh. *And even if he weren't, he's the boss.*

"All right, Mircea," he said. "You're right. We do have to come to an understanding with the other enclaves, at least the local ones, and that probably does mean sharing what we have if some of the others are flat up against starvation. So, yeah, I can see why it makes sense for us to share inventories with each other. And it makes sense for us to agree to help each other out if looters or raiders come after them. I understand that. I'll admit I hate the thought of planning to help other people kill human beings when there are Shongairi around to kill, instead, but I'm not an idiot, and it's not as if I haven't had to shoot at the occasional other human being over the past couple of decades. In fact, I guess the real problem is that there's a part of me that hates letting *anyone* know what we've got tucked away in the larder, because people are still people. If their kids start starving, then any parent worth a single solitary damn is going to do anything it takes to feed them. I understand that, and I'll give *any* kid the last slice of bread I've got. But if any of those other enclaves out there decide to sell us out, or throw us to the wolves to save their own asses by pointing somebody who comes after what *they've* got in our direction—or if they're stupid enough to try and use your agreement just to get close enough to us to hit us themselves—then I'm going to be really, really unhappy, you understand. And they won't like me when I'm unhappy. Hell, *I* don't like me when I'm unhappy!"

He shrugged, and Basarab nodded. Then the Romanian chuckled softly.

"What?" Buchevsky raised an eyebrow at him.

"It is just that we are so much alike, you and I." Basarab shook his head. "Deny it as you will, my Stephen, but there is a Slav inside you!"

"Inside *me?*" Buchevsky laughed, looking down at the back of one very black hand. "Hey, I already told you! If any of my ancestors were ever in Europe, they got there from Africa, not the steppes!"

"Ah!" Basarab waved a finger under his nose, green eyes gleaming with unusual warmth in the candlelight. "So you have said, but I know better! What, 'Buchevsky'? This is an *African* name?"

"Nope. Probably just somebody who owned one of my great-great-granddaddies or grandmamas."

"Nonsense! Slavs in nineteenth-century America were too poor to own anyone! No, no. Trust me—it is in the blood. Somewhere in your ancestry there is—how do you Americans say it?—a Slav in the straw pile!"

Buchevsky laughed again. He was actually learning to do that once more—sometimes, at least—and they'd had this conversation before. Besides, Basarab was the only man in any of the villages under his protection who'd ever been to America. It was obvious he'd enjoyed the visit, but it was equally obvious he hadn't got all of the slang quite correct. His most recent sally had been considerably less mangled than most, as a matter of fact.

Buchevsky hadn't realized Basarab had ever visited the United States. Not for a while, anyway. But he'd discovered that despite the dark places behind Mircea Basarab's eyes, the man had a naturally warm, sly sense of humor. He could still remember the first night when they'd heard the wolves howling in the mountains' untouched forest and Basarab had looked at him, laid one forefinger against the side of his nose, and—perfectly deadpan—dropped his voice at least one full octave and solemnly declaimed: "Ah! The children of the night! Hear how they sing!"

Buchevsky had been drinking some of the villagers' home-brewed beer at the moment, and he'd sprayed a quarter of a mug or so of it across Calvin Meyers. Then the two of them had glared as one at Basarab, who'd shrugged with a devilish smile.

"I saw that film in Chicago years ago," he'd said. "It was a . . . what do you people call it over there? Ah, yes! It was a *film festival* at the public library there. As a native of Wallachia, I was, of course, deeply impressed by the film's total fidelity to the land in which I was born." His smile had gone even broader, and he'd shrugged. "I do not believe they actually got a single thing right, of course, but I have always loved that particular bit of dialogue. It is so delightfully overdone, do you not think?"

"I believe the term you're looking for at this particular moment is 'haystack,' not 'straw pile,' Mircea," Buchevsky said now. "And while I realize Jasmine Sherman, Lyman Curry, and I are probably the only blacks within two or three hundred miles, it's still just a *little* bit politically incorrect."

"Oh, and you are *so* devoted to this 'political correctness' of yours, are you?"

"Honestly? No, not so much," Buchevsky admitted, and Basarab chuckled. But then the Romanian's expression sobered, and he reached across the table to lay one hand on Buchevsky's arm.

"Whatever you may have been born, my Stephen," he said quietly, "you are a Slav now. A Wallachian. You have earned that."

Buchevsky waved dismissively, but he couldn't deny the warmth he felt inside. He knew Basarab meant every word of it, too, just as he knew he truly had earned his place as the Romanian's second-in-command through the training and discipline he'd brought the villagers. Basarab had somehow managed to stockpile impressive quantities of small arms and infantry support weapons, but however fearsome Take Bratianu and the rest of Basarab's original group might have been as individuals, and however devoted they might have been to their chieftain, it was obvious none of them had really understood how to train civilians. Stephen Buchevsky, on the other hand, had spent years turning pampered *American* civilians into US

Marines. Compared to that, training tough, mountain-hardened Romanian villagers was a piece of cake.

I just hope none of them are ever going to need *that training,* he reflected, his mood turning grim once again.

"Go ahead and sit down with the others, Mircea," he said. "However much you decide you have to tell them, I'll back you. I'd rather you didn't go into too much detail about our own defensive plans and positions, though. They might not do much good against the *puppies,* but I'd just as soon have them come as a surprise if any of our neighbors decide to get all . . . acquisitive this winter."

"'Acquisitive'?" Basarab tilted his head to the side, one eyebrow cocked. "This is a word most Marines use a great deal? Or have you been saving it for a special occasion?"

"I know all kinds of big words," Buchevsky assured him. "I just don't know very many of them in Romanian yet. I'm sure it'll come, though . . . assuming those floppy-eared bastards leave us alone, at least."

His voice had hardened again with the final sentence, and Basarab reached across the table to touch his forearm again.

"Agreed," he said, and shrugged. "I know it goes as much against the grain for you as it does for me, my Stephen. Yet sooner or later, unless they simply intend to kill all of us, there must be some form of accommodation."

Basarab's sour expression showed his opinion of his own analysis, but he continued unflinchingly.

"The people of this land have fought back against conquerors before, my Stephen. Sometimes with success, and other times . . . not so successfully. Indeed, Vlad Tepes himself once had his main fortress, Cetatea Poenari, atop a mountain at Cortea-de-Argeş, barely thirty kilometers from here. I realize Vlad has not been much beloved in history outside Romania, although some see him differently in this land because of how much he did to resist the Turks, how successfully he held them at bay—for a time, at least—and it was to Cetatea Poenari he retreated when enemies forced him to yield ground.

"Yet that only underscores the point, does it not? Not even he, despite all the horrific measures to which he was willing to resort—and although my people venerate him in many ways, those measures *were* horrific, my Stephen; far worse, I fear, than anything you have seen in Afghanistan or other lands in your own lifetime—could defeat the Turks in the end. How then shall *we* defeat an invader from beyond the stars themselves?"

Basarab shook his head.

"No. To dream of such foolishness would but bring the destruction it has brought elsewhere, yet if the Shongairi had intended simple butchery rather than conquest, then they would have begun by destroying *all* of our cities and towns from space. To me that suggests we are at least marginally more valuable to them alive than dead. I fear one could scarcely have said more for the Turks or the Soviets, and no one truly knows how many thousands and millions of Romanians died resisting those purely human conquerors. Now it would seem we must turn our thoughts once more to surviving conquest, and what our people have done before, no doubt they can do again. But I will not subject *my* people to these new conquerors from beyond our world without first holding out for the very best terms we can obtain. And if they prove me in error—if they demonstrate that they are, indeed, prepared to settle for butchery rather than conquest—then they will pay a higher price than they can possibly imagine before they rule *these* mountains. As you say, they will not like *either* of us when we are angry."

He sat for a moment in cold, dangerous silence. Then he shook himself.

"Well, it seems we are in accord, then. But if we are to have true agreement with our neighbors—and if I am to be certain the agreement is upon *my* terms—I shall have to go in person to negotiate with each of the enclaves and its leaders."

"Now, wait a minute!" Buchevsky said. "I'll agree it's something we need to do, whether I'm all that crazy about it or not, but I'd just as soon not have you out wandering around the woods all alone, Mircea. I've gotten a little fond of you, and on a purely selfish note, you're the one holding this entire arrangement together. We can't afford to lose you."

"I am not so easily lost as all that, my Stephen," Basarab assured him. Buchevsky only glared at him, and after a moment, the Romanian sighed. "Very well, you stubborn American! I will take Take and his men with me. For that matter, it probably would hurt nothing for me to arrive with a suitable . . . retinue to impress my fellow leaders with my importance and formidable military resources." He made a face. "Will that reassure you?"

Buchevsky opened his mouth to protest again, but then he closed it once more, objection unspoken. He'd discovered he was always uncomfortable when Basarab went wandering around the mountains out from under his own eye. And a part of him resented the fact that Basarab hadn't even considered inviting *him* along on this little jaunt. But somebody had to stay home and look after things, and that was logically his job if Basarab was away. Besides, the truth, however little he wanted to admit it, was that he would probably have been more of a hindrance than a help.

Take Bratianu and the rest of his formidable little band all seemed able to see like cats and move like drifting leaves. He couldn't even come close to matching them when it came to sneaking through the woods at night, and he knew it . . . however little he liked admitting that there was *anything* someone could do better than he could.

Hey, cut yourself some slack, Stevie! he scolded himself. *Take must be, what—forty or fifty years old? And I'll bet you he's spent every month of those years wandering around in the woods. That probably gives him just a* teeny *bit more experience than* you've *got, now doesn't it? And under the circumstances, it makes sense for Mircea not to invite a great big clumsy Marine with him. Even if it does piss you off a little.*

He chuckled and shook his head at the thought, and Basarab smiled at him.

"I think we have a few days yet before the written invitations can reach all of the others," he mused. "Next week, I think. Wednesday, perhaps. And while I am away, you will keep an eye on things for me, my African Slav, yes?"

"Yeah, I'll do that," Buchevsky agreed.

. XXX .

Rain pelted down, not so much pattering on the leaves as battering its way through them, and thunder rumbled somewhere beyond the coal-black sky which had draped itself over the mountain summits like a lumpy, billowing roof. It felt more like October than the first week of September, Dave Dvorak thought, squatting in the scrub woods west of US-64. And it felt more like seven or eight in the evening than it did like four in the afternoon, too.

He didn't like being here. Rob Wilson didn't like being here, either, and neither of their wives had been happy about their going. Yet they hadn't argued, and despite the unpleasant weather and something roiling around within him which felt entirely too much like terror, he was proud of them for *not* arguing.

"Of course you're going," Sharon had said unhappily, meeting his gaze with level blue eyes which refused to weep. "They need you. But don't you dare get yourself killed, Dave Dvorak! And do what you can to bring my idiot brother back with you, too."

He'd wrapped his arms around her, holding her close, feeling her nestle under his chin and press against him almost as if she wanted to crawl inside his skin with him and become one being. And he'd discovered that he had to remind those arms of his that her ribs were breakable.

The weather had already been turning bad, but one good thing about fanatic deer hunters—they had the foul weather gear to stay at least moderately comfortable even in a downpour. And, frankly, Dvorak had wished the afternoon and evening would be ripped by tornadoes and pumpkin-sized hail, battered by lightning and blizzards—hell, invaded by frigging clouds of giant locusts! Anything to keep any rapid-response Shongair shuttles thoroughly grounded.

But that wasn't going to happen. He'd lost his Google weather bug along with the rest of the Internet, yet he hadn't really needed the Internet or the now defunct National Weather Service to tell him the day was going to be thoroughly miserable but nowhere near as miserable as he wished it would.

Just have to make do as best we can with what we get, he'd told himself, relaxing his embrace at last and standing back from his wife, cupping her cheeks in his hands, tilting her head back so he could gaze down into her eyes and drink up every square inch of that beloved face.

She'd been making preparations of her own—preparations both of them hoped fervently would never be needed—and her weapon of choice lay on the kitchen table: a PSN90, the civilian semiauto version of the fully automatic P90. Developed by FN Herstal of Belgium around its proprietary 5.7-millimeter cartridge, the bullpup-configured weapon really defied traditional definitions. The manufacturer had referred to it, at least initially, as a submachine gun, intended to provide serious emergency firepower for vehicle crews and other military personnel who weren't normally supposed to need conventional rifles. Eventually, it had come to be referred to as a "personal defense weapon," which made a certain degree of sense given its designed function. Yet the majority of militaries which used it actually employed it as an assault rifle, instead, and although the PSN90 had been limited to a civilian-legal thirty-round magazine, it could also use the fifty-round magazine of the military and law enforcement version of the weapon.

There were lots of things to like about the weapon, in Dvorak's opinion, although he generally preferred his guns a little bigger, more comfortably suited to his large frame, and he didn't much care for the ejection port's location. Sure, putting it on the bottom simplified the design of a truly ambidextrous weapon, but he didn't like lying in his own spent brass firing from a prone position. He had some doubts about the round's stopping power, too, although it certainly had excellent penetration! And he had to admit Sharon was deadly accurate with it. In fact, she'd always been a good shot—the first real gift he'd bought her, when they'd both been in college (she at Furman, he at Clemson, which had offered altogether too many opportunities for mutual verbal sniping) had been a Taurus PT-92 automatic. He'd given it to her as a Valentine's Day present, which hadn't really been as weird as it sounded. (All right, *some* weird. He'd give it that much. But not *as* weird as some people might have argued. He'd given guns to quite a few women over the years, on the basis that if Colonel Colt had made all men equal, he could damned well make *women* equal, too.) Nonetheless, there'd been some truth to Sharon's boast that he'd bought it for her because he'd be damned if he'd let her go on outshooting him with his *own* handguns after he'd taught her how to shoot in the first place!

Despite all that, the real reason she'd wanted a P90 was because she'd been a devotee of the series *Stargate*. She had the entire series—all three iterations, although she still liked the original best—on DVD, and she'd thought the fearless team of adventurers' P90s had been "so cute." Dvorak had winced a lot whenever she'd said that. Then she'd discovered that not only was a civilian version of the P90 available, but so was the FN Five-seveN pistol, firing the same round from a twenty-round magazine, and she'd just had to have one of both. Nor had it done Dvorak any good at all to point out that the pistol's name was obviously an example of cutesy marketing gone berserk, which had no place in the serious world of firearms. Especially not when she'd been prepared to smile sweetly and point out that even though the PSN90 *was* a bit pricey, it cost a *lot* less than certain firearms from a company named "Barrett" she could have mentioned. If, of course, she'd been the sort to bring up past conspicuous expenditures. And, of course, her brother (who'd still been in law enforcement at the time and had bought himself an all-up P90 of his own just because he'd thought it would be cool to play with) had been only too willing to share his perfectly legal (or, at least, legally purchased) fifty-round mags with her.

At that moment, however, as he'd held her in his arms and looked over her head at the weapon on their kitchen table, he'd felt absolutely no desire to tease her about her "cute little gun" the way he usually did.

He'd experimented with the captured Shongair weapons and body armor, although he'd discovered that weapons designed around the aliens' six-fingered hands and proportionately longer, double-jointed arms were very poorly proportioned for human use. The iron sights were a pain, too, and he'd come to the conclusion that there had to be some fairly significant differences between human and Shongair eyes. Nonetheless, he'd been able to test them from his Ransom Rest on the outdoor range below the cabin, and he was confident about the overall accuracy of his evaluation.

Bullet diameters didn't match perfectly with any human measurement system, which had hardly surprised him. His calipers made it about 7.54 millimeters for the assault rifle, though, with a bullet weight of approximately a hundred and thirty grains, and his chronograph indicated an average muzzle velocity of about two thousand feet per second. That worked out to a muzzle energy of a shade over eleven hundred foot-pounds, which was within about two hundred foot-pounds of the smaller (but also much *faster*) 5.56 NATO from the M16A4. On the other hand, it was less than half the standard 7.62 NATO's 2,470 foot-pounds, far less the 2,700 foot-pounds of the heavier 168-grain round launched from Rob Wilson's M1A. Of course, it didn't even compare to the 11,000-plus foot-pounds of his own Barrett's mammoth 647-grain bullets (or the even heavier 660-grain bullet for the same weapon), but that was a specialist's weapon, not to mention a *heavy* son-of-a-bitch. Definitely *not* the kind of gun someone wanted to schlep around in the field on any kind of regular basis.

That information had been fascinating to the gun nut in him, but the discovery that Shongair body armor was even more inferior to its human counterparts than he'd thought was of far more practical value.

Made of some sort of advanced composite, it was lightweight, well articulated, and undoubtedly more comfortable than most military-issue human body armor. Those were its good points.

Its bad point—its *really* bad point, actually—was that while it would stop medium-caliber pistol fire with a fair degree of reliability at ranges over twenty-five yards or so, virtually *every* rifle round he'd tested against it blew straight through. Sharon's P90 certainly did, even firing civilian-legal loads. And the higher velocity steel penetrators of the SS190 law enforcement loads Rob Wilson had left lying carelessly about penetrated both front and back plates at ranges out to two hundred yards, almost three times the weapon's official effective range.

Which might turn out to be of vital importance if things went as badly that evening as they had the potential to go.

"I hate this," he'd said softly. "Especially leaving you and the kids behind without me. And I know it scares them whenever I'm gone."

"Of course it does," she'd said, reaching up and touching the side of his face. "They're *smart* kids, despite their father's genetic contribution. But Nimue's about ready to drop those pups of hers, which should help distract them at least a little this time."

"Good." He'd smiled down at her, but then his smile had faded and he'd shaken his head. "Good," he'd repeated more softly. "But if something goes wrong, I ought to be *here*, taking care of them—and you—not gallivanting around off in the rain somewhere!"

"Nobody's ever managed to be in two places at once," she'd replied. "And you told Sam and Dennis you'd be *there,* not here. Alec and Ronnie and Jessica and I will be waiting for you—with the kids—when you get back.

For that matter," she'd managed a smile, "I'll even have hot soup for you. I'm sure Ronnie and Jessica can manage that if I stay out of their way in the kitchen."

"You're sure about this?" he'd asked quietly, looking deep into her eyes once again. "I already found out it's not like shooting deer. It's not as bad as I'd always thought it might be, maybe because of everything I know they've already done, and maybe because I still don't really think of them as 'people.' But it was bad enough. Are you ready for that if it comes down to it?"

"If those long-eared freaks ever get this close, my kids—*our* kids—are going to be hiding inside that cave, scared out of their minds," she'd said, looking back unflinchingly. "Those kids are our lives, Dave. They're our future. Hell," Sharon Dvorak, unlike her brother, almost never swore, but she did this time, and her eyes gleamed with unshed tears, "they're our hearts and *souls,* and you damned well know it! And if anything happens to you, I'll see you in their faces, hear the echo of you in their voices. *Nothing* is going to take that away from me. Nothing on God's green earth—and I don't *care* how it got here!—is getting past me to hurt those kids! Don't you worry about what *I'm* ready for, David Dvorak. Not when our kids are involved!"

And so, now, he sat in the rain with his brother-in-law, waiting. Hoping they wouldn't be needed. Praying that if they were, nothing they or anyone else did would lead the Shongairi to that cabin and the cave beyond it.

"Backstop, Front Door," a voice said suddenly from the handheld radio Wilson carried. "Nanny's here."

"Front Door, Backstop copies," Wilson replied softly into the radio, then looked across at Dvorak. "And about damned time, too!" he muttered. "They're two frigging hours late as it is!"

Dvorak nodded in heartfelt agreement and relief, although using radios made him acutely unhappy. Still, they had to be able to communicate somehow, and the handheld, encrypyted units the North Carolina SBI had somehow misplaced had an effective range of less than ten miles even under optimum conditions, which these weren't. That should make them hard for any direction finders to pick up, especially in these mountains and with everyone limiting himself to the absolutely shortest transmissions possible. And if Dennis Vardry's contacts were right, the Shongairi weren't very good at hunting for them, anyway.

Of course, if Dennis is frigging wrong. . . .

Dvorak shoved that thought aside, as well. Besides, Dennis probably wasn't wrong. Over the last month or so, a lot of information about the Shongairi had started filtering down through the network of law enforcement personnel still managing to maintain something like order throughout the state. And so far almost everything they'd been able to test had checked out as accurate.

It was pretty obvious North Carolina was immensely better off than most of the country. Governor Howell could take a lot of the credit for that, as could people like Dennis Vardry and the sheriff's deputies and the state highway troopers who'd stayed put and fought the good fight. All the same, and much though it irked Dvorak to admit it, their success probably owed at least as much to the fact that the Shongairi had established that base of theirs near Greensboro, too. The aliens had made the state one of their occupation zones, and they'd concentrated enough manpower—and enough of their damned shuttles—to be pretty confident no one was going to argue with them very strongly.

There were undoubtedly those who were going to accuse Howell of selling out to the enemy. Dave Dvorak wasn't one of them, though, since he didn't see where Howell had had any particular choice when the Shongair base commander—Teraik, or whatever his name was—gave him his options: "submit" and cooperate, or see his capital and every other town and city in North Carolina go the same way as Charlotte.

Nope, Dvorak thought now, *not a lot of wiggle room in that.*

Apparently, however, the Shongairi were better at making people *agree* to cooperate than they were at enforcing actual obedience, and there was a lot of passive resistance going on. Not just spontaneously, either. Superiors—from the governor's own office on down, as far as Dvorak could tell—were actually *directing* subordinates to creatively "assist" their Shongair "guests" into . . . less than fully successful outcomes. No one was stupid enough to put anything into writing (e-mail didn't come into it, since the Shongairi had flatly refused to allow the Internet back up even among humans who'd "submitted"), but it didn't seem to have occurred to the Shongairi that bugging "their" humans' communications might be a good idea. In fact, the aliens seemed blissfully unaware of the human tendency to do end-runs around superiors they didn't much care for.

When Dvorak was a boy, his father had introduced him to an English translation of the Czech author Jaroslav Hašek's illustrated novel *The Fateful Adventures of the Good Soldier Švejk During the World War.* Švejk had been a complete idiot . . . *or* he'd been highly skilled at sabotaging his superior officers and the war effort in general by doing exactly what he'd been *ordered* to do rather than what they'd *intended* him to do. Dvorak had always liked that book. And from what he'd been able to pick up from Dennis and Mitchell, the entire state of North Carolina seemed to have become suddenly filled with Czech expatriates, all resolutely following the exact letter of their orders and not one of them able to find his own posterior with both hands and a flashlight if it involved doing something he thought was a Bad Idea.

The Shongairi didn't appear to have caught on yet, either. It was possible they realized what was going on and simply hadn't chosen to do anything about it, but Dvorak was damned if he could come up with any logical explanation for why they might have done something like that. Ridiculous as it might be on the face of it, it actually seemed more likely to him that they really and truly hadn't realized the humans whose world they'd invaded would promise faithfully to do one thing and then do something entirely different, all the while swearing it was what they thought they'd been *supposed* to do all along.

They also seemed unaware that huge quantities of information about their operational patterns, their plans, and their capabilities were hemorrhaging from their "submissive" human minions to the "wild humans" who had no intention of submitting. It didn't seem to have occurred to them, for example, that they couldn't coordinate with human agencies without at least partially briefing in the human agencies involved . . . and that some of the humans working for those agencies would then immediately make it their business to pass those briefings on to others.

Despite the ongoing passive (and not so passive) resistance, it had all made for an enormous easing of tension, of course, and Dvorak wasn't going to pretend he wasn't grateful. Governor Howell's government had somehow managed to keep essential services at least minimally online throughout most of the state and provided an interface between the invaders and the humans, as well. Quite aside from any successes in sabotaging Shongair activities, it was in a position to at least mitigate the worst conditions and to represent humans' desires and needs to the aliens. In fact, it had occurred to Dvorak that if the Shongairi had only been smart enough—or, at least, understood humans well enough—to have offered the same sort of arrangement to the world in general when they first arrived, things might have been very different.

Starting right out by killing a couple of billion people before you even announce your presence, though, he reflected now. *I don't know, but somehow I think* that's *likely to get you off on the wrong foot with their surviving brothers, sisters, cousins, fathers, mothers, and aunts and uncles.*

The thought flickered below the surface of his mind as he checked his weapon. He'd gone ahead and brought the Barrett, even though in this miserable weather any kind of really long-range shooting was out of the question. He simply couldn't *see* far enough through such heavy rain to make any really long shots. On the other hand, the rifle still offered all of its stopping power, and he'd had ample proof it was as capable of knocking out Shongair vehicles—and recon drones—as it was of knocking out *human* vehicles.

Which hopefully, he thought in a distinctly prayerful tone, *isn't going to matter one way or the other.*

"Jesus, I hate this frigging weather," Wilson muttered, and Dvorak snorted.

"Don't much like it myself," he acknowledged. "On the other hand, if Dennis and Sam are right, it's going to do a lot to knock back their thermal detectors. And I don't think their optical and low-light equipment is even as good as ours is."

"Yeah, yeah," Wilson grumbled. "Yada, yada, yada." He turned his head and grimaced at his brother-in-law. "Sorry," he said a bit contritely. "I know you really get into that kind of stuff. And I guess it's good to know. But I keep thinking about kids whistling in graveyards, know what I mean?"

"Damn straight I do," Dvorak muttered back. "And you're right. I sure as hell do *want* to believe that's the way it is. But it's not *just* wishful thinking, you know."

Wilson's eyes were back on the junction where Hannah Ford Road ran into US-64, but he nodded. Somehow, without their ever intending to do anything of the sort, the two of them had become a kind of clearinghouse for information. No more than thirty or forty people outside their immediate family knew about the cabin (or its exact location, anyway), but those thirty or forty people knew an amazing number of other people who were engaged in things of which the Shongairi no doubt would have disapproved. And the other people *they* knew, knew still other people, who knew still *other* people. Their web of direct and indirect contacts spread throughout the western portions of both Carolinas and well into eastern Tennessee, now, and quite a few people had figured out that if they dropped a word to the Dvoraks and Wilsons about a problem or a question, somehow that word would eventually reach the person they needed it to reach and answers would come back to them the same way.

At first, Dvorak and Wilson hadn't even realized that was happening. In fact, if they had realized they might well have tried to stop it, since the whole object of building the cabin had been to provide a bolthole for their family, not to set up some sort of guerrilla resistance organization! By the time they did realize, though, it was really too late to do anything about it. Besides, they'd been careful to keep the more . . . active aspects of the local resistance's operations as far away from home as possible.

Even without the involvement of their wives and children, that would have made sense from an operational perspective. Dvorak had never served in the military, and while Wilson had been a designated marksman, he'd never done any kind of special operations work. Nonetheless, it seemed obvious to both of them that the very first order of business had to be protecting your own side's communications nodes. And if that was an added reason to keep *their* kids as far away as possible from anything that might bite them, so much the better!

They'd both ventured considerably farther from home than Rosman as they became more actively involved, and Wilson had damned nearly gotten himself killed on one of those little escapades all the way over near the town of Clemmons, ten miles outside Winston-Salem and a hundred and sixty miles from the cabin. Dvorak was still convinced the raid on a Shongair convoy—which had destroyed fifteen of the limited number of APCs in North Carolina, not to mention two more GEVs—had been worthwhile, but they were lucky as hell they'd gotten Wilson back alive afterward. In fact, three of the eight other men from the upstate with him *had* been killed before the survivors managed to disengage and elude their pursuers. And that time they'd been careful to make sure they were outside the retaliation radius which the Shongairi had established for human towns too close to attacks. But this time, they were both painfully aware that they were barely eleven miles from the cabin. If the Shongairi got really pissed, if they decided to lob in a few KEWs just to teach the locals a lesson. . . .

"Come on," Wilson muttered now. "It's only three more frigging miles, Sam. *Come on!*"

Dvorak turned his own head to glance at his brother-in-law, but he didn't say anything. He understood exactly what Wilson was thinking at that particular moment.

"Front Door" was an Avery County deputy by the name of Paul Scanlon.

Scanlon's brief, five-word transmission had been confirmation that the refugees they were out here to meet had finally reached his position three miles to the east, where Connestee Road met US-276. At the moment, those refugees were somewhere between them and Scanlon, hopefully headed their way through a network of backcountry roads between US-276 and US-64 without anyone else the wiser. The land between the two highways was primarily farming country, cut by belts of woodland, so it wasn't like any of the back roads in question were anything like remotely *straight*, but west of Highway 64, the farms ended and the Pisgah National Forest began. The trick was to get the refugees the rest of the way into the national forest without anyone suffering a mischief, and the two of them were only one picket post established to watch the planned route ahead of Mitchell and his charges to be sure the coast was clear.

"Wish I knew why the puppies wanted these guys in the first place," Dvorak muttered now.

"You think I've suddenly figured that out? Or are you just talking to pass the time?" Wilson inquired sardonically, and he chuckled.

"Talking to keep my teeth from chattering, really. And, no, *not* because I'm cold."

"What I thought." Wilson snorted. "Don't think you're the only one feels that way, either."

Dvorak turned his head again to give his brother-in-law an affectionate smile, but he really did wish he knew what the Shongairi were up to. The only things he *did* know were that the Shongair base commander had ordered Howell to have his police round up a minimum of four hundred humans and deliver them to his base, and that Howell had declined. Which had been pretty ballsy of him, all things considered, although according to Vardry and Mitchell, the way he'd phrased it was basically that while he himself, of course, was completely willing to do whatever the Shongairi desired, it was likely to have less than desirable repercussions. Without any explanation of why the humans were wanted and at least some assurance of their ultimate safety, after all, it was bound to create uncertainty and anxiety among the humans who had submitted to the Shongairi. The consequences could be that some of those humans would renounce their submission, with the sort of results the Shongairi had seen elsewhere.

Given that guerrillas from outside had recently begun operating inside the state, the Shongair commander had apparently decided it would be just as well not to add any fuel to that particular fire by encouraging local participation. Instead, he'd informed Governor Howell that his own troops would secure the necessary humans from outside North Carolina. The governor had agreed that that was a much better idea, and suggested that if he knew the route by which the humans in question would be transported to Greensboro, his own police officials would be in a much better position to help provide for the transport convoy's security once it reached North Carolina.

The Shongair had decided that was a good idea, too, given his own increasing acute shortages of both troops and vehicles, and Howell had clamped down iron security all along the roadways between the South Carolina border and Greensboro. Any Shongair convoy that got into *his* state would by God get to Greensboro *intact*!

Of course, that hadn't said anything about any citizens of North Carolina—or raiders from outside the state who'd somehow come into contact with any citizens of North Carolina—who might somehow inadvertently find themselves south of the border on the day the transport convoy was due to arrive. Which was how somewhere in the neighborhood of two hundred Shongairi had been killed in a most unfortunate ambush on Interstate 26, three and a half miles southeast of Landrum, South Carolina . . . and three miles *south* of the state line. The guerrillas who'd actually hit the convoy had then headed down I-26 South, towards the ruins of Columbia, obviously fleeing deeper into the area of South Carolina the Shongairi hadn't occupied. They'd even abandoned a few "broken down" vehicles (with weapons still aboard) along their route to be sure any Shongair pursuers would know which direction they'd gone. But the humans the convoy had been transporting had headed south*west,* down South Carolina 14 to Highway 11, instead, then across to pick up US-276 above Slater and turn north again, towards Brevard by way of Caesar's Head. Hopefully, the Shongairi would be busy chasing after the guerrillas—once they realized the convoy had been attacked, at any rate—while the liberated prisoners were herded towards relative safety as quickly as possible along those narrow, twisty, tree-covered secondary highways.

As the bird flew, the ambush site was less than thirty-five miles from where Dvorak and Wilson squatted in the rain, but it was over fifty miles by road, and even in clear weather without any Shongair patrols or overflights to worry about, the drive would have taken an hour and a half. Under the conditions which actually obtained, it had taken one hell of a lot longer.

Without reliable, secure long-distance communications, it had been impossible to know whether or not the Shongairi had managed to keep to their intended schedule. If they *had,* however, then the attack should have occurred over five hours ago, and Mitchell and his little convoy of fugitives had been well overdue. Nobody's nerves had gotten any less tense as the minutes and the hours had dragged past, either. But so far, at least—

"Backstop, Corner Post," the radio said suddenly. "Puppies, headed south!"

"Oh, *fuck,*" Wilson whispered with soft, almost prayerful fervency.

"Get on the horn," Dvorak said tersely, already gathering up his rifle and moving to his left, where the belt of trees in which he and Wilson were positioned made a sharp corner and angled back to the west along the southern edge of a small industrial building's parking lot. "Tell them we've got company. They'd better either get a move on or turn the hell around!"

Wilson nodded and picked up the radio.

"Nanny, Backstop," he said. "Say time to Backstop."

"Backstop, Nanny," Sam Mitchell's voice replied from the SUV in which he was leading the caravan of two buses, a pair of two-and-a-half-ton flatbed trucks, and half a dozen vans, all of them crammed full of refugees, towards safety. "I make it four minutes. Say again, four mikes."

Wilson looked at Dvorak, who'd settled into his alternate firing position, facing up Highway 64 instead of across it, and raised his voice.

"What do I tell him, Dave?"

Dvorak thought hard, staring into the north. The rain wasn't quite as heavy as it had been, and the wind was driving it from the southeast, so at least it was at his back and he wasn't facing into it. Despite that, visibility was limited, to say the least. There was no sign yet of the Shongair patrol—and it almost had to be one of their routine patrols, he told himself, not someone specifically dispatched to intercept the refugees—"Corner Post" had just reported. Probably out of their satellite base in Old Fort, between Asheville and Hickory. They made fairly frequent sweeps in this direction, and they timed them randomly to keep the humans guessing. So. . . .

Four minutes, Mitchell estimated. That didn't seem like very long. On the other hand, "Corner Post" (an Asheville city policeman named Grayson) was only seven miles north, on the far side of Brevard, watching the interchange where US-64 peeled off to the east towards Hendersonville and US-276 headed west towards Waynesville. Shongair patrols normally moved at about forty-five miles an hour. In this weather, they'd probably be a little slower . . . call it forty; that'd be about right, judging from other reports on their operations. So, seven miles at forty miles per hour came to . . . about *five* minutes.

Oh, crap.

"Tell him to fucking floor it," Dave Dvorak said. "Then get your ass over here. I'm afraid things are going to get . . . busy."

.XXXI.

Senior Squad Commander Laifayr sat in the commander's seat of the APC with his feet propped on the heater and tried not to shiver in the raw, wet chill.

His vehicle wasn't *really* an APC, of course. Losses in those—and even more in the GEVs—had been the next best thing to catastrophic. In fact, even though Laifayr wasn't supposed to be thinking about things that far above his own rank, he had the distinct impression that "catastrophic" might actually be too anemic an adjective. At any rate, the *real* APCs had mostly been assigned to ground bases where the local population was more unruly than in Ground Base Two Alpha's ZOR. And the handful which *had* been made available to Ground Base Commander Teraik were reserved for critical assignments.

Which, unfortunately, Laifayr's routine patrol wasn't.

That was why he was driving along through this miserable rain, watching it blur and splatter on the windshield, in what was basically a standard cargo vehicle to the sides of which Ground Base Two Alpha's maintenance techs had tacked jury-rigged armor plate. Only, of course, it wasn't real armor plate, either, just tripled layers of old-fashioned building composite. It was probably tougher than its human equivalent—he understood they used something called "plywood," a natural cellulose product, for similar building purposes—and three layers of it would stop fire from the Shongairi's own small arms handily. Laifayr was less confident about how well they would stop *human* small arms fire, however. And he was *positive* it wouldn't stop those damned shoulder-fired disposable rockets of theirs.

Of course, no one had done anything about providing them with overhead cover, had they? The "armored" trucks' cargo compartments still had only their fabric covers, so they remained completely vulnerable to overhead fire, although he supposed he should be grateful his troopers at least had firing ports cut through their "armor." They could fire from cover against anyone who *wasn't* in a position to shoot down at them from above. And there was a light auto-cannon mounted on the "APC's" cab, as well. There was a downside to that, too, naturally, since nobody had provided a hatch to seal the access trunk to the gun position in bad weather. The best he'd been able to do was rig a tarp across the gun and snug it down, and even then icy rainwater kept dripping down onto the driver and the communications tech squeezed up against the right side door.

And did we get any RC drones? Laifayr asked himself sardonically. *Of course we didn't!* They're *getting too thin on the ground, too, aren't they? Cainharn! I don't think I've ever heard of a colonizing expedition a* twelfth part *as fucked up as this one!*

He wasn't supposed to know just how bad the equipment shortages had become, but he doubted any officer anywhere had ever managed to keep the regular troopers from knowing things they "weren't supposed to know." That was the nature of reality in the Emperor's service. And, to be fair, he was pretty sure—well, maybe not quite *that* sure—that the shortages were worse in Ground Base Two Alpha's zone than elsewhere. Things had been so much quieter around here, at least until recently, that the other ground bases had been assigned a higher priority for already scarce equipment.

Yeah, and the last *damned thing you want, Laifayr, is for the situation to change enough that they suddenly decide they have to start transferring combat equipment back into* your *zone to deal with it!*

That wasn't the way a Shongair trooper, a Shongair hunter, was supposed to think, but Laifayr had become a sadder and a wiser Shongair. It was one thing to hunt aborigines armed with flint-tipped arrows or even iron swords and spearheads. It was quite another to hunt somebody who not only had firearms but personal weapons which were actually *better* than one's own. And, frankly, the sooner he got far, far away from these lunatic humans, the better he'd like it!

He grimaced and leaned closer to the windshield, rubbing at the mist which had condensed on its inner surface, and peered through the water-streaming crystoplast.

They were rolling into one of the humans' towns—the one called "Brevard" on the maps. There didn't seem to be many of the aliens about at the moment, though. Not too surprisingly, probably, in this weather. He knew they were virtually out of fuel for their vehicles, and *he* damned well wouldn't have been out walking in rain like this unless he absolutely had to!

He thought about ordering the communications tech up onto the auto-cannon, given the opportunities for ambushes the town's buildings afforded. On the other hand, the one thing even humans weren't stupid enough to do anymore was to actually ambush Shongairi inside one of their towns. They'd had ample evidence of what would happen to any town within two of their miles of where something like *that* happened!

No, if anything was likely to happen, it wouldn't be inside one of their towns or cities. On the other hand. . . .

"Slow down a little," he told the driver, scrubbing off more condensation—this time on the side window—and looking into the rain-blurred rearview mirror on his side for the headlights of the other two semiarmored cargo haulers of his outsized squad. He could see only one set of lights, and he grimaced. "Let the others catch up a bit before we head back out into the country."

"Yes, Senior Squadron Commander," the driver replied, and Laifayr returned his efforts to peering through the windshield once more as the vehicle slowed a little.

He couldn't see much, and he glanced at his awkwardly mounted thermal viewer. It was a standard infantry model, fitted to the "APC" as best the techs could manage, and squeezing it in hadn't been easy. He had to bend over and crane his neck uncomfortably to use it, which was probably one reason he didn't spend more time looking through it. Besides, the infantry model wasn't worth much compared to the ones normally mounted in the real APCs and GEVs. It was shorter ranged and less sensitive, and rain like this really hammered its range back. Under *these* conditions, he'd probably see anything worth seeing with his unaided eyes before he'd pick it up with that piece of junk!

Not that there is *anything to see right this minute,* he thought grumpily, and sat back once more, thinking longingly of the patrol's end.

• • • • •

SAM MITCHELL'S SUV came scooting out of Hannah Ford Road onto US-64. Its headlights were off, despite the bad weather and limited visibility, and Dave Dvorak and Rob Wilson felt a huge surge of relief as they saw it. Unfortunately, the game plan had been for the convoy to turn to the right and travel another mile to the point at which 64 intersected Island Ford Road and Cathey's Creek Road. From there, it would head up Cathey's Creek to the National Forest Road, a little over three miles northwest of Brevard.

That twisting, circuitous, heavily overgrown road would take them deep into the Pisgah Forest, where concealment would be much more easily come by. Eventually, they would reconnect with US-276 around Waynesville, then head across into Tennessee by way of the back roads that ran up over Eaglenest Mountain.

Which would have been just fine . . . if it hadn't required them to go *north* first—directly towards the oncoming Shongair patrol.

Wilson was waiting outside the tree line with a Maglite flashlight, and he speared the windshield of Mitchell's SUV with the light's diamond-bright beam the instant he saw it. Mitchell braked hard, then leaned out the driver's window.

"*What?*" he shouted.

"Take 'em south!" Wilson shouted back. "Pick up 215, then take it up to the Parkway and cross into Tennessee that way!"

Mitchell didn't hesitate, despite the abrupt change in plans. He only nodded back, then accelerated south along the divided highway in a splattering slipstream of rain. The buses, trucks, and vans of the rest of his little convoy came hurtling out of Hannah Ford Road right behind him, following his taillights, and Wilson ran sloshingly through the rain to join his brother-in-law.

"Any sign of them yet?" he panted, flopping down in the sodden leaves, and Dvorak shook his head without looking away from the road. He had his big rifle's bipod firmly settled, and he'd laid out his extra magazines.

"Nope," he said now. "I expect they'll be along any minute, though. Question is, what do we do about them?"

"If they're willing to leave us alone, then I move we leave *them* alone," Wilson replied, wiggling into a comfortable firing position of his own. "I think Sam's got a pretty good head start. If they aren't coming pretty fast, I doubt they'll spot any of his vehicles. And once he gets off 64 onto 215, he'll have that ridge between him and the highway."

"Agreed," Dvorak said, and looked at him. Neither of them wanted to admit the fear they felt. The new route Wilson had just sent Mitchell along ran within less than eight miles of the cabin and their family. If the Shongairi *did* spot the escaping convoy and went in pursuit. . . .

Would it be better to go ahead and ambush them here? Dvorak wondered tensely. *We're five miles from Sam's turnoff. If we were to nail them here, would it keep them from following him up, closer to the cabin? But on the other hand, we don't have a clue how many of the bastards there are. For that matter, if they never even notice us, if they just drive on by, then. . . .*

. . . . .

THE PATROL'S VEHICLES had closed up nicely again, Senior Squad Commander Laifayr decided, watching the headlights of the other two vehicles in the mirror. Another day-twelfth or so, and they could turn around and head back towards their home base at the human town of Old Fort . . . not that he was looking forward to that horrible stretch of the humans' "interstate" between there and Black Mountain. The only good thing about Old Fort Mountain was that they'd be going *down* it this time, although that had its own drawbacks in weather like this.

Cainharn, this whole damned planet *has its drawbacks!* he grumbled to himself.

. . . . .

HIS NAME WAS Jamison Snelgrove. He was a thirty-six-year-old lawyer who'd enjoyed a promising career before the Shongairi arrived, and his wife Melanie was pregnant with their second child.

Neither of them had wanted the nightmare which had enveloped their world over the last three and a half months, and they'd done their best to ride out the storm at Melanie's folks' North Carolina farm. They'd been making out fairly well—not everybody was well fed, and none of them were looking forward to the coming winter, but they'd been making it.

Until Melanie went into premature labor, anyway.

The phones were down, of course, and the nearest doctor they knew about was in Brevard, so that left only one thing to do. Fortunately, they'd been hoarding gasoline against exactly this sort of an emergency.

Which is how Jamison and Melanie Snelgrove came out of Hannah Ford Road onto US-64 barely three minutes behind the convoy of refugees and just as Senior Squad Commander Laifayr's patrol came down it from Brevard, headed south in the northbound lane.

. . . . .

***"SHIT!"* ROB WILSON** hissed as the pickup truck came hurtling out of Hannah Ford so fast it fishtailed on the wet pavement when the driver turned north.

"Take it easy!" Dvorak responded. He'd flipped up the lens covers on his rifle sight and was peering through it towards the headlights which had just appeared to the north of their position. "May be the best thing that could've happened. If the patrol stops these folks and they've got a legitimate reason to be out here, it'll delay the puppies long enough for Sam to get his people completely out of sight."

"Yeah, we can *hope*," Wilson muttered.

• • • • •

SENIOR SQUAD COMMANDER Laifayr blinked as he saw the headlights appear suddenly in front of him. They were headed directly towards him, and they had that peculiar blue-white intensity only humans' headlights had. It was the first time he'd seen a human vehicle on his patrol route in the last five days, though, and he felt himself perking with curiosity.

Probably one of the local government's official vehicles, he thought. *No one else would have the fuel to be out here.*

• • • • •

"JIMMY!" **MELANIE SNELGROVE** screamed as she saw the trio of headlights suddenly coming directly towards them on their side of the road. The color didn't look right to her, and then her eyes went even wider as she made out the poorly seen silhouettes behind them. She'd never seen anything quite like them, and she knew—without question or doubt—that those weren't *human*-designed trucks.

Jamison saw them, too. He stared at them for half a heartbeat, then wrenched his head around towards his wife. Melanie was white-faced with fear, hands clutching her abdomen as another of those terrifying, premature contractions ran through her.

Half a hundred chaotic thought fragments flashed through Jamison's brain. There wasn't time for any of them to truly register, be completely thought out. They were bits and pieces. His terrified wife. Their unborn child. Rain beating on the pickup's windshield and side windows. The uncertainty of how the aliens would react. Hum of hot air through the defroster vents. Fear for what might happen to Melanie. Fear that even if the aliens had no hostile intent, they would delay him, keep him from reaching the doctor in time. Clicking sound of windshield wipers. Reports and rumors about clashes with the Shongairi. Pickup tires hissing on wet pavement as they carried him towards the alien vehicles. . . .

All of that flashed and chattered and yammered in his brain, and his hands acted without command. He slammed the wheel hard around to the left, stamped on the gas pedal, and accelerated desperately south, away from the oncoming patrol.

. . . . .

LAIFAYR SHOT BOLT upright in his seat as the human vehicle suddenly turned away. It accelerated with amazing speed, rocketing away from him like a Deathwing with its tail on fire. He'd heard that the absurdly overpowered human vehicles had better acceleration rates than anything except a GEV, but this was the first time he'd actually seen it demonstrated. Still. . . .

"After them!" he snapped at his driver.

. . . . .

"FUCK, FUCK, *FUCK!*" Wilson snarled as the pickup truck abruptly whirled around.

He had no idea why the driver of that vehicle had decided to run for it. Maybe the idiot had a perfectly good reason—a reason even Rob Wilson would have approved of, or at least sympathized with, if he'd only known what it was. But at this moment, the only thing Wilson could think of was that fleeing pickup truck leading the Shongair patrol straight towards Sam Mitchell's convoy.

"Wh—?" he began, but the deafening blast of his brother-in-law's rifle answered the question before he ever got it asked.

. . . . .

DAVE DVORAK HAD spent hours studying diagrams and sketches—even a few digital photos—of Shongair vehicles. Most of the photos only showed the vehicles driving by, and even the ones that showed them parked and motionless were usually taken from far enough away to show considerably less detail than he would have preferred. The diagrams had helped a lot, though, and between them he'd established clearly in his mind where the driver of any given vehicle was likely to be. More than that, one of the diagrams Sam Mitchell had brought him had given him a detailed feel for where the Shongairi kept the radios, and the range was barely a hundred and fifty yards.

A corner of his brain had already noted that *these* trucks seemed to be covered in something he hadn't seen before. Probably it was the improvised armor Mitchell and Vardry had described to him. If so, it wasn't likely to stop one of the Barrett's big slugs, but it might pose a problem for Wilson's lighter .308s.

Deal with that when you get there, that same corner of his brain told him. The open front lens cover gave his sight some protection from the rain. The fact that the rain was coming from his right rear, rather than directly towards him, helped even more. He could just make out a shadowy, blurred, indistinct form through the windshield where the diagrams told him the driver ought to be, and the recoil of the big, bellowing rifle came as a surprise to him, exactly the way it was supposed to.

. . . . .

LAIFAYR'S "APC" WAS just beginning to accelerate when the 647-grain bullet blew a head-sized chunk of the windshield into fragments and the rest into a crazy-quilt web of cracks, then struck his driver just below the center of his chest.

The sheer concussion of being that close to a bullet that big traveling that fast when it struck something solid would have been bad enough. The finely divided spray of blood and tissue that blasted out behind it was even worse.

The senior squad commander's eyes went huge in shocked disbelief as about half his driver's total blood supply exploded across him, and that shock turned rapidly into something far worse as the vehicle swerved wildly. The bullet's impact had half-disintegrated the upper portion of the driver's torso, and the improvised "APC" responded by going completely out of control and turning sharply to its left.

The good news was that the driver's sudden and violent demise had thrown his entire body back, away from the Shongair equivalent of the gas pedal, as well as the steering. The sudden swerve, coupled with the abrupt disappearance of any pressure on its accelerator, told the truck's onboard computer something had gone wrong. It was a simpleminded device, but it knew what to do in that case. It applied the brakes automatically, and the armored truck began slowing rapidly before it could hurtle completely off the highway and into a rain-soaked patch of trees east of the road.

That was the good news. The *bad* news was that the flesh-and-blood driver of the patrol's second vehicle didn't have time to react before it plowed broadside into Laifayr's. The impact drove the lead vehicle the rest of the way off the road and into the trees after all. It also locked both of them together, and the senior squad commander heard shouts of panic—and pain—from the troopers huddled together for warmth under the cargo bed's fabric cover.

The *worse* news was that whoever had just killed his driver was still shooting from a bunch of trees three hundred *urma* to the south and on the *west* side of the highway.

. . . . .

DVORAK WATCHED THE two lead trucks run into each other and slide off the road. From the screeching sound—funny, a part of him noted even now, how Shongair brakes and human brakes sounded exactly the same in a situation like this—and then the echoing sound of impact, they'd hit at a high enough rate of speed he could pretty much ignore the two of them for the moment.

He switched his point of aim to his left and, sure enough, the third truck's driver decided to come around the collision on that side, where the highway's median and southbound lanes offered him more clearance.

Idiot, the human thought coldly. *Last thing he needs to be doing is charging straight into my sights!*

His finger stroked the trigger again.

. . . . .

IN FAIRNESS TO the third driver, he had no idea what was going on. All *he* knew was that both of the vehicles in front of him had abruptly accelerated and then, for reasons unknown, the two of them had collided. Dvorak's position was completely invisible from his position at the rear of the short column, and it never occurred to him that the "accident" might have been the result of hostile action.

It might well have occurred to him a second or two later, but he was too busy avoiding the two trucks in front of him to think about it at the moment. And, unfortunately, the unanticipated arrival of Dvorak's second shot meant it never *would* occur to him, after all.

. . . . .

ROB WILSON WAS less confused than the unfortunate Shongair driver. As a consequence, he knew exactly what he should be doing. Like Dvorak, however, he'd realized what the peculiar slab-sided layers of material on the Shongair trucks had to be and, also like Dvorak, he had no idea whether or not his fire would penetrate it.

One way to find out, he told himself philosophically, and opened a rapid, aimed fire. From over a hundred yards away, in the rain, he couldn't tell whether or not his rounds were penetrating, but at least he didn't see any of those dramatic, sparkling ricochets the movies had always loved.

. . . . .

DVORAK SWITCHED BACK to the first truck, putting a round through the area where the radio was supposed to be. He was shooting blind this time, because the vehicle had turned partly away from him with the impact, presenting him with a three-quarter view of the solid rear of the cab. On the other hand, there wasn't much question about whether or not *his* fire was getting through. Even in the poor light and the rain, his telescopic sight clearly showed him a sudden hand-sized patch of bare alloy or composite where whatever the Shongairi used for paint had been literally blasted away by the bullet's impact. There was a dark hole in the center of that bare patch, and he moved his point of aim to the second truck, punching bullets through *its* cab.

· · · · ·

SENIOR SQUAD COMMANDER Laifayr crouched as low as he could, sandwiched between the mangled bodies of his driver and his communications tech. If anyone had told him someone was shooting at him with a mere rifle, he would never have believed it. And, in fact, the bullets coming at him from Dave Dvorak's rifle were actually larger than the high-explosive shells of the ten-millimeter cannon on the roof of his "APC."

But what they were being launched from was far less important to Laifayr at that moment than the consequences of their arrival.

Panic yammered at the back of his brain. Without an RC drone, and with his communications tech dead (not to mention the shattered hole the bullet which killed him had punched through the com unit itself) there was no way to summon assistance. None of their personal units had the range or the power for that kind of work, anyway. He could only hope one of the other vehicles had managed to get off a message, and whether it had or not, no help was going to get here in time to save any of them unless they did it on their own.

He crawled and squirmed across the seat, kicking and pummeling the driver's mangled corpse out of his way, and managed to open the door on the far side from whoever was shooting at them. Thoughts of the autocannon did flicker through his mind as he rolled out into the painful scratchy embrace of the tree limbs, but he brushed them aside quickly. He'd left his own rifle in the cab, and his sidearm couldn't possibly reach whoever was shooting at him. A little voice suggested he should go back and get it, but he brushed that voice aside even more quickly than he had the thought of the cannon.

It wasn't his responsibility to get tied down in a firefight, he told himself. No, it was his responsibility to impose some sort of order on this ravening chaos. And if that just happened to keep him out of the direct line of fire of whatever demon had torn apart the other two troopers in the cab with him, so much the better.

He fought his way through the clinging branches of the scrubby trees which had enfolded the "APC," then reached up and pounded on the improvised armor of the cargo bed and started bellowing orders at the troopers he hoped were still alive inside it.

• • • • •

THE SECOND "APC'S" commander—braver (or stupider) than Laifayr—did force his way up through the access trunk and grabbed the firing grips of his auto-cannon. Unfortunately, his movements attracted Dave Dvorak's eye. A moment later, the commander himself attracted another of Dvorak's bullets.

Rifle barrels were beginning to thrust out of some of the firing ports cut through the vehicles' "armor." The Shongairi behind those rifles had strictly limited fields of view. One or two of them, though, had seen the impressive flash from Dvorak's muzzle brake in the gathering darkness, and their fire started sizzling back towards the two humans belly down in the sodden woods.

• • • • •

***JESUS, THERE'S* A** bunch of them! Rob Wilson thought as Shongair muzzles began to flash.

He didn't know whether or not the Shongairi had gotten off a contact report. If the information they'd been provided by the state troopers who'd had more contact with them was correct, their communications weren't very good without those drones of theirs, and he'd neither seen (nor heard) one of them. It looked like Dvorak had ripped hell out of the trucks' cabs, too. It seemed unlikely there was anyone alive in there, anymore, and if there were, it struck him as a pretty fair bet Dvorak had taken out their internal radios.

Which, unfortunately, left what looked and sounded like thirty or forty *really* pissed-off Shongairi inside the trucks' cargo compartments.

"Hey!" he shouted at his brother-in-law. "I don't know if I'm even getting through! Start ripping up the truck beds—I'll handle any runners!"

• • • • •

***SWEET DAINTHAR!* LAIFAYR** thought as he heard the bloodcurdling shriek and saw one of Dvorak's slugs punch right through the *far* side of the truck's "armor."

He could hear the steady, measured reports of the human's monster rifle now, and his spirit quailed at the thought of facing that sort of destructive power. Another round slammed into the troop compartment. At least this one didn't come all the way out the other side, but more screams told him it had found a target anyway.

"Out of the trucks!" he heard himself shouting. "*Out of the trucks!* Don't just sit there—we've got to go *after* them!"

. . . . .

DVORAK AND WILSON saw the Shongairi come boiling out of the tangle of vehicles. It didn't look as if most of the aliens had a very clear fix on their enemies' positions, but they obviously had at least a general notion of where the fire was coming from. Some of them clearly *did* know where to look—probably from Dvorak's muzzle flashes—and they'd obviously figured out that sitting in place wasn't going to work for them.

Now thirty-seven Shongair troopers started towards the two humans, a football field and a half away, firing their weapons as they came.

. . . . .

***SHIT,* WILSON THOUGHT.** *I feel like fucking Butch and Sundance in Bolivia!*

Shongair bullets began to whine and crackle entirely too close for comfort. He made himself ignore the sound, concentrating on servicing targets and wishing for the first time that his rifle had a full-auto setting.

A hundred and fifty yards didn't seem like all that far with forty or so murderous aliens charging towards you across it.

. . . . .

IF, IN FACT, the Shongairi had simply charged—charged as quickly as they could possibly move, taking their losses to close the distance—it would all have been over in a hurry. Human troops, realizing they were taking fire only from a pair of semiautomatic weapons, might well have done just that. The Shongairi weren't accustomed to taking aimed rifle fire at *all*, however. There were very few veterans of combat against humans in Laifayr's patrol, and even their experience was limited. So instead of charging, or even using one squad to lay down suppressing fire while the other one charged, *both* squads surged forward in a sort of half run, half trot, firing as they came.

It gave them the worst of both worlds. They were moving too rapidly to aim, but moving slowly enough to give the humans more time to engage them.

. . . . .

DVORAK EJECTED A spent magazine and slapped in another.

"Next-to-last!" he shouted to Wilson.

"*Told* you those big-assed bullets took up too much frigging space!" Wilson snarled back.

"Squinchy little Irish bastard!" Dvorak replied, squeezing off another round and watching yet another Shongair fly backward. "At least when I hit one of them, the fucker goes down!"

"*When* you hit one of them!" Wilson agreed as Dvorak's next target stumbled just as he fired. The bullet missed completely, and Dvorak snarled, readjusted his point of aim, and fired again.

"Better!" Wilson congratulated him.

"Glad you liked—"

The bullet wasn't aimed, not really. In fact, the Shongair trooper who'd fired it was already going down with one of Rob Wilson's .308 slugs in his chest when his finger jerked convulsively at his trigger.

None of which made any particular difference when it slammed into Dave Dvorak.

Wilson heard a hard, slapping sound. Then his brother-in-law grunted explosively and he felt something that wasn't rain—something hot, not cold—splash the left side of his face.

He couldn't turn his head and look, not then. Not with the Shongairi still coming for them.

"Dave?" he called. *"Dave?!"*

. . . . .

LAIFAYR REALIZED ONE of the human weapons—the heavy one which had punched so effortlessly through anything in its way—had fallen silent, and he felt a sudden surge of hope. Despite the fear still hammering through him, he'd been listening, and he'd realized what none of the rest of his troopers had. The weapons firing at them were firing *single* shots, not automatic. And now it sounded like there was only one of them left! So if he could just get his own warriors across the remaining twenty *urma* or so of wet grass and pavement between them quickly enough—

"Yes!" he shouted, coming to his feet behind the twelve and a half of his remaining troopers. "*Yes!* Now—*charge* the vermin!"

. . . . .

ROB WILSON SAW them coming.

Steam rose from his rifle's barrel in the rain, and he'd lost track of how many rounds were left in the current magazine. There wasn't much time to think about things like that, either.

As the Shongairi came to their feet in a single wave and started forward, he rose on one knee, firing with deadly precision, speed, and accuracy as he worked his way across their line. One of them went down, then another. A third. A fourth.

He knocked them down like wooden bowling pins in a Friday night pin-shooting contest against Sam Mitchell back at the range, but for every Shongair that went down, the survivors gained another half stride. It was a race between how quickly he could kill them and how quickly they could get to him—or one of them could finally manage to put a bullet *in*to him—and it was a race he was losing.

He fired again, and his ninth—or was it the tenth?—target went down, but the bolt locked back on an empty magazine. There was no time to load another one, if he still had one left—he wasn't sure, anyway—and he dropped the rifle.

Over the years, Rob Wilson had instructed more Marines and cops than he could count in the proper use of handguns, and he'd always made a point of depressing the pretensions of any would-be two-gun pistoleros who crossed his path. That kind of fancy shit looked good in movies, he'd told them cuttingly. Of course, in that case both the writers and the director were on the side of the hero as he unerringly picked off individual targets with each hand while simultaneously hurling his body in a graceful, headfirst, slow-motion, midair roll of a leap through a solid hail of automatic fire. In real life, the hurlee would almost certainly end up shredded and dead, he'd pointed out. And even if the idiot survived—miracles *did* occasionally happen, after all, and he'd been told God sometimes took pity on lunatics, drunks, and fools—all he'd really achieve was to totally waste the ammunition from both of the guns in question. Even standing *still* he'd waste most of his shots because the human brain had this odd little quirk: it found it quite difficult to focus on two separate sight pictures simultaneously.

Especially if the targets weren't standing conveniently side by side where the shooter could actually *see* both of them at once.

He couldn't remember the number of times he'd said that, and every time he said it, he'd meant it. Which was one of the reasons his brother-in-law had ribbed him mercilessly when he tucked one .40 caliber HK USP automatic into his old USMC shoulder holster and a second into a tactical drop holster on his left thigh before setting out on their current excursion.

He'd told Dvorak the second gun was only a backup, but they'd both known that wasn't quite the truth. Because, while it was absolutely true that nine pistoleers out of ten couldn't hit the broad side of a barn with their off hands if they tried to fire two handguns at once, Rob Wilson was the *tenth* pistoleer.

His hands found the grips without any conscious thought on his part. The pistols cleared their holsters, coming up, settling into position, even as he stood fully upright. Something whizzed viciously past his left ear, but he paid no attention at all.

He had other things on his mind.

. . . . .

LAIFAYR SAW THE single human come to its feet. Its hands didn't even seem to move, but suddenly there was a big, black pistol in each of them. The sight registered on the senior squad commander with strange, almost frozen, crystalline clarity.

And then those pistols began to spit fire.

. . . . .

IF EVEN ONE of the six surviving Shongairi had thought to pause long enough to actually take aim it might have been different.

But they didn't. Instead, obedient to Laifayr's order, they hurled themselves forward . . . directly into Wilson's fire at a range so short their body armor was completely useless.

. . . . .

THE LAST OF Senior Squad Commander Laifayr's troopers went down, and Laifayr gawked across their fallen bodies at the demon who'd killed them. The half-twelve of shots had come so close together they'd been a single fist of sound, like some angry giant ripping a sheet of fabric in half, and so far as he could see, not *one* of them had missed its target.

You should have stayed up closer behind them, a little voice told him as he brought up his own sidearm in the prescribed two-handed shooting position. Maintaining a little extra distance had seemed like a good idea, but now—

You're too far away to hit anyone from here with a handgun, you fool!

He squeezed off a shot, then another one. The human didn't even seem to notice. Instead, he turned slightly away from Laifayr, raising one hand in the Shongair's direction in a movement that seemed oddly elegant, graceful despite the squatness of the human's chunky, alien body.

Then Rob Wilson's raised hand flashed fire, and Laifayr discovered he wasn't too far away to *be* hit with a handgun, after all.

. XXXII .

"Yes, Fleet Commander? How may I serve?" Ground Base Commander Shairez asked, folding her ears respectfully as Thikair's image appeared on her comm display.

"If even a quarter of the rest of my personnel served as well as you do, Ground Base Commander," Thikair replied, "we would conquer this Cainharn-bedamned species after all!"

His voice was hard, sharp-edged with anger, and the tips of his canines showed. But then he drew a deep breath and visibly forced himself to calm, if not to relax.

"Unfortunately, they do not . . . and we won't," he said more heavily.

"Should I assume there have been additional . . . unforeseen problems, Sir?" she asked quietly.

"Indeed you should," he told her, and rubbed the bridge of his muzzle with one hand.

He looked old, she thought. Not simply older, but *old*. The thought sent a pang through her, and she felt one hand stir at her side, as if to rise and extend itself in a gesture of sympathy. But she would only have shamed him if she had allowed it to do that, and so she simply waited.

"Our efforts to collect the necessary research subjects for Ground Base Commander Teraik . . . have not prospered," Thikair said finally. "I don't know how much of 'Governor Howell's' advice was sincere and how much of it was more of the humans' 'sabotage,' but Teraik believed—and I agreed—that there was logic to it. Whatever Howell's actual attitude may be, Ground Base Two Alpha's ZOR is the only one on the entire planet we can really consider relatively tranquil. Please do note that I used the qualifier 'relatively.'"

His ears twitched in a wry smile which contained at least a ghost of the dry humor Shairez had always associated with the fleet commander before their arrival in this star system.

"At any rate, Howell pointed out that if we began collecting research subjects in the necessary quantities from within his state of North Carolina it would generate unrest. Given your recent discoveries about this species' psychology, I think he was probably correct about that. Dainthar only knows how these humans' 'family groups' would react if we started dragging off their cubs or their sires or dams! And, of course, if we were to experience general unrest in Teraik's zone, that would tend to undercut any future claim on our part that the area had been thoroughly pacified and so, of course, we would never have deliberately released a bioweapon within *it,* of all places.

"Because of that, I instructed Teraik to collect his specimens from outside North Carolina. He attempted to do so. Unfortunately, his first two convoys of captured humans were both ambushed before they could reach his zone. Indeed, before they ever crossed the border into North Carolina, at all." The fleet commander's ears grimaced. "I fear we've had very little luck trying to locate Teraik's prey after it bolted, either. It would appear one of our routine patrols *may* have stumbled into contact with the humans who ambushed the second convoy. We can't be certain, since there were no surviving troopers from either the convoy *or* the patrol."

Shairez felt her own ears pressing close to her skull, and Thikair snorted.

"I'm inclined to believe Teraik is correct that none of the human Howell's personnel were involved in the attacks upon the convoys themselves. I'm less confident that none of them were involved in hiding the escaped specimens or helping them to escape afterward. Analysis of the attacks themselves, however, suggests that they were carried out by one of the band of raiders we've been tracking as best we can. They appear to have been working their way south for some time now, and we've amassed an unfortunate degree of familiarity with their handiwork. They routinely display a high degree of precision in both their timing and their maneuvers, and they obviously have an excellent appreciation of our doctrine and tactics, and Teraik has assigned them responsibility for the attack on the basis of their . . . style, for want of a better word. I think I agree with his assessment, based on the reports I've seen so far. The attackers seem to have used their shoulder-launched antiair missiles to destroy the convoys' RC drones in the same pattern that band has previously employed, and their evasion techniques—fleeing into areas we've already devastated and going to ground, probably in preselected positions, in the ruins—also fit what we've seen from them in the past.

"I've diverted additional personnel to Teraik to assist in hunting down those raiders. Unfortunately, in their attacks on his convoys, they've already destroyed an additional eight GEVs and a full twelve of APCs, in addition to perhaps twice that many cargo vehicles. We can ill afford to continue sustaining such losses, and so I've instructed Teraik to suspend the gathering of specimens until the raiders have been located and destroyed. Frankly, given the persistent survival of this particular group of vermin, I have no idea how long that will take.

"In the meantime, however, I see no reason why we should allow this to delay the development of the necessary bioweapon. Have you sufficient specimens on hand in Ground Base Seven to begin the required research there, instead of in Ground Base Two Alpha?"

"I think . . . yes, Fleet Commander," Shairez said slowly, considering resources and availability even as she spoke. "I have approximately a double-twelve of humans left from my experiments with the neural educators. That should be enough to make a start, but, obviously, it would be grossly insufficient for a development program on the scale we'll require. I would have to collect more."

"Will that be a problem?" Thikair asked.

"I think not, although I'd like to consider the best approach to the operation for a few day-twelfths before I respond definitively, Sir," she said. "Things have been so quiet here in my zone—relatively speaking, at least"—his ears twitched in amusement as she allowed herself to use his own qualifier, and she smiled back—"that a considerable proportion of my combat equipment and troops have been redeployed to Ground Base Six. Ground Base Commander Fursa has been having a far worse time dealing with the numerous human attacks in his ZOR."

She was too tactful, Thikair noticed, to point out that the real reason she'd been forced to send her armored vehicles to Fursa had less to do with the *number* of human attackers in Fursa's zone than with their *effectiveness*. The truth was that the Cainharn-damned humans—and not just in Ground Base Six's zone, although losses had been heavy there—had shot up enough of Ground Force Commander Thairys' original inventory of combat equipment to leave him spread desperately thin. There simply wasn't enough of it to go around; *no one* had the GEVs and APCs he really needed, far less the cushion the TO&E normally assigned.

"In addition," Shairez continued, "I share some of Ground Base Commander Teraik's concerns. Particularly in light of my . . . shortage of ground combat power, I would much prefer not to agitate the humans in my immediate ZOR. I think it would be wiser if I collected my specimens at some distance from the base itself."

"Do you have a specific supply of specimens in mind?" Thikair asked.

"Not at this moment," she admitted. "That's one of the points I wish to consider, and I'd prefer to confer with Regiment Commander Harah and seek his advice, as well. It would be best, I think, to select some relatively isolated area where there would be few human eyes to notice we were collecting specimens at all. That would be one way to minimize the . . . disturbing effect throughout my zone. And, to be honest, at this point I have more assigned shuttles and shuttle lift capacity than I have troopers or equipment to move about." She allowed her ears to stir in a sardonic smile. "Transporting my catch, even from a relatively distant hunting ground, would not pose any significant problem."

"Very well, Ground Base Commander." Thikair's ears nodded in agreement. "I'll leave you to your conference. As soon as you've satisfied yourself as to the best fashion in which to proceed, by all means do so. Report back to me when you're prepared to begin actual development. In the meantime, hopefully Teraik will have some success against these elusive raiders of his. Whether he does or not, however, I see no reason why the 'accidental release' shouldn't still occur in his ZOR. Bear that in mind during your research. It would be well for your documentation 'proving' all of the work was carried out in Ground Base Two Alpha to be in order from the very beginning."

"Of course, Fleet Commander."

. XXXIII .

Ouch! *Easy* there, Florence Nightingale!"

"Oh, shut up," Sharon Dvorak said tartly as she finished adjusting the pillow. "And stop being such a *baby*! I swear, *Malachai* whines less than you do!"

The universe, Dave Dvorak decided grumpily as he tried to settle himself into something like a remotely comfortable position, wasn't exactly running over with justice where the wives of heroically wounded warriors were concerned. Somehow he didn't think Penelope had given Odysseus such a hard time when *he* got home to Ithaca.

"You wouldn't think I was whining if *you* had to put up with this," he told his wife severely.

"I don't *think* you're whining; I know you are," she retorted. "Besides, I told you to be careful out there and you come back *this* way?" She shook her head with a disgusted expression. "You're not going to get any sympathy out of me because you didn't do what you were told to do in the first place. You and Rob—idiots the pair of you! Who did you think you were, anyway? Butch Cassidy and the Sundance Kid?"

Since his brother-in-law had shared his very thought to that effect with him, Dvorak wisely maintained silence.

Sharon glared at him for a moment longer, hands on her hips. But then her blue eyes softened and she leaned forward, resting one hand on his uninjured right shoulder, and kissed him gently on an unshaven cheek.

"Now stop carrying on like a big baby and get better," she whispered in his ear, her voice going husky. "And don't do something like this again. I was . . . that is, the *kids* were worried about you."

"I'll try not to," he promised her, reaching up with his good arm and hugging her briefly.

The acute discomfort in his left shoulder turned into something much sharper and hotter when he moved, but he ignored that and concentrated on how sweet her freshly washed red hair smelled. There was gray in it now, he realized with a pang, and he didn't have any business adding more to it.

He turned his head, pressing his lips to her cheek, then let himself settle back again with a carefully hidden sigh of relief as his injured shoulder returned to its familiar dull throb.

"I *heard* that," she said, with an unusually gentle smile, and patted him on his unkissed cheek.

"Was worth it," he replied, and was rewarded with a much broader smile. Then she looked at her wristwatch and grimaced.

"You'd better get some rest while you can," she told him. "Rob says Sam and Dennis have someone they want you to talk to. They're supposed to be here in about an hour. And I promised the kids they could have an hour with you before supper, too. I think Morgana and Maighread are afraid elves are going to carry you off if they don't keep an eye on you, and Keelan says Uncle Dave promised to finish telling her that story about the technicolor monster. Oh, and *Malachai* says the two of you are three chapters behind on *David and Phoenix*."

Dvorak smiled. He'd read to all three of their children every night, virtually from the moment they came home from the hospital. More recently, the three of them had been taking turns reading to *him* as their literary skills improved. Morgana and Maighread were old enough now that they took the occasional glitches in the schedule in stride, but Malachai was still insistent that he was supposed to read to Daddy when he was supposed to read to Daddy, and little things like alien invasions weren't supposed to intrude on that sacred duty.

"He's probably right," the Daddy in question said out loud.

"No, he's cutting you some *slack*," Sharon retorted. "He's not even counting the week or so when you were too drugged up to recognize our children when you saw them. You are *so* lucky he had brand new puppies to distract him!"

Dvorak grimaced, but she had a point.

"All right, I'll take a nap," he promised. "But did Rob drop any hints about just who it is that wants to talk to us?"

"Stop trying to wheedle information and go to sleep!" she commanded in awful tones, then turned and stalked out.

At least there was no door to slam behind her for emphasis, he thought.

Since it might have been just a little awkward trying to explain to any Shongair patrol who wandered by how one of the adult males of the household happened to have acquired a bullet hole entirely through the bony part of his left shoulder about the time one of their *other* patrols had been ambushed and killed less than fifteen miles from the cabin, they'd moved him out to the cave. He couldn't say the decor appealed to him. Somehow he didn't think most hospitals built the walls of their patients' rooms out of crates of food, standing rifle racks, cases of ammunition and reloading supplies, racked M136s and M240s, and storage tanks of gasoline. Big as the cave was, it was also so crowded now as to make him feel almost claustrophobic. The rock roof didn't do a lot for him, either, and he was getting heartily tired of the fluorescent light.

Besides, he'd become rather uncomfortably aware of what would happen if someone inadvertently dropped a match or something in here. Sure, the gas tanks were independently vented to the outside world, but still. . . .

Whatever its drawbacks, however, it was dry, warm, and about as securely hidden as any place they could have parked him. They were damned lucky they had it, when all was said, and he knew it.

In fact, "damned lucky" was a pretty good description of everything that had happened from the moment he was careless enough to get himself shot.

He'd come to the conclusion that he was never going to know exactly what had happened after he was hit, since Wilson had been the only witness and obviously wasn't going to tell him. Although his brother-in-law was perfectly prepared to strike a properly heroic pose, chin lifted and steely eyes fixed on an invisible horizon with noble determination, whenever Dvorak asked him, he'd actually provided exactly zero in the way of details. Which led Dvorak to suspect things had been even dicier than he'd thought.

What he did know was that he was inordinately fortunate that the bullet had managed to miss any of the major arteries on its way through. He was also fortunate that Wilson had spent the last five years of his Marine career in search and rescue. The SAR training had bobbed to the surface when Dvorak was hit, and he'd managed to apply pressure bandages and get the bleeding stopped. Mostly, anyway.

After that, he and Dennis Vardry had somehow gotten Dvorak away from the scene of the shootout and back to the cabin—well, to the *cave,* if he wanted to be picky—before any Shongairi turned up.

They *had* been visited by a Shongair patrol, accompanied by a North Carolina state trooper "guide," the next day. Fortunately, the trooper in question had passed along his entire agenda ahead of time, so Sharon and Jessica had "just happened" to have the kids down at the dam, swimming, and both shepherds banished to the cave with Dvorak, when they arrived.

Both of the big dogs had always been intensely protective of "their" people. Nimue had turned even more protective than usual since giving birth to her six puppies, and Sharon had decided—wisely, in Dvorak's opinion—that it would be just as well to keep both of the dogs away from the aliens under the circumstances. The last thing they'd needed was to get one or both of the shepherds shot because they growled at the wrong Shongair.

They'd also had time to move every weapon, other than a pair of shotguns, Dvorak's old sporterized SMLE .303 deer gun, and four handguns none of them had ever been particularly fond of out to the cave, as well. There certainly hadn't been any fancy, long-ranged weapons or anything that could possibly have punched bullets through even improvised vehicle armor lying around, anyway. Which was probably a good thing since, predictably, the Shongairi had confiscated every firearm they'd found. They hadn't found anything else, though, and they'd settled for interrogating Wilson and Alec (Veronica, who'd been trained as a nurse's aide, had been in the cave, keeping an eye on Dvorak), rather than hiking the rest of the way to the dam to question Sharon and Jessica—or the kids—as well.

Dvorak was just as happy he'd been only intermittently conscious when that happened. There were some things, frankly, which he'd discovered he lacked the courage to face, and he would have been terrified out of his mind lying there in the cave, not knowing what was happening with his family . . . or if one of the kids might inadvertently let something slip.

They were all good, smart kids, but that was the point. They were *kids*, and smart grown-ups all too easily trapped or tricked kids into saying more than they thought they were saying. Especially scared kids, and only a child who was invincibly stupid—which none of theirs were—*wouldn't* have been scared in the face of what was happening to their world. Whether they wanted to admit it to their parents or not, all the children had bad dreams and occasional nightmares, and he knew it had gotten worse since he'd been shot. He and Sharon had always made it a point to answer their children's questions, whether it was convenient or not, and they'd followed that same policy since fleeing to the cabin. Oh, sure, there were some things they'd skated their way around, but by and large, they'd leveled with their children. So the kids had always known what was going on, understood why their parents were so grim and focused these days. Yet that hadn't been the same as seeing Daddy brought back to them bloody on a shutter. No, that had brought it home to them in a way he would have given his left arm—hell, his *right* arm, and it was the one that still worked!—to spare them.

No wonder they want to spend time with me, he thought now, once again trying futilely to find a comfortable way to lie. *And I want time with* them, *too! I just wish I didn't catch them with that* scared *look in their eyes when they don't realize I'm watching them.*

He growled with fresh frustration at that thought. He wanted up. He wanted out of bed, out of this cave, back spending time with his family where his children could see him—and he could see them—and all of them could know the others were all right.

Not going to happen until you can actually stand up and walk more than fifty yards at a time, boy-oh, he told himself sternly. *Last thing we need is for the Shongairi to drop back in unexpectedly and find you lying around with this damned hole in your shoulder after all!*

He reached across his body with his right hand, touching the back of his left hand where the immobilizing straps held it across his chest. He found himself doing that quite a lot. He could wiggle the fingers of his left hand, but he'd discovered that he needed to reassure himself that he still had feeling in it, as well. That it could feel the pressure of his right hand's fingertips.

Of course, the real question was whether or not he'd ever actually be able to *use* that hand again. At the moment, the odds didn't seem all that good.

The Shongair bullet might have missed arteries and veins, but there was a lot of bone in the human shoulder. "Flesh wounds" to the shoulder were far rarer in real life than in bad fiction, and Dave Dvorak's shoulder had been pretty thoroughly pulverized.

Once Wilson had him home and realized how bad it really was, he'd headed straight back down the mountain. Veronica's training had been a priceless asset from the very beginning, but their medical supplies had never been intended to deal with something like *this.* For that matter, Veronica hadn't managed to fully stop the bleeding, and it had been obvious to Wilson that without proper medical assistance, they were still going to lose his brother-in-law. So he'd done what Marines always did when they needed help—he'd called on another Marine.

Or, rather, on the cousin of a Marine, in this case. Which was how Dvorak had come to wake up—mostly—and find himself looking up into a very black face wearing a surgical mask and a professionally competent expression.

"Hosea?" he'd gotten out.

"In the flesh," Dr. James Hosea MacMurdo had replied.

Why a young black man had preferred "Hosea" to "James" when he was growing up was something which had always puzzled Dvorak, but MacMurdo had been insistent about his given name from the time he was six. Maybe because he'd had an uncle named James that no one in the family had ever liked very much. Dvorak didn't know about that, but he'd known MacMurdo for almost fifteen years. His cousin, Alvin Buchevsky, was a Methodist pastor who'd been a frequent visiting preacher in Dvorak's own church. More to the point, Alvin had been one of Rob Dvorak's best friends since the two of them had been Marines together. Rob was almost ten years younger than the other man, but they'd been from the same hometown, they'd known a lot of the same people, and they'd kept ending up assigned to the same duty stations, especially before Buchevsky had become an officer, a squid, and a chaplain.

Which, Wilson had explained to Dvorak some years ago, while he, Alvin, and Dvorak had watched steaks turning brown on a grill, had been something of a shock to him. But despite Alvin's defection to the Navy—and as an *officer,* at that—they'd discovered they could remain friends. As long as no one else found out about it, at least.

While his cousin had been shooting people, then getting a divinity degree and a commission, however, Hosea MacMurdo had been getting his *medical* degree. Several of them, in fact. He was the senior and founding partner in MacMurdo Orthopedic Associates and generally regarded as one of the finest orthopedic surgeons in the entire state of South Carolina, and Dvorak was far from the first recent gunshot victim to whose side Rob Wilson had chauffeured him.

"What . . . are you . . . ?" Dvorak had gotten out groggily, and MacMurdo had snorted.

"Oh, *puh-leeze!*" he'd replied, rolling his eyes. "You got shot in the shoulder, not the *head,* Dave! What d'you *think* I'm doing here?"

"When you care enough to send the very best," another voice had said, and Dvorak had rolled his head and seen Rob and Veronica Wilson standing on the other side of the bed. His brother-in-law wore a surgical mask, as well, Dvorak's oddly floaty brain had observed. So did Ronnie, now that he noticed, but she was wearing surgical gloves, as well.

"Spare my blushes," MacMurdo had said dryly. "Oh, and Al sends his regards, too."

"Thanks," Dvorak had whispered.

"And now, despite the somewhat primitive nature of my facilities," MacMurdo had continued, nodding to Ronnie to start the IV inserted into Dvorak's right arm, "we're going to do something about that shoulder of yours. So go to sleep, and let me get on with it."

Dvorak knew how fortunate he'd been to have someone with MacMurdo's skill and experience working on him. And he'd been almost equally fortunate in that MacMurdo and Sam Mitchell between them had been able to come up with almost enough in the way of painkillers, given that morphine and its derivatives weren't exactly widely available anymore. Unfortunately, MacMurdo hadn't been joking about the "primitive nature" of his facilities. There was only so much skill could do without the right kind of backup, and he'd warned Dvorak soberly that he was going to suffer serious loss of mobility in the shoulder.

"I've done what I can," he'd said just before Sam Mitchell drove him the forty-odd miles home, "and as long as nothing gets infected, I don't see anything coming up that Ronnie can't handle. But I couldn't begin to do all I'd like to have done." He'd made an unhappy face. "It's going to take you months to come back from this, Dave. I want you to take it easy along the way, too, because you may have noticed we're just a little short on the kind of follow-up care I'd normally prescribe. I'll be in touch with Ronnie again in a week or so, see how you're coming along, maybe start thinking about what kind of physical therapy we can manage under the circumstances. The truth is, though, that I wasn't able to do anything like a full rebuild on that shoulder. You were lucky in a lot of ways, but that bullet . . . well, let's just say it didn't do the skeletal structure of your shoulder any favors."

"Can't say that comes as much of a surprise," Dvorak had replied, his voice calmer than he'd actually felt.

"I didn't think it would, somehow." MacMurdo had flashed a brief smile. "Anyway, what we really need is a properly equipped operating room and the time to do the job right. I could fix you up with a nice replacement shoulder joint if I had those, but I don't. And somehow, I don't think either of them's going to come our way anytime soon."

He'd smiled again, sadly, then shaken Dvorak's good hand and departed, leaving his patient with his thoughts.

Not very happy thoughts, really.

All the same, intellectually, Dvorak had realized then—as now—that he was unbelievably lucky to be alive at all. And when he thought about the fact that he *was* alive, and that so were Sharon, Morgana, Maighread, and Malachai, little things like whether or not his left arm was ever going to work properly again quickly dropped back into their proper perspective.

None of which, he thought now, drowsily, did anything to make him any less curious about whoever was coming to visit.

. . . . .

"ARE YOU DECENT, dear?" Rob Wilson called in a high-pitched falsetto from the far side of the partition of ammunition cases which had been arranged to give Dvorak his own little cubicle.

"No, but I've got a gun under the pillow, you dirty old man," Dvorak replied.

"Yeah? Well, I guess the good news is that a lousy shot like you couldn't hit anything, anyway!" Wilson retorted, poking his head around the corner. "Seriously, ready for your visitors?"

"Ready as I'm going to be, anyway," Dvorak replied, scooting to sit up a little straighter against the pillows despite the hot throb in his shoulder.

"Good." Wilson looked back over his shoulder and nodded to someone Dvorak couldn't see yet. "This way, gentlemen," he said in a considerably more businesslike voice.

Dvorak's eyebrow arched as his brother-in-law's tone registered, and then Wilson led three other men into his sleeping space.

Things seemed a lot more crowded all of a sudden, Dvorak noted, but his attention was on the newcomers. Sam Mitchell was no stranger, but he had no idea who the compactly built fellow with the black hair and green eyes or his taller, bearded companion might be.

"Sam," he said, nodding in agreement to the one visitor he knew, and then looked at the others with a politely inquiring expression.

"Dave," Mitchell said, "let me introduce our friends here. This here"—he indicated the green-eyed man—"is Dan Torino, Major Dan Torino, who goes by 'Longbow' for some reason. And this"—he nodded to the considerably taller and much darker-skinned stranger—"is Abu Bakr bin Muhammed el-Hiri."

Both of Dvorak's eyebrows rose, and the bearded man chuckled.

"Really is my name," he assured Dvorak. "And for a hick cop, Sam didn't do all that *bad* a job of pronouncing it!"

"Hey, six months ago I'd've been checking to see if the Feds had gotten around to issuing an arrest warrant on you yet," Mitchell retorted, grinning down at el-Hiri, who, despite his height, was still a good two inches shorter than *he* was. "And they probably would have!"

"Let's not be bringing up the past, gentlemen," the man named Torino said in a chiding tone, and Mitchell and el-Hiri snorted almost in unison.

"Anyway," Mitchell said, "to complete the introductions. Major, Abu Bakr, meet Dave Dvorak."

"Pleasure," Dvorak said, holding out his good hand to each of them in turn.

Both of them showed signs of strain and fatigue, he thought. Most people did these days, of course. But Torino and el-Hiri had that wary look, as well. The one that combined the awareness of the hunted with the tightly leashed violence of the predator. He was pretty sure *they* hadn't been sitting around in cabins up in the mountains for the last three or four months, he thought with something very like a sense of guilt.

"I imagine you're wondering what brings our two visitors up to see you," Mitchell continued, and Dvorak nodded.

"The question had crossed my mind," he admitted.

"Well, fact is, these two are the leaders of the guerrillas Governor Howell's been feeding info to for a while now. In fact, you may not realize it, but you've already met Major Torino, in a manner of speaking."

"I have?" Dvorak thought for a moment, then shook his head. "If I have, I don't remember it."

"I guess I should've said you've seen him on TV," Mitchell replied, and his voice was much more sober than it had been. "Major Torino was leading the fighters Admiral Robinson sicced on those puppy shuttles on Day One."

Dvorak's eyes widened, then narrowed in quick speculation as they darted back over to Torino's face. What he was most conscious of, for a moment, was how little like a figure out of legend Torino actually looked. But then he recognized something else—the weary sorrow and loss behind the steely determination in those green eyes.

"It's an honor," he heard himself say quietly, and Torino shrugged. It was an uncomfortable gesture.

"We couldn't have done it without Robinson," he replied after a moment. "In fact, I kind of doubt people would have fought back as hard as they have anywhere without him."

"I think you're right," Dvorak agreed. "Do you know if he's still alive?"

"I'm pretty sure he's not," the ex–fighter pilot said heavily. "I know they took out Dahlgren, and we've actually managed to establish a halfway decent communications net. I'm pretty sure I'd have heard by now if he'd gotten out in time."

"Damn," Dvorak said softly.

"Amen, brother," Wilson agreed in an equally quiet voice.

"Well," Dvorak said a moment later, giving himself a shake, "I won't embarrass you by going on about it, Major, but I will say thank you. I'm pretty sure I speak for most of the human race when I say that, too. But I'm also pretty sure you didn't hike all the way up here into the mountains just to introduce yourself?"

"No," Torino agreed, obviously happy to put that whole subject behind him. "As it happens, I have something else on my mind, and Mr. Mitchell here"—it was his turn to nod his head sideways at the tall ex–police officer—"tells me you and your brother-in-law are the major communications hub for the bloody-minded mountain folks here about."

"I don't know that I'd go that far," Dvorak said. "I mean, we—"

"Don't be an idiot," Mitchell interrupted brusquely. "You know damned well you are. If anybody has somebody they've got to hide, they mention it to you, and you guys find somebody to do the hiding. Somebody's looking for ammo to hit the Shongairi, they mention it to someone, and sooner or later a friend of a friend mentions it to you, and you mention it to *me*. Somebody else needs a doc, they come to you, and you guys find 'em one. Hell, you know as well as I do that you and Rob are the ones who really arranged the escape route—and found contacts in Tennessee—for those poor bastards the Major and his people busted out! And just who was it got us turned around in time to avoid running right into that frigging puppy patrol which *someone* then took out completely?"

Dvorak started to argue, then stopped.

He's right, he thought almost wonderingly. *Damn.*

It was odd, really, he supposed. He'd been aware that he and Rob were acting as a sort of clearinghouse, but he'd never really thought of themselves as "the" clearinghouse. Yet now that he considered it, there was actually quite a bit of truth to it. Maybe he hadn't noticed because it had never been planned. It had just happened, and he hadn't really realized until this moment just how heavily the people who knew where to find them had come to rely on them to pass information and help with planning. Without ever noticing, they'd become . . . facilitators, he supposed might be the best word for it.

Of course, his own "facilitating" days appeared to be over. He realized his right hand was touching the back of his left again and made himself stop.

I imagine a "communications hub" is about all *I'm going to be good for from now on,* he reflected.

"I hadn't really thought of us that way," he said out loud, "but I guess Sam does have a point. So, what can we do for you?"

"We need you to pass some information for us, as widely as you can," Torino replied, and his voice was harder, flatter.

"What sort of information?" Dvorak asked a bit cautiously, looking back and forth between their visitors.

"We took two of the puppies alive when we hit that convoy of theirs," el-Hiri said. "Thanks to info from the Governor and his friends, we know those belt translators of theirs don't have radio links built in. That means we don't have to worry about their phoning home for help on them. And that we can go ahead and . . . ask them questions and *request* answers even if they can't speak our language and we can't speak theirs."

There was an ugly light in his eyes. Somehow Dvorak didn't doubt that any Shongair from whom he "requested" answers would provide them.

And it doesn't bother me one damned bit, either, he thought grimly.

"Should I assume you're here about whatever they had to say?" he asked.

"Absolutely," Torino said grimly. "I don't think either of them was supposed to know why Teraik wanted those humans they were delivering to him. One of them—the senior one—was an officer, though. About what we'd call a first lieutenant, I'd guess. He knew more than he was supposed to. He couldn't tell us everything, but I think we've been able to pretty much fill in the blanks or connect the dots or whatever the hell you want to call it. And what it comes down to is that we need to get the word out that going along peacefully if the puppies come calling isn't a very good idea anymore. They told everyone in the convoy that they'd been drafted as part of the human labor forces the Shongairi have been using to try and clean up some of the worst wreckage in their occupation zones, but that wasn't what they really had in mind for them at all."

. XXXIV .

Regiment Commander Harah didn't like trees.

He hadn't always felt that way. In fact, he'd actually *liked* trees until the Empire invaded this never-to-be-sufficiently-damned planet. Now he vastly preferred long, flat, empty spaces—preferably of bare, pounded earth where not even a *garish* or one of the humans' "rabbits" could have hidden. Any other sort of terrain seemed to spontaneously spawn humans . . . all of whom appeared to have guns or some *other,* improvised sort of weapon none of his troopers had ever before heard of or experienced. The sheer bloodthirsty inventiveness of these creatures was simply impossible to believe without firsthand experience, and there seemed no end to their creativity.

He hadn't needed Ground Base Commander Shairez's psychological analysis to tell *him* humans were all lunatics! It was nice to have confirmation, of course, and he'd been simply *delighted* when the ground base commander's conclusions led Fleet Commander Thikair to change his plans. Once every last human had been expunged from it, this would probably be a perfectly nice place to live.

He grimaced at his own thoughts as he sat gazing at the plot in the command GEV moving steadily west above the vast lake's broad blue waters.

Actually, Harah, part of you admires *these creatures, doesn't it?* he thought. *Once you get past their total lack of any concept of honor, at least. And according to the Ground Base Commander, that's not really their fault.* He couldn't even begin to wrap his own mind around a psychology that bizarrely twisted, but he trusted Shairez's analysis. *If you can ever accept that they truly don't realize how completely and utterly dishonorable it is to refuse submission to a proven superior, it all looks a bit different, doesn't it? After all, we've killed thousands of them for every Shongair we've lost, and they* still *have the guts—the absolutely insane, utterly irrational, totally dishonorable, mind-numbingly* stupid *guts—to come right at us. If they only had half as much* brains, *they would've acknowledged our superiority and submitted months ago, psychology or no psychology, of course. But, no! They couldn't do that, could they? That would be the* reasonable *thing to do!*

He growled, remembering the forty percent of his original regiment he'd lost attempting to subdue the eastern portion of what had once been the state of Pennsylvania in the nation the humans had called the "United States." Brigade Commander Tesuk had gone in with three regiments; he'd come out with barely one and a half, and Fleet Commander Thikair had ended up blasting every major city in Tesuk's area of operations from orbit, anyway.

Harah had been delighted when he was transferred to Ground Base Seven, away from *that* madhouse. The transfer made sense for a lot of reasons, of course. Tesuk's brigade had initially been assigned to Ground Base Two, which was supposed to be Ground Base Commander Shairez's command from the outset. That hadn't worked out too well, either, as Harah recalled. Tesuk himself had been assigned to the replacement, improvised ground base—Ground Base Two Alpha, they'd decided to call it—along with both of the brigade's other two regiments. Harah suspected that his understrength command had been chosen to replace the two regiments initially assigned to Ground Base Seven when they were transferred to North America because he'd taken heavier losses in Pennsylvania than either of his sister regiments. As such, he'd represented less of a loss of combat power.

He'd tried to convince his warriors that the reassignment was actually a compliment and a reward. He'd pointed out that their single, depleted regiment was being tasked to perform duties which would normally have fallen to twice their number of *full-strength* regiments, which hardly counted as a sinecure. And he'd argued that being chosen for such an important assignment represented a recognition not simply of how disproportionately heavily the burden of fighting in North America had fallen on their shoulders, but of how well they'd done when it had.

He didn't think they'd believed him. In fact, he knew they hadn't, and there'd been quite a bit of ill feeling. Resentment that they were being cast aside, relegated to a secondary theater, because they'd been incompetent enough to suffer more casualties than the other units of their brigade. It was hard for any warrior to stomach that kind of thought, and the jeers of Tesuk's other regiments as they prepared to board shuttles for the flight here hadn't helped.

Harah suspected those other regiments had stopped jeering since. According to one of his litter-brothers on Ground Force Commander Thairys' staff, their casualty rates had long since surpassed his own. In fact, Tesuk was at substantially less than half strength despite the priority which had been assigned to replacing losses among the units operating in North America. The ground force commander had even been forced to begin completely disbanding his worst-depleted units, breaking them up and using their survivors to reinforce other units which had taken lighter losses, and he *still* couldn't bring Tesuk back up to strength. The thought was sobering, but it didn't really surprise Harah very much. As far as he'd been able to tell during his own time in hell, those lunatic "Americans" actually had more guns than humans!

At least their initial experiences had taught the expedition's senior officers to economize on forces by occupying open terrain, where surveillance could be maintained effectively, whenever and wherever possible. The redeployment of their ground combat forces to support Fleet Commander Thikair's revised strategy of concentrating the troop strength necessary to subdue North America first had made that necessary, not optional, for the other ground bases which had been forced to give up so many of their own troopers to make up the needed numbers, but that didn't make it any less wise.

And the decision to allow lower levels of command to call in kinetic strikes on organized resistance instead of kicking every request clear up to fleet command level for clearance had been another wise move. In fact, Harah had come to the conclusion that it was one the Empire should consider incorporating into permanent doctrine during the drastic revision which was inevitably going to follow this debacle. It was an improvisation which had been forced upon them, true, yet allowing an officer as far down the chain of command as a lowly regiment commander to specify his own KEW targets had enormously reduced the response time. They were actually managing to catch some of the accursed human raiders—"guerrillas" they called themselves—before they had time to scatter and start scampering out of the strike area. Which was arguably a more effective, if less satisfying, tactic than reprisal strikes against nearby towns and villages which had already been largely deserted anyway.

Of course, the brigade commanders and division commanders will all scream at the very notion of permanently allowing mere regiments to control their own supporting fire, he thought sardonically. *I wonder how they'd react if I suggested giving* battalion commanders *that kind of control? Dainthar! Talk about heretical notions!*

His ears twitched in amusement at the thought, although he was more than half convinced it really would be a good idea. He was sure there were others to be discovered from any systematic analysis of what had happened here on KU-197-20. There had to be hundreds—thousands!—of lessons to be found, and he supposed they owed the humans a vote of thanks, in a perverse sort of way, for how much the Empire was ultimately going to learn from them.

Not that any of them will be around to be *thanked,* he reflected a bit more grimly, returning his thoughts to the task at hand.

He found himself strongly in agreement with Ground Base Commander Shairez's decision to collect the necessary specimens from someplace outside her core zone of responsibility. He wasn't that worried about long-term consequences—it shouldn't take all that long to develop the bioweapon and obviate all future consequences—but it would certainly be inconvenient in the short term if the humans in Ground Base Seven's ZOR started turning as restive as those in, say, North America. Or in Ground Base Six's zone, to the northeast. Harah simply didn't have the personnel to deal with that sort of unrest without either substantial reinforcements or calling in a *lot* of KEWs. Unfortunately, the reinforcements didn't exist, thanks to their casualties, and that sort of bombardment would be . . . a bad idea. Ultimately, it wasn't going to make much difference to the local humans whether they were vaporized by kinetic impact or died later of whatever plague Shairez developed, but Shairez had briefed him (partially, at least) on Fleet Commander Thikair's ultimate strategy.

We shouldn't have to skulk around and go to such ridiculous lengths just to disguise a simple matter of pest control, he thought grumpily. *Anybody who ever* met *a human would understand the galaxy could only be an enormously better place without any of them in it. But, of course, those sanctimonious, bleating,* bigoted *weed-eaters on the Council will never admit that! And you can be damned sure the hypocritical bastards would jump on any excuse to criticize* us *like a* hasthar *on a* garish*! So instead we have to bend ourselves all out of shape arranging a suitably deniable "accident" to accomplish something every sane sentient ought to fall at our feet* thanking *us for!*

Well, no one ever said the galaxy overflows with justice, he reminded himself as both prongs of his attack force approached their jump-off positions. *And at least the satellites' thermal imagery's told us exactly where* these *humans are. They've been left completely alone, too.* Their *herd hasn't been culled yet, and we haven't picked up any electronic emissions from them at all, not even a miserable little auxiliary generator, so probably they were never even connected to the humans' "Internet" in the first place.*

His lips wrinkled back, exposing his canines in a hunter's anticipatory smile, as he remembered the backward parochialism still to be found in similarly remote villages even back on Shongair Prime itself. Given the humans' uneven distribution of technology, even before the expedition had arrived, his targets' situation had to be even worse.

Isolated this far up in the hills, they may not even realize what's been going on! And even if they'd heard rumors about the invasion, they should still be fat, happy, and stupid, compared to the miserable jermahk *we've been trying to dig out of the woodwork elsewhere on this continent. Not to mention having a lot less guns than those crazy "Americans"! And*—his ears flattened more grimly—*if they* do *want to fight,* we've *learned a lot ourselves since we first started running our snouts into them.*

• • • • •

STEPHEN BUCHEVSKY SWORE with silent, bitter venom.

The sun was barely above the eastern horizon, shining into his eyes as he studied the Shongairi through the binoculars and wondered what the hell they were after. After staying clear of the mountains for so long, what could have inspired them to come straight at the villages this way?

And why the hell do they have to be doing it while Mircea's still away discussing his glorious vision of cooperation with the others? a corner of his mind demanded.

It was at least fortunate the listening posts had detected the approaching drones so early, given how close behind them the aliens had been this time. There'd been time—barely—to crank up the old-fashioned hand-powered warning sirens, and at least the terrain was too heavily forested for any sort of airborne op. If the Shongairi wanted them, they'd have to come in on the ground . . . which was exactly what they seemed to have in mind. A large number of APCs and a handful of GEVs were assembling on the low ground at the southern end of the lake, about a kilometer below the dam, while a smaller force of GEVs came in across the lake itself, followed at a cautious interval by over a dozen of their huge orbital shuttles—the ones which could carry a dozen of their APCs apiece—and he didn't like that one bit.

The villages were scattered along the rugged flanks of a mountain spine running east to west on the lake's southeastern shore. The ridgeline towered over thirty-two hundred feet above sea level in places, with the villages tucked away in dense tree cover above the eighteen-hundred-foot level. He'd thought they were well concealed, but the Shongairi clearly knew where they were. Not only that, they were coming in in a pincer movement which obviously intended to squeeze the villagers between the force coming in over the lake and the second force, hooking up from below the dam along the deep valley between the villages' ridge and the even taller one to the valley's west, where his forestry service cabin lookout post was located. If their maneuvers succeeded, they'd bag every human being in all three of the villages.

That much was clear enough. Among the many things that *weren't* clear was how well the aliens' sensors could track humans moving through rough terrain under heavy tree cover. He hoped the answer to that question was "not very," but he couldn't rely on that.

"Start them moving," he told Elizabeth Cantacuzène. "These people are headed straight for the villages. I think we'd better be somewhere else when they get here."

"Yes, Stephen." The teacher sounded far calmer than *Buchevsky* felt, and she nodded, then disappeared to pass his instructions to the waiting runners. Within moments, he knew, the orders would have gone out and their people would be falling back to the position he'd allowed Ramirez to christen "Bastogne."

It was an Army dance the first time around, he thought, *and it came out pretty well that time. I guess it's time to see how well the Green Machine makes out.*

• • • • •

REGIMENT COMMANDER HARAH swore as the icons on his plot shifted.

It appears we weren't close enough behind the drones after all, he thought grumpily.

HQ had been forced to factor the humans' bizarre ability to sense RC drones from beyond visual range into its thinking, and his operations plan had made what *ought* to have been ample allowance for it, based on intelligence reports from higher up. Unfortunately, it hadn't been, and he was already losing sensor resolution as they went scurrying through those accursed trees.

That was the bad news. The good news was that his northern group of

GEVs had secured the shore of the lake without difficulty. This far from any major population center, the chance of there being any of those pestiferous shoulder-launched SAMs down there was effectively nil. They'd all learned painful lessons about making assumptions where humans were concerned, however, and he watched approvingly as the point GEVs moved far enough inland to secure the shuttle landing zones. There wouldn't be any SAMs bringing down *his* APCs while they were helpless in their shuttle bays, by Dainthar!

"They're moving along the ridge," he said over the regimental net. "They're headed west—towards those higher peaks. Second Battalion, get those APCs ashore and swing farther up the lake before you cut inland. Try to come in on their flank. First Battalion, get moving up that valley *now*."

. . . . .

BUCHEVSKY MUTTERED ANOTHER curse as the drones' unpleasant vibration kept pace with him. Clearly, the damn things could track through tree cover better than he'd hoped. On the other hand, they seemed to be coming in close, above the treetops, and if they were—

. . . . .

"CAINHARN SEIZE THEM! Let them rot uneaten like the vermin they are!"

A quartet of dirty fireballs trickled down the sky, and four of Harah's drones went off the air simultaneously. Which pointedly contradicted at least *one* part of his pre-attack enemy forces estimate.

Damn it! What in Cainharn's Third Hell are villagers up in these damned mountains doing with SAMs*?!*

. . . . .

BUCHEVSKY BARED HIS teeth in a panting, running grin as Macomb's air-defense teams took out the nearest drones. He still felt vibrations from other drones, farther away, but if the bastards kept them high enough to avoid the Gremlins, it might make their sensor resolution crappier, too.

. . . . .

HARAH TRIED TO master his anger, but he was sick unto death of how these damned humans insisted on screwing up even the simplest operation. Dainthar be praised he'd established a safe shuttle zone anyway, but that had been simple auto-reflex by now. He wasn't supposed to *have* to do that kind of crap, because there weren't supposed to be any SAMs or heavy weapons up here in the first place! That was one of the main reasons they'd come clear out here looking for Ground Base Commander Shairez's specimens.

Only the humans *still* refused to cooperate! It was as if the accursed creatures had known he was coming!

He considered reporting to headquarters. Given the expedition's already astronomical equipment losses, HQ was unlikely to thank him if he lost still more of it chasing after what were supposed to be unarmed villagers cowering in their mountain hideouts. But they had to secure specimens *somewhere,* and he had *these* humans more or less in his sights.

Besides, he admitted harshly to himself, *I will be* damned *if I turn around and back off again. This time, I'm going to drive right through these creatures and show them why they should* never *have refused to submit!*

"We're not going to be able to bring the drones in as close as planned," he grated to his battalion commanders. "It's up to our scouts. Tell them to keep their damn eyes open."

Fresh acknowledgments came in. He heard his own anger, his own frustration, in those responses, and he watched his own icons closing in on the abruptly amorphous shaded area representing the drones' best guess of the humans' location.

We may not be able to see them clearly, he thought angrily, *but even if we can't, there aren't that many places they can* go, *now are there?*

. . . . .

BUCHEVSKY WAS PROFOUNDLY grateful for the way hard work had toughened the lowland refugees. They were managing to keep up with the villagers, despite the elevation and despite the steepness of the terrain, which they never would've been able to do without that toughening. Several smaller children (not all of them lowland-born) were beginning to flag anyway, of course, and his heart ached at the ruthless demands being placed on them. But the bigger kids were managing to keep up with the adults, and there were enough grown-ups to take turns carrying the littlest ones.

The unhealed wound where Shania and Yvonne had been cried out for *him* to scoop up one of those tiny human beings, carry *someone's* child to the safety he'd been unable to offer his own children.

But that wasn't his job, and he turned his attention to what was.

He slid to a halt on the narrow trail, breathing heavily, watching the last few villagers stream past. The perimeter guards came next, and then, last of all, the scouts who'd been on listening watch. One of them was Robert Szu.

"It's . . . pretty much like . . . you and Mircea figured it . . . Top," the private panted. He paused for a moment, gathering his breath, then nodded sharply. "They're coming up the firebreak roads on both sides of the ridge. I figure their points are halfway up by now."

"Good," Buchevsky said.

. . . . .

"FARKALASH!"

Regiment Commander Harah's driver looked back over his shoulder at the horrendous oath until Harah's bared-canines snarl turned him hastily back around to his controls. The regiment commander only wished he could dispose of the Dainthar-damned humans as easily!

I shouldn't have sent the vehicles in that close, he told himself through a boil of blood-red fury. *I should've dismounted the infantry farther out.* Of course *it was as obvious to the humans as it was to me that there were only a handful of routes vehicles could use!*

He growled at himself, but he knew why he'd made the error. The humans were moving faster than he'd estimated they could, and he'd wanted to use his vehicles' speed advantage. Which was why the humans had just been able to destroy six more irreplaceable GEVs and *eleven* more APCs . . . not to mention something like half the hundred and thirty-two troopers who'd been *aboard* the troop carriers.

And let's not forget the APC drivers and gunners while we're at it, Harah! he thought viciously. *And there's no telling how many* more *little surprises they may have planted along any openings wide enough for vehicles.*

"Dismount the infantry," he said flatly over the command net. "Scout formation. Vehicles are not to advance until the engineers have checked the trails for more explosives."

. . . . .

BUCHEVSKY GRIMACED SOURLY. From the smoke billowing up through the treetops, his handful of scavenged mines and jury-rigged IEDs had gotten at least several of their vehicles. Unfortunately, he couldn't know how many.

However many, they're going to take the hint and come in on foot from here . . . unless they're complete and utter idiots. And somehow, I don't think they are. Damn it.

Well, at least he'd slowed them up. That was going to buy the civilians a little breathing space.

Now it was time to buy them a little more.

. . . . .

HARAH'S EARS FLATTENED, but at least it wasn't a surprise this time. The small-arms fire rattling out of the trees had become inevitable the moment he'd ordered his own infantry to go in on foot.

. . . . .

AUTOMATIC WEAPONS BARKED and snarled, crackling in a score of small, vicious, isolated engagements scattered across the heavily forested mountainside, and Buchevsky *wished* they hadn't been forced to deep-six their radios. His people knew the terrain intimately, knew the best defensive positions, the possible approach lines, but the Shongairi had heavier support weapons, and their communications were vastly better than his. Their inherent ability to maneuver far exceeded his own as a consequence of their ability to remain in constant, instant contact with one another. And adding insult to injury, some of their infantry were using captured human rocket and grenade launchers to thicken their own firepower.

The situation's bitter irony wasn't lost upon him. This time, *his* forces were on the short end of the "asymmetrical warfare" stick, and it sucked. On the other hand, he'd had painful personal experience of just how effective guerrillas could be in this sort of terrain.

. . . . .

THERE WAS MORE satisfaction to accompany the frustration in Harah's growl as he looked at the plot's latest update.

The advance had been enormously slower than he'd ever contemplated, and morning had become afternoon, but the humans appeared to be running out of SAMs at last. That meant he could get his handful of surviving drones in close enough to see what the hell was happening, and his momentum was building.

Which was a damned good thing, since he'd already lost over twenty percent of his troops. He was sure he could rely on Ground Base Commander Shairez to take his part and support him when he had to face his superiors and explain that, but he was also unfortunately certain how unhappy that kind of loss rate was going to make Ground Force Commander Thairys. Particularly in light of the notion that this was supposed to be a *low*-casualty operation.

Well, maybe I have *gotten hammered,* he thought harshly, *but I'm hardly the only commander* that's *happened to since we got here! And I've cost them, too, by Dainthar's Gleaming Fangs!*

Real-time estimates of enemy losses were notoriously unreliable, but even by his most pessimistic estimates, the humans had lost over forty fighters so far, and from the size of the thermal signatures the fleet had plotted from orbit, they couldn't have had all that many of them to begin with.

That was the good news. The bad news was that they appeared to be remarkably well equipped with infantry weapons for a batch of primitive, backward, uneducated mountain villagers, and their commander was fighting as smart as any human Harah had ever heard of. His forces were hugely outnumbered and outgunned, but he was hitting back hard—in fact, Harah's casualties, despite his GEVs and his mortars, were at least six or seven times the humans'. The other side was intimately familiar with the terrain and taking ruthless advantage of it, and his infantry had run into enough more concealed explosives to make anyone cautious.

Whatever we've run our snouts into, and whatever the satellites might have said, he reflected, *these damned well* aren't *just a bunch of villagers. Somebody's spent a lot of time training them—and reconnoitering these mountains, too. They're fighting from positions that were preselected for their fields of fire. And those explosives . . . someone picked the spots for* them *pretty damned carefully. Whoever it was knew what he was doing, and he must have been preparing his positions almost since the day we first landed.*

Despite himself, he felt a flicker of respect for his human opponent. Not that it was going to make any difference in the end. The take from his drones was still far less detailed than he could wish, but it was clear the fleeing villagers were running into what amounted to a cul-de-sac.

. . . . .

BUCHEVSKY FELT THE momentum shifting.

He'd started the morning with a hundred "regulars" and another hundred and fifty "militia" from the villages. He didn't have that many anymore. He knew everyone tended to overestimate his own losses in a fight like this, especially in this sort of terrain and without reliable communications between his positions, but he'd be surprised if he hadn't lost at least a quarter of his people by now.

That was bad enough, but there was worse coming.

The Bastogne position had never been intended to stand off a full-bore Shongair assault. It had really been designed as a place to retreat in the face of attack by *human* adversaries trying to pillage the villages' winter supplies. That meant Bastogne, despite its name, was more of a fortified warehouse than some sort of final redoubt. He'd made its defenses as tough as he could, yet he'd never contemplated trying to hold it against hundreds of Shongair infantry supported by tanks and mortars.

Stop kicking yourself, an inner voice growled. *There was never any point* trying *to build a position you could've held against that kind of assault. So what if you'd held them off for a while? They'd only have called in one of their damned kinetic strikes in the end, anyway.*

He knew that was true, but what was *also* true was that the only paths of retreat were so steep as to be almost impassable. Bastogne *was* supposed to hold against any likely human attack, and without its stockpiled supplies, the chance that their civilians could have survived the approaching winter would have been minimal at best. So he and Mircea had staked everything on making the position tough enough to stand against anything *less* than an all-out Shongair assault . . . and now it was a trap too many of their people couldn't get out of.

He looked out through the smoky, autumn-bright forest, watching the westering sun paint the smoke the color of blood, and knew his people were out of places to run. They were on the final perimeter now, and it took every ounce of discipline he'd learned in his life to fight down his despair.

I'm sorry, Mircea, he thought grimly. *I fucked up. Now we're all screwed. I guess I'm just as glad you didn't make it back in time after all.*

His jaw muscles tightened, and he reached out and grabbed Maria Averescu, one of his runners.

"I need you to find Gunny Meyers," he said in the Romanian he'd finally begun to master.

"He's dead, Top," the teenaged girl replied harshly, and his belly clenched.

"Sergeant Ramirez?"

"Him, too, I think. I know he took a hit here." Averescu thumped the center of her own chest, just below the bosom which was never going to have time to fully develop after all.

"Then find Sergeant Jonescu. Tell him—"

Buchevsky drew a deep breath. Jonescu commanded his entire reserve, the only people he'd have available to plug any Shongair breakthroughs on the final perimeter. If he sent Jonescu off. . . .

"Tell him I want him and his people to get as many kids out as they can," he said harshly. "Tell him the rest of us will buy him as much time as we can. Got that?"

"Yes, Top!" Averescu's grimy face was pale, but she nodded hard.

"Good. Now go!"

He released the young woman's shoulder. She shot off through the smoke, and he turned in the opposite direction and headed for the perimeter command post.

. . . . .

THE SHONGAIR SCOUTS realized the humans' retreat had slowed still further. Painful experience made them wary of changes, and they felt their way cautiously forward.

They were right to be cautious.

. . . . .

BASTOGNE HAD BEEN built around a deep cavern that offered protected, easily camouflaged storage for winter foodstuffs and fodder for the villages' animals. Concealment was not its only defense, however.

. . . . .

BUCHEVSKY BARED HIS teeth savagely as he heard the explosions.

In a lot of ways, he still wished he'd been able to get his hands on US mines, since that was what he'd been trained with. On the other hand, Basarab had managed to lay his hands on an amazing quantity of Soviet-style ordnance. Some of it had been sadly obsolete, packed in crates that looked like they'd probably been tucked away in the bottom of a warehouse somewhere since World War II and old enough he'd had serious doubts abouts its reliability or even safety. But most of it had consisted of much more modern equipment, and no one had ever accused the Ruskies of being slouches when it came to mine warfare.

The bulk of the antipersonnel mines had been the Russian MON-50, a directional mine which was basically a copy of the US-designed M18 Claymore with a few uniquely Russian refinements, including a peep sight to replace the original's simpler open sight when it was being "aimed" on initial emplacement. Tactically, there was nothing to choose between the two, though: a rectangular, slightly concave plastic body containing a shaped charge of plastic explosives designed to throw a hurricane of lethal fragments in a fan-shaped pattern fifty yards or so deep. The variant Basarab had been able to provide threw five hundred and forty steel balls as opposed to the seven hundred slightly smaller balls of the Claymore.

In addition, there'd been several crates of the more powerful MON-100, a circular sheet metal mine shaped like a large bowl and designed to throw four hundred and fifty steel rod fragments to a lethal range of over a hundred yards. There'd even been a couple of dozen MON-200s—much bigger and heavier (over fifty pounds) siblings of the MON-100, powerful enough to be effective against light-skinned vehicles and helicopters, as well as personnel. He'd used most of those up booby-trapping the fire roads, though. It looked like they'd been at least reasonably effective against the Shongair APCs, but he found himself wishing he had more of them left now.

Not that he supposed the Shongairi were going to complain.

The outer mine belt wasn't as deep as he would have liked, but the Shongairi obviously hadn't realized what they were walking into. Their infantry advance had come to a sudden stop as his forward troops set off the command-detonated mines, and he listened with bloodthirsty satisfaction to alien shrieks as solid walls of shrapnel scythed off limbs and shredded torsos.

He didn't expect the delay to last very long, but he'd take what he could get. Besides, the *inner* mine belt was considerably deeper, with tripwire mines placed to thicken the command-detonated ones.

I may not stop *them, but I can damned well make them pay cash. And maybe—just maybe—Jonescu will get some of the kids out after all.*

He didn't let himself think about the struggle to survive those kids would face over the coming winter with no roof, no food. He couldn't.

"Runner!"

"Yes, Top!"

"Find Corporal Gutierrez," Buchevsky told the young man. "Tell him it's time to dance."

. . . . .

THE SHONGAIRI STALLED along the edge of the minefield cowered even closer to the ground as the pair of 120-millimeter mortars Basarab had scrounged up along with the mines started dropping lethal fire in on them. Even now, few of Harah's troops had actually encountered human artillery, and the thirty-five-pound HE bombs were a devastating experience for troopers whose ranks had already been riven by the blast zones of Stephen Buchevsky's land mines.

. . . . .

REGIMENT COMMANDER HARAH winced as the communications net was flooded by sudden reports of heavy fire. Even after the unpleasant surprise of the infantry-portable SAMs, he hadn't anticipated *this.*

His lead infantry companies' already heavy loss rates soared, and he snarled over the net at his own support weapons commander.

"Find those damned mortars and get fire on them—*now*!"

. . . . .

HARAH'S INFANTRY RECOILED as rifle fire from concealed pits and camouflaged, log-reinforced bunkers added to the carnage of mortar bombs and minefields. But they were survivors who'd learned their lessons in a hard school, and their junior officer started probing forward, looking for openings.

Three heavy mortars, mounted on unarmored transports, had managed to struggle up the narrow trail behind them. Now they tried to locate the human mortars, but the dense tree cover and rugged terrain made it impossible. The Shongairi had never provided their artillerists with the specialized radar human artillery used to track incoming fire back to its source. After all, there'd never been any *reason* for them to develop the capability before they ran into the infernally inventive humans. Instead, they'd always relied upon their RC drones to overfly the local primitives' positions and direct their fire while they themselves stayed safely out of range and shelled the enemy with impunity. When they tried that in this case, however, they discovered that the humans weren't *entirely* out of Gremlins after all. And even if that hadn't been the case, Gutierrez's weapons had been dug-in and camouflaged with extraordinary care.

Finally, unable to actually find the corporal's mortar pits, the Shongairi resorted to blind suppressive fire. Their mortars were more powerful than their human counterparts, and white-hot flashes began to walk across the area behind Buchevsky's forward positions.

One of his forward bunkers took a direct hit and exploded, and another Shongair mortar round stripped the camouflage from a second bunker. Three captured human antitank weapons slammed into it, and he heard screams ripping out of some wounded human's throat from the ruins.

He heard screams rising from behind him, as well, but the Shongairi had problems of their own. Their vehicle-mounted weapons were confined to the trail, while the humans were deeply dug-in, and Buchevsky and Ignacio Gutierrez had preplotted just about every possible firing position along the trail. As soon as the Shongairi opened fire, Gutierrez knew where they had to be, and both of *his* mortars retargeted immediately. They fired more rapidly than the heavier Shongair weapons, and their bombs fell around the Shongair vehicles in a savage exchange that could not—and didn't—last long.

Ignacio Gutierrez died, along with one entire crew. The second mortar, though, remained in action . . . which was more than could be said for the vehicles they'd engaged.

. . . . .

HARAH SNARLED.

He had over a twelve more mortar-carriers . . . all of them still far behind the point of contact, at the far end of the choked, tortuous trails along which his infantry had pursued the humans. He could bring them up—in time—just as he could call in a kinetic strike and put an end to this entire business in minutes. But the longer he delayed, the more casualties that single remaining human mortar would inflict. And if he called in the kinetic strike, he'd kill the specimens he'd come to capture along with their defenders . . . which would make the entire operation—and all the casualties he'd already suffered—meaningless.

That wasn't going to happen. No. If this bunch of primitives was so incredibly stupid, so lost to all rationality and basic decency that they wanted to die fighting rather than submit honorably even now, then he would damned well oblige them. And when he was done, he'd drag the specimens they were trying to protect from him back to Ground Base Commander Shairez as payment for every one of his own losses.

He looked up through a break in the tree cover. The light was fading quickly, and despite their night-vision equipment, the Shongairi had discovered that fighting humans in the dark was a losing proposition. But there was still time. His infantry had managed to blow at least one gap through the humans' well-concealed, well-dug-in infantry. There was an opening, and they could still break through before darkness fell if—

He started snapping orders.

. . . . .

STEPHEN BUCHEVSKY SENSED it coming. He couldn't have explained how, but he knew. He could actually *feel* the Shongairi gathering themselves, steeling themselves, and he knew.

"They're coming!" he shouted, and heard his warning relayed along the horseshoe-shaped defensive line in either direction from his CP.

He set aside his own rifle, settled into position behind the KPV heavy machine gun, and swung it to cover the gap where his bunker line had been at least partially breached.

There were a dozen tripod-mounted PKMS 7.62-millimeter medium machine guns dug in in the bunkers and individual strongpoints around Bastogne's final perimeter, but even Mircea Basarab's scrounging talents had limits. He'd managed to come up with only one heavy machine gun, but it was one hell of a heavy, Buchevsky thought. Bulky and undeniably awkward—the thing was six and a half feet long (which made it twenty percent longer than even the US M2A .50 heavy MG Buchevsky was used to), and mounted on a two-wheeled cart—it looked more like some kind of fieldpiece than any machine gun Buchevsky had ever used. As far as he knew, the infantry version had been withdrawn from Soviet service in the 1960s, and the obsolescent weapon looked like a refugee from World War II, but at this time, in this place, he wasn't about to complain, and the spade grips felt solid and welcome in his hands.

The Shongairi started forward behind a hurricane of rifle fire and grenades. The second mine belt staggered them, disordered them. For a moment, it stopped them completely while their wounded shrieked and writhed in mangled agony. But there simply weren't enough mines, and they came on again. In fact, their rate of advance increased as they realized they'd gotten too close to the defenders for the single remaining mortar to engage.

Then the medium machine guns opened up.

More Shongairi shrieked, tumbled aside, disappeared in sprays of blood and tissue, but a pair of wheeled APCs edged up the trail behind them. How they'd gotten here was more than Buchevsky could guess, but their turret-mounted light energy weapons quested back and forth, seeking targets. Then a quasi-solid bolt of lightning slammed across the chaos, blood, and terror. Another human bunker exploded, and two of the machine guns suddenly stopped firing.

But Stephen Buchevsky knew where that lightning bolt had come from, and the Soviet army had developed the KPV around the 14.5-millimeter round of its final World War II antitank rifle. The PKMS' 185-grain bullet developed three thousand foot-pounds of muzzle energy; the KPV's tungsten-cored bullet weighed almost a *thousand* grains . . . and developed twenty-four thousand foot-pounds of muzzle energy.

He laid his sights on the vehicle which had just fired and sent six hundred rounds per minute shrieking into it.

The APC staggered as the tungsten-cored, armor-piercing, incendiary bullets slammed into it at better than thirty-two hundred feet per second, capable of penetrating almost an inch and a half of rolled homogenous armor at five hundred and fifty yards. The APC's light armor had been reinforced by the external appliqués Shongair maintenance techs had fitted to every one of Harah's vehicles, and it had shrugged off human small arms fire all day long.

It never had a chance against *that* torrent of destruction, and the vehicle vomited smoke and flame.

Its companion turned towards the source of its destruction, and Alice Macomb stood up in her rifle pit. She exposed herself recklessly with an RBR-M60, and its three-and-a-half-pound rocket smashed into the APC . . . just before a six-round burst of rifle fire killed her where she stood.

Buchevsky swung the KPV's flaming muzzle, sweeping his fire along the Shongair front as the aliens' point drove forward, pouring his hate, his fury, his desperate need to protect the children behind him, into his enemies.

He was still firing when the Shongair grenade silenced his machine gun forever.

.XXXV.

He woke slowly, floating up from the depths like someone else's ghost. He woke to darkness, to pain, and to a swirling tide-race of dizziness, confusion, and fractured memory.

He blinked—slowly, blindly, trying to understand. He'd been wounded more times than he liked to think about, but it had never been like this. The pain had never run everywhere under his skin, as if it were racing about on the power of his own heartbeat. And yet, even though he knew he had never suffered such pain in his life, it was curiously . . . distant. A part of him, yes, but walled off by the dizziness. Held one imagined half step away.

"You are awake, my Stephen."

It was a statement, he realized, not a question. As if the voice behind it were trying to reassure him of that.

He turned his head, and it was as if it belonged to someone else. It seemed to take him forever, but at last Mircea Basarab's face swam into his field of vision.

He blinked again, trying to focus, but he couldn't. He lay in a cave somewhere, looking out into a mountain night, and there was something wrong with his eyes. Everything seemed oddly out of phase, and the night kept flashing, as if it were alive with heat lightning.

"Mircea."

He didn't recognize his own voice. It was faint, thready.

"Yes," Basarab agreed. "It is a good sign that you are awake again. I know you may not believe it at this moment, but you will recover."

"Take . . . your word . . . for it."

"Very wise of you."

Buchevsky didn't have to be able to focus his eyes to see Basarab's fleeting smile, and he felt his own mouth twitch in reply. But then a new and different sort of pain ripped through him.

"I . . . fucked up." He swallowed painfully. "Sorry . . . so sorry. The kids . . ."

His eyes burned as a tear forced itself from under his lids, and Basarab gripped his right hand. The Romanian raised it, pressed it against his own chest, and his face came closer as he leaned over Buchevsky.

"No, my Stephen," he said slowly, each word distinctly formed, as if to be certain Buchevsky understood him. "It was not *you* who failed; it was I. This is *my* fault, my friend."

"No." Buchevsky shook his head weakly. "No. Couldn't have . . . stopped it even if . . . you'd been here."

"You think not?" It was Basarab's turn to shake his head. "You think wrongly. These creatures—these *Shongairi*—would never have touched my people if I had remembered. If I had not held my hand, decided to stand upon the defensive to avoid provoking them instead of seeking them out. Instead of teaching them the error of their ways, warning them in ways even *they* could not have mistaken to stay far from my mountains. If I had not spent so long hiding, trying to be someone I am not. Trying to forget. You shame me, my Stephen. You, who fell in my place, doing my duty, paying in blood for *my* failure."

Buchevsky frowned. His swirling brain tried to make some sort of sense out of Basarab's words, but he couldn't. Which probably shouldn't have been too surprising, he decided, given how horrendously bad he felt.

"How many—?" he asked.

"Only a very few, I fear," Basarab said quietly. "Your Gunny Meyers is here, although he was more badly wounded even than you. I am not surprised the vermin left both of you for dead. And Jasmine, and Private Lopez. The others were . . . gone before Take and I could return."

Buchevsky's stomach clenched as Basarab confirmed what he'd already known.

"And . . . the villagers?"

"Sergeant Jonescu got perhaps a dozen children to safety," Basarab said. "He and most of his men died holding the trail while the children and their mothers fled. The other villages have already offered them shelter, taken them in. The others—"

He shrugged, looking away, then looked back at Buchevsky.

"They are not here, Stephen. For whatever reason, the vermin have taken them, and I do not think either of us would like that reason if we knew it."

"*God.*" Buchevsky closed his eyes again. "Sorry. My fault," he said once more.

"Do not repeat that foolishness again, or you will make me angry," Basarab said sternly. "And do not abandon hope for them. It is in my mind that this entire attack was designed to secure prisoners, not simply to destroy a handful of villages in the remote mountains. If all they wished was to kill, then the others' bodies would be here as well. And, having taken prisoners, surely they will transport them back to their main base in the lowlands. That means we know where to find them, and they are *my* people. I swore to protect them, and I do not let my word be proven false."

Buchevsky's world was spinning away again, yet he opened his eyes, looked up in disbelief. His vision cleared, if only for a moment, and as he saw Mircea Basarab's face he felt the disbelief flow out of him.

It was still preposterous, of course. He knew that. Only, somehow, as he looked up into that granite expression, it didn't matter what he knew. All that mattered was what he *felt* . . . and as he fell back into the bottomless darkness, what the fading sliver of his awareness felt was almost sorry for the Shongairi.

. . . . .

PRIVATE KUMAYR FELT his head beginning to nod forward and stiffened his spine, snapping back upright in his chair. His damnably *comfortable* chair, which wasn't exactly what someone needed to keep him awake and alert in the middle of the night.

He shook himself.

None of Ground Base Seven's officers were particularly cheerful at the moment. It wasn't quite as bad as it had been immediately after Regiment Commander Harah's return, three days ago, but it was bad enough to be going on with. The regiment commander's casualties and equipment losses had been at least as bad—probably worse, actually, Kumayr suspected—than anything the brigade's other two regiments might have suffered in North America. His unhappiness was obvious, and his junior officers reflected his unhappiness. They weren't being outstandingly patient and understanding these days, especially with garrision troopers who hadn't been in the field with the regiment. In fact, Kumayr decided, if he didn't want one of those junior officers to come along and rip his head off for dozing on duty, he'd better find something to do.

Something that looked industrious and conscientious.

His ears twitched in amusement at the thought, and he punched up a standard diagnostic of the perimeter security systems. Not that he expected to find any problems. The entire base had completed a wall-to-wall readiness exercise only two days before Regiment Commander Harah had departed to collect Ground Base Commander Shairez's specimens. All of his systems had passed their checks with flying colors then, and he hadn't had a single fault warning since. Still, running the diagnostic would look good on the log sheets . . . and save his ears if Squad Commander Reymahk or one of the others happened along.

Kumayr hummed softly as the computers looked over one another's shoulders, reporting back to him. He paid particular attention to the systems in the laboratory area. Now that they had test subjects, the labs would be getting a serious workout after all. When that happened—

His humming stopped, and his ears pricked as a red icon appeared on his display. That couldn't be right . . . could it?

He keyed another, more tightly focused diagnostic program, and his pricked ears flattened as more icons began to blink. He stared at them, then slammed his hand on the transmit key.

"Perimeter One!" he snapped. "Perimeter One, Central. Report status!"

There was no response, and something with hundreds of small, icy feet started to scuttle up and down his spine.

"Perimeter Two!" he barked, trying another circuit. "Perimeter Two—report status!"

Still no response, and that was impossible. There were *fifty troopers* in each of those positions—one of them had to have heard him!

"All perimeter stations!" He heard the desperation in his voice, tried to squeeze it back out again while he held down the all-units key. "All perimeter stations, this is a red alert!"

Still there was nothing, and he stabbed more controls, bringing up the monitors. The displays came alive . . . and he froze.

Not possible, a small, still voice said in the back of his brain as he stared at the images of carnage. At the troopers with their throats ripped out, at the Shongair blood soaking into the thirsty soil of an alien world. Heads turned backward on snapped necks, and dismembered body parts scattered like some lunatic's bloody handiwork.

Not possible, not without at least one *alarm sounding. Not—*

He heard a tiny sound, and his right hand flashed towards his sidearm, but even as he touched it, the door of the control room flew open and darkness crashed over him.

. XXXVI .

"What?"

Fleet Commander Thikair looked up at Ship Commander Ahzmer in astonishment so deep it was sheer incomprehension.

"I'm . . . I'm sorry, Sir." The flagship's CO sounded like someone trapped in an amazingly bad dream, Thikair thought distantly. "The report just came in. I'm . . . afraid it's confirmed, Sir."

"*All* of them?" Thikair shook himself. "*Everyone* assigned to the base? Even Shairez?"

"All of them," Ahzmer confirmed heavily. "And all of the Ground Base Commander's specimens have disappeared, as well."

"*Dainthar,*" Thikair half whispered. He stared at the ship commander, then shook himself again, harder.

"How did they do it?"

"Sir, I don't know. *No one* knows. For that matter, it doesn't . . . Well, it doesn't look like anything we've seen the humans do before."

"What are you talking about?" Thikair's voice was harder, impatient. He knew much of his irritation was the product of his own shock, but that didn't change the fact that what Ahzmer had just said made no sense.

"It doesn't look like whoever it was used *weapons* at all, Fleet Commander." Ahzmer didn't sound as if he expected Thikair to believe him, but the ship commander went on doggedly. "It's more like some sort of wild beasts got through every security system without sounding a single alarm. Not one, Sir. But there are no bullet wounds, no knife wounds, no sign of *any* kind of weapon. Our people were just . . . torn apart."

"That doesn't make sense," Thikair protested.

"No, Sir. It doesn't. But it's what *happened.*"

The two of them stared at one another. Then Thikair drew a deep breath.

"Senior officers conference in one day-twelfth," he said flatly.

. . . . .

"THE GROUND PATROLS have confirmed it, Fleet Commander," Ground Force Commander Thairys said heavily. "There are no Shongair survivors. None. And"—he inhaled heavily, someone about to say something he really didn't want to—"we found exactly eleven expended rifle cartridges. *Eleven.* Aside from that, there's no evidence a single one of our troopers so much as fired a shot in his own defense. Most of them died in their beds, obviously without ever waking up at all. And as for the duty sections . . . It's as if they never saw, never heard, a *thing*. As if they all just . . . *sat* there without even *noticing* that someone—or some *thing*—was about to tear them apart."

"Calm down, Thairys." Thikair put both sternness and sympathy into his tone. "We're going to have panicky rumors enough when the *troops* hear about this. Let's not begin believing in night terrors before the rumor mill even gets started!"

The other officers gathered around the table looked distinctly uneasy, and Thikair flicked his ears in an impatient shrug.

"I have no more idea than you do about how they did it," Thikair replied. "Not *yet*, at any rate. On the other hand, we've encountered one surprise after another ever since we entered the star system. So far, we've survived all of them, however painful some of them have been. And we've always managed to unravel what happened—and how—eventually. How they managed *this* one is more than I can say at this time, of course. If no weapons were used, perhaps what we're looking at is the use of some sort of trained animals! I know that sounds absurd, but these creatures have done nothing *but* come up with one absurd, preposterous tactic or weapon after another. For that matter, it's not as if we haven't seen other primitives use war animals. Remember those trained cat-apes on Bashtu? They got those past all of our precautions because the troops thought they'd make such marvelous 'pets'! Or what about those poisonous crawlers the Rashinti managed to introduce into our garrisons' food supplies? No one saw that one coming, either, did they? Oh, and let's not forget the bigger ones they used to fire at us with their Dainthar-cursed catapults!" His ears wagged emphatic negation. "I'm certainly not prepared to rule out the possibility that these damned humans have done something of the same sort!"

Thairys looked at him for a moment, then managed a chuckle that was only slightly hollow.

"You're right, of course, Sir. And your point about how they got the cat-apes and the poison crawlers into our ground bases is well taken. It's just that . . . Well, it's just that I've never seen anything like this. And I've checked the database. As nearly as I can tell, no one in the entire *Hegemony* has ever seen anything like this."

"It's a big galaxy," Thikair pointed out. "And even the Hegemony's explored only a very small portion of it. I don't know what happened down there either, but trust me—there's a rational explanation. We just have to figure out what it is."

"With all due respect, Fleet Commander," Squadron Commander Jainfar said quietly, "how do we go about doing that without at least some information on what actually happened?"

Thikair looked at him, and the squadron commander flicked his ears.

"I've personally reviewed the sensor recordings and logs the Ground Force Commander's patrols retrieved, Sir. Until Private Kumayr began trying to contact the perimeter strongpoints, there was absolutely no indication of any problem. For that matter, according to his computer logs, the initial alarm from his diagnostic programs had nothing to do with hostile incursions. It simply indicated that some of the perimeter positions were no longer manned as they were supposed to be. I'm sure he assumed the fault was in the software, not the hardware, at least initially. When he got no response to his attempts to contact those perimeter points manually, however, he activated the internal security cameras to check on them, and *that's* when he hit the general alarm. Whatever happened, it apparently managed to kill every single member of the garrison—except for Kumayr—without being detected by any heat, motion, pressure, radar, or audio sensor. It avoided not simply the passive sensors, but the *active* ones, as well."

"What about the visual *records* from the cameras, Squadron Commander?" one of the division commanders attending electronically asked. "Surely they must have shown *something*, if whatever Kumayr saw prompted him to sound a general alarm," he continued, and Jainfar lowered his ears.

"The cameras might actually have offered us at least some insight," he said. "Unfortunately, all visual records from the base archives were erased. Or, to be more accurate, all visual records from the period beginning approximately a quarter day-twelfth before Kumayr sounded the alarm were erased from the master computer banks . . . and the backup recording chips were physically removed."

There was a moment of silence as all of Thikair's officers digested that particular bit of information, then Jainfar turned back to the fleet commander and shrugged. There wasn't a trace of disrespect in that shrug, only frustrated ignorance.

"The fact of the matter is, Sir, that we have no data. No information at all. Just an entire base full of dead personnel. And with no evidence, how do we figure out *what* happened, far less who was responsible for it?"

"I think the Squadron Commander has raised a significant point, Fleet Commander," a new voice said respectfully. "May I address it?"

Ground Base Commander Barak was down on the planetary surface, attending the conference electronically from the communications center in Ground Base One, and Thikair flicked his ears at the other officer's com image in permission to speak.

"With all due respect, Sir," Barak said, his ears lowered in a position of profound submission, "I doubt that this situation is going to lend itself to the sort of explanations we've found for all of this planet's other surprises. I agree that the condition of the bodies indicates they weren't attacked with sophisticated *weapons*, but only a very sophisticated *attacker* could have penetrated Ground Base Seven's defenses in the first place. And while the wounds may appear to have been inflicted by some sort of animal, the attackers—or whoever directed the animals in question, if animals were truly involved at all—were clearly not simply sentient, but *technologically* sophisticated. They managed not simply to locate and remove the physical recordings of what was presumably a visual record of their actions inside the ground base, but to erase that same imagery from the base computer net. That implies a level of familiarity with our systems and technology which far surpasses anything we've seen out of these creatures. I don't say they wouldn't have been aware of the probable existence of such records, but simply that they're neither trained on nor familiar with our own cybernetics and data storage *methods*. Without that training and familiarity, how would they even *find* those records, much less erase them from the master computers?

"Moreover, I think we must ask ourselves another significant question. If it was the humans—if humans were capable of this sort of thing, had this sort of ability and the technological sophistication to penetrate our cyber systems and erase or extract information—would they have waited to use it until we'd killed more than half of them? For that matter, why there? Why Ground Base Seven? Why not Ground Base Commander Fursa's? Why not one of the other bases here in North America, where the humans appear to have been more technologically advanced and we've experienced so much difficulty in asserting control in the first place? Unless we wish to assume that the humans somehow figured out what Shairez was going to be developing and wanted to prevent it, why employ some sort of 'secret weapon' for the first time against a base whose ZOR has been so relatively tranquil rather than in one of the areas where the fighting has been both prolonged and intense?"

"Those are all intriguing questions, Ground Base Commander," Thairys said. "Yet what I seem to be hearing you suggest is that it was not, in fact, the humans at all. And if not the humans, then who do you suggest it might have been?"

"That I don't know, Sir," Barak said respectfully. "I'm simply suggesting that what we *do* know clearly implies relatively high technological capabilities and that, logically, if humans could do this in the first place, they would already have done it . . . and on a considerably larger scale than a single ground base."

"Are you suggesting some other member of the Hegemony might be responsible?" Thikair asked slowly.

"I think that's possible, Sir." Barak shrugged again. "Again, I have no idea of who it might actually have been, but the sophistication required to penetrate Ground Base Commander Shairez's defenses strongly suggests that it could have come only from another advanced species."

"I don't really see how it could have been another member of the Hegemony," Squadron Commander Jainfar objected, rubbing the bridge of his muzzle thoughtfully. "Our technology is as good as anyone else's—probably even better, in purely military applications—and I don't think *we* could have penetrated Shairez's security so seamlessly."

"Wonderful." Thairys grimaced. "So all any of us have been able to contribute so far is that we don't have a clue who did it, or how, or even why! Assuming, of course, that it wasn't the humans . . . whom we've all now agreed don't have the capability to do it in the first place!"

"Wait."

Thikair tipped back his chair, grooming the tip of his tail while he pondered, and the others sat respectfully silent. Several minutes passed before the fleet commander brought his chair back upright and flipped his ears at Barak in a nod of appreciation.

"As Ground Force Commander Thairys has said, Ground Base Commander, I believe you've raised several telling points. In particular, your observation that even if the humans somehow managed to train some unknown animal to break into our fortifications and slaughter our personnel, animals could neither have gotten past that many separate layers of sensors without *something* being detected nor subsequently erased and removed any visual record of their presence."

He paused, expression grim, then lowered his ears in mingled anger and harsh determination as he gazed around the table at his other officers.

"As Ground Base Commander Barak has so ably pointed out, simply defeating the perimeter sensors would require a level of sophistication in advance of anything we've yet seen on this planet. Indeed, it would require a level of sophistication in advance of our *own,* and while the humans' capabilities have surprised us several times, it's always been primarily because of the way in which those capabilities have been *applied,* not because their technology is inherently superior. They've done things it never occurred to us to do because we'd never faced the problems they were solving, but we *have* faced the problems involved in creating sensors and security systems to protect our bases not simply against overt attack, but also against undetected incursions, even by the spies of another advanced species. On the other hand, like anyone else, we build our defenses on the basis of the threats we anticipate. Which means we don't always give equal emphasis to defeating both types of threats *simultaneously,* now do we?"

He paused, looking around at their expressions, then shrugged.

"I find myself beginning to wonder if perhaps all of us—including His Majesty's ministers—have underestimated the full depth of Vice-Speaker Koomaatkia's purposes in this case," he said very softly. "Clearly, she intended to suggest we would receive the sub-rosa support of her own species, and possibly some of the others, if there were any . . . irregularities in our conquest of the humans. The question which has just occurred to me, however, is whether or not she was being honest. For that matter, was she as ignorant as we of the true state of affairs here on KU-197-20?"

"What do you mean, Sir?" Thairys asked respectfully, watching the fleet commander's expression intently.

"I'm not certain I know what I mean." Thikair's ears twitched a humorless smile. "One possibility which has occurred to me, though, is that perhaps the Kreptu—especially if they were made sufficiently nervous about the humans by the original survey report—dispatched one of their own vessels to examine the planet themselves while the various bureaucracies were still considering and processing Survey's information. If so, they would certainly have realized how aberrant the humans' rate of technological advancement has been. In which case, by acceding to our colonization request—by *encouraging* our efforts in that direction—they might have specifically intended for us to run our snouts into a *shengar* nest in the hope we might lose at least one eye to the creatures' claws. Conversely, if they were aware of the humans' capabilities, they might have felt even more anxiety about the potential danger the species represented, in which case their desire to see that danger neutralized would have been even greater . . . and we would have provided them with the most readily applied blunt object with which to do the neutralizing.

"But suppose their actual intent goes even deeper than that. Suppose they want the humans neutralized, but that they've also become aware of the Empire's ultimate plans for the remainder of the Hegemony? If they've finally awakened to at least a portion of our long-term strategy, they would certainly oppose it. And one step in doing that would be to turn public opinion among the other races of the Hegemony even more strongly against us.

"So suppose they also saw this as an opportunity to significantly embarrass us before the rest of the Hegemony? If the Kreptu have developed a stealth technology superior to anything our intelligence services have reported, and if they actually have dispatched an expedition of their own to this star system, then it would be distinctly possible that they could have a vessel present even now, without our detecting it. In that case, they may have been surreptitiously recording all of our actions since our arrival. For that matter, we know what data was *erased* from Ground Base Commander Shairez's systems, but we have no way to know what information might have been *extracted* from them. Although they contained no details on the Empire's grand strategy, for obvious reasons of operational security, it would be difficult to overestimate how embarrassing some of the other data from her secure files might prove.

"With such records, particularly after a little judicious editing, they might find themselves in a position to convince the Hegemony's weed-eaters that our species is even more 'degenerate' and 'vicious' than our most vociferous critics have ever claimed. They might hope they could actually encourage some of the other races to begin taking steps to build a genuine military capability of their own with which to oppose ours. They would be unlikely to succeed on any large scale, given the weed-eaters' and most of the omnivores' abhorrence of all things military, but such 'revelations' could still inflict enormous damage on our status within the Hegemony, with potentially serious consequences for the Emperor's long-term plans."

Some of his officers looked skeptical, to a greater or a lesser extent. Others were beginning to look even more alarmed, and he shrugged.

"I may well be seeing shadows within shadows, plots and threats where none exist," he conceded. "For that matter, focusing on Koomaatkia and the Kreptu might well be an error . . . especially if some *other* advanced race is working against us. It's even possible that that hypothetical other advanced race—the Liatu, for example, who aren't much fonder of the Kreptu than they are of us—is working against *both* of us. If the Kreptu could be maneuvered into having 'connived' with us Shongairi, and if we could be demonstrated to have egregiously violated the Constitution as a result of the *Kreptu's* actions, then the Kreptu's status within the Hegemony might be seriously undermined, as well."

One or two sets of ears were waving slowly in tentative half agreement with him now, but Jainfar's ears frowned, instead.

"I agree those are interesting possibilities, Sir," the blunt old space dog said. "Yet it sounds very much to me as if you are suggesting that it was the Kreptu—or someone—and *not* the humans who attacked Ground Base Seven. That would require them to act far more directly, and get far more blood on their claws, than they've ever done before."

"Unless they're actively *cooperating* with the humans on the ground, Squadron Commander," Ground Base Commander Barak said thoughtfully. "Providing the humans with technological support to get them through our defenses, then standing back and allowing the humans to do the actual bloodletting."

Thikair looked at him, and the ground base commander shrugged.

"I'm not saying that's the case, you understand, Sir. But consider this. If we do, indeed, have a significant enemy within the Hegemony who's finally awakened to the Empire's long-term plans—whether the Kreptu or one of the weed-eaters, like the Liatu—they might be seeking more than one quarry in a single hunt. Embarrass and discredit us, yes. Perhaps even attempt to build some countervailing military power or faction within the Hegemony. But suppose they also see this as an opportunity to more directly evaluate our own military capabilities in order to decide how dangerous we truly are? Is it not possible that, in such an instance, they might provide the humans with assistance against us? Especially if they believed that seeing how we responded to the enhanced threat might tell them a great deal about *our* capabilities. For that matter, might it not be possible they would use our automatic assumption that it must be humans who attacked Ground Base

Seven as cover for an incursion of their *own* personnel, whereby our systems and their capabilities might be directly evaluated and tested?"

"I can't see the Liatu getting that close to so much bloodletting," Jainfar replied. "They're almost as squeamish as the Barthoni. The Kreptu, now . . . I might see *them* in that role. Or the Garm or the Howsanth, for that matter."

"I realize I'm the one who initially started us down this scent," Thikair said. "I think we've wandered about as far in speculation as we profitably can at this point, however. All we truly know at this stage is that Ground Base Seven has been attacked and that the attack clearly exceeds the capability of anything we've previously seen out of the humans. Beyond that, all we can do is wander through the realms of hypothesis, which seems unlikely to lead us to any hard and fast conclusions. For that, we will require additional information—more evidence."

His subordinates all looked at him, and he bared his canines in a frosty challenge smile.

"Don't misunderstand me. I'm as . . . anxious about this as anyone. But let's look at it. We've been hurt—badly—and as yet we actually know very little about how it was done. One thing is crystal clear, however: whatever happened, it took Shairez's entire base completely by surprise. The first step, then, is to see to it that *no one* can surprise us a second time. Whether this represents the use of some previously unknown human capability or the work of another member of the Hegemony is immaterial in that regard."

He turned his attention to Ground Force Commander Thairys.

"If, indeed, this is someone seeking to evaluate our technology, obviously we should take the opportunity to evaluate *their* technology, in return. As good as Ground Base Seven's security systems were, none of them were specifically directed at Hegemony-level threats, so it's distinctly possible we left ourselves vulnerable to a more sophisticated incursion. I believe our first step, then, should be to completely reassess our systems' vulnerabilities. Improving our existing capabilities can't possibly hurt anything against the humans, and if in fact one of our fellow members of the Hegemony is playing games with us, a sufficient upgrade of our systems may just come as an unpleasant surprise for them.

"So we start by putting all of our bases and personnel on maximum alert. Next, we emphasize to all of our personnel that whoever was responsible may have some form of stealth technology. They won't like hearing that, but it will at least begin putting events into a familiar frame of reference, and that can't hurt. Better they be concentrating on a threat which fits into their existing . . . mental landscapes, as Shairez might have put it, than spending their time fueling the rumor mill with all manner of wild speculation!

"Next, since we apparently can't rely on our sensors until we've upgraded them suitably, we'll put our own physical senses online. When I say I want *maximum* alertness, I mean precisely that. I want all of our ground bases to integrate every unit assigned to them into real-time, free-flow communications nets. All checkpoints will be manned, not left to the automatics. Regular roving patrols and additional fixed, *manned* security points will be established, and all detachments will check in regularly with their central HQs. At the same time as we announce those measures to all personnel, I want all officers above the rank of battalion commander informed we may be looking at covert operations by enemies within the Hegemony. I want them ready to recognize that if they see evidence of it, and to respond decisively. If in fact we have . . . rivals creeping about in our backyard, I want them identified and neutralized. I'd prefer that they be taken alive and fully interrogated, but at this particular moment, I'm not feeling too particular about that, either." He bared his canines again, briefly. "For that matter, even a *dead* Kreptu or two would make a fairly convincing bit of evidence if it becomes necessary to demonstrate their manipulation of the situation to the Council."

"And if it *isn't* another member of the Hegemony, Sir?" Thairys asked quietly. "If it turns out the humans *did* somehow breach Ground Base Commander Shairez's security without outside assistance?"

"To be honest, in many ways, I'd be relieved to have that proved," Thikair admitted. "It would be much less alarming in terms of the Empire's long-term strategy than discovering that our intended prey has become aware we intend to stalk it in the fullness of time. And if it turns out this was, indeed, simply another example of the humans having applied their more primitive technology more innovatively than we'd anticipated or allowed for, improvements in our own sensors' sophistication are bound to catch them at it in the end. Ultimately, our capabilities are simply too much greater than theirs, even if we haven't yet applied them sufficiently to the problem, for any other outcome.

"In the short term, however, while we're reassessing and improving our systems' capabilities, our hardware will remain vulnerable to similar penetrations by whoever managed this one, which is why I want such special emphasis placed on manned surveillance during our reassessment. For that matter, I have greater ultimate faith in the senses and alertness of our own people—of sentries aware of their responsibilities and concentrating upon them—than I do in any automated systems, however capable. Even if our sensors can't detect these people—whoever they are—on their way in, we can at least be certain our own eyes, ears, and noses will tell us when they've *arrived*."

He looked around the table again.

"Our warriors, our officers, are *Shongairi*. We will not allow this episode to stampede us like a weed-eater fleeing the hunter! With duties to concentrate upon, our troopers will settle down despite the rumors, and looked at from a proper perspective our other ground bases actually become bait. Our people are predators—hunters—and the canny hunter shapes his method to the prey he seeks. For the *hasthar,* the spear, the coursing beast, and the horn. For the *garish,* the snare. For the *binarch,* the concealed pit and beaters to drive him into it. For the great *tharntar,* the staked-out *mahrlar,* as bait. And for taking the most dangerous or elusive prey of all, the hunter's greatest weapon is often patience. Very well, we will *be* patient, but we will also remember that sooner or later the time always—*always*—comes for the hunter to pounce. And pounce we shall, when that moment arrives. Whatever human trick this may be, whatever advanced stealth another member of the Hegemony may be able to bring to bear, we will find a way to detect it. Have no fear of that. And once detected, we *will* track it down and kill it!"

. . . . .

"YES, THAIRYS?" THIKAIR said.

The ground force commander had lingered as the other senior officers filed out. Now he looked at the fleet commander, his ears half folded, and his eyes were somber.

"There were two small points I . . . chose not to mention in front of the others, Sir," he said quietly.

"Oh?" Thikair managed to keep his voice level, despite the sudden cold tingle dancing down his nerves.

"Yes, Sir. First, I'm afraid the preliminary medical exams indicate that Ground Base Commander Shairez was killed at least two day-twelfths *after* the rest of her personnel. And there are indications that she was . . . interrogated for quite some time before her neck was broken."

"I see." Thikair looked at his subordinate for a moment, then cleared his throat. "Two points, I believe you said?"

"Yes, Sir. I did. And the second point is that all of the base's neural education units are missing, Sir."

He met Thikair's eyes, and the fleet commander drew a deep breath of comprehension.

"I think there's considerable merit to the points you raised about possible involvement by other members of the Hegemony, Sir," Thairys continued quietly. "I don't know if your concerns are justified, but I do know all of us are groping for clues at this point. Obviously, until we know more the possibilities are endless. Nonetheless, I must admit that the loss of those education units . . . concerns me. Deeply. I find myself wondering if any other member of the Hegemony could be so completely mad, so *insane,* as to have simply handed such devices to a species like the *humans.* On the other hand, if not to hand them to the humans, why take them at all? Their utility to any other of the advanced races would be negligible, as they already possess educator technology of their own, but Ground Base Commander Shairez had determined that humans were neurally educable even without implants. Indeed, that was why the units were present in her base in such numbers. And that's why their absence concerns me so deeply. If they've fallen into human hands—whether they were initially seized by the humans themselves or simply given to them by someone else—and if the humans know how to operate them. . . ."

The ground commander's voice trailed off. There was, after all, no need for him to complete the sentence, since each of the education units contained the basic knowledge platform of the entire Hegemony.

. XXXVII .

"Pieter, there's someone looking for you."

Ushakov looked up, eyebrows arching in surprise.

"Looking for me?" he repeated, and Ivan Kolesnikov shrugged.

There was something a bit peculiar about that shrug, Ushakov thought, although this was scarcely the first time someone had come seeking them. They'd lost Fyodor Belov four days ago, and even counting Ushakov and Kolesnikov, there were only seven of his original Ukrainians left. Yet despite those losses, his overall strength had actually increased, because they'd attracted a steady trickle of Russians, most of whom couldn't have cared less whether their leader spoke Russian, Ukrainian, or Swahili. All *they* cared about was his ability as an alien-killer.

There were times when Ushakov suspected that the brutality the Shongairi had shown in his area of operations stemmed directly from the effectiveness of those operations. That was the way it usually worked when "partisans" or "guerrillas"—or "terrorists," he supposed, since one man's guerrilla was another man's terrorist—proved successful. Whatever occupier they were attacking at the moment lashed out at the civilians in the area. In the process, a lot of civilians got killed . . . and a lot of survivors became guerrillas. And of course, the reverse was sometimes true. If he'd been willing to leave the Shongairi alone, they might have been willing to be less brutal to the Russians in the area.

They might.

But he wasn't going to leave them alone, and most of the locals who'd managed to survive this far seemed to share his bitter, unwavering hatred for the aliens. They didn't really care whether or not his operations were provoking reprisals, because almost all of them had joined his band because they no longer had anyone left for the Shongairi to retaliate *against.*

In the process, he'd become a marked man in the resistance, and he knew it. Even the Shongairi had identified him—by name, anyway—and the handful of Shongair prisoners Ushakov's men had taken and interrogated had made it clear enough (before their own inevitable deaths) that their superiors wanted Pieter Ushakov's head on a stick.

The thought didn't exactly fill him with terror. Nothing did that anymore, he'd discovered. If anything, it pleased him as proof of how badly he'd hurt them. Still, he'd been careful to maintain operational security. If the Shongairi really wanted him, and if they were smart enough to figure it out, they'd be trying to capture one of his guerrillas who could lead them to him. Or the family member of one of his guerrillas, perhaps. Someone they could . . . convince or coerce into betraying him to them. And there was no point in pretending they couldn't do that, if it occurred to them. Enough pain, enough starvation, or—far worse—enough threats to someone a human being loved—to a daughter or a son, a wife or a husband—would eventually find the chink in anyone's armor.

Unless, of course, they'd already lost everyone they'd ever loved.

"Who is this 'someone,' Vanya?" he asked.

"I don't know," Kolesnikov said unhappily. "He just . . . turned up outside Fetyukov's bunker." The young lieutenant who no longer looked young shook his head. "I don't like it," he admitted.

"Is he looking for *me,* me, or is he looking for 'the rebel commander' me?"

"He asked for you by name."

Kolesnikov didn't seem to be getting any happier, and Ushakov didn't blame him.

"Where is he now?"

"He says he'll be back at Fetyukov's in a couple of hours. He wants you to meet him there."

"Don't go, Pieter! *Please!*" a voice said, and Ushakov turned his head and looked at the child sitting on the other side of the table from him.

Her name was Zinaida, and she was seven years old. A heartbreakingly wise and frightened seven years old.

He reached out a hand, and she took it, squeezing his thumb in one small, tight fist and his little finger in the other. His Daria had held his hand that way, before she became "a big girl," he remembered, and smiled at her.

"I'm not going anywhere right this minute," he promised her in Russian.

"But you *are* going," she said, tears welling in her blue eyes. "I know you are!"

"Perhaps I am," he agreed, then cocked his head. "But if I do, what did you promise me?"

"That I'd let you," she said in a tiny voice.

"Yes," he agreed. "And that you would take care of your mother and Boris and Kondratii. That's what big girls do."

She nodded mutely, still staring up into his face through a blur of tears, and he felt the heart he'd thought had died in Kiev melt inside him.

Stupid, he thought again. *Stupid! What in God's name are you* thinking, *you lunatic? You've been on borrowed time for months now, and you know it.*

Yes, he was, and he did. But when he looked into those eyes, he couldn't help himself.

And so he had done the unforgivable. He'd let himself start *feeling* again, even if it was the worst thing he could possibly do.

His mind went back to the day they'd met, when Zinaida had clung to him so desperately while the explosion sealed the water main behind them. It turned out they *had* been deep enough to survive the kinetic bombardment which had turned the woods through which they'd run into a cratered, seared wasteland almost exactly on schedule. The "tunnel" had run far enough to get them safely out of the immediate area, as well, and he'd used the same tactic twice more since then. Of course, one couldn't always find a convenient water main when one needed one, but he and Kolesnikov had trained their Russian recruits into competent combat engineers in their own right. And along the way they'd taught them that there was nothing magic about kinetic bombardments. Explosions were explosions, and a deep enough hole far enough away from the point of impact was what made explosions survivable.

But what had changed for Pieter Ushakov on that day was the way in which the aching hole in his heart had suddenly found something to fill it. A frightened, half-starved little girl. Her younger brother, who never spoke anymore, except in whispers to their mother. Her baby brother, born after the Shongairi's arrival. And the courageous young woman who had managed, against unimaginable odds, to keep both of her older children alive while she found enough sustenance, somehow, to produce the breast milk her baby needed.

Larissa Karpovna didn't talk about that very much. In fact, she said little more than her son Boris, but she'd attached herself to Ushakov. It wasn't a romantic attachment. He didn't think he'd have another one of those—not like the one he'd had with Vladislava, at any rate. No man was blessed enough by God to have two loves like that. And he didn't think Larissa really thought of him as a *man*—not in any sexual sense, at any rate. He was . . . he was her *rock,* he thought. He was the solidity she clung to, the only faint promise of safety for her children in a world gone far worse than simply insane.

He respected her deeply. In fact, he'd been a bit surprised when he realized just how much he did respect her and her accomplishment in preserving her children as long as she had. And he'd found that he did love her, but it was as if she were Zinaida's older sister, not someone old enough, if barely, to have been his own wife. All four of them had somehow become his children, and that was a terrible thing, because it gave him something to *live* for.

You've made me vulnerable again, little one, he thought now, looking down into Zinaida's face. *You're my Achilles' heel . . . my Achilles' heart. I can't* afford *that weakness, and I know it, but I can't*—won't—*give you up, either. I never had the chance to save my own babies, but perhaps I* can *save you, and as God is my witness, I will. Somehow, I* will. *And that's what makes you my weakness. Because with you and your mother and your brothers inside my heart, it's not enough just to kill Shongairi anymore. Not now.*

"Fetyukov's bunker, you said, Vanya?" he said out loud, and used the tip of his free hand's index finger to brush a tear from Zinaida's cheek.

. . . . .

"PIETER USHAKOV?"

Ushakov couldn't see the speaker very clearly. It was too dark in the tangled, shadowed woods beyond the camouflaged bunker. That didn't disturb him all that much, in itself. What did disturb him more than a little was that the stranger had somehow reached this point without a single one of the sentinels Ushakov had deployed challenging him.

Not good, Pieter, a corner of his mind thought. *Your people are supposed to be better than that! In fact, they are. Or they'd damned well* better *be if any of you want to be alive this time next week, anyway!*

"Yes," he said out loud. "And your name is—?"

"My name is less important than why I wanted to speak with you," the stranger replied in only slightly accented Ukrainian. He spoke the language remarkably well for a nonnative speaker, Ushakov thought, but his accent was odd. One he couldn't quite place. It certainly wasn't Russian, at any rate, and eyes narrowed.

"And what do you want to talk about?" he asked, more than a little irked by the stranger's avoidance of his question and letting an edge of suspicion sharpen his tone in response.

"Because I understand you have been attacking the aliens' convoys and working parties around this base of theirs for some time," the other man replied. "This is correct, no?"

"I think if you know enough to ask for me by name, you already know that, too," Ushakov replied tartly.

"I think so, too," the stranger agreed. He sounded amused by Ushakov's tone, yet rather to the Ukrainian's surprise, the amusement didn't irritate him. Perhaps because it wasn't a dismissive or denigrating amusement. Indeed, it seemed to invite him to share its joviality in a way that was almost . . . soothing.

"So suppose you tell me the reason you wanted to speak with me," he said.

"Very well. I intend to attack and destroy that base, and I seek information about the vermin who garrison it. About their movements and their numbers." Ushakov had the strong impression of a smile, although he couldn't see it in the darkness. "It will not matter all that much in the end in most ways, I suppose. But a wise commander, as I am sure you yourself have learned, scouts the terrain before an attack."

"You think you can *destroy* their base?" He couldn't quite keep the incredulity out of the question. "I've been attacking them, hurting them every way I could, for three months now, and you think you can walk right through their defenses? Past the automated gun emplacements? Through the sensors they've set up on every approach?"

"Yes, I think I can, my troops and I. And we will."

Ushakov had never heard such iron certainty in a human voice. The man behind that voice might be—probably was—mad, but there was no doubt in him.

"Then I want to go with you," he heard his own voice say.

"No, you do not," the stranger replied, almost gently.

"I do." The echo of that same steely certitude sounded in his own voice, and he realized why. It wasn't just his thirst for vengeance anymore, either. It was more than that—a way to neutralize the threat looming over the human beings he'd been foolish enough to allow himself to love once more.

"I'll help you, tell you what I know. And no one alive knows the approaches to that base the way I do. I'll guide you in. But only if I go with you."

"You do not realize what you are asking me for," the stranger said.

"Then tell me."

. . . . .

"I ALMOST WISH something else would happen," Ground Base Commander Fursa said. He and Ground Base Commander Barak were conferring via communicator, and Barak frowned at him.

"I want to figure out what's going on—and who's doing this to us—as badly as you do, Fursa. And I suppose for us to do that, 'something else' *is* going to have to happen. For that matter, I even agree with the Fleet Commander that we should be looking upon this as an opportunity to bait a trap for our enemies. But while you're wishing, just remember, *you're* the next closest base."

"I know." Fursa grimaced. "That's my point. We're feeling just a *bit* exposed out here." His ears wiggled sourly. "It's been bad enough with the attacks on my supply columns and patrols. To be honest, my troopers would like an opportunity to get our claws into more than a human raider here, or another one over there. Dealing with an enemy who actually stands up—who attacks where we can get *at* him for a change, instead of just disappearing again afterward, like smoke—would make us all feel better."

Barak felt his own ears perk in understanding. Outside of North America, Ground Base Six's ZOR had been the most lively—and the most costly—of them all. The local human resistance leader had demonstrated an infuriating ability to plan and execute attacks with lethal precision, and he'd cost Fursa heavily. That was one reason Ground Base Seven had been so lightly garrisoned at the time it was attacked; most of Ground Base Commander Shairez's deployable combat forces had been on loan to Fursa. So, yes, Barak understood, even sympathized, but still. . . .

"I'm inclined to suspect that the anticipation is at least as bad as beating off an actual attack would be," Fursa continued. "In fact, my warriors are getting more than a little edgy because things have been quieter than usual the last couple of days." The ears moved grumpily again. "You know how the common troopers are! The rumor mill's been busy ever since our local pests stopped buzzing quite so furiously around our ears. It's all part of whatever happened to Ground Base Seven, you know. The ominous forces which destroyed it so mysteriously are gathering about us now, and their very presence is frightening the *local* humans into hiding, like *garish* trying to hide themselves from a thunderstorm."

The irony in Fursa's voice was withering. In fact, it was so withering

Barak found himself wondering if at least part of its scorn for the "common troopers'" rumormongering wasn't an effort to conceal—perhaps even from Fursa himself—the depth of the ground base commander's own anxiety.

Well, if it was, the other ground base commander had a certain justification, Barak supposed. Unlike Fursa's, his own base sat in the middle of what had once been called "Iowa," which put an entire ocean between him and whatever had happened to Shairez. Of course, on the debit side of that particular account, it put him right in the very midst of the maddeningly inventive and endlessly destructive "Americans." His own losses had been significant, especially when he'd begun extending his ZOR eastward into the states of Wisconsin and Illinois. Missouri hadn't been any great prize, either, although at least he hadn't had to resort to the sort of general bombardment which had reduced most of Pennsylvania and New York to wastelands. According to the fleet's orbiting sensors, there were actually quite a few starving, ragged humans still creeping about in the wreckage over there, but there was very little left worth the Shongairi's time or attention.

And there aren't going to be any humans left creeping around anywhere *much longer,* he told himself.

Of course, the loss of Ground Base Seven had put a crimp into those plans, as well. Shairez had been Fleet Commander Thikair's favorite ground base commander for a lot of reasons, and Barak suspected the fleet commander had regarded her as a potential future mate, whether he'd ever realized that himself or not. But even if that were the case, it had been only a single factor in his reliance upon her, and the raw ability she'd brought to almost any task had been a much greater factor. Deservedly so, too. Picking someone to replace her in charge of the bioweapon project hadn't been easy. In the end, however, the fleet commander had decided to return it to Ground Base Two Alpha, as originally planned. Given the difficulty getting convoys of specimens through to the base, though, Thikair had also decided to use Starlanders to shuttle them in, instead. That would both avoid the maddeningly effective raiders who seemed to swarm around Ground Base Two Alpha's outer perimeter like goading insects and let him collect them from farther away, as well.

Like Barak's ZOR, for example.

Which means a third of my troopers are out crawling through the ruins around what used to be Chicago hunting for humans to bring back alive, and isn't that *fun? Cainharn! I think every human still out there has at least two guns!*

The good news was that the fleet technicians had finally come up with a capture gas which worked pretty well. They hadn't had one of those before—only lethal agents, tailored on the basis of the original Survey physiological reports. Now they were busy manufacturing the capture gas in quantity. He ought to be receiving the first mortar shells loaded with it within a few days, and after that supplying Ground Base Commander Teraik with his specimens should be a far simpler task.

And it better be, too. Almost three local weeks had passed since Ground Base Seven's destruction. That was a lot of time, yet no one in the entire expedition had been able to come up with a workable explanation for what had happened. Personally, Barak was inclined to think Fleet Commander Thikair was on to something when it came to analyzing who might be behind it, but he couldn't quite shake the feeling that there was more to it. Or perhaps less. Try though he had, he'd been unable to come up with a better way to describe his . . . amorphous sense of dread even to himself, and he wondered if perhaps he, too, was subject to some of the same unformed fears that drove the rumor mill Fursa had been talking about. But still. . . .

"You may have a point," he said now. "And, yes, trust me—my rumor mill over here is as . . . fertile as yours is over there. But if I'm going to be honest about it, I can't say I'm really looking forward to the other side's next move. In fact, if I had my way"—his voice lowered—"I'd already be cutting my losses. This planet's been nothing but one enormous pain in the ass, and when you come down to it, it's not even *that* pleasant a place to live. If we're going to kill all the humans off in the end, we might as well just pick a nice empty planet that doesn't have anyone living on it in the first place and take the expedition over there. In the meantime, where *this* world's concerned, I say take all our people off and level the place. See how whoever attacked Ground Base Seven likes *that*!"

The base commanders' gazes met, and Barak saw the agreement hidden in Fursa's eyes. Any one of Fleet Commander Thikair's dreadnoughts was capable of sterilizing any planet . . . or of reducing it to drifting rubble, for that matter. Of course, actually *doing* that would raise more than a few eyebrows among the Hegemony's member races. The sort of scrutiny it would draw upon the Empire might well have disastrous consequences, and if Thikair's suspicion that one of the Hegemony's member races was deliberately manipulating the situation, providing their unidentified enemy with that kind of ammunition would probably be a mistake. On the other hand. . . .

"Somehow I don't think that particular solution's going to be very high on the Fleet Commander's list," Fursa said carefully.

"No, and it probably shouldn't be," Barak agreed. "But I'm willing to bet it's running through the *back* of his mind already, and you know it."

. . . . .

"TIME CHECK," BRIGADE Commander Caranth announced. "Check in."

"Perimeter One, secure."

"Perimeter Two, secure."

"Perimeter Three, secure."

"Perimeter Four, secure."

The acknowledgments came in steadily, and Caranth's ears twitched in satisfaction with each of them . . . until the sequence paused.

The brigade commander didn't worry for a moment, but then he stiffened in his chair.

"Perimeter Five, report," he said.

Only silence answered.

"Perimeter Five!" he snapped . . . and that was when the firing began.

Caranth lunged upright and raced to the command bunker's armored observation slit while his staff started going berserk behind him. He stared out into the night, his body rigid in disbelief as the stroboscopic fury of muzzle flashes ripped the darkness apart. He could see nothing—nothing at all!—but the flickering lightning of automatic weapons . . . and neither could his sensors. Yet he had infantry out there shooting at *something,* and as he watched one of his fixed heavy weapons posts opened fire, as well.

"*We're under attack!*" someone screamed over the net. "Perimeter Three—we're under attack! *They're coming through the—*"

The voice chopped off, and then, horribly, Caranth heard other voices yelling in alarm, screaming in panic, cutting off in mid-syllable. It was as if some invisible, unstoppable whirlwind was sweeping through his perimeter, and strain his eyes though he might, he couldn't even *see* it!

The voices began to dwindle, fading in a diminuendo that was even more terrifying than the initial thunder of gunfire, the explosion of artillery rounds landing on something no one could see. The firing died. The last scream bubbled into silence, and Caranth felt his heart trying to freeze in his chest.

The only sound was that of his staff, trying desperately to contact Ground Base Commander Fursa's command room or even *one* of the perimeter security points.

There was no answer, only silence. And then—

"What's *that?*" someone blurted, and Caranth turned to see *something* flowing from the overhead louvers of the bunker's ventilation system.

Gas! he thought. *Is* that *how they've been doing it? But it's a sealed system. How could they—?*

His brain was still trying to formulate the question when the flowing gas seemed suddenly to solidify and darkness crashed down on him like a hammer.

. XXXVIII .

"You've got to be kidding me," Abu Bakr el-Hiri said, shaking his head as he looked across the garage at Dan Torino. Torino looked back, and el-Hiri grimaced.

"Are you *listening* to this shit you're spouting?" he demanded. "I mean *suicide truck bombs?* If I'm remembering correctly, that method of attack wasn't exactly high on you folks' list of acceptable tactics!"

"Mainly because we had other means of delivery," Torino replied. "And because we liked ones that killed a few less innocent bystanders, if I want to get nasty about it. But we don't have those other means of delivery anymore, do we? And as for killing innocent bystanders—"

He shrugged. Not happily—because if there was one thing he wasn't, it was happy about proposing such an attack—but without much hesitation, either.

They hadn't been able to absolutely confirm it—they hadn't had any handy Shongair prisoners to interrogate lately—but all the evidence suggested Ground Base Commander Teraik was about to start up his little biological warfare lab after all. They'd managed to put a severe crimp in the Shongairi's ability to transport in his "specimens" by road, but the aliens appeared to have found a solution to that one. They were flying in their hapless research subjects by shuttle now, and security in the ground base's immediate vicinity was too tight for anyone to have a hope of smuggling in a Stinger to take down one of the shuttles on approach. And, as an added benefit from the aliens' perspective, the fact that they were capturing their "specimens" from other Shongair bases' operating zones meant the humans being captured hadn't even received the warning Dave Dvorak and Rob Wilson had transmitted through their net of contacts.

"We don't know how much longer it's going to take them to start churning out their bugs or their poisons or whatever it is they're going to use," Torino said now. "I don't think we can afford to assume it's going to take them all that long, though. And then there's the question of what's *happening* to the people they've dragged in there." He showed his teeth in a snarl. "I don't know, but I don't think being the subject of a research project looking for the most efficient way to kill everybody on the frigging planet is likely to be a very *enjoyable* experience."

"Longbow," el-Hiri said in a much quieter voice, "I'm not arguing with you about that. Nobody is. But face it, man. Even if we stop them *here,* what's going to stop them from doing the same thing somewhere else? I'm not ready to give up on Allah yet, but I have to admit, it's getting harder to believe." He shook his head, his eyes dark. "It's pretty clear from the ones we've questioned that we've hurt them a hell of a lot worse than anyone else ever did, but the writing's on the wall. In fact, I've been thinking maybe the best thing we could do is ask Governor Howell to negotiate our surrender."

"What?" Torino looked at him, unable to believe he'd heard him correctly.

"I'm talking about *us*—you and me, not the whole planet," el-Hiri said. "I've been with you every step of the way. I still am, even if you *are* one of those crusader bastards Allah's going to burn in hell forever. But the truth is, I've been thinking about something you said a long time ago. About that chart or graph you were thinking about. Maybe it's time for us to see what kind of terms we can buy for everybody else if we're willing to hand ourselves over to them."

Torino started a quick reply, then stopped. He looked into el-Hiri's eyes and realized that the other man, the Muslim extremist, had become his friend. More than his friend, almost his brother. And as he realized that, he also realized el-Hiri was serious. For that matter, the more he thought about it, the more it seemed to him el-Hiri might actually have a point.

Except, of course, that it was too late.

"I don't think it would do any good," he said now, softly. El-Hiri looked at him, and he shrugged.

"They've made up their minds," he said. "And it's not just us—not just you and me—and you know it. The Shongairi we've interrogated made that clear enough. Oh, you and I've been unmitigated pains in the ass as far as they're concerned—I don't doubt that. And from what those bastards had to say before we cut their throats, they've had more trouble here in North America than anywhere else. Course, that may be because this is where they decided to concentrate, which meant we just naturally had more shots at them than anybody else did. But that's my point, really. Even if we stopped—you and I, I mean—and handed ourselves in tomorrow, the rest of the human race wouldn't. It's not *in* us, Abu Bakr. Hell, look at the way your own lunatic fringe was still making IEDs and still walking into mosques and synagogues wearing suicide belts when the Shongairi got here! I know as well as you do that most Muslims would never have dreamed of doing anything like that, but the true believers, the hard-core radicals, did. Because they were *committed.* Because what they were committed to was more important than anything else they could imagine.

"Human minds *work* that way. It's who we are and the way we think and feel and believe. No matter what we do—no matter what the *Shongairi* do—there's always going to be some human somewhere who'll be perfectly happy to die as long as he gets to cut one Shongair throat first. God knows different groups of humans have given one another plenty of reasons to hate each other over the centuries, and I think we've pretty amply demonstrated that we can hate each other for a long, long time, even over things that are pretty frigging silly, when you come right down to it. But *these* bastards have killed better than *half the entire human race* when none of us—*none* of us—had ever done a damned thing to them! Do you seriously think anyone, anywhere on the face of this planet, is ever going to forgive them for *that*?"

El-Hiri looked back into his eyes, then drew a deep breath and shook his head.

"Guess not," he said, and Torino nodded.

"I'd have to say that, for interstellar conquistadors, the Shongairi seem dumber than rocks when it comes to really understanding other species, but I think they've finally got *that* part figured out in our case. That's why it's not going to make any difference in the long run. They've decided to wipe us out, and they're going to do it. So it seems to me that about the only decision left to us is whether or not we're going to make it easy for them. And I've got to tell you, Abu Bakr, I'm not. It may not make one damned bit of difference in the end, but if they're going to murder my entire species, then before they do, I am *damned* well going to kill every single one of them I can."

"Put that way, it makes sense to me," el-Hiri said, "but I still say you shouldn't be driving any 'suicide truck bombs.' I mean, think about your image, man! The hero of the Air Battle of Washington going out as a *suicide bomber*? That's the kind of thing us lunatic towel heads are supposed to be doing, not you calm and collected infidels."

"No way in hell," Torino shot back. "The only way we're going to get this"—he twitched his head at the enormous weapon they'd forged—"inside their main base is in a real *truck,* and the only kind of truck we're going to get past their perimeter security is one of their own. And there is no way in hell somebody as tall as *you* are is going to fit into one of their trucks well enough to drive it."

El-Hiri glowered at him, yet there was a certain unanswerable logic to his argument. They'd captured three of the Shongair cargo vehicles, and figuring out how to operate them hadn't been all that difficult. In fact, their controls were downright simpleminded. Humans found the peculiar "tiller" steering arrangement a little hard to get used to, initially at least, but it wasn't that hard for a competent mechanic to swap it out for a human-style steering column.

The real problem was that there just wasn't very much room for the driver. The wiry Shongairi were shorter and far more slender than the average human. That probably could have been adjusted for, but their limbs were also double-jointed and the joints didn't even come in the same places they did for humans. By the time a cargo truck's controls were altered for human operation, no human much over five feet tall could fit into the available space with any degree of comfort. Torino could cram himself into it, but it wouldn't be anything remotely like *comfortable* for him. For that matter, although he wasn't about to admit it to el-Hiri, he was a little afraid the cramping would be bad enough to affect his ability to control the vehicle during the approach. He wasn't worried about simply slamming down the accelerator and driving it into its target when the time came; he was concerned about getting it to the target and through the outermost ring of sensor posts without attracting Shongair attention by driving erratically.

But if it might be a problem for him, it damned well *would* be a problem for el-Hiri, who was almost seven inches taller than he was.

El-Hiri glowered at him, then looked back at their bomb which, Torino thought, was probably the biggest Claymore mine anyone had ever built. It was essentially a huge triangular-shaped form, as if they'd chopped off an old-fashioned barn's peaked roof, covered first with explosives and then with thousands of nails, bolts, nuts, and screws scavenged from abandoned hardware stores and building supply centers all over North Carolina. The angled shape would direct the blast upward, and the explosion alone ought to suffice to destroy the cargo bay he'd selected for his target at the base of the Shongair ground base's central structure. He was pretty sure destroying the bay would bring the entire building down—despite everything, he couldn't quite get the vision of the collapsing Twin Towers out of his head when he thought about that—but even if he was stopped short of his ultimate target, he was confident the shrapnel, blasting through the flimsy fabric cover over the flatbed cargo area, would kill every exposed Shongair within a hundred yards or so.

"You're both wrong," another voice said, and the two of them turned to face the speaker. It was a young black man, no more than fifteen or sixteen years old. "You're both too tall," he continued. "Whereas me. . . ."

He shrugged and indicated his own height . . . which was four inches shorter than Torino's five feet eight.

"Forget it, Mus'ad," Torino said instantly. "I am not sending a fifteen-year-old kid in with a suicide bomb!"

"I'll be *sixteen* in another month and a half," the young man replied levelly. "Or I would be, anyway. And I ain't no 'kid,' either!"

Torino opened his mouth, then paused.

Mus'ad had a point. Two of them, really. The odds of his ever living to be more than sixteen were nonexistent, anyway, given Fleet Commander Thikair's decision to exterminate the human race. And even if that hadn't been true, he was scarcely a "kid." He'd killed his first six Shongairi before he and his brother ever met up with Longbow Torino. And he'd shot down more of the Shongair recon drones than any other two members of Torino's band combined. In fact, his skill with the Stingers had earned him the nickname el-Rumat—"the Archer."

But even so, even now, something inside Dan Torino cried out against sending someone so young on a mission of death which could end only in his *own* death even if he succeeded.

Sure you don't want to do it, a voice told him. *But how much of that is worry about Mus'ad, or even about what losing Mus'ad would do to Abu Bakr, and how much of it's the fact that* you *want to do it? You* want *this. Admit it. Everything you just said to Abu Bakr is true enough, but what it comes down to is that you personally want to kill these bastards. And there's a part of you that wants to be dead, anyway. So why not wrap it all up in one great big package with a bow on it? Kill as many of them as you can and kill* yourself *at the same time? "Happy Birthday Longbow!"*

"Look," he heard himself say, holding up both hands in a stopping motion, "let's not the three of us get carried away here. I mean, we haven't even got it in the damned truck yet. We don't have to make up our minds tonight about who gets to drive it in. Except, of course, that it can't be *you*, Abu Bakr. You're still too damned tall!"

"So are you," Mus'ad shot back.

"I don't think so. But I *am* big enough to kick your butt if *you* try to drive it!" The young man glowered at him, and he shrugged. "Hey, I'm not saying that's the way it's going to be. I'm just saying we don't have to make our minds up tonight. I'm sure we can settle it in some civilized fashion when the time does come, too. If we can't do it any other way, we can always do rock-paper-scissors or something to decide, okay?"

"This has to be the craziest conversation I've ever sat in on," el-Hiri said. "And I've sat in on some weird ones."

"Don't even tell me," Torino retorted.

"Well, that's—" el-Hiri started, then paused as someone else poked his head into the garage.

"There's someone here looking for you, Longbow," the newcomer said.

"Who?" Torino asked.

"Didn't give his name. Big black guy, though—taller'n you, Abu Bakr. And he says he wants to talk to you guys about attacking the base."

. XXXIX .

Fleet Commander Thikair felt a thousand years old as he sat in the silence of his stateroom, gazing at the blank display screen and cursing the day he'd ever had his brilliant idea.

It seemed so simple, he thought almost numbly. *Like such a reasonable risk. But then it all went so horribly wrong, from the moment our troopers landed. And now this.*

First, Ground Base Seven—Shairez and all her personnel, dead.

Then, three of the humans' weeks later, it had been Fursa's turn and Ground Base Six and every one of its troopers had died. In a single night. In the space of less than one day-twelfth, two fully alert infantry brigades and an entire armored brigade—one that had been made up to full strength, despite the expedition's losses in GEVs and APCs!—had been just as utterly slaughtered as Ground Base Seven.

And they'd still had absolutely no idea how it happened.

They'd received a single report, from a platoon commander, claiming he was under attack by what looked like humans. But humans who had completely ignored the assault rifles firing into them. Humans who'd registered on no thermal sensor, no motion sensor. Humans who *could not* have been there.

Thairys had to have been right about that, Thikair thought now. *Whoever it is who's helping the humans, they must be projecting holo images to distract and confuse—and terrify—our troopers. Of* course *our warriors fired at the threat they* saw *without asking themselves if perhaps the reason it wasn't appearing on their motion sensors or thermal sensors was because it wasn't really there! These humans have been such a nightmare to them from the very beginning, it's no* wonder *the rumor mill is starting to call them outright night demons! And while our troopers are busy shooting at electronic ghosts, our* real *enemies, the ones operating under stealth, are slipping right past them.*

He told himself that yet again, but deep inside, it didn't really matter. Not anymore.

Not now that Ground Base Two Alpha had gone the same way as Ground Base Seven and Ground Base Six. And this time, there hadn't been *any* reports from inside the base. Only a sudden silence, more terrifying than any report. And instead of moving instantly, on his own authority, to relieve the base—or at least find out what had happened to it—Thairys had commed him to ask for orders. To *ask* for orders! A senior ground force commander of the Shongair Empire whose troopers had been attacked had asked for *orders* before responding.

Thikair never knew how long he simply sat staring at the display. But then, finally, he punched a button on his communicator.

"Yes, Fleet Commander?" Ahzmer's voice responded quietly.

"Bring them up," Thikair said with a terrible, flat emphasis. "I don't care who's down there helping them. I don't even care if there's no one at *all* down there helping them, Cainharn seize them! If there is, they can go the same damned way as the humans. I want every single trooper off that planet within three day-twelfths. And then we'll let Jainfar's dreadnoughts use the Dainthar-cursed place for *target practice*."

. . . . .

IT WASN'T THAT simple, of course.

Organizing the emergency withdrawal of an entire planetary assault force was even more complicated than landing it had been. But at least the required troop lift had been rather drastically reduced, Thikair reflected bitterly. Well over half his entire ground force—including maintenance and support techs, not just combat troops—had been wiped out, and he'd be bringing back less than one in twelve of his combat vehicles. However small his relative losses might have been compared to those of the humans, it was still a staggering defeat for the Empire, and it was all his responsibility.

He would already have killed himself, except that no honorable suicide could possibly expunge the stain he'd brought to the honor of his entire clan. No, that would require the atonement of formal execution. Even that might not prove enough, yet it was all he could offer the Emperor. And perhaps—just perhaps, threadbare though the hope might be—if he was right and the Shongairi's enemies had deliberately arranged this disaster, his execution might offer the Emperor some flimsy cover. A way to assert that all of it, from first to last, had been the consequences of a single, feckless utter incompetent's having exceeded both the letter and the intent of his orders.

It wasn't much. It was simply all he had to give.

But before I go home to face His Majesty, there's one last thing I need to do. Jainfar's main batteries will reduce this accursed world to asteroids. *If there* are *any Kreptu or Liatu hiding down there, they'll never have expected* that *or prepared their hideouts to survive it, so. . . .*

"Are we ready, Ahzmer?"

"We are according to my readouts," the ship commander replied. But there was something peculiar about his tone, and Thikair looked at him.

"Meaning what?" he asked impatiently.

"Meaning that according to my readouts, all shuttles have returned and docked, but neither *Stellar Dawn* nor *Imperial Sword* have confirmed recovery of their small craft. All the transports have checked in, but we haven't yet heard from either industrial ship."

"What?"

Thikair's one-word question quivered with sudden, ice-cold fury. It was as if all his anxiety, all his fear, guilt, and shame suddenly had someone *else* to focus upon, and he showed all of his canines in a ferocious snarl.

"Get their commanders on the com *now*," he snapped. "Find out what in Cainharn's Ninth Hell they think they're doing! And then get me Jainfar!"

"At once, Sir! I—"

Ahzmer's voice stopped abruptly, and Thikair's eyes narrowed.

"Ahzmer?" he said.

"Sir, the plot. . . ."

Thikair turned to the master display, and it was his turn to freeze.

Six of the expedition's seven dreadnoughts were heading steadily away from the planet.

"What are they—?" he began, then gasped as two of the dreadnoughts suddenly opened fire. Not on the planet—on their own escorts!

Nothing in the galaxy could stand up to the energy-range fire of a dreadnought. Certainly no mere scout ship, destroyer, or cruiser could.

It took less than forty-five seconds for every one of Thikair's screening warships to die . . . and every one of his transport ships went with them.

"Get Jainfar!" he shouted at Ahzmer. "Find out what—"

"Sir, there's no response from Squadron Commander Jainfar's ship!" Ahzmer's communications officer blurted. "There's no response from *any* of the other dreadnoughts!"

"*What?*" Thikair stared at him in disbelief, and then alarms began to warble. First one, then another, and another.

He whipped back around to the master control screen, and ice smoked through his veins as crimson lights glared on the readiness boards. Engineering went down, then the Combat Information Center. Master Fire Control went off-line, and so did Tracking, Missile Defense, and Astrogation.

And then the flag bridge itself lost power. Main lighting failed, plunging it into darkness, and Thikair heard someone gobbling a prayer as the emergency lighting clicked on.

"Sir?"

Ahzmer's voice was fragile, and Thikair looked at him. But he couldn't find his own voice. He could only stand there, paralyzed, unable to cope with the impossible events.

And then the command deck's armored doors slid open, and Thikair's eyes went wide as a *human* walked through them.

Every officer on that bridge was armed, and Thikair's hearing cringed as a dozen sidearms opened fire at once. Scores of bullets slammed into the human intruder . . . with absolutely no effect.

No, that wasn't quite correct, some numb corner of Thikair's brain insisted. The bullets went straight *through* him, whining and ricocheting off the bulkheads behind him, but he didn't even seem to notice. There were no wounds, no sprays of blood. His *clothing* rippled as if in a high wind, but his body might as well have been made of smoke, offering no resistance, suffering no damage.

He only stood there, looking at them. And then, suddenly, there were more humans. Three of them. Only *three* . . . but it was enough.

Thikair's mind gibbered, too overwhelmed even to truly panic, as the three newcomers seemed to blur. It was as if they were half transformed into vapor that poured itself forward, around and past the first human, streaking through the command deck's air with impossible speed. They flowed across the bridge, *enveloping* his officers, and he heard screams. Screams of raw panic which rose in pitch as the Shongairi behind them saw the smoke flowing in *their* direction . . . and died in a hideous, gurgling silence as it engulfed them.

And then Thikair was the only Shongair still standing.

His body insisted that he had to collapse, but somehow his knees refused to unlock. Collapsing would have required him to move . . . and something reached out from the first human's green eyes and forbade that.

The green-eyed human walked out into the body-strewn command deck and stopped, facing Thikair, his hands clasped behind him, and his three fellows gathered at his back, like guards of honor.

The green-eyed human was the shortest of the four. Two of the others were much taller than he—both of them in garments bearing the mottled camouflage patterns the humans' militaries favored, although the patterns were different. One of them—the taller one, in the pale, almost dusty-looking camouflage pattern—had brown eyes and a skin dark as night. The other could have been designed as his antithesis: clad in a darker, more forestlike pattern, with blue eyes, fair skin, and wheat-colored hair. The third was only a very little taller than their chieftain, and he, too, had green eyes, but terrifying as the hate in those eyes was, they lacked the power and dark fury crackling in the ones which held Thikair motionless.

Silence hovered, twisting Thikair's nerves like white-hot pincers, and then, finally, the human leader spoke.

"You have much for which to answer, Fleet Commander Thikair," he said quietly, softly . . . in perfect Shongair.

Thikair only stared at him, unable—not allowed—even to speak, and the human smiled. There was something terrifying about that smile . . . and something wrong, as well. The teeth, Thikair realized. The ridiculous little human canines had lengthened, sharpened, and in that moment Thikair understood exactly how thousands upon thousands of years of prey animals had looked upon his own people's smiles.

"You call yourselves 'predators.'" The human's upper lip curled. "Trust me, Fleet Commander—your people know nothing about *predators*. But they will."

Something whimpered in Thikair's throat, and the green eyes glowed with a terrifying internal fire.

"I had forgotten," the human said. "I had turned away from my own past. Even when you came to my world, even when you murdered billions of humans, I had forgotten. But now, thanks to you, Fleet Commander, I *remember*. I remember the obligations of honor. I remember a Prince of Wallachia's responsibilities. And I remember—oh, *how* I remember—the taste of vengeance. And that is what I find most impossible to forgive, Fleet Commander Thikair. I have spent five hundred *years* learning to forget that taste, and you have filled my mouth with it once more."

Thikair would have sold his soul to look away from those blazing emerald eyes, but even that was denied him.

"For an entire century, I hid even from myself—hid under my murdered brother's name. But now, Fleet Commander, I take back my *own* name. I am Vlad Drakulya—Vlad, Son of the Dragon, Prince of Wallachia—and you have *dared* to shed the blood of those under *my* protection."

The paralysis left Thikair's voice—released, he was certain, by the human-shaped monster in front of him—and he swallowed hard.

"Wh-what do you—?" he managed to get out, but then his freed voice failed him, and Vlad smiled cruelly.

"I could not have acted when you first came, even if I had been prepared to—*willing* to—go back to what once I was," he said. "There was only myself and my handful of closest followers, and we would have been far too few. But then you showed me I truly had no choice. When you decided to build a weapon to destroy every living human, when you seized those under my protection upon whom to experiment for that purpose, you made my options very simple. I could not permit that—I *would* not. And so I had no alternative but to create more of my own kind. To create an army—not large, as armies go, but an army still—to deal with you.

"I was more cautious than in my . . . impetuous youth. The vampires I chose to make this time were better men and women than I was when I was yet breathing. I pray for my own sake that they will balance the hunger you have awakened in me once again, but do not expect them to feel any kindness where you and *your* kind are concerned.

"They are all much younger than I, new come to their abilities, not yet strong enough to endure the touch of the rising sun. But, like me, they are no longer breathing. Like me, they could ride the exteriors of your shuttles when you were kind enough to recall them from Romania and Russia to North America. When you used them to evacuate all of your surviving personnel to your transports . . . and to your dreadnoughts. And like me, they have used your neural educators, learned how to control your vessels, how to use your technology."

That terrible voice paused for a moment, and the fire in those eyes turned colder than the space beyond the dreadnought's hull.

"I learned much in my . . . conversation with your Ground Base Commander Shairez," Vlad said then. "Oh, yes, she was *eager* to tell me anything I might possibly wish to know before the end. And I learned still more probing the history in your educators' data banks. Interrogating your other base commanders one by one as your installations fell. I know your Empire's plans, Fleet Commander. I know how the Hegemony came to be, how it is organized. And I know how its Council has chosen to regard the human race—how *casually* it tossed this entire planet into the hands of the murderous vermin who have killed two-thirds of those who lived upon it. Who would have killed *all* of them out of frustrated ambition and fury at their having *dared* to defend themselves against unprovoked invasion.

"Oh, yes, Fleet Commander, I have learned a great deal, and I will leave your educators here on Earth, to give every single breathing human a complete Hegemony-level education. And, as you may have noticed, we were very careful not to destroy your industrial ships. What do you think a planet of humans will be able to accomplish over the next few centuries, even after all you have done to them, from that starting point? And how do you think they will respond to what the Hegemony Council allowed—*encouraged*—you to do to their world and to their people. Do you think the Council will be pleased?"

Thikair swallowed again, choking on a thick bolus of fear, and the human cocked his head to one side.

"For myself, I doubt the Council will be very happy with you, Fleet Commander. But do not concern yourself with that. I promise you *their* anger will have no effect upon your Empire. After all, each of these dreadnoughts can shatter a planet, can it not? And which of your worlds will dream, even for a moment, that one of your own capital ships might pose any threat to it at all?"

"No," Thikair managed to whimper, his eyes darting to the plot where the green icons of his other dreadnoughts continued to move away from the planet. "No, *please* . . ."

"How many human fathers and mothers would have said exactly the same thing to *you* as their children died before their eyes?" the human replied coldly, and Thikair sobbed.

The human watched him mercilessly, but then he looked away. The deadly green glow left his eyes, and they seemed to soften as they gazed up at the taller human beside him.

"Keep me as human as you can, my Stephen," he said softly in English. "Keep me sane. Remind me of why I tried so hard to forget."

The dark-skinned human looked back down at him and nodded, and then the green eyes moved back to Thikair.

"I believe you have unfinished business with this one, my Stephen," he said, and it was the bigger, taller, darker, and infinitely less terrifying human's turn to smile.

"Yes, I do," his deep voice rumbled, and Thikair squealed like a small, trapped animal as the powerful, dark hands reached for him.

"This is for my daughters," Stephen Buchevsky said.

EPILOGUE

PLANET EARTH

YEAR 1 OF THE TERRAN EMPIRE

Dave Dvorak stood gazing up into the frosty, moonless night sky with one arm wrapped around his wife's shoulder. The other arm was still immobilized, but it was getting better. And it looked like Hosea MacMurdo was going to get the opportunity to rebuild his left shoulder, after all.

In fact, a lot of things were going to happen "after all." His children were going to live and grow up, have children of their own. His country was going to emerge from the wreckage and the carnage once again. Other nations around the globe would live once more, mourning their dead but *alive*. His entire world was going to survive.

After all.

"Hard to believe, isn't it?" Sharon murmured, and he looked down and smiled at her.

"Always believe three impossible things before breakfast every morning," he told her.

"That's silly, Daddy," another voice said, and he turned to look at his son. Malachai Dvorak had a dark mustache of hot chocolate from the supply of instant still tucked away in the cave and broken out for the occasion, and he shook his head, red hair gleaming in the light of the quietly hissing Coleman lantern.

"Impossible things aren't real," he informed his father with impeccable six-year-old logic. "And if they aren't real, you shouldn't believe in them."

"You think?"

Malachai nodded firmly, and Dvorak took his arm from around Sharon to ruffle the boy's hair, then looked across at his daughters. Maighread looked back at him, but Morgana appeared to be bobbing for marshmallows in her huge mug of hot chocolate. She had her face buried in it, anyway.

"What do you think, Maighread?" he asked. "Should you believe in impossible things?"

"Well . . ."

His daughter cocked her head to one side, obviously pondering, then turned to the even smaller, blond-haired girl standing beside her. Zinaida Karpovna was looking down into her own hot chocolate with an almost reverent expression.

"What do you think, Zinaida?" Maighread asked.

"About what?" Zinaida responded, looking up from the mug. "I wasn't listening."

The Russian girl spoke flawless English, but that was fair enough. Maighread could have asked the question in equally flawless Russian if she'd wanted to, thanks to the neural educator installed in the cave. They'd pulled a few strings—Dvorak was prepared to admit it, if anyone asked—to get that educator, but there hadn't been too much argument about it. There were upward of three thousand of them scattered about the world at the moment, and producing more of them would be one of the first priorities of the world's rebuilt infrastructure. In the meantime, Dave Dvorak had every intention of going ahead and realizing his desire to be a history teacher . . . especially now that he had the history of a whole interstellar civilization (such as it was) at his mental fingertips.

The kids certainly thought it had been a good idea, too. They'd come to think of the neural educator as the biggest and best encyclopedia in the entire known universe, and their craving for knowledge seemed bottomless. In fact, the adults had to be careful about cramming knowledge too quickly into children; there were physiological limitations on how much neurally delivered information a still-maturing brain could absorb without cognitive and psychological damage. Besides, the educators provided only *knowledge,* not the ability to *grasp* that knowledge or handle complex concepts. It would be some time before any of the kids were old enough for a *complete* neurological education, and they didn't seem to have fully realized—yet, at any rate—that they were still going to have to go to school to develop those cognitive skills, learn to handle those concepts. But they already had a well-developed set of *language* skills, and since Zinaida and her family were going to be living with them for a while, all of the parents involved had decided it only made sense to make all the children bilingual.

"Daddy was asking if people should believe in impossible things," Maighread explained now, and Zinaida shrugged.

"Of course they should," she said simply. "If we didn't believe in impossible things, we wouldn't be here. I mean, if anyone had asked if I thought I'd ever drink something like this . . . hot chocolate," she pronounced the words cautiously, despite her new English fluency, "I would've thought *that* was pretty impossible."

She shrugged again, and Dvorak nodded.

"Good answer, kid," he told her, reaching out to tug teasingly on her right earlobe. Then he looked at his son again.

"You know, Malachai, *everything's* impossible until somebody believes in it enough to *make* it real."

"An excellent observation," another voice said, and the adult Dvoraks turned just a bit quickly as they realized the night's guest of honor had arrived.

He smiled at them, and reached out his left hand to Zinaida. She smiled back, then cuddled her cheek into his palm, catching his hand between her face and shoulder in a handless embrace that was somehow unutterably tender.

"And as Zinaida has observed," Pieter Ushakov continued, looking across her bent head at Dave and Sharon Dvorak, "if we did not believe in impossible things, we would not be here, would we?"

My, oh my, but have you got that *one right*, Dvorak thought wryly. *Legends and myths and monsters, oh my! Count—I'm sorry*, Prince—*Dracula?* Good guy *vampires riding to the rescue of all humanity? Who would've thunk it?*

He looked at the blond-haired, blue-eyed man whose breath wasn't producing the vapor clouds everyone else seemed to be exhaling. Which had a little something to do with the fact that Pieter Ushakov no longer exhaled. Or inhaled, for that matter, unless he needed the air to speak.

Dvorak glanced back up at the sky. Most of humanity's heavens were still blacker than black, without the high-tech sky glow which had once been so much a part of its major cities. There were places where those cities were already coming back, though, and whatever human authority had managed to preserve itself through the nightmare of the Shongair invasion was trying desperately to bring some sort of order to a world coping with starvation, disease, and—for the northern hemisphere, at least—the rapid onset of winter.

It was going to be bad, he knew. Not as bad as it could have been, but even with all the goodwill in the world, and with all of the captured Shongair resources which were being converted and applied to the problem as quickly as possible, millions more were still going to die. It couldn't be any other way with the planetary infrastructure so hammered and battered and broken.

But bad as this winter was going to be, spring would follow, and new growth would emerge from the killed-back winter roots. And perhaps—just perhaps, he thought, following up that metaphor—something newer and stronger and better would grow out of the rich, sustaining soil of the past.

God knows it's been manured with enough blood, he thought soberly. *And we know we're not alone, anymore. Not only that, I don't think we're going to like our neighbors very much. So, since humans seem best at burying their differences in the face of some mutual, outside threat. . . .*

He watched the larger of the two bright, shining motes sweeping slowly across the night sky. He thought it actually looked bigger to the naked eye than it had just the night before, although that could be only his imagination. After all, he knew it *was* getting bigger, even though nobody's unaided vision should be able to pick that up just yet.

The Shongair industrial vessels didn't care that they'd changed ownership and management. They just went steadily ahead, completing their automated assembly process, preparing to begin construction of an entire Hegemony-level industrial infrastructure for Earth's tattered survivors. By the time the various planetary governments got themselves reorganized, that industrial infrastructure would be just about ready to begin rebuilding mankind's home, and an old line from a not particularly great science-fiction television series ran through the back of Dave Dvorak's brain.

"We can rebuild it, we can make it better," he misquoted quietly, and Sharon laughed.

"Thank you, Colonel Austin!" She shook her head at him. "You do realize none of our kids—or our guests—are going to get that one, don't you?"

"They don't have to understand the *original* reference," he replied, and her smile faded.

"No, they don't," she agreed softly. "The question is whether or not we can pull it off this time."

"We can," Ushakov said, facing them squarely. "I need my hand, Zinaida," he said, and she smiled up at him and released it.

He smiled back, then used his liberated hand to stroke the small, sleepy bundle of night-black fur cradled on his right forearm. The puppy stretched and opened his mouth in a prodigious yawn, showing needle-sharp little white teeth, and Ushakov chuckled. Then he looked back at his hosts.

"We can, and we shall," he said simply. "I believe the English idiom is 'Failure is not an option.'" He shrugged, still stroking the back of the puppy's delicate skull. "Vlad and Stephen will deal with the Shongairi. That will still leave the remainder of the Hegemony, however, and I doubt they will react calmly to the notion that someone far worse—as *they* see things at any rate—than the Shongairi has burst upon the scene. Worse still, from their perspective, I think with the lesson of the Shongairi before us here on our own world, we will not be quick to accept the Hegemony's authority. I doubt they will react calmly to that, either."

He shrugged again.

"One may quibble about the historical forces in play at any single moment—for example, Marx was a dunce, in my own opinion, although I admit that may be prejudice on my part—but the dialectic remains a valid method of analysis, does it not? In this instance, the thesis is the Hegemony's prejudices and mania for stability, while humanity's insatiable hunger for change and our fury over what was done to us represent the antithesis. I do not think they can coexist for very long. So the question becomes who will survive in the coming synthesis, and I believe the Hegemony will discover that humanity is very, very *good* at surviving."

Yes, we are, Dvorak thought, then looked up quickly as he heard a soft, whooshing sort of sound and Keelan Wilson suddenly squealed with laughter.

Boris Karpov still didn't talk a lot, but he and Keelan had been almost inseparable ever since his mother and his siblings had arrived to join Ushakov. Now the two of them were "helping" Jessica and Veronica set the table while Rob and Alec lit the bonfire. Normally, that was Dvorak's job, but with only one good arm, he'd agreed—reluctantly—to delegate it to Wilson.

Apparently his reluctance had been well placed.

It had rained heavily for the last couple of days, and he and his brother-in-law had somewhat different approaches to coaxing recalcitrant, wet wood into flame. It looked to Dvorak as if Wilson must have used the better part of a quart of their precious gasoline to "encourage" the kindling. At any rate, when he'd tossed in the match, he'd gotten a *most* impressive ignition.

He jumped back, expressing himself in vehement Marine-ese and smacking hastily at the tiny dots of flame busy singeing his Mackinaw's fuzzy surface, and Keelan laughed again.

"You're all *sparky,* Daddy!"

"Yeah, and he doesn't have any *eyebrows* anymore, either!" Alec put in. He sounded rather less amused than his much younger half sister. Probably because he'd been in closer proximity to ground zero and his own eyebrows had just gotten a little frizzy-looking, Dvorak decided, shaking his head with resignation.

"Only in America," he muttered, and it was Ushakov's turn to chuckle.

"Oh, I think you could find his like elsewhere." His smile faded and he looked back at Dvorak. "And a good thing, too. A strong man, your brother-in-law. The kind we need more of."

He met Dvorak's eyes levelly, the implication unstated, and Dvorak nodded slowly, thinking of a conversation he'd had with another strong man.

A good man.

. . . . .

"ARE YOU SURE about this, Stephen?" Dave Dvorak asked. "I don't like lying to your dad, even by omission."

"Yeah." Stephen Buchevsky gazed up at the silver disc of the moon. "Yeah, I'm sure, Dave." He turned back from the moon, folding his arms across his massive chest. "Maybe the time will come to tell him—and Mom—I'm still alive . . . in a manner of speaking, anyway. Right this minute, though, I don't think he'd be ready to deal with it."

"What? Why *ever* would you worry about that?" Dvorak shook his head. "A Methodist pastor with a vampire for a son . . . Where could the problem possibly be in *that*?"

"Exactly." Buchevsky shook his head, but he also smiled very slightly. "I love my dad and my mom more than anything else in the world." His smile faded as he remembered the only people who had ever matched his parents' place in his heart, but his voice didn't falter. "I love them, but it's going to take them time to adjust, and I don't want them worrying about it, agonizing over it, when I'm not even here."

"*Should* they adjust, Steve?" Dvorak asked very quietly.

"What? You mean all the 'damned souls of the undead' and like that?"

Buchevsky sounded more amused than anything else, but Dvorak faced him squarely and nodded.

"Don't think for one moment I'm not grateful," he said. "And don't think I didn't go down on my knees and thank God when I heard about what happened. But, you know, that's kind of the point of my concern. I take God just as seriously as your dad does. And that means I can understand why he might have some of the same . . . questions I do."

"Course you do." Buchevsky nodded. "Couldn't be any other way. But. . . ."

Stephen Buchevsky reached inside his shirt. When his hand came back out, it held the small, beautiful silver cross Shania had given him less than a year ago. It lay across his broad, dark palm, shining in the moonlight, and he held it out to Dvorak.

"You see?"

Dvorak looked at the cross, then reached out and touched it gently. The hand across which it lay was cool. Not cold, he thought—simply cool. The skin was neither shriveled nor leathery. It felt just like any hand's skin . . . except that there was no warmth.

"Hollywood got most of it wrong, Dave," Buchevsky said. "Vampires are still . . . human. We've changed, and I'm not going to tell you the change is a pleasant process, because, trust me, it isn't. And I'm not going to tell you there aren't things I'm going to miss—a lot—now that I'm no longer what Vlad calls 'a breather.' But we're not automatically monsters."

"Not *automatically*," Dvorak repeated, and Buchevsky nodded.

"That's a choice we all make, isn't it? Monster, angel, or maybe just . . . man, do you think?" He looked levelly into Dvorak's eyes. "Anybody can choose to become a murderer. Anybody can choose to become a doctor. One of them requires more discipline and more study, but they're both *choices*. I chose to be a Marine, and I killed quite a few people in the service of my country. So did your brother-in-law. So have you, assuming you want to consider Shongairi 'people.' Did that make me a murderer or just a Marine?"

"So you're saying that even *Vlad Drakulya* is just misunderstood?"

"Of course I'm not." For the first time what might have been a trace of anger flickered around the edges of Buchevsky's voice. "In fact, he'd be the first to tell you that wasn't what happened. The truth is, Vlad *was* a monster . . . but that was true even before he stopped breathing. Becoming a vampire didn't *make* him a monster; it only meant he could do even more monstrous things, and for a while, that's exactly what he did. Ask him about it."

"No thanks."

Dvorak shivered. He'd met Drakulya twice now, and while he suspected that he felt less uncomfortable around him than many might have, there was a vast difference between "less uncomfortable" and anything remotely like "*comfortable.*"

"That man—and whatever else he may be, he is a *man,* Dave, trust me—has spent five centuries learning *not* to be a monster. He thinks he hasn't pulled it off yet, but *I* think he's wrong. I've seen him, I've watched him. You know, we *can* enter churches. We can pray—I still do that fairly regularly. And I've seen him in a church, seen how he stares at that cross, seen how he still thinks of himself as unclean. I'm not going to tell you he's a 'nice' man, because he was born in the flipping *fifteenth century,* and he's still got more than a few fifteenth-century attitudes in him. I don't think he's ever likely to care much for 'Turks,' for example. Had what you might call an unpleasant boyhood experience with them, which doesn't even consider the way they treated Romania while he was still a breather. Or the way his own brother, Radu, converted to Islam and invaded Wallachia under Mehmed II. And you might want to take a look at what the boyars did to his father and his older brother, too. He's been in some really *bad* places—inside his head, as well as physically—in the last six hundred years or so, and he's never going to be what you might call a very forgiving sort. But whatever he may once have been, he's not a monster anymore. And I won't let him be one again."

Dvorak's eyebrow rose.

"That's why I can't stay and work this out with Dad and Mom," Buchevsky said, putting the cross gently back inside his shirt and buttoning it once more. "Vlad needs me. I promised to keep him sane, and I'm going to. But I know what we're going to be doing to the Shongairi, too, and that's why I have to be with him. He needs me, I think, as the proof that he can make another vampire who *isn't* a monster. Because, maybe, if there's *one* vampire in the universe who isn't a monster, *he* can not be a monster, too. And as long as he needs me for that, I'll be there. Because I owe him that. Because *every surviving human being* owes him that. And because he damned well deserves it."

· · · · ·

NOW DAVE DVORAK'S attention returned to the present, looking into the lantern-lit eyes of yet another vampire.

No, he told himself. Into the eyes of another good *man* who simply happened to be a vampire, as well. One of the two or three dozen vampires—no one knew exactly how many, and the vampires weren't telling—who'd been left behind as Vlad Drakulya's deputies. Not to rule the planet in his name, not to terrorize the living, but simply to be there. To be sure that in the turmoil and upheavals certain to accompany the world's rebuilding and the adjustments to all the new technology and capabilities about to pour down over humanity, the "breather" monsters were held in check.

You know, he reflected now, *if I'm a corrupt strongman somewhere, or a warlord who hates to let a good crisis go to waste and thinks it would be really cool to build a new little empire all my own, and somebody like Pieter Ushakov pours himself through my keyhole in a column of smoke and suggests I really ought to think about changing my ways, I'd probably do it. I mean, I don't know for* sure, *but . . . probably.*

He chuckled at the thought, then gave himself a shake.

We're going to have to get used to the notion of a galaxy with other intelligent species in it. I don't think we're going to like all of them very much, either. But maybe what we really need to do is get into the habit of recognizing that our lowly little planet is actually home to two *intelligent species all its own. One that breathes, and one that doesn't. If we're going to avoid the Shongair pattern—or the Hegemony's, for that matter—and learn to really* coexist *with other folks, maybe we should start practicing right here at home.*

"Well," he said out loud, "now that 'Sparky's' stopped blowing himself up, I suppose I should go see whether or not the charcoal's ready." He smiled at his wife. "It's been—what? Six *months* since I grilled a steak? God, that really brings it home somehow."

"So does the fact that Mr. Steak Nazi Dvorak is about to grill steaks that he actually *froze,*" she retorted.

"Hey, if I hadn't stuck them in the freezer before all this started, we wouldn't have them today. I mean, sure, *freezing* a steak comes under the heading of an unnatural act, but sometimes you just don't have a choice. And as far as grilling them today—or, rather, tonight, now that Pieter's been able to join us—I'll simply point out that today is the girls' birthday, and Tuesday is my birthday, and next Friday will be the first day of the new school year. The *schools* are going to be open again, Sharon! If all of that isn't grounds enough to thaw out some of the world's few remaining sirloins, I don't know what is!"

"You're right," she said much more gently. "You're right. Of course, school's never going to be quite the same again, is it?"

"Nothing is, and we're just damned lucky Howell managed to hold so much of North Carolina together. I was talking to Sam about it yesterday, you know. They're talking about going ahead and merging North Carolina and South Carolina into one state, at least for a while." Dvorak shook his head. "Hard to believe we're about to become the wealthiest, most stable, best educated state—or states—in the entire Union. They're even talking about putting the new national capital in Raleigh! Somewhere down to the cemetery John C. Calhoun and Daniel Webster must be spinning up a storm. And don't even get me *started* on William Tecumseh Sherman!"

"I know little about this Calhoun or Webster," Ushakov said, "but Sherman I have heard of. And from what I have seen and heard so far, I would not be at all surprised if your Governor Howell does not become even more famous than he, when the history books are finally written. For that matter, I suspect he will become *President* Howell as soon as your nation can organize new elections. It would seem to me that he truly deserves it."

"Well, maybe he does," Dvorak agreed, "but I'll tell you right now, Sam and Longbow and Howell are out of their damned minds if they think *I'm* going to agree to run for the Senate." He shuddered. "Oh, no, you're not getting *me* into Washington—or Raleigh, or wherever the hell *else* we put the capital when we get around to rebuilding it! I've got me a cabin up in the hills with a bunker, by God, and I'm a-stayin' in it!"

"Amen, Lord! *Amen,*" his wife said fervently. Then whacked him on his good shoulder. "Now get your lazy nonsenatorial butt over there to the kitchen and start cooking!"

"Yes, Ma'am. To hear is to obey," he said, and the two of them and Ushakov started across towards the bonfire, followed by Zinaida and their own children.

"You know, Pieter," Dvorak said, looking over his shoulder at the Ukrainian, "before he left, Stephen said there were things he was going to miss about breathing. I have to say, one of the things I'd hate to give up is eating. Especially"—he grinned at Morgana—"steak."

"Yeah, *steak*!" Morgana agreed with a huge grin.

"I want mine well done, Daddy," Malachai said, and Dvorak shook his head.

"Such sacrilege," he murmured.

"Well," Pieter said, running one finger down the muzzle ridge of the sleepy puppy still stretched out along his right forearm, "I may not partake of your meal myself, but I always enjoy the conversation. And perhaps if I cut the pieces up small enough, Renfield here might enjoy a nibble."

Dvorak and his wife stopped dead, turning to look at him in disbelief.

"What?" he asked, eyebrows rising.

"*What* did you just call that puppy?" Sharon Dvorak demanded. "I don't know if the records are still around anywhere, but Merlin and Nimue are both AKC-registered, and I'm not sure *that* name is going to fly, you should pardon the expression, for one of their offspring!"

"What are you talking about?" Ushakov asked, his expression puzzled.

"You just called that puppy '*Renfield*,' " she said, reaching up to jab a finger under his nose, deadly creature of the undead or not. "Don't pretend you didn't, Pieter Stefanovich Ushakov!"

"Of course not!" he said, cradling the puppy protectively closer to his chest. "That is his name—Milo Renfield!"

"*No!*" Sharon cried. "*Don't* tell me you named one of *my* dog's puppies *Milo Renfield*! What did you think you were *doing?*"

"I thought it was a fine name," Ushakov protested.

"Funny, you don't look depraved," Dvorak observed, then cocked his head thoughtfully. "Tell me, just how did you come up with that particular name, Pieter? Did someone, oh, *suggest* it to you, by any chance?"

"Perhaps." Ushakov tilted his own head to one side, narrowed eyes speculative.

"Well, I was just wondering. Was it Stephen . . . or Vlad?"

"Vlad," Ushakov replied. "Why? He said it was the name of a character in a film he saw once. A character he felt rather close to."

Dave Dvorak covered his eyes with his good hand and shook his head.

"I should've guessed," he said.

"Guessed what?" Ushakov demanded.

"Who suggested it." Dvorak shook his head again, then lowered his hand and put it on Ushakov's shoulder, urging him on towards the waiting charcoal grill and the steaks. "Don't worry, we'll explain." He shook his head again. "And you know, that suggestion just goes to prove Stephen was wrong."

"Wrong about what?" his wife asked, still clearly torn between outrage and amusement by the name which had been bestowed upon her four-footed grandson.

"Well, I hope Pieter here won't take me up wrongly on this, but if Vlad Drakulya, of all people, could bestow *that* name on a puppy that's busy adopting a vampire, then deep down inside, he *is* still a monster."